Tales from my
Welsh Village

'Captures a time gone by. Everyone in Wales and other parts of the UK who live in a semi-rural community will have their own version of the characters portrayed.'
– Jeff Davies, lecturer at Cardiff Metropolitan University

'A fascinating read, captivating and often difficult to put down, as I wanted to find out what escapade Fred was involved with next.'
– Philip J Grant, author

Tales from my
Welsh Village

KEN SMITH

This book is dedicated to the memory of Trefor Plough,
Fred and Colin Howells (the 'Partners')
and all the other local characters who inspired this story.

First impression: 2018
Second impression: 2018
© Ken Smith & Y Lolfa Cyf., 2018

Cover design: Y Lolfa
Cover illustration: Mumph

ISBN: 978 1 78461 525 3

Published and printed in Wales
on paper from well-maintained forests by
Y Lolfa Cyf., Talybont, Ceredigion SY24 5HE
e-mail ylolfa@ylolfa.com
website www.ylolfa.com
tel 01970 832 304
fax 832 782

Foreword

THIS STORY, FOR the most part, is fiction loosely based on some of the local characters in the village of Rhigos, where I grew up from the age of eight until I emigrated to Canada in 1975.

Over the years, for whatever reason, I had made notes about events as they happened and thought that one day I would put them all together as a personal memory of days long ago.

Then one day, I was at home following surgery after an accident at work and was reading through a local newspaper. I came across an article regarding some night courses on creative writing and I thought briefly about my old notes. On the spur of the moment, I got into my car and drove about 30 miles to the college in Edmonton to find out a bit more about the classes. I was asked to write a chapter on any subject and submit it that day, it being the last day for submissions. Driving home, I thought again about my scribbling, and wrote a chapter about the Plough Inn. I made a return journey to the college and dropped off my submission at the tutor's office.

I had just returned home when the phone rang and a voice said: "This is Scot Morrison. I am the creative writing course tutor and I would like you to sign up right away!" Which I did. In all I must have driven more than 180 miles that day.

Later, I found myself in a class of 13 people, 12 of whom were published authors. What a revelation and an introduction into the secret world of creative writing.

This book is the inspiration for and result of those classes.

Grateful thanks:

To my wife, Avril, for her patience and understanding about the amount of time spent alone while I disappeared for hours on end scribbling and burning the midnight oil.

To Jen Llywelyn for her diligence in editing this book.

To the staff at Y Lolfa for all their work in the production of the book.

Also to Fred Howells' daughters, Sheila and June, for their support and advice during the writing of the book.

Ken Smith
July 2018

CHAPTER I

Fred 'Rats' Howells

THE LATE AFTERNOON sun was casting long shadows on the north face of the mountain behind the Globe Inn as Fred downed his final pint of the day and took his leave from the smoke-filled main bar of the pub. He was a little unsteady, which was not surprising considering he had been drinking heavily for the past four days, while spending most of his afternoons betting on the unlikely performance of his selection of racehorses. He stumbled slightly as he went down the uneven slope to the nearby bus stop.

The proximity of the Globe Inn to the bus stop, a mere few yards, had little to do with the reason he had spent most of the day in that particular pub. No, the overriding attraction was the off-track betting shop operated by a well-known turf accountant from the large neighbouring town of Merthyr Tydfil. For many years this building, prior to it being turned into a betting shop, had been the storage area for copious amounts of coal, fuel for the many fireplaces scattered throughout the inn. But with the advent of natural gas into the area, central heating was now readily available, and the building had fallen rapidly into a sorry state of disrepair. It was during this period that off-track betting was introduced, and with it individually licensed betting shops. No time had been lost in turning the dilapidated lean-to building into a veritable gold mine. Hard-earned money had been taken with consummate ease from the likes of Fred and his cronies as their selections, based on 'form', failed, with monotonous regularity, to win.

Needless to say, the landlord of the inn also saw benefit from the close ties with the betting shop, via the constant ebb and flow of patrons wishing to quench their thirst, and witness the results of their individual endeavours on the large colour TV strategically perched above the main bar.

There also appeared to be a direct correlation between the patrons winning or losing and the health of the cash till. If a punter won a few pounds or so he was more or less obliged to buy a beer or two for those in his company who had supported his winning choice in horseflesh. If, on the other hand, he lost his money, then his compatriots would invariably buy him a pint and commiserate with him on his latest misfortune. In either event, or so it appeared, the landlord saw a profit.

Fred, who failed in his selections more times than he cared to think about, unfortunately didn't receive any tangible benefit from either side of the equation. This being the case, he had resigned himself to accept a minor role in life's endless stream of ups and downs.

However, on this particular weekend he had gained some measure of success on his choice of horses, and was in a happy frame of mind as he strolled the extra few yards to the bus stop. He looked as unkempt as usual, tops of his wellies turned down the regulation few inches, coarse grey working trousers, thick woollen shirt, a nondescript jacket from some long forgotten suit, and his favourite flat chequered ratting cap perched jauntily at an angle to one side of his head. He was a man who had never been overweight throughout his adult life, remaining within a pound or two of ten and a half stone. While broad-shouldered, he was a sparely-built individual, standing just a shade over medium height. His features, in general, were sort of flattish and slightly elongated, complimented by a fairly long sharp nose; this was set between keen bright blue eyes, which did not miss a thing if it was to his advantage; the pupils were mere pinpoints. To complete the picture, his hair, at this time in his life, was grey and slightly grizzled, and invariably cropped close to his skull (or as some wag unkindly remarked to his face one day, "It's right down to the bluddy wood, Fred").

Lost in thought, or so it would appear to the casual observer, he leaned against the stone wall of the open bus shelter which adjoined the garden wall of the Globe Inn, his hands thrust deep in the pockets of his trousers.

Eventually the dull roar of the nearby river to his right broke into whatever he had been thinking about, and he sauntered in the direction of the sound to peer over the wall at the small stream, now in full flood after days of heavy rain. This stream marked the boundary between the two parishes as it wended its way through the village of Waun-gron.

Waun-gron had been a thriving industrial ironworks town of some 40,000 people during the early part of the nineteenth century, a bustling town when the now capital of the country had been nothing more than a large riverside village with a large wharf at the mouth of the river Taff, from which steamships, laden with iron and coal, the products of Waun-gron's industry, had sailed to distant markets throughout the world. Now, though, Waun-gron was nothing more than a sprawling village of less than 5,000 souls. The industry had long gone, leaving in its place a sense of dereliction.

Fred stared down at the swirling waters and in his mind's eye traced its wandering banks back up the mountainside to its source, a cluster of tiny springs that thrust their way forcefully through the grey hillside shale, ice cold and sweet to the taste. 'Damn,' he thought, 'I've drunk my fill from there so many times while walking the mountain.' His eyes swept across the darkening green backdrop as the shadows lengthened and he grinned to himself. "Aye," he mused out loud. "If I could have a penny for every drop I've tasted, I would be a bluddy rich man by now."

Turning his back on the wall and his memories, he rested his elbows between the upright stones that formed a jagged tooth-like line across the length of the road bridge. He lifted one knee and propped the sole of his wellington boot against the wall, affording him some measure of support as he studied each passer-by with interest. He was hopeful of seeing someone who knew him, and who would perhaps congratulate him when given the good news of his good fortune on the horses. Fred had been raised not more than a few hundred yards from where he was standing, and as he nodded in passing acknowledgement to each one as they walked by, he received a similar friendly nod in return.

Fred cast his mind back over the last three (or was it four?) days since he had been home, and he thought fleetingly of Annie, his long-suffering wife of many years. "I 'spect she'll be off with me again. Ahhh! What the 'ell, she's been off enough before," he muttered under his breath, grinning slightly as he remembered all too vividly some of their more infamous confrontations, which had ended in a full-scale shouting match out on the street for all the world to witness. As usually happened on those occasions, he had done exactly as he had planned to do anyway, even explaining his reasons to anyone who was prepared to listen.

CHAPTER 2

A shock for Fred

ANNIE, FRED'S WIFE, weaving slightly from fatigue and the mortal shame which had just been heaped on her frail shoulders, made her way slowly up the steep hill towards the shabby looking house they rented on a weekly basis from the local District Council. Like all the other council houses, it wasn't much of a place but it was, with the few sticks of furniture she possessed, a place to call home.

She had struggled, with the tenacity of a bull terrier, for many years against ever-mounting odds, to keep a roof over their heads, food on the table and more importantly her family together... that is, until today. The shopkeeper's refusal had been the final blow to whatever remnants of pride she had clung to.

It wasn't unusual in those parts to run up a bill in Shop John; the current owner of the shop, being of a generous nature, was seen by many as a sort of public benefactor and part-time philanthropist. He would, when things became difficult for some of his customers through unemployment or some other form of distress, allow them to have what they needed from his shop on credit, sometimes carrying their debt for months on end until the situation improved for them. He, in the style of the old company shops, knew he had a captive market and would eventually receive his due, paid in full, and his customer's integrity intact.

Today, being Friday morning, Annie had gone down the hill to Shop John for a few essentials to add to their ever-increasing debt. There were never any luxuries in her additions to the bill: a loaf of bread, some cheese, butter and a bit of bacon to boil (it went further that way). Arriving at the counter with her selections, she had placed them on the glass counter in front of him.

But today, the grocer, looking more than a little embarrassed, gently, politely and apologetically refused any more credit until such time that part or all of the existing debt had been squared away.

There was nothing Annie could say in defence. The grocer was a local man, born and bred in the village. He knew well enough all about Fred's activities in the village and beyond. There was no way in the world that anyone could blame him for making a stand on the issue to perhaps force Fred to accept some of his rightful responsibilities.

At that moment, Annie felt totally humiliated; all this, even though he had spoken very quietly, was in front of a shop full of people who knew her. Devastated, she stared at the items on the glass counter top through tear-filled eyes. Then, her thin shoulders sagging with the shame of it all, she turned away, pushing blindly past the other customers to the partly open door. She felt a surge of anger, not because of the refusal by the grocer, but because that bluddy Fred was off somewhere again, enjoying himself on money that was desperately needed to clear their debts at Shop John.

She sat in the chair beside the empty fireplace and stared vacantly into its depths, warm tears of unhappiness trickling slowly down the lines in her sunken cheeks. She took a crumpled cigarette packet from the pocket in her apron and pushed the flap through the sleeve. Absentmindedly she glanced down, tears for an instant distorting her vision: 'Just two left,' she thought, 'and no money for anything else. A few cigarettes and little else is all I seem to get out of life, and now I can't have that either.'

An arm looped around Annie's bony shoulder and she looked up, startled. Lost in her despair she hadn't heard anyone come into the house. Her youngest daughter Joann knelt beside her, making soft comforting sounds as she hugged her mother close to her. Annie felt slightly embarrassed, because she was not one to show much in the way of affection, having suffered rebuttal for so many years at the hands of Fred.

"It's okay, love," she murmured. "I'm all right now, honest." She wiped the tears from her lined face with the back of her hand. She stood up and stared distantly across the mountainside through the curtain-less windows. "So what shall I do now then?" she muttered softly, without realising her resolve was gaining strength.

"What was that, Mam?" Joann asked, looking up into her mother's face.

Without replying to her question, she turned towards the young girl. "Do you think you can ride a bike all the way to Waun-gron? You will have to be very careful, mind, because the main road will be very busy at this time of the day. P'raps you should ride on the path, not the road." Waun-gron was about five miles away and was the village where Annie and Fred had first set up home, and where their five children had been born.

"I think so, Mam. Why then?"

"Never mind the why at the moment. Here's what I want you to do for me." Her voice was suddenly strong with an inner determination. "Go round to Mrs Thomas's and ask if you can borrow Susie's bike for a while. Then, I want you to ride down to our Raymond's in Waun-gron and ask him to please come up here with his van. He promised to help me if ever I was in trouble."

CHAPTER 3

Fred's return
to an empty house

FRED PUSHED HIMSELF upright as his bus turned the corner. Dismissing all thoughts of past battles of will, and the one he was certain would be waiting for him the moment he stepped through the back door, he joined the other passengers waiting patiently to board the bus. In preparation he counted out, from a handful of small change, the exact fare for the five-mile journey to Rhyd-y-groes. Flopping down in the first available seat, he closed his eyes and thought again about the past few days. A secret smile played along the edge of his thin lips as he recounted in his mind all the fun he had had, not forgetting the tally of his 'winnings'. 'Damn,' he thought, with more than a little satisfaction, 'it looks as if my luck has begun to change for the better.' He let out a sigh of contentment as he felt in his pocket for the few remaining crisp banknotes left over from this particular run of good fortune. "And I've still got a bit left over too," he murmured. "Huh?" he said in surprise.

The portly woman in the seat beside him repeated her question. "I said: What did you say?"

"It was nothing. I was just talking to myself, that's all," Fred replied a bit sheepishly. At that moment he felt reluctant, which was unusual for him, to explain his pleasant thoughts to a complete stranger.

"That's a very bad habit you have, if you ask me," she said with a toss of her head. "You could end up in Bridgend," she added, nodding her head again in confirmation. Bridgend is a town in the southern part of the county where a large psychiatric hospital is situated.

"Hey, missus! Now you just hold on there," he said with a grin. "There's nothing wrong with my bluddy head. Anyway, this is where I get off." Rising quickly from his seat before she could add anything else, he made his way to the exit. Glancing back up the aisle he saw the woman still staring at him so with a broad grin he raised his cap to her and she quickly looked away.

He sat for a while on the wide stone window sill of Shop John and watched the bus until it disappeared over the rise in the direction of the Plough Inn. 'Hmm,' he thought, 'it's a bit late in the day to go up there for a few pints and anyway, that old so-and-so of a landlord might not even be there yet.' Trefor, the landlord of the Plough Inn, one of Fred's favourite haunts (especially when he was short of ready money), divided his duties in the pub with running the family farm in the next parish and occasionally he would be forced by circumstances beyond his control to bend the licensing laws just enough to accommodate whichever task required his attention the most.

I'll go up there later, Fred decided, rising from the sill, concluding that it might be better if he put in an appearance at home first. He stretched with his arms out wide and turned for home, half yawning as he made his way up the hill to his house. Arriving at the wrought-iron gate, he paused with his hand on the latch and quickly surveyed the windows facing him; they in turn stared vacantly back at him, showing no sign of life from within. He sucked in a deep breath and squared his shoulders, preparing for the inevitable fray he knew would be waiting as he walked down the path at the side of the house. Entering the back yard he took a quick look into the kennels; the dogs, recognising him in an instant, set up a clamour of barking and tail wagging in welcome. He grinned fondly at them, brushing his hand along the top of pens, and made a mental note that they still had food and water in their bowls. He pulled a face. "I wonder if I will get the same welcome in there," he mused, glancing towards the closed back door.

He stood with his back to the house surveying the mountains that reared their mass steeply to the sky behind the council houses. "Damn," he murmured softly, "it's lovely up here, except for the bluddy winters. Lots of fresh air and open space."

He loved the mountains and the sense of freedom they gave him, a freedom in complete contrast to the daily claustrophobic existence of his working life as a rat catcher, deep underground in the dust-filled tunnels of the local coal mines. He sucked in a deep breath, letting it out slowly, savouring the cool freshness of the mountain air. At that particular moment he was in no hurry to face the inevitable wrath of Annie's sharp tongue and felt he needed to postpone the encounter for as long as humanly possible.

Without moving, he looked over the thick privet hedge at Tŷ Cwm farm and the rushing waters of the small river that bisected the green fields some 300 feet below, down the steep slope dotted with clumps of bright yellow gorse.

'Finally,' he thought, 'the moment of truth has arrived.' With a visible effort, he dragged himself away from the view and turned towards the house, muttering to himself as he did so, "I wonder what gems she'll have on her bluddy tongue this time."

He opened the back door stealthily, pausing for an instant to listen for any sound, then called out in a normal tone, "Helloo! It's meee. I'm home!" He waited a moment or two then called out louder. "Annie! It's me! I'm home!" He still stood on the doorstep, one hand on the door handle, head and shoulders through the half open door, just in case he had to avoid some swiftly flying object or flee in a hurry, as he listened intently for a caustic response to his breezy greeting.

There was no reply. He frowned, staring down at the red bare earthenware tiled floor of the tiny kitchen. He was still unsure of what sort of welcome awaited him when he noticed the old coloured raffia mat which had always graced the centre of the room was not there. His brow furrowed in puzzlement as he stepped away from the doorway and glanced down the garden, noting the empty clothes line. For some reason he couldn't explain, he had fully expected to see the old mat hanging there.

"That's funny," he muttered, feeling a brief surge of annoyance that things were not turning out exactly as he had anticipated. Mentally, he had prepared himself for an argument and at this point there was nothing forthcoming.

'Something is not quite right here,' he thought. Taking a ring of keys from his pocket, he opened the garden shed. Poking his head around the edge of the door, he quickly cast his eyes over the shelves and the wooden bench in front of the single window, not knowing exactly what he expected to see wrong. "Funny," he repeated, returning to the house. Entering, he shouted again, "Hello! It's me!" The uneasiness he had felt earlier was much stronger now that he was fully inside the house. "This place sounds more empty than usual," he muttered. As he turned to close the back door he discovered that the ancient electric stove, which for years had stood in the alcove, slightly behind and to the right of the back door, had disappeared.

"Bluddy 'ell. What the 'ell has been going on here, then?" he shouted, as he ran through into the living room and found it completely bare. "Where's my bluddy sideboard, then?" he yelled, running on into the front room. "Empty!" he shouted. "Bluddy empty. We've been robbed, that's what!" Anger was quickly replacing any feeling of remorse or apology he might have felt or had for his wife. In his mind, at that moment, she was to be held totally responsible of taking care of things while he was away from the home. Where was she when all this happened? "Annie! Where the 'ell are you woman?" He dashed from room to room again, as if he couldn't believe the evidence of his own eyes. Suddenly, he stopped in mid-stride as a singular thought struck him.

"Hey! Wait a bluddy minute here. She can't have gone off and left me, can she?" He groaned in disbelief, his jaw hanging open. He ran outside, slamming the door behind him. He jumped over the low fence separating his house from next door and began rapping frantically on the neighbour's front door.

"Mrs Thomas! Mrs Thomas! Quick, open the door, please," he shouted, his mouth close to the door panels. The front door opened slowly and a frail-looking, grey-haired woman peered at him from the gloom of the hallway. Jinny Thomas, Fred's neighbour's wife, was barely five feet tall and her thin pinched features and pale complexion bore the ravages of a hard life raising seven children on a farm labourer's wages.

"Oh, hello, Fred," she said in soft tones, staring up into his agitated features. "What can I do for you today, then?"

"Well, to tell you the truth of the matter, Mrs Thomas. I think we've been robbed or something. Did you, by any chance, see anything or anyone around our house today? I need to know right away if you have, so I can run down to the post office to call the police to come up as soon as they can." His words came tumbling out one on top if the other, his eyes wide in agitation.

"Now, now, Fred," Mrs Thomas said calmly, stepping forward and patting his arm gently. "I don't think you need to bother the police about this, or anyone else for that matter."

Fred stared at her, momentarily puzzled by her softly spoken words. "And why the 'ell not?" he demanded.

"I think you know well enough why, Fred, without me saying another word." Her words were still softly intoned but at the same time were slightly admonishing as she added. "We haven't lived next door to you all these years without hearing and seeing a few things, mind." She clasped her work worn hands in front of her, almost but not quite, as a symbol of compassion.

"Aw, Mrs Thomas, fach. You don't think she 'ave left me, do you?" He had a pained expression on his face as he uttered the very thought that had occurred to him earlier, but which he had been too stubborn and proud to admit until this very moment.

"Well, it certainly looks that way, Fred, doesn't it? Let me tell you what I saw today and you can judge for yourself the truth of it, okay? There was a large blue van outside your house today and I saw a couple of chaps loading a lot of stuff into it. Bits of furniture and stuff like that. Your Annie was there too and she got into the van with them. Then they left and that's the last I saw of them. I was a bit surprised, mind: after all, we've been neighbours for a good many years now, and she left without even saying goodbye to me or anyone else, as far as I know anyway."

"Well, I go to 'ell. And there's me thinking my luck had changed for the better."

Visibly shaken by her revelation he sat down on the edge of the doorstep, arms resting across his knees as he studied his fingernails and the backs of his gnarled hands as if seeking a solution to his problems there. "That bluddy Raymond," he muttered, half to himself.

"Would you like a nice cup of tea, Fred? The kettle has just boiled. Come on in, mun. A cup of tea will do you the world of good. Come on," she coaxed, not unsympathetically. Fred looked up over his shoulder at the little woman as she stepped back and held the door open a little wider.

"Um, yes, please, if you're sure it's no bother. I could do with a bit of a lift, I can tell you." He rose to his feet and walked behind her down the gloomy hallway into the warmth of the cosy back kitchen. Without being asked, he seated himself at the small table, looking more than a little dejected at this turn of events, while Mrs Thomas busied herself getting cups and saucers ready on the snow-white table cloth. She poured the boiling water onto a heaped spoonful of loose tea leaves, stirring them rapidly, as if to make them brew all the quicker.

It was quiet in the warmth of the kitchen. Later, as Jinny poured the tea, she asked Fred what he intended doing about his wife's sudden and hurried departure. "Are you going to go and look for her, Fred? Ask her to come home, p'raps? Do you think she would come home if you did?"

"I dunno," he said glumly, his bottom lip pushed out as he thought about it. "She's a very stubborn woman, see, an' if she's taken into her head to go this far, there's no telling what she'll do now. To be truthful, I can't see her ever coming back here. In my mind I'm pretty sure of that now. What do you think?"

"Well, what if you went to her and said you were sorry or something?" she pressed. "P'raps she'd see things in a different light. P'raps she'd take you and Colin in, wherever she is?"

"Oh aye, sure to be," Fred said somewhat disparagingly, then he added with bitter emphasis. "Listen. She wouldn't even dream of doing something like that. Oh no, Mrs Thomas. The more I think about it, the more I am convinced that she has been planning this for a while now."

Colin was Fred and Annie's eldest son, who had had little choice but to return home to his parents after his own marriage failed. Colin's wife, who had refused to put up with him joining his father in gallivanting all over the place, day and night, on the flimsiest of pretexts, had left him for the stability of a more responsible older man and had moved away from the district.

Colin was, in general, much like his father. Although slightly taller, his shoulders were narrower and he had his mother's narrow pinched features, with long blond hair swept back from a high forehead and plastered down with any Brilliantine he could lay his hands on; goodness knows why, because he invariably sported a flat cloth cap pulled down firmly to his ears. In every other way he was the double of his father, and just like Fred he was in his element when he was in the outdoors. He worked in the same coal mine as his father, but was a trained mechanic, skilled in the repair of anything mechanical underground. Fred and Colin went everywhere together and did most things as one, except playing cards, in which Fred had not the slightest interest. Apart from that, the two men were seen more as firm friends than father and son. They called themselves 'the Partners'.

Fred sipped slowly at the hot liquid, going back in his mind over the years they had spent raising their five children.

True, it hadn't been easy, but things weren't all that bad either, and we had managed. I was working regular, but the money was small. Annie was home all the time then, and that little house in Waun-gron sparkled and the brass-work was polished til it gleamed like gold.

Aye, then me and our Colin going after rabbits down in Carmarthen with George and the boys, coming home with a sackful of rabbits to sell around the village for little more than the price of a cartridge. We had a lovely garden there too, beautiful black dirt you could grow anything in, not like the bluddy rubbish we've got up here, half clay and full of stones. What the 'ell happened to us.

Fred's thoughts turned to Eva, his first-born child. She's been married for quite a few years now. They do say that time flies and it does, by damn. I wonder if she knew anything about all this nonsense while I was staying there these past few days? I wonder what the others will have to say about it, especially when they think about all the arguments me and Annie have had in front of them. Nothing, I suppose. Well, our Roland has his own life now with a wife and children, without me pestering him about his mother leaving me in the lurch.

Mentally he shrugged as his thoughts turned to Shirley, his middle daughter, who was at present out in America working for some rich family as a nanny; the lucky so-and-so to be away from all this, living it up in the sunshine. His lips twitched into a wry smile. So, that only leaves our Joann to worry about. What age is she now? 14? I suppose she left with her mother too.

He replaced the empty cup carefully in the centre of the saucer and said: "I'm sorry to bother you like this, Mrs Thomas, but I wonder if you can remember something for me. Did you, by any chance, see our Joann go with them in the van? See, I wouldn't want her to come home to an empty house like I did. It wouldn't be right, you know, for that to happen."

Jinny Thomas stared at him for a moment or two, slightly taken aback, until she realised that somewhere deep inside he still had a little spark of decency and wasn't quite the rascal that everyone thought he was. "Well, yes I did, Fred. Now that I come to think of it, I remember she came out of the house carrying a couple of small cases. Then she got into the van with one of the chaps that were helping your wife. Yes, that was it. It was a big dark blue van."

"From your description that sounds like our Ray's van from Waun-gron," Fred grunted. He leaned on his elbow at the table, forehead resting on the palm of his hand as he stared unseeing at the fine lines in the white tablecloth. It was quite obvious that his thoughts were elsewhere at that particular moment.

Mrs Thomas attempted to raise him from his reverie. "Hey, Fred! How about another cup of tea? I'm sure it will make you feel a lot better. C'mon."

He looked up with a weak grin. "Aye, I suppose I could at that. I have to thank you, Mrs Thomas, for your kindness in my moment of trouble." He sighed heavily, as if all the woes in the world had suddenly descended on his shoulders alone.

She pursed her lips and proceeded to busy herself about the kitchen, effectively ignoring Fred. She was in no mood to commiserate or otherwise with him regarding Annie's sudden departure. She wouldn't tell him as much, unless pushed, but she had seen enough of his antics over the years to believe that his wife had no doubt done the right thing this day. 'P'raps this will shake a bit of sense into him,' she thought, glancing quickly at him and then away from his sorry expression, but feeling little sympathy for his present predicament.

Suddenly, as if coming to a momentous decision, Fred picked up the cup of tea and drained it, gulping down the hot fluid without batting an eyelid. "Well, Mrs Thomas, thanks again for the tea, it was great. Now, I had better go and take a closer look at what she has left behind. Just wait until our Colin comes home from work. He'll be tampin' about today's nonsense, that's a certainty."

"I don't think so, Fred." She studied his features shrewdly and added, "And, to be quite honest with you, Fred, if truth be known, I don't think that *you* are all that aggrieved about it either." She gave a disapproving lift to her chin as she spoke.

Fred stood sideways on the doorstep, looking first at his accuser then out into the street and back again, his features breaking slowly into a lopsided grin. "Well, we'll just have to wait for the outcome of that, won't we, Mrs Thomas? Thanks a lot for the information, though." She pursed her lips tightly to prevent herself adding a few more barbs of her own, then nodding briefly, she closed the door on his retreating figure.

Fred stood for a few moments on the front step of his house before fishing in his pocket for his key ring. He opened the door and went in, closing it carefully behind him. He leaned with his back against the door in the darkness as he listened to the overwhelming silence of the almost empty house. A feeling of remorse, followed by anger at his predicament swept over him. Suddenly, in the midst of his rollercoaster of emotions a horrifying thought struck him and he muttered angrily, "My bed! I hope she's left me a bluddy bed to sleep in!" He ran clattering up the bare wooden stairs two at a time, almost falling on his face in his haste. "Now then, let's see what she's left up here..." Gasping for breath, he pushed open the door to their former bedroom and, hanging onto the door handle for support, he surveyed the room in an instant. "Uh," he grunted. "Thank God for that. It's still bluddy here!"

The sagging iron frame bed stood forlornly in the centre of the bare unpainted wooden floor. A couple of threadbare woollen blankets and a single lumpy pillow were thrown in a heap on the equally lumpy striped mattress. There were no bed sheets to be seen. The small amount of other furniture that had once graced this room had gone, as had the tiny strip of worn carpet in front of the empty tiled grate. He had seen enough. He spun on his heel and poked his head into Colin's room, and noted there was some sort of bed in there too but precious little else. No mats or furniture, just cold bare linoleum. Not even curtains hung over the slightly rusty steel-framed windows.

"Clever," he said aloud. "Bluddy clever!" The sound of his own voice echoed eerily in the almost empty room. He descended the stairs at a much slower pace as it really began to sink in that his wife had indeed left him – and, what's more, had left him and his son only the barest of essentials. He gave out an involuntary sob and leaned against the stairwell wall for a few moments, his eyes tightly closed to prevent any tears of self pity from escaping. "Bluddy 'ell," he muttered tensely, at the same time gritting his teeth to fight the emotion that suddenly welled up in him. "What am I going to do now? What a bluddy mess to come home to."

Downstairs, the large front room was empty too, except for the cracked and torn linoleum and some faded yellow curtains. The living room wasn't much better off. A small work table, that had once been in the kitchen, now stood in front of the window facing the mountain, a rickety chair placed on each side. Fred tilted one of them up on two legs to examine it. "These bluddy things are not ours," he growled, a surge of anger rapidly building once more within him. "She must have brought these things from somewhere else so she could take ours. Oh, the rotten so-and-so. I can't believe she had the gall to do this to me!"

Out in the tiny kitchen he rummaged through the drawers in the built-in cabinet. "Just look at this, will you," he yelped in disbelief. "There's just two of every bluddy thing!" He looked around wildly, flinging this door and that door open, briefly examining the contents and getting angrier by the second. There was no food to speak of in the pantry, just a few seedy potatoes and some rubbery looking carrots. The electric stove was missing too.

"What am I going to do?" he ranted. "What am I supposed to cook on? If I do any cooking at all!" He answered his own question out loud. "On the bluddy fireplace, I suppose." The sound of his bitterness echoed again in his ears. Angrily he returned to the living room, his eyes lingering momentarily on each stick of furniture that remained.

"Well, I don't bluddy well know," he said aloud. "P'raps it is all my fault, but at least she could've said something, mun." His anger fizzled out as quickly as it had formed. Feeling thoroughly miserable with his lot in life at that particular moment, he sat down heavily in one of the two dilapidated chairs beside the combination oven/fireplace and contemplated the long-dead fire. "Damn it all!" he said aloud. "Even this has gone out and left me." He laughed out loud at his own joke and something of his former good humour from earlier in the day began to return. 'Well, let's face it, Fred,' he thought, 'the job has been done now and maybe this is not a bad thing, after all is said and done. At least I can't get into any arguments with myself, can I?' He got to his feet and set about re-lighting the fire. When it was burning brightly he put the kettle on the hob with the intention of making some tea. He settled back into the chair, his stockinged feet propped against the oven door for extra warmth, while he waited for Colin to come home from work. Slowly his eyes closed in the radiant warmth of the fire as he imagined, in his mind's eye, how he and his 'Partner' Colin could best make use of all their spare time from now on…

Fred awoke with a start. The room was in total darkness. "Bluddy 'ell. What time is it, I wonder?" he muttered, climbing stiffly to his feet and groaning with the pangs of pain behind his knees. He switched on the light, the bare bulb shining starkly against the yellowed ceiling. He stared open mouthed at it for a few seconds. "And where the 'ell is the… Oh, aye. She 'ave taken that too, by damn!" He groaned again as he stretched. "I wonder where our Colin is, then? Stopped off somewhere for a pint, I suppose."

He paused in thought. "At least I hope that is where he is. If I find out they have all ganged up on me there will be a bluddy row, I can tell you." He smiled, suddenly remembering. "Nah! She 'ave left two of everything so he doesn't know a thing about this yet." He paced back and forth, at the same time rubbing the backs of his legs vigorously in an effort to restore some circulation, pausing only to pick up the kettle, which had boiled dry while he slept. "Damn it all," he muttered, bitterness in his tone. "It seems like I can't take my eyes off anything for a second around here, without something going wrong. Ah, well. What the 'ell, I say." He moved across the room to stand in front of the window, hands resting on the rickety table. From where he stood, he could see the headlights of some cars moving along the road which led to the next valley, and the thin line of street lamps twinkling in the darkness on the same road that led to the Plough Inn.

"Now then, let me see," he said to himself mockingly. "What shall I do tonight?" It was not as if he was some kind of millionaire with a multitude of avenues open to him just begging to be explored. He had just £5 in his pocket, not including a handful of loose change, which at that particular moment was threatening to burn a large hole in it. First of all, he decided, a wash and brush up, then a quick shave and I'll be as right as rain.

He glanced towards the now dead fire. Well, I'm not lighting you again tonight. To 'ell with it. I'll just have to shave in cold water, I've done it before. He laughed out loud, his spirits rising by the second. "I'll have a few pints of liquid inspiration in the Plough and I'll feel better."

He was out of the house in less than ten minutes, walking briskly down the hill to join up with the road which would take him to the Plough Inn. The road up to the pub was narrow and winding with barely enough room for two cars to pass each other, and as he walked between the tall hedgerows, his thoughts dwelt again on the day's happenings. I'm going to make the most of this bit of freedom, he vowed to himself. You never know with our Annie, she might decide to come back home. Which would be okay, but not for a while, is it. He grinned to himself. "To 'ell with that bluddy nonsense," he said aloud, quickening his steps towards the Plough.

As he crested the hill, he could see the light over the front door of the pub, which in his imagination appeared to be beckoning to him from almost half a mile away. His spirits continued to rise and the closer he got to his destination, the more jaunty his step became. He chuckled to himself. If nothing else comes of it, you can guarantee we'll have a few laughs out of it, somewhere along the line. "To 'ell with all of them, especially 'er."

CHAPTER 4

The Plough Inn

THE PLOUGH WAS an ancient inn. The silent three-foot thick walls of stone and mortar, and its cool, dimly-lit rooms gave one the impression of it having stood on this site forever. There was a pervading smell of beer and stale pipe tobacco, and you felt in the stillness, if you listened intently with your imagination, you could still hear the faint tramp of miners' nailed boots as they moved across the slate and stone-flagged floors.

The décor of the men's bar was not much to look at. The regulars, who were there on a daily basis, showed little concern for the numerous patches of peeling paint, the faded and yellowed wallpaper, or the half dozen or so battered tables surrounded by an incredible mixture of rickety chairs, collected, or so it would appear, from every rummage sale under the sun. The most redeeming feature of the Plough Inn, however, was, without doubt, the selection of draught beers. They were all exceptionally good and although the place was a bit untidy, and sometimes a little dusty from the passing traffic from the nearby opencast mine, the glasses the amber nectar was served in were never less than sparkling clean. Trefor, the landlord, made sure that anyone coming down from the mountains behind the pub, or miners on their way home from labouring in the nearby coalmines, each and every one, found warmth and friendly hospitality within the confines of the Plough.

The pub itself had been in the hands of Trefor's family for more than a century, and, without doubt, had been part of the village for a lot longer than that. In earlier times the ale had been served from a large chipped enamel jug, the froth off the beer foaming and bubbling over the brim as it was poured into quart glasses. It was a jug that had seen a lot of service over the years; it needed to be filled with great frequency from the oaken casks standing like sentinels on wooden racks in the cool back room.

A few years before the time of this tale, one of the major breweries in Wales had attempted unsuccessfully to purchase outright control of the pub from the family, but they had closed ranks and staunchly refused to become a one-brewery establishment. Trefor Plough (as he was known to everyone in the area) liked the look of the sign above the front entrance which proclaimed for all the world to see that it was a Free House; besides, most of his regular patrons expected to have freedom of choice when they frequented the Plough, for their moods changed as quickly as did their preference for a different taste in beer.

The only major event that had occurred in living memory was when the landlord's family decided to bring the Plough somewhat closer to the twentieth century, with their idea of modernisation. Two of the larger rooms were made into one long room; the magical cool back room, where the oak barrels had stood, disappeared for ever. The familiar flag-stoned floor of grey north-Walian slate had been taken up and replaced with concrete and covered over with plain plastic tiles. A plastic facsimile of a bar was installed, replacing the familiar oaken counter across which so many hundreds of ales had passed, sporting a pair of plain pull pumps; the familiar enamel jug was no more.

The final step towards 'modernisation' was the removal of the two pot-bellied, black-leaded stoves that had stood in good stead for so many years past. These had been strategically placed well away from the outer walls, allowing, on cold winter nights, sufficient room for the patrons to crowd close to them on all sides. Unfortunately for the regulars, the new coal burning unit, even though it was still in the men's bar, stood almost flush against the wall and therefore didn't offer the same warmth or appeal the old black-leaded stoves had given. To some of the older men who patronised the Plough with unfailing regularity, this was a mistake of immense importance and they lost little time in letting the landlord know how they felt about it.

Trefor, to be fair, had made a genuine effort to make some amends for the disruption to the peace and quiet of before. He installed a pair of tall-backed oaken settles, one on either side of the offending heating unit. These well-worn seats were intended to bring some sort of cosiness to the area around the stove, and also to form a focal point in the long room centring on the largest table, where most of the action seemed to take place when a card game was in progress. In part, for a few of the older men at least, the settles had the desired effect, as they took possession of a particular spot on each settle, by virtue of their daily and nightly attendance at the pub: a right that was accepted without any resentment from the other patrons of the men's bar (but woe betide anyone who transgressed that right).

However, such major upheavals did not sit at all well, at first, with some of the older men, since any deviation from what they considered to be their traditional way of life was bound to be, for them personally, something of a traumatic experience, and was accepted only after much grumbling and copious quantities of free beer from the landlord.

Eventually, as all things do, the newness of the alterations wore off, and everything gradually settled back into the old ways. Peace and quiet reigned once again. For the time being...

CHAPTER 5

Return of the prodigal

"FIFTEEN TWO, FIFTEEN four and two is six and not a penny more, boys." In quiet tones a voice was calling out his score in the game of four-handed crib being played on the large farmhouse table situated in front of the shuttered window, facing the road which ran through the hamlet of Cwm Du.

Arwyn, a tall, bespectacled, avuncular-looking farmer who frequented the bar after his daily work was completed, sat perched in an ungainly fashion on a tall wooden stool. He was sitting sideways to the bar, leaning on his elbow with one long leg outstretched towards the centre of the room as he half-listened to the latest news reports on the TV and tried unsuccessfully to oversee the card game at the same time. However, his divided attention was further distracted by something going on at the other end of the bar. The TV was unusually subdued, as were the rest of the Saturday night crowd of regulars.

Johnny Wills, a man in his early thirties built like a rugby prop forward, a position he had played for a while with one of the local clubs, was in his usual spot at the far end of the long bar. He was, at present, the chairman of the local parish council and also the elected representative for the parish on the Neath Rural

District Council. He typified the average Welshman: slightly less than medium height, dark-haired with sharp dark eyes. He had a firm set to his solid jaw which did little to belie the aggressive nature lurking just below the surface. He was, at that moment, in close but quiet conversation with the landlord.

Trefor was leaning forward listening intently to something Johnny was saying, his forearms resting comfortably on top of the bar, his meaty hands clasped lightly together. He was a short, portly, complacent man in his middle fifties, round-featured with distinctive ruddy-coloured jowls. He was blessed with a small snub red nose and sharp, intelligent eyes under very dark bushy eyebrows. He was a confirmed bachelor and a born practical joker, as everyone who knew him was well aware.

Arwyn squinted his eyes sideways at the two men, then twisted slightly on the stool to get a better view of the object of their attention. He had noticed that in the midst of their conversation they would occasionally cast surreptitious glances in the direction of Old John Shinkins, who was seated in his usual place on the far side of the stove. He too, had caught some of their glances but appeared to be unconcerned by pretending to watch the card game from a distance. However, he was very much aware of the landlord's close scrutiny, and knew full well that Trefor was angling for something. He also knew, if this was anything like his usual little tricks, he was attempting to get an argument going amongst some of the regulars over some touchy local issue, with the councillor at his elbow providing the necessary ammunition for him to fire. It was Trefor Plough's usual method of creating what he believed was the right kind of noisy Saturday night atmosphere.

Old John was a retired mineworker who bore ample witness, through the many blue-tinted scars which marred the backs of his gnarled hands and his florid features, to a lifetime spent toiling in the bowels of the earth. He stole a glance across the room at the landlord from under the brim of his cap and felt a sudden surge of irritation. He turned his attention back to the card game, tucking the ends of his woollen muffler impatiently down the front of his old grey cardigan. He nodded to himself, the muscles on his jaw tightening briefly, as he said under his breath, "Well, he's not bringing me into any old nonsense here tonight." Involuntarily, he raised his voice, pointing an accusing finger at the landlord. "Hey, Trefor! Don't you go thinking for one minute you are going to bring me into any old row here tonight! I'm damned if you will. So there!"

"Who, me?" Trefor smiling broadly, raised his eyebrows in mock surprise, while at the same time pointing a stubby forefinger at himself. "Now come on, John bach. You know me better than that, don't you?"

"Oh, aye. I know you, all right!" Old John suddenly realised, his quick temper rising nicely to boiling point, that he had done exactly as Trefor had wanted him to and taken the bait, hook, line and sinker. He clamped his mouth tight and pulled the brim of his cap down hard, shading the anger in his eyes. He had fallen for that old trick of Trefor's once again, he thought angrily.

"You lost him, Tref," Johnny murmured in an aside.

"No, I 'aven't. Give 'im a couple of minutes to cool down a bit, then we'll wind 'im up again."

Trefor Plough was well aware that Old John, one of the catalysts he was attempting to prime, could be counted on (most of the time) to argue the toss over the slightest thing when he was in the right frame of mind. It also meant that the beer would begin to flow more readily as tempers began to flare; the participants became more and more agitated as they postulated and argued over a specific issue that was dear to them. These animated discussions never came to blows or anything even approaching that, but it was extremely good for the business of selling beer and more especially if Trefor managed to add a few barbs of his own as he served beer to the different factions. On this particular night, however, he was having little success in achieving his objective, when the heavy oak door into the bar swung open. It was Fred. He stood in the centre of the doorway, his face beaming, with one hand on the doorknob and the other held up high in a kind of salute to everyone in the room.

"Here I am, boys!" he said loudly. "I'm back. Fred is back!" The card game continued as if no one had entered the room, the four players calling out their scores in the same quiet tones.

"Hoy! Remember me?" Fred tried again for recognition without success.

Trefor's ruddy feature lit up with a broad smile. "Well, well. Look at this, will you? Return of the prodigal son, by damn. Where have you been, Fred? We've all missed your noise."

"And his lip," Johnny said in an aside, grinning at the landlord's gleeful expression.

Fred still stood in the open doorway in all his glory, including his ratting cap perched jauntily to one side of his head.

"Shut the bluddy door, Fred," ordered one of the card players with his back to Fred. He knew very well who it was the moment he had spoken. "There's a 'ell of a draft coming through yere and only since you came in, too." He winked broadly at the other players.

"Awright, awright. Please your bluddy selves then. Take no notice, boys, It's only Fred!" He dropped his arm and swung the door shut behind him with a quick twist and a shove of his hip.

"A pint, landlord, as quick as you like. I'm just dying of thirst. And I want a pint of your best too," he added, turning to survey the rest of the patrons in the bar.

"Let me see the colour of your money first, Fred!" Trefor spoke in his sternest tones. Fred had materialised like the answer to an unspoken prayer. 'Now,' he thought, 'we'll have ourselves a bit of fun to liven up the night.'

Fred was the product of the old parish, raised there, the first-born son of his mother's second marriage. He had arrived into a ready-made family of two older brothers and two older sisters, who from the very beginning had done their best to make him feel totally unwelcome. He had grown up during the Depression years, a time when many people were unemployed and had little or no money coming into their homes, and so from a very early age he had been forced by circumstances to scrounge and forage for just enough to survive. Conditions were such that if the parish council had work that needed doing, it was first offered to unemployed men with families to support, then to unemployed married men. Finally, if anything was left over, it was offered to single able-bodied men. Fred hadn't felt it necessary, at that stage in his life, to get married to secure some occasional employment, and he became quite adept at surviving in other ways.

One of the absolute necessities for survival during that stage of his young life was finding sufficient food on a daily basis. To this end, he began to develop a routine. He called on each of the local farmers in turn throughout the district and sometimes beyond, to offer his services for a day or even half a day in exchange for a meal or two. Since he never quite knew when or from where his next meal would come, he developed an incredible capacity to eat twice as much as the average man whenever the opportunity presented itself.

There was also another distinct advantage to this planned strategy. As he began to be more and more well known to the farmers in the district, he became more and more familiar with the untold acres of fields and woodlands owned or managed by them. He had freedom to roam as he pleased; he quickly learned not only the ways of hunting and trapping small game, but also the means for the destruction of vermin that preyed on the farmer's flocks. As he grew in stature, so did his reputation as a hunter (or, as some of the old-timers of the day said of him: "He could live where crows would starve.") Fred always took these disparaging comments as something of a compliment and bragged openly about it at every opportunity.

"I have to tell you about it, boys. I am a survivor and a legend in my own time." He plonked a handful of coins on the bar top and began to lift the glass to his lips. The skirt of his jacket thrown back to one side and one hand on his hip, he surveyed the room again. 'Hmm,' he thought, 'no strangers in tonight then.' He was always on the lookout for the unwary traveller to regale with some story or other about himself, in the hope of them buying him a pint or two, just to get rid of him. He didn't mind taking the odd insult or two along the way, especially if it meant a free beer at the end.

"Well, Fred, where you been, then?" Willi Bray's curiosity had been piqued. He wasn't really nosy in the general sense of the word; he just liked to be in the know regarding everybody's business, just in case someone should ask. He was one of Fred's equals in knowing everything about everybody and nothing about anything at all.

Absentmindedly Fred replied, "I've just come back from Waun-gron, mun." He took another swig then paused in mid-swallow. A slightly puzzled expression passed over his broad features and he smacked his lips as he held the pint glass up to the dim light overhead. He turned and faced the brighter light over the card table and again lifted the glass to study the slightly clouded liquid.

"Wait for it," Trefor murmured to the councillor at his elbow. "Here we go, boys."

"Trefor!" Fred yelled at the top of his voice. "What's this bluddy rubbish you've served me? First bluddy pull, by damn. You've done it again to me, 'aven't you. I've a good mind to report you to someone. You're always doing this to me. It's not bluddy fair!"

"Oh aye," said Trefor dryly, "and I notice that you always drink more than half a pint of it before you complain, too. Is *that* fair?"

"That's not the point, Trefor!" Fred yelled, storming back across the floor to the bar. "Here, 'ave the bluddy stuff back and give me a pint of the best bitter I asked for."

"Oooh? Best is it? You didn't pay me for best. I suppose you didn't notice that either, did you?" Trefor's voice was now rising to match Fred's tone in mock anger.

"Hey! Keep the bluddy noise down, will you?" Roy shouted above the din. "Hey, Fred! You haven't been in here more than five minutes and already there's a bluddy row. Now shut up for goodness sake, so we can have a bit of peace and quiet here, okay?" Turning his attention back to the card game he said, "Whose deal is it, boys? Damn it all, that Fred is a noisy sod and no mistake."

Roy Childs was usually a fairly placid man. He was in his middle years, above average height and always well turned out in dark grey flannels, sports jacket, white shirt and regimental tie, which for the working men who frequented the Plough Inn could be considered a bit over-dressed. He had dark wavy hair complimenting a full almost-black beard, which at certain times gave him a fierce pirate-like appearance. He was a well-educated, professional man, employed as a civil engineer at one of the local opencast coal mines. Unfortunately, he wasn't very civil as far as Fred was concerned. He had a hard rasping voice and frequently used the edge of it when speaking to or talking about Fred. He seemed to derive some sort of perverse satisfaction from making fun of him in front of others.

Fred was well aware of Roy's feelings. He turned to pull a face at Roy's back then banged his glass loudly on the bar, splashing the remaining beer in all directions.

"Fill 'er up, landlord," he ordered gruffly. "And, in a fresh glass, if you please." He returned to the warmth of the stove, where he stood rubbing the backs of his legs in the fierce heat of the open door.

"Well go on, Fred! Tell us all what you've been up to, then! We 'aven't seen hide or hair of you f'rages." Willi Bray was a tiny man in every sense of the word, except in voice. It was often said of him, sometimes a little unkindly perhaps, that he could talk a glass eye to sleep and still have enough breath left over to exhaust anyone who was prepared to listen. Speculation was that this peculiar affliction was the direct result of not being able to get a word in edgeways at home and therefore he hoarded every scrap of energy he had until he arrived at the men's bar in the Plough Inn. At that particular moment though, he wanted, more than anything else, to hear exactly what Fred had been doing over the past few days.

"Aww, come on, Fred," he said persuasively. "There's more to it, isn't there?"

"Oh aye. There's more to it all right." He stared at Willi, his thoughts obviously elsewhere at that moment. "Oh yeh, I've been stopping in my daughter's house in Waun-gron since last Wednesday, and on Thursday I went up to the Legion for a few pints and was jammy enough to win some money on bingo, so I decided, since my luck seemed to in, to stay down in Waungron a bit longer, and on Friday I had a bit of decent luck on the horses. I tell you boys, my luck seemed to be in at last," he bragged, rubbing his hands together gleefully. Few of the other patrons had any interest at all Fred's revelations of his good fortune, except one.

"You winning on the horses, Fred?" Roy cut in derisively, his back to Fred. "You couldn't pick your nose tidy, never mind picking a winner from a bunch of nags you have never seen before."

"Hey! Fair play, Roy!" Old John interrupted angrily, jumping to his feet. "Why don't you just leave 'im alone to tell about his old nonsense in Waun-gron and you just get on with your game of cards. All right?" Ruffled by Roy's scathing remarks and Trefor's attempts to wind him up, Old John continued to glare at Roy's back as he slowly resumed his personal seat on the settle next to the stove.

"Aye, that's right," Fred added, grateful for any support at that moment, his thoughts dwelling momentarily on his wife. "You just wait till I tell you what 'ave happened to me, boys. Just you wait a minute." He paused, fighting desperately to hold back the hurt that grew like a knot in the pit of his stomach. He drew in a deep breath as he looked at the expectant faces of the men around him, then said, letting out his pent-up breath: "Well, boys. She've bolted. When I came home today, she'd bluddy gone. Gone!" He laughed with a touch of bravado. Suddenly, Fred became the centre of interest as they all stared silently at him in momentary shock.

Roy turned in his chair to look at Fred, shaking his head with something akin to sympathy in his eyes. "I'm really sorry to hear that, Fred."

Fred nodded acknowledgement and said, "Aye. She 'ave bluddy bolted, boys. Gone and left me she has." His tone of voice became a little bitter and more subdued. "Well, what do you think of that, then?"

"Who has?" Willi asked stupidly. "Your daughter, is it?"

"'Ell no! Our Annie, my wife, that's who, you daft sod!" He began laughing but the sound had a hollow ring to it as he pretended to wipe a tear of mirth from the corners of his eyes. He thrust his hands deep into his trouser pockets and stared down at the floor rocking gently back and forth on his heels.

"Well, go on, mun, what's the rest of it?" Willi prompted unfeelingly.

"For God sake, Willi!" Fred exploded. "That's bluddy it! I came home, opened the back door and saw the mat was missing, so I looked outside and it wasn't there. So, when I went back in I found just about everything else was gone too. At first I thought we had been robbed, and to tell you the truth I was on the point of calling for the police."

Roy, his brief moment of compassion for Fred's misfortune spent, muttered, "I think they would have to be hard up to steal from you, Fred."

"What was that, Roy?" Fred's hearing was still quite sharp.

"I said, you must be feeling in a bad way," he sniggered, bowing his head.

"Nah! It's just me and our Colin now," he replied nonchalantly, deciding to gloss over Roy's snide remark, which he had heard quite clearly. "Colin and me, we're Partners, you know, and we'll manage okay, so don't you worry yourselves on our account, boys."

Roy shrugged, grinning at the others around the table, as Fred went on. "We've got a table and a chair each, some dishes and a we've got a bed each. What more do we need, I ask you?" He shrugged his broad shoulders. "Hey, Mr Landlord!" he shouted from his spot in front of the stove. "Where's my pint?"

"Tip up first, Mr Howells. I want to see the colour of your money before you get any beer in this establishment." Trefor shouted his reply as he served Old John, then with his head bowed he said in a quiet aside: "Watch me have him going on this one, John bach. I guarantee it will take 'is mind off his troubles in double quick time." Raising his voice he said loudly and in his sternest tones. "I want to see the coin of the realm first, Fred, or you're going to be out of luck for any more beer tonight."

Without replying to the taunt Fred sauntered casually over to the bar and, taking a handful of coins from his pocket, proceeded to count out the exact amount of coins onto the bar. "How's that, Mr Landlord," he smirked. "I heard you clear enough the first time."

"Well, now then, let me see." Trefor held the pint glass tightly onto the bar top with one meaty fist while he laboriously counted Fred's pile of coins with the other, turning each one's face value as he did so.

Fred meanwhile had grabbed the handle and vainly tried to lift the glass off the bar without spilling any of the amber fluid, with Old John grinning like a Cheshire cat beside him. "Hey, c'mon, Trefor. Let it go, mun."

"Be quiet, Fred. Can't you see I'm counting your money?" Fred tried once again to lift the firmly held glass and failed, much to the amusement of the other men standing at the bar waiting to be served. Suddenly tiring of Trefor's obstructive tactics, he raised himself on tip toe and like a horse to water, he leaned over the bar and lowered his mouth to the glass and sucked in as much beer as he could hold in his mouth. Amid laughter from the onlookers, Trefor let go of the glass and swept Fred's coins uncounted into the open till drawer. He smiled apologetically as Fred glowered at him. "I'm sorry about that, Fred, but I had to count it a few times because you kept on interrupting me with your old nonsense." He shrugged, and knew at once his ploy had had the desired effect when Fred growled, "I'll get you for that, Trefor Plough." He turned away from the bar with the start of a grin, which Trefor was just able to see, then he stopped dead in his tracks. "Hey! Wait a minute here! What's the game, Trefor?" He spun around to face him, pointing a finger accusingly at the pint glass in his hand. "This is the second one I am paying for and I haven't finished one pint yet. What about that rubbish you served me first then?"

"Oh, yes. I am so sorry, Fred." Trefor raised his eyebrows in all innocence "It was a pure lapse of memory on my part. You know that." A slow knowing smile lit up his round features while his eye sparkled with amusement. He had accomplished exactly what he had set out to do.

"A lapse of memory? Is it by damn? Not on your part, Trefor Plough, I know that well enough. On my part you mean! See that boys!" He turned to the room in general. "John, you'll be my witness. He just tried to do me, a poor working man, out of a pint of best bitter while I was gassin' about my troubles with our Annie."

"Hey, now then Fred! Hold it right there. Don't you bring me into your squabbles." Old John rose to his feet waving his arms back and forth erratically thereby denying any connection with Trefor's little scheme to get Fred's mind off his present problem. "I don't watch what you do, mind!"

"Don't you, by damn?" Fred's head thrust forward aggressively. "John, you are always watching somebody, an' minding their business too, sometimes." He turned his attention back to the landlord, his marginal dispute with Old John completely forgotten. "Now then, Trefor. You still owe me a pint of best bitter, right?"

"Right you are, Fred. A pint it is and I'm not going to mention in front of everyone here tonight how much you OWE ME, on the slate, right?"

"Haisht, Tref! That's something between you and me and nobody else, right?"

"Right."

Honour satisfied for the moment, Fred took another long swallow. "Damn, now that is a good pint," he said licking his lips appreciatively, then with one final gulp he emptied the glass. "Right then, Tref. I'll 'ave the other one now then. The one I just paid for, right?" He paused grinning at the landlord. "It's just in case I forget, see... I think there is something wrong with my memory tonight. Too much excitement, I 'spect." His glass now refilled to his satisfaction, he returned to his place in front of the stove. Sweeping the room with his eyes, he realised that the interest the regulars had shown in his misfortune had been, as usual, very short-lived. He nodded to himself, somewhat disillusioned but not really surprised by their attitude. After all, how could he expect them to know what it feels like to find yourself alone after so many years of married life. 'Aye, you sods,' he thought, 'only interested in what Fred says and does when I'm in a spot of bother. But wait on, we'll see what happens from now on.'

"Hey, Fred." Old John tugged at the edge of Fred's jacket. "Come and sit down by yere and tell me what has been going on then".

He looked down at the older man for a moment, then at the vacant spot beside him on the settle, then shrugged, as if it didn't matter very much what he did or said now, it wasn't going to change anything. He squeezed between the two tables and sat down heavily beside Old John. "Aye, John bach, that's it in a nutshell. She 'ave left me in the lurch after all these years together. I never thought for one minute she would do that, mind. But there you are. You never bluddy-well know, John". His remorse showed briefly in his eyes as he sighed.

"So, what brought all this to a head then?" John inquired softly. He didn't want anyone else to join in on this quiet discussion. He had known Fred since he was a young lad, having been born and raised in the same area of the old parish where Fred had been born, and felt a certain kinship towards him. He didn't agree with many of Fred's antics and money-making schemes but nevertheless he felt it wasn't right that everyone seemed to pick on him just for a bit of fun. Although (he grinned briefly to himself) Fred sometimes brought retribution on himself without even trying and then joined in the fun in making sport of himself. He turned sideways to face him.

"Say, Fred, had you been having rows or something like 'at? You know, nasty like?"

"Oh aye, but not really nasty like. You know how it happens. We was always 'aving a row over something or other, mostly about money, but so does everybody else, don't they? Another thing she was always on about was me being out all over the place. She didn't like that, but she knew what I was like. Even before we were married, I was always out somewhere," he said defensively. "Anyway, John bach, it don't matter a bit now. She's done it and gone somewhere else to live and I don't care. Good luck to her, I say. It's just me and our Colin now. The Partners," he added, his sombre features lighting up as he laughed. Old John couldn't help but laugh with him in this sudden change of mood. "Damn, John, I had a good win on the horses on Friday." Fred rubbed his hands together gleefully. "I had a treble come up for me at Kempton Park."

"Ooh. So what did you do, then?" Old John only had a passing interest in horse racing, except for the Derby and the Grand National, in keeping with everyone else who speculated no more that a few pennies on each way bets on their selections.

"Well," Fred paused to get his facts right. "What I did was a three-to-one in the first race, a six-to-four favourite in the third race and a nine-to-one outsider in a six-horse race in the last race of the day."

Old John, keeping an eye on the card game just an arm's length from where he sat, nodded absently, as if he understood completely the details of what Fred had just described. "Ooh, and how much did you bet on this um, treble?"

"Two bob, cos I was down to my last few shillings, too." Fred's eyes gleamed in triumph as he remembered. "I was on pins waiting for the result of the last race, cos by that time, I had a pound riding on a nine to one." He gripped the sleeve of Old John's jacket tightly, reliving that brief moment of excitement.

"Der, it was great! And like I say, I thought my luck was in. Then I came home to this nonsense." He waved a hand vaguely in the general direction of his home. "Ah well, never mind, is it? We'll do okay."

He rose to his feet and downed the remaining half a pint in one gulp then stood swivelling his hips while he crooned, "'m the oldest teenager in the county. Just you wait, John bach. Me and our Colin are going to 'ave some fun together when all this has been settled. You'll see. Everyone will see." He spread his arms wide and began: "Mammy, waitin' for ya, waitin' for ya…"

Old John laughed, then grabbed him by the tail of his jacket and began to pull him backwards. "Sit down, you daft so-and-so, before they come to take you away to the nuthouse in Bridgend."

Fred resisted, leaning his weight against the pull and began to sing even louder. "I'm in the money. I'm in the money…"

"Then let me have some of it to clear your slate, Fred," Trefor called out, smiling broadly from across the room, where he was busy collecting empty glasses off the other tables.

"Singing I am, not bragging, Trefor." Fred's rebuttal was instantaneous.

"And that makes a change for you, Fred." Roy had turned in his chair at the card table to grin at him.

Fred stopped gyrating. "One of these days, Roy! One of these days you'll say just a bit too much for your own good, mate. Just remember that."

"Aye, aye, Fred. One of these days. I've heard it all before. You are forever saying that." He laughed out loud and returned to his game.

Fred glared angrily at his back. "Just you bluddy wait, that's all." Then he muttered under his breath, "If only I was twenty years younger."

CHAPTER 6

Fred's story of 'Blucher'

DURING THE EARLY part of the following week, Fred, and his penchant for creating a commotion almost everywhere he went, was conspicuous by his absence in the men's bar of the Plough Inn. Trefor, who gleaned most of his knowledge of the ins and outs of village gossip via the daily passage of customers to the pub and betting shop, which was located in the nearby tumbledown cottage owned by the landlord, had his own views on Fred's disappearing trick. It was his belief that Fred, taking full advantage of his wife's recent departure for greener pastures, was roaming the district in search of fun at any time of the day or night. Unless of course he was flat broke and had decided to give the Plough a wide berth. This was, however, extremely unlikely, since Fred needed people around him, if only to play foil to his peculiar sense of humour. He needed people as much as a plant needs an occasional splash of water, lest it should wither and eventually die. And so it was, for the better part of that week, that the men's bar in the Plough retained its atmosphere of quiet, if restrained, solitude… a time without Fred relating or exaggerating some yarn about his own experiences as a young man.

But the peace and quiet of the previous few days were soon put to rest when late on Friday evening, Fred and his son Colin literally rolled off the last bus through the village. Both of them were three sheets or more to the wind and it was quite obvious to all and sundry in the crowded room that the Partners had over-indulged somewhere.

"Coupla pints, Tref." Fred slurred the words together as he pushed his way unceremoniously through the crowd and up to the bar, squinting while trying to focus his gaze on the landlord's familiar portly figure.

Trefor glanced up briefly from under bushy eyebrows whilst busily filling a pint glass for one of his regular patrons. "Look at the state of him, Roy." He nodded his head sideways at Fred, who was holding onto the edge of the counter and swaying gently back and forth on his heels. "Just look at who's been drinking elsewhere, and pretty heavily too from the looks of him, and thinks he can come back here to good ol' Tref and drink on strap while he still owes me money." He placed the foaming pint on the bar in front of Roy, winking broadly as he did so. This was his method of using someone else as a foil to the barbs he was throwing in Fred's direction.

"Well, you've got a damn cheek, Fred, I'll give you that. If that is the case here." Roy grinned at Fred's rapidly changing expressions, then lifted the foaming beer very slowly towards his lips. Fred's bleary eyes followed the path of the glass, as if mesmerised by the movement of the glistening bubbles, then shook his head in sudden irritation as Roy's words struck home. His jaw thrust forward belligerently and he gripped the counter a bit harder to steady himself.

"Hey! Now wait a bluddy minute, Roy! What the 'ell do you mean by that, then?" he blustered, the muscles in his jaw working as he ground his teeth in anger. "I didn't ask 'im for beer on strap, did I? Or you either, you nosy sod!"

"That's as maybe," Trefor cut in, before things got any more personal. He needed a distraction right away to defuse the situation. Fred had arrived in time to liven things up a bit, but had come to the boil far too quickly for it to be funny.

"Do you see the time, Fred?" He pointed to the old fashioned clock fastened to the wall at the far end of the bar, the brass pendulum of which swung steadily to and fro as it ticked off the seconds. "It will be stop tap in five minutes, and ten minutes after that it will be chuck out time. *Chi'n deall?* Understand?"

"Like that, is it, Trefor?" Fred squared his broad shoulders, while keeping a firm grip on the edge of the bar, preparing himself to make an issue over the time.

Before he could corral his thoughts into some sort of order, Trefor said, "Two pints is it, Fred?" The mild tone in his voice defused Fred's ire in an instant. Trefor placed both glasses on the bar in front of him and then, while still holding the handles in a firm grip, added in a loud stage whisper. "Coin of the realm first, if you please, Mr Howells."

Fred, through a haze of beer fumes, tried his best to glare at his adversary and failed miserably. This futile attempt at bravado brought a quick smile to Trefor's round features. Fred's antics never failed to amuse him, and the fun he had at his expense was completely without malice. In fact, Fred, usually received the benefit of a free pint or two from him when the fun was over, and Trefor's generosity made it good for business too, for his customers always saw a sort of friendship between them despite their raised voices to each other.

Fred's features, at that moment, were a picture of concentration as he began to rummage through each of his pockets in turn in a slightly uncoordinated manner, first down the right side and then down the left side, only to repeat the process. He was still fishing for sufficient funds when Colin, grinning impishly and shaking his head in despair at his father's futile efforts, reached over his shoulder and placed a crumpled pound note on the bar. "You'd better take it out of that, Tref," he said. "I could die of thirst in yere if I 'ave to wait for him to find enough cash." He grinned at his father affectionately and clapped him on his back, almost knocking him off his unsteady feet.

"Thank you, Colin," Fred mumbled. "Thank you very much indeed. See, he's good to me, Tref. Good to his poor old father in his time of need. So there you 'ave it, Tref. Coin of the realm." He pointed to the crumpled note, and grabbing the now-released glass with both hands, he pushed his way through the crowd to stand in his favourite spot in front of the stove.

Invariably, the general discussion got onto the subject of rabbiting, terriers, and all other forms of hunting and trapping. Fred, being the only expert on the subject in the room, in his own mind anyway, at once took charge of the debate. He began by relating some of his experiences as a young man in the company of a renowned character from Waun-gron. This man's nickname was 'Blucher'. Nobody still living in the village could remember what his given name had been. Blucher was named after Field Marshall Blucher, a Prussian soldier in the last century who had favoured a certain type of knee-high boot.

Blucher was one of the most colourful characters of the time. He lived in a hovel at the edge of the woods near the parish boundary. He wore close-fitting cord trousers, knee-high leather boots and a home-cured moleskin waistcoat, which he complemented with a nineteenth-century military coat of scarlet and blue that had faded almost beyond recognition. He also sported a large moleskin hat and was, most of the time, unshaven with extra long mutton-chop whiskers of grizzled black and grey, which made it difficult to tell the true shape of his face. He had deep-set animal-like eyes, slanted, dark and piercing, topped with black bushy brows, which seemed to disguise his features even more. He didn't mix at all well with any of the villagers, with the exception of Fred and his cronies in the hunting fraternity.

However, he was held in high esteem by the local squire and the rest of the local fox-hunting gentry. It became a well-known fact that if the squire's pack of hounds were unable to raise a fox to chase down, Blucher would have one already hidden in a sack, ready to release on command, much to the delight of the squire and his friends, and in so doing he earned himself quite a reputation as a hunter. It went without saying that the gold sovereigns slipped into his hand by the grateful squire became incentive enough for a repeat performance when Blucher was called upon to do so. It was this kind of recognition, from an early age, that Fred aspired to.

"I'm telling you, boys. This man could live off the land and could survive anywhere, and under any conditions too," Fred boasted, grabbing suddenly at the back of Roy's chair for support as he lurched forward unsteadily, then went on, "Why, I remember..."

"Come off it, Fred," Roy interrupted harshly. "You're damn-well at it again and you're more than half drunk into the bargain."

"No, no. This what I'm telling you, boys, is gospel," Fred insisted, pleading his case to the back of Roy's head. "One time, as I remember it, Blucher got a lift for me and 'im over to Brecon and all we 'ad with us was two of 'is best terriers. We 'ad no gun, no food, nothing. Well, we got out of this chap's car, just outside the town on this side of the iron bridge. 'Right,' he said. 'Now we'll walk back 'ome.' 'What about food?' I asked him."

"Always on about your belly, Fred!" Roy chipped in, pulling a face and winking at the other players. He was having fun baiting Fred at every opportunity.

Exasperated, Fred stood looking down at him. "Will you keep quiet for a bluddy minute!"

"Aye, okay. Just for you, Fred." Fred sucked in a deep breath as if he was about to say something vindictive to Roy, but changed his mind.

"C'mon, Fred. I want to hear the story, even if he doesn't," said Willi Bray, pointing a tiny finger at Roy.

Fred looked from one to the other. They were both grinning like a pair of Cheshire cats. "No, by damn. To 'ell with the lot of you," he said angrily, turning away from the card table and almost falling over Old John Shinkins' legs. John quickly pushed him back onto an even keel.

"Aw, c'mon, Fred, tell us the rest of it, mun," said Roy pleadingly, while trying desperately to stifle his laughter at Fred's bumbling antics.

"To 'ell with you, Roy," he replied angrily, gnarled fists clenched as he glared at his tormentor.

"I'll tell you what, Fred," Old John said in quiet tones, intent on placating Fred. "If – I'm saying IF, mind – *if* it's a good story, I will buy you a pint of the best ale in the house. How does that sound, then?"

Fred stood unsteadily in the centre of the room, debating with himself whether it was worth the trouble or not. Deciding that it was, mainly because Old John wasn't all that free with his money, he moved back towards the card table.

"Well, all right," he said grudgingly. "But, you 'ave to let me finish my story. Right!" He stared at the crowd with a lopsided serious expression. He sucked in a deep breath and went on with his tale. "Blucher said, 'Don't worry boy, we'll find food on the way.' I was a boy to 'im I suppose," he added, winking conspiratorially. "Anyway, he started walking back up the road we'd just came down, just as fast as he could manage. I can tell you, boys, I had a job to keep up with 'im. After a long spell of this I was out of breath. We came to a gate that opened onto a steep field, which looked as though it might lead us to the bottom of the mountains. He grabbed my arm and said: 'Now, what we have to look for is some straight pieces of hazel. Look for stems about two inches thick, Fred, and cut two of them about four feet long'. I asked 'im what for," he continued to his now captive audience. "I was pretty new to all this in those days, see."

At this point, Roy was visibly tempted to make some remark, but Old John raised a hand, palm outwards, just in time to forestall his interruption.

"'They'll come in handy, you'll see,' was all Blucher would say. Well, I'm telling you boys, that was a 'ell of a walk. Twenty miles over the mountains, as the crow flies, and it's a lot more than that climbing up and down the bluddy rocks. Anyhow, we climbed pretty steady through the rocks in one place and that stick did come in handy too, I can tell you.

"Well, next thing, we were almost at the top, where the ground was getting a bit more level, when he stops suddenly and sniffs the air, like a dog. He grabbed the terriers by the scruff of their necks and squatted down quickly, holding them against his knees with his arm around them. They didn't move an inch, boys, just sat there, eyes bright and sharp, looking and listening for a sign of the bluddy fox. Damn," Fred said in admiration, "they were well-trained dogs. Blucher – you should 'ave seen, boys."

Caught up in his own storytelling, Fred began to imitate his hero's actions. Squatting down slightly, he peered intently around the room. In his mind and at that moment he was back on the crest of that mountain with Blucher. "He raised a finger to his lips and whispered to me, 'There's a fox here somewhere, and I think it's very close to us.' Hah!" Fred gave a short laugh and rose to his feet to continue his story. "I don't think I 'ad enough breath left after that climb to say anything anyway, so I just nodded my head and leaned on my walking stick and watched 'im and the dogs looking for the fox."

"You've come on a bit since then, Fred. In talking, I mean,"

Trefor called out from across the room, causing everyone to start laughing.

"Haisht a minute, boys," Roy said sharply. He was now in the depths of Fred's story. "Go on, Fred!"

"Well, next thing he had turned the terriers loose, and they started working back and forth, quartering the ground in front of them. Suddenly, one of them, the little Jack Russell, I think it was, leaped up in the air and disappeared from sight in the tall grass. You couldn't see the little so-and-so but you could hear 'im well enough. Next thing, this big fox jumps out of a clump of reeds and went over a wide bank where a stone wall had been before. Well, boys, Blucher and me, we ran over the top of it, just in time to see 'is terrier's arse-end disappear down the hole and into the fox's den."

It was deathly quiet around the table. Even the card game had come to a halt with the intensity of his tale. Fred paused and took a long swig of his beer, smacking his lips with satisfaction as he looked at the expectant faces of his audience. Carefully, he replaced his glass on the corner of the table and continued. "'Right you are, Fred,' Blucher said to me, whispering." Fred had dropped his voice to suit the occasion. 'You stand right by there, just a bit to this side of the 'ole and get ready to 'it 'im with that stick of yours if he comes this way. I'm going over by there to look for the other way out. These things are pretty crafty, mind, and they always have another way to escape. Now listen careful, Fred', he told me. 'When I give you the thumbs-up signal, you start beating the ground beside the hole for all you are worth.' Well, boys, I have never seen anything like it in my life." He looked around the rapt faces of his audience. "Never. *Byth.*"

He paused, then in dramatic tones went on: "There was Blucher, boys, laying flat out on the ground at the far end of the bank with one hand held up in the air. Suddenly, he gave me the thumbs-up signal, and I started beating the bank just as hard as I could. Oooh, I must have 'ammered the ground for at least two minutes solid, when up jumps Blucher with the bluddy fox wriggling in 'is hand. By damn, he 'ad caught 'im by the scruff of 'is neck as 'e ran out. I couldn't believe it, boys. I'm telling you now that's what happened."

"Get away from yere, Fred! You, and your damn fairy stories. I ought to have my head read for listening to you and your nonsense." Willi Bray turned away in disgust, making his way to the bar for a refill. "What do you think of him, Tref?"

Trefor shrugged. "No comment," he replied with a grin. It was at times like this that Fred was worth every drop of free beer he gave him.

"It's right enough, boys!" Fred was shouting now, above the pretended chorus of boos and jeers. "It's the bluddy truth I'm telling you."

"That's a hard one to swallow, Fred," said Roy, shaking his head in a solemn fashion. He picked up the pack of cards and began shuffling them.

"Whose deal was it, anyway, lads?"

"He caught that fox barehanded," Fred insisted, looking from one to the other, searching for anyone even slightly sympathetic to his pleas. "And he stuffed it into a sack before he got over his surprise an' bit 'im. I know cos I..."

"I was there," Roy cut in, his tone loud and sarcastic.

"No, Roy!" Fred rounded on him angrily. "Cos I had to carry the bluddy thing all the way home, that's why! You boys know nothing about hunting and trapping like I do, otherwise you would believe me!" Fred wiped a few droplets of spittle from his lips with the back of his hand as he glared at his detractors. "It was an education just to be with that man, I can tell you." He picked up his beer and turned towards Old John, then sat down beside him.

He was silent for a few moments, then said. "I'm half sorry I said anything at all now, John bach, but it is all true what I am saying, you know."

"Aye, I know, Fred," John grinned lopsidedly. "I remember him too, mind."

"Oh aye, I forgot. You lived in Waun-gron too." He grinned, some of his good humour returning. "Der, you should have seen, John bach. For food he dug up roots and dandelions, collected stinging nettles. He broke them up with his bare hands too and put everything into one of those folding billy cans he had in his pocket. He lit a small fire of grass and cut up thick clods of grass, like peat, from the bank of a small brook, then he put a few drops of water with all the leaves an' roots an' things to boil it all up for a while. It doesn't sound like much but when you're bluddy starving, it tastes great. It *was* great too," he added with some conviction. Lifting his glass he finished off what remained of his beer, which by this time had gone flat. "Damn," he said, getting to his feet, "that was thirsty work." He made his way a little unsteadily to the bar, while casting a swift glance at the big clock on the far wall and noting that it was well past closing time. "Pint, please, Trefor," he called out optimistically.

"Look at the time, Fred." Trefor replied instantly, without looking up from his task of filling a pint glass for someone else.

"Aw, c'mon, Tref," he pleaded. "You're already pulling a..."

"Hey, Fred! He was two hours late opening up tonight!" Willi Bray, in his usual busybody fashion, called out the information from across the room.

Fred's features lit up in a broad smile. "Well now. Is that so? Is that so indeed, Trefor?" Trefor merely grinned in reply. "Then I'll have a pint of the best beer in the house, Mr Landlord, if you please," he said politely.

"I'll pay for that one, Trefor. Fair play, it was a pretty good story." Old John smiled at Fred's look of surprise. "Well, I did say I would pay, Fred. Is your memory that bad tonight?"

"No, it isn't, but I will thank you very much all the same, John bach." He raised the brimming glass in salute, then made his way through the crowd to his favourite spot, where the discussion at the table had somehow got onto the subject of rabbits. His ears pricked up at the sound of the word and he moved a bit closer to sit on the settle beside Old John as he waited to get in on the debate.

"I'll tell you what, boys," Fred chipped in moments later. "There isn't a farm around here, or in Breconshire for that matter, where I am not welcome to hunt on their land. Years ago, when some of you were just pups, I was working hard on every farm around, and trapping rabbits by the sack-full in my spare time. I was working then, not for money, but the price of a meal just to survive. Things are easy today, not like when I was young," he said boastfully.

"Okay, Fred. That's it. I for one am just about fed up with your constant bragging around here." Jimmy Drew, scowling, looked up from the card game. He was one of two brothers living nearby, who were close enough in age and looks to have been easily mistaken for twins, except that Titch, his brother, had the unfortunate habit of pushing his bottom set of false teeth in and out with alarming frequency. He had lost most of his teeth when a cow he was about to milk took exception to his ministrations and lashed out, catching him full in the mouth. The brothers were roughly five feet tall, although Jimmy, being the eldest, always claimed to be the tallest. They were almost as round as they were tall, with tight curly blond hair capping round ruddy features. Titch wasn't his given name, but it's doubtful that anyone in the village, with the exception of his parents, could remember the name he had been christened with.

"Well Fred, how about it then? Why don't we go tomorrow morning, first thing if you like, and pick up a few of these rabbits that are so plentiful in the places you know." Unsmiling, he winked at the others around the table and baited Fred still further. "And if you're so bluddy clever at catching them, as you keep on telling us, we'll only be out of the house about ten minutes."

"Now wait on a minute, Jimmy..." Fred jumped to his feet.

"I thought so," Jimmy said, cutting him off, and then loud enough for everyone else in the room to hear, "He's all bluddy noise, this one is, and no go at all."

"Now, fair play, boys," Fred pleaded, looking around at their unsmiling faces. "First of all, we haven't got a car 'ave we? And it's a bit late to start organising things tonight. P'raps some other time, is it?"

"Well, that's a pretty convenient excuse, Fred. Not one of your best, mind, but I suppose it will get you out of the pickies this time." Jimmy looked up from the game, a broad grin creasing his round features.

Fred, relieved to get away from the pressure of having to back up his bragging with something tangible, nodded agreement, his eyes moving blearily across the faces around the table.

"Hey, wait a minute!" Bobby, Jimmy's playing partner in the game, a thin-faced, dark-haired mineworker who lived near Fred, put his cards face down on the table. "Okay, listen to this. I've just had a great idea, boys. We all know that Alan is always game for a bit of fun. So, why don't we," he paused for effect. "Why don't we ask him to take the Great White Hunter here," nodding his head at the dumbstruck Fred, "on a safari with a few of the boys tomorrow morning?" Bobby watched as Fred's mouth opened but no sound came out. He glanced quickly at his watch and added, "I'll bet you he'll be here in a couple of minutes."

Laughter rippled quietly around the table as Fred glared balefully at the engineer of his misfortune.

He toyed with the idea of leaving before things got out of

control, but at the same time was unwilling to leave the bar at that moment while there was still an off-chance of a few free pints. 'P'raps Alan won't want to have anything to do with rabbiting tomorrow,' he thought optimistically.

Alan George was the Councillor's brother-in-law, although in truth they acted more like brothers. They belonged to the same organizations and were both members of the present Parish Council, where Johnny Wills sat as a chairman and his brother-in-law was vice chairman. He looked towards the end of the bar where the councillor usually stood and caught the amused eyes of Johnny Wills watching him. Fred grinned a bit sheepishly and moved away from the area near the card table to another spot where horse racing, the second love of his life (when he had money to spare) was being discussed. Within minutes, he had become quite loud, and he was in the midst of projecting to all and sundry his own particular forecasts from the following day's racing card, when the bar door opened slowly and Alan George's head appeared round the edge. For a moment or two he surveyed the assembled crowd, then with a broad grin came into the room.

Johnny, through a blue, smoky haze of cigarette smoke, spotted Alan the instant he entered. "A pint of the best in the house for that man, Trefor, and I'm paying, remember," he called out with a grin, pointing a finger at Alan's stocky figure as he eased his way through the crowd.

Trefor looked up quickly, and following the line of Johnny's finger, lost no time in seizing his chance to liven things up even further. "Hey, Fred!" he shouted above the noise. "Here's the man of the moment. Now's your chance to ask 'im, first hand. Go on, don't be shy. Ask the man. Ask 'im!"

Fred, who up to that point had failed to notice Alan entering the room, looked up from the racing page, open-mouthed, to see him standing at the bar, pint in hand. "Okay, okay. Righto!

I will now, just as soon as I've finished picking my winners for tomorrow." He was in a corner now and knew it; he should have left the Plough when he had the chance. The last thing in the world he wanted to do at that moment was ask Alan about using his car.

"Ask me what, Fred?" Alan, all innocence, took a sip of beer while catching the landlord's eye. In that instant, he knew that Fred had somehow got himself into a situation, and was now trying his best to get out of it. It was also fairly obvious, from the shifty look in Fred's eyes that things were not quite going his way. "C'mon, Fred! You can tell me."

"Aye, I know. I will in a minute, Alan. I 'ave to tell Trefor something confidential first." Fred's mumbled words were indistinct.

"That's okay, Fred. I'm not sure exactly what you said but I am sure I can wait a few minutes longer," he replied, grinning at Fred's apparent reluctance to discuss his needs.

"*We* can't, though," Jimmy called out from the card table, taking an immediate interest in the repartee between Alan and Fred.

Alan moved closer to where Jimmy sat and asked quietly, "Quick, tell me what's going on, while he's up at the bar."

"Well, it's like this," Jimmy said in low tones and proceeded to fill in the details of Fred's boasting.

"Ahh. I see." Alan moved slowly towards the bar to stand directly behind Fred. "When you have a free moment, Tref, I'll have a small bottle of light ale to top up this pint." The sound of Alan's voice right in his ear, caused Fred to look around in sudden alarm. It also did wonders for his memory, or so it would appear.

"Hey, Trefor! I just remembered what I was going to tell you earlier, in confidence," he added, lowering his voice and almost covering his mouth with a cupped hand.

"So, Fred. What is so important and confidential? You know I have no secrets here. These people are all my friends. You too," Trefor's tone held a touch of sarcasm and his eyes went up to the ceiling in supplication.

Fred glanced momentarily from side to side then leaned forward slightly as he spoke. "I heard tonight that Twm Mawr... you know Twm Mawr, don't you?"

"Yes, yes. I know Twm Mawr," Trefor cut in testily "Go on Fred, for goodness sake, we haven't got all blessed night, you know." He glanced up at the clock. "Listen, I'm a long way past closing time already."

"Well, he's taken over the Lamb Hotel as manager. So I was told, anyway." Fred had that sort of smug look about him as he imparted the choice snippet of gossip and knew at once, from the look of surprise on Trefor's round features, that the rumoured story was probably true.

"Is that so? And where, might I ask, did you get that little bit of news from, then? I'm not sure if what you're spouting is even true." Trefor chose to act as if he wasn't all that interested in Fred's chit chat. He knew Twm Mawr as a man about town and a close friend of the local butcher but he couldn't quite picture him in the role of a pub manager. He appeared to be the type more suited to the other side of the bar.

"It's confidential, Trefor. My lips 'ave been sealed." Fred gave a slow wink, slurring his words slightly as he spoke.

"Damn you, Fred!" Trefor shook his head in exasperation. "You're at it again, aren't you?"

"No, I'm not! Honest to God," he protested. "If you really want to know, Trefor, I heard it in a pub down in the valley tonight, that's all."

"Oooh! So that's where you've been to spend my money!"

"Wait a minute, Tref. You know I'll pay you every single penny just as soon as I can. Anyway, listen. I heard Twm Mawr has some big plans to put the Bont on the map, so to speak."

The Bont, as it was known to the locals, was a scenic area of great natural beauty on the north-western border of the parish, in the adjoining county of Breconshire. "And I also heard," Fred continued, lording it a little while he had the stage, "he's gonna put a café in it too."

"A café in a pub? Don't talk daft." Alan started chuckling, shaking Fred gently by the shoulder. "You must mean a restaurant, Fred." He began chuckling again.

"Café, restaurant? What's the difference? You get food in both of them don't you? Now stop bothering me with daft questions, boys. I've told you all I know about it, so there. I just want to be left alone for a little bit, cos I feel a bit lucky on the horses this week and I want to finish picking my winners." He was still doing his best to get away from the subject of rabbiting.

Alan, ignoring Fred's request to be left alone, followed him through the crowd to sit beside him at the table where he had been busily scribbling the names of horses on minute scraps of paper when Alan had first come in. He sat in silence for a while as Fred pretended to be totally engrossed in the racing form of certain horses and their trainers, then he said quietly.

"Well, now then, Fred, tell me what all the commotion is about here tonight."

"To tell you the truth, Alan," he began hesitatingly, rubbing the side of his jaw pensively. "We was thinking, Jimmy and me, that is, of going after a few rabbits tomorrow morning. Trouble is, it's over in Brecon county, at a good place I know of, see."

"Oh, yeh?" Alan took a sip of his beer and waited.

"Aye. We was thinking of goin' early too!" Fred emphasised the early start, while casting a sly sideways glance at him, to see what sort of reaction it had. "And we was thinking about that big car of yours," he finished lamely, lifting his shoulders in a sort of non-committal shrug.

Alan, being forearmed with the facts leading up to this moment, had had sufficient time to plan in his mind, how he would lead Fred on a little dance first, then deflate his balloon a little bit. "Aw, Fred! Now this is a bit of bad luck. It so happens I have to work tomorrow and I don't..."

"Hey boys, listen!" Fred interrupted, without waiting for any further explanation. "Alan's working tomorrow, so we can't go. Right?" His mournful expression rapidly changed to one of delight as he turned towards Jimmy a wide grin spreading across his face. The group gathered around the other table shook their heads in disgust at Fred's delighted expression. They were, like Fred, unaware that Alan was just about to drop his bombshell.

"Just look at 'im," Jimmy growled, glowering at Fred. "He's as pleased as anything now, the old so-and-so."

Alan, grinning, watched the brief exchange of looks between Fred and Jimmy then said, while trying desperately to keep a straight face, "There is one other possibility, though." He paused. Fred had spun around to face him, his expression changing by the second. He had realised, even in his tipsy state, that his plans for putting one over on Jimmy and his pals had just gone down the drain.

"I'll tell you what I can do, just to put things right for you, Fred," Alan continued, keeping him in suspense. "I can lend my big car to Johnny, over there, so you can show these boys," he waved his hand in a wide circle encompassing everyone in the room, "some of these good places for rabbits which only you know about. So, what do you say to that plan, Fred? Personally, I don't think it would be right or proper to disappoint them after all you have said about it and all those smashing places you've been. Now would it, Fred? Now c'mon, be honest."

The crowd around the table began to cheer as the realization dawned on them of what Alan had just done. Instinctively Fred already knew, and his face collapsed into a picture of dismay. 'Damn Alan and his big car,' he thought miserably.

"So Fred, we'll be on the road by six in the morning then, is it?" Jimmy's gruff voice cut into his thoughts. "Johnny, you, me, Titch, your Colin, and the dogs." He laughed. "We got you this time, you old so-and-so."

"Aye, I suppose you did, this time," he agreed reluctantly, his features breaking into a sheepish grin. "But we'll have a good day out and some fun too, don't you worry 'bout that. Right, Colin?"

"Right, Daddy!" At the bar, Colin turned and swept his cap off, bowing in tribute towards his father. "Boys! My father is the best," he said to the room at large, then resumed his attack on a fresh pint.

Trefor, not wanting to be left out of the fun, shouted across the room. "And I will pay double for the first rabbit caught tomorrow. You hear that, Fred? Johnny can be the referee, cos he won't put up with any old nonsense from you. Have we got a deal?"

Fred looked at the expectant faces around him and knew he had no other choice but to agree. 'Aye, okay, Tref. The first one is yours, for sure."

Alan slapped him on the back, laughing at the same time. 'C'mon, Fred! It's not the end of the world for you, is it? A man of your experience can catch rabbits in his sleep without even waking up. C'mon, drink up quick before Trefor closes the bar and I'll buy you a pint of best bitter. A pint of the best for the Great White Hunter, landlord," he called out, winking broadly at Trefor, who was now grinning from ear to ear.

"Time, boys bach. Time!" he shouted above the noise, at the same time throwing the cloth towels over the pumps, signifying to everyone there would be no beer more served this night. The noise and the fun had been exactly to his liking tonight, and all because Fred loved to be in the limelight.

"Just a minute, Tref."

He glanced up. Fred had rushed up to the bar, empty glass in hand, but not quickly enough. He stared at the bright linen cloths covering the pumps in front of him. "What about that pint Alan just put over for me, then?" he bleated. "What about that, Tref?"

"Sorry, Fred! I think you have had more than your fair share of beer tonight, and from the look of you a while ago you'd already had too many by the time you got here. And, that's without the ones you've drunk since. I don't want to jeopardise my chances of getting a rabbit tomorrow because you've got a hangover. I want you to be in top form, otherwise, if you fail, I will get the blame for serving you too much beer. You can have that pint tomorrow, with interest, after I get my rabbit. We have an agreement, remember! Besides, Fred, look at the time! I'm already two hours over the limit." His hands full of empty glasses, he nodded his head towards the clock. "And just for your information, Fred, I did not open two hours late."

Fred, who had been desperately trying to get a word in, was poised, one hand on the bar and the first finger of his other hand raised to emphasise some point which he thought would give him a reasonable excuse to get that last free pint, but Trefor, losing patience with his antics, brushed his hand away and rang the closing bell.

"Okay, that's it, boys. Everybody out! You too, Fred!" Slowly the remaining crowd in the room dispersed until only Johnny and Alan remained.

They were not drinking anything so it didn't really matter if they were in the pub after hours. "Well, I suppose you'll be up early in the morning, then? "Alan grinned at his brother-in-law.

"Aye. About 5.30 or something like that, I suppose. You're a pair of bluddy rascals, that's what, winding him up like that.

I hadn't planned on getting involved with any of Fred's damn nonsense. I have better things to do with my Saturdays. But, all things considered, despite himself, we can undoubtedly expect him to get into some sort of scrape somewhere along the line tomorrow. He always does. So, the day out will probably be worth the effort, if only for the laughs we get out of it later. And him too," he added.

"You know, it's funny, Fred seems to be delighted when he's got into some mess or other, then tells everyone what he has done so that he can have a laugh too. Personally, I wouldn't dream of telling anyone if I had done something silly. Not Fred though, he seems to relish it. Perhaps he's just lonely?" he grinned. "So, Alan! Now that you have so readily volunteered my services to drive your car on this dark and dangerous expedition, just as a matter of interest, how are you getting to work? You are going to work, aren't you? This isn't some scheme where I'm off with Fred and his gang on safari tramping around the countryside up to my ankles in cow shit, while you are laying warm and *cwtch*ed up in bed, because if it is…"

"Oh yes," he replied grinning. "I'm going to work all right, honest."

Alan worked on the same opencast coal site as Roy. It was situated on the south side of the mountain about five miles or so from the village and Alan was in charge of security on most weekends.

"Okay, I believe you – thousands wouldn't. Do you want my car?"

"Nah! It's all arranged so I don't need a car at all this weekend." He grinned at Johnny's mystified expression. "Listen to this. Before I came here tonight, I had already asked Dai Williams, he's one of the maintenance men on the site, to pick me up in the morning on his way to work. He lives down in Waun-gron somewhere."

"Well, all I can say is, you must be psychic."

"Something like that," Alan chuckled. "I think you've got to be in here, just to keep your sanity."

Trefor came back into the bar, his round features beaming. "Hey, boys, did you see the look on old Fred's face when he knew there was no way out? That'll teach him to brag about the place."

Chapter 7

Brecon Hotel and the chocolates

Johnny rolled over and quickly hit the stop button on the alarm clock so as to not disturb his peacefully sleeping wife. Dressing quietly, he went downstairs and put the kettle on. By the time he had poured his second cup of tea he was wide awake and ready to deal with any of Fred's nonsense.

Switching his mini for Alan's big car he arrived at Fred's house just after 5.30 and hammered on the front door until Fred's sleepy head poked out of the upstairs window.

"All right, all right, I heard you. Be quiet or you'll wake up the whole bluddy street," he grumbled. "I'll be right down, don't bother." Moments later he opened the front door, staring bleary-eyed at Johnny, then turned and shouted up the hollow-sounding stairwell, "C'mon, Colin! Time to get up, our driver is here. Damn, it's chilly this morning," he said looking out into the street and rubbing his arms vigorously.

"Its no wonder, Fred. You've only got a vest on."

"Oh aye," he replied with a grin, looking down at himself. "I'd better get dressed then, right away." He went scampering up the stairs, calling over his shoulder. "Go into the kitchen, Johnny, and see if the fire is still alight to make us a cup of tea."

Johnny opened the door into the kitchen. "The fire is out, Fred!"

Fred and Colin came clattering, as one, down the bare wooden stairs into the hallway. "Never mind that now," Fred said hoarsely, coughing like a broken-winded horse. "Did you call the other two yet?"

"No, but they'll be ready to go, don't worry. Jimmy won't miss a chance like this."

"Well, he'd better be bluddy ready after all the fuss he made about me last night."

Outside, the car was made ready quickly. Guns, wrapped carefully in cloths, were placed on rags in the boot; the ferret in its cage was tucked into a corner for safety. The dogs, with Colin in charge, were on the back seat, lying on Fred's best (and only) woollen blanket. "Okay, that's it, we're ready. Let's go," Fred ordered, settling himself in the passenger seat.

Johnny let out the clutch and the car began to roll down the hill. Colin from the back seat called out, "Have you put the purse nets in, Daddy?"

"No, by damn! I forgot about them. WAIT! Wait a minute, Johnny." He was out of the car and running back up the hill almost before the car had come to a halt. He ran down the side of the house to the garden shed. Swiftly unlocking it, he grabbed the bundle of green string nets and tucked them under his arm. Out of breath from the exertion, he climbed back into the car. "I'll put these in the boot when you stop for the other two, right," he said, pushing himself back down into the seat. "Let's get cracking, then."

Stopping briefly for Jimmy and Titch and their guns at the bottom of the hill, Fred informed them that he would be the navigator, that's why he was in the front seat. "Cos, I know this county like the back of my hand, okay?"

They had driven about twenty miles across the mountain

in relative silence when Fred shouted out, "We never had any breakfast this morning!" rudely waking the others, who had been dozing in the warmth and comfort of the car.

"Fred, bluddy shut up, you noisy sod!" Jimmy mumbled, his eyes still closed.

Fred ignored the comment and went on. "Tell you what, Johnny, we'll stop in Brecon at a place at I know of. We can get some tea and toast there pretty reasonable." Fred, it appeared, was also wise in the ways of early morning travel.

"Go to the Brecon Hotel. It's on the right as you go into the town near that big church. They open for breakfast at half past six every morning except Sundays. I'll pay for this one, okay, boys? I always like to pay first," he looked sideways at Johnny, winking broadly.

"Well, I've never heard that one before, Fred!" Johnny took his eyes off the road for a second or two to look at him.

"We'll have to post a notice about it in the Plough right away. Right boys? How does this sound: 'Fred always likes to pay the first round!' Sounds okay too," Jimmy replied. "And when we get back there later today, I vote we send Fred in front of us to buy the first round of beer. How does that sound, Fred?"

"Aw, c'mon, boys," he moaned. "By damn, I can't even open my mouth now..."

"Without putting your foot in it," finished Johnny, laughing.

"I think I'd better shut up altogether." Fred leaned against the door and closed his eyes. Entering the market town of Brecon some ten minutes later, Johnny soon found the hotel on the main street, just as Fred had described it. The Brecon Hotel was a fairly posh establishment and one of the better hotels in the town, frequented with regularity by commercial travellers and local businessmen. Parking the car on the street a short distance beyond the main entrance, Johnny looked up at the front of the hotel and thought, 'This isn't the sort of place for us, a group of part-time rabbit hunters dressed in shabby work clothes, seeking early morning tea and toast.'

"Okay, Fred! Wake up!" He switched off the engine. "Here we are, boys. Fred's hotel."

Everyone stirred sleepily and stretched. Opening the doors, they climbed out onto the pavement, brushing some of the creases from their crumpled clothing.

"Right, boys, follow me," Fred ordered briskly. "Colin, are the dogs okay?

"Yes, Daddy. I 'ave spread the blanket over the seat just like you said."

"Hey. This is a bit posh, innit?" Jimmy was looking up at the red carpet on the steps, the gleaming glass and the highly polished brass on the rails and revolving door.

"Don't worry about that, boys," Fred said, full of confidence. "Me and Georgie Mounts 'ave been here hundreds of times." He was of course stretching the truth a bit. With Fred leading the way, they pushed through the revolving glass door and entered the early morning stillness of the carpeted foyer. Standing a little self-consciously to one side of Fred, they looked around at the richness of the décor.

The Manageress, suddenly aware of the disreputable-looking travellers, moved rapidly from her position behind the reception desk to stand directly in front of Fred, as if in protection of her other guests. Looking haughtily down her nose at Fred, she said "Yersss? How can I assist you, gentlemen?" her hands clasped across her ample waistline.

Fred immediately took command. In his very Sunday best voice he said: "A very good morning to you, ma'am," sweeping his cap off with a flourish. "We've been travelling for hours and hours and we haven't had anything to eat or drink since sometime yesterday. We've been told that this hotel," he waved his hands, while looking around appreciatively at the décor, "is the best place in Brecon for tea and toast." He grinned, at the same time raising his eyebrows, which Johnny thought was a fair impression of Stan Laurel. The icy stare melted just a little.

Jimmy nudged Colin, his eyes cast up to the ceiling. "Hundreds of times," he muttered behind his hand, and then added. "I'm willing to bet this is the first bluddy time in yere for him."

"So, if you could find us a little corner, sort of out of the way, like," he continued, smiling all over his face, "we would be most grateful." He was doing his best to sound sincere while the others stood around shuffling their feet as if they were completely uninterested in the proceedings.

"Well." (It was a long, drawn-out 'well'.) "Well, if you are not too long about it..."

"Oh no, we won't be!" Fred cut in quickly. "Just tea and toast all round and we'll be off like a shot. I promise." He grinned, a mischievous glint in his eyes as he looked at her.

"Wait here," she commanded. "I'll see what I can do." She moved quickly away from the group and stood in the doorway of the dining room. She appeared to be looking for a suitable table well away from the early-morning breakfasters. Turning in the doorway she beckoned Fred's party with a flick of her hand, directing them to a small table set in an alcove with a tall curtained window, or so it appeared. Seating themselves quickly, the manageress looked at each of them in turn, as if regretting what she had just agreed to do. Little did she know then what was about to happen.

"Tea and toast for everyone, if you please, ma'am," Fred said grandly. Moments later he got up from his seat at the end of the table, pushing past Johnny and Jimmy to open the curtain an inch or two, and found he was looking directly down into the back seat of Alan's car.

"Damn, this is handy," he muttered to himself. "I can keep an eye on things from here."

"Hey, Fred! I thought you said you had been here hundreds of times. How come she didn't recognise you then?" Johnny gave Jimmy a nudge.

"Aye! Tell us Fred! Hey, boys, p'raps he didn't give 'er a tip last time and she's in a bit of a pout."

"That's easy," he replied, ignoring the jibe. "She's new to this place. Listen," he went on, changing the subject. "If we are quick about it in here, we can be on the land in Llyswen while there is still dew on the fields." He got to his feet once more to part the curtains again to check on his dogs. Back in his chair he said, expansively, thumbs hooked in his braces, "Just follow me today boys and we'll have some fun."

"No doubt we will," Johnny said drily, leaning on his elbows, hands clasped. "What I need right now though is a nice cup..." Just then, the tea and toast arrived at the table, piping hot.

"Now, there's service for you. Didn't I tell you? See, they know me, even over here," Fred boasted, a broad smile wreathing his features.

Jimmy chuckled. "It's not you, Fred! They just want us out of here in double quick time. I'm willing to bet, somebody out there," he nodded towards the main dining room, "is still waiting for their breakfast toast!"

"Aw, shut up, Jimmy. You just don't believe. That's your trouble," Fred spoke through a mouthful of buttered toast as he rose once again to peer through the gap in the curtain.

"Hey! Watch it, Fred! You're like a jack-in-the-box. Why don't you just move your chair to that end, then you wouldn't be pushing back and forth. See what you've done now?" Johnny had been pouring his tea as Fred pushed past and the tea had spilled in a wide circle across the snow-white tablecloth. "Damn it all, Fred! I don't know about you."

"Oh. Sorry, I think," he grinned mischievously, "but that's a good idea though. He lifted his chair over the table and now sat with his back to the window. "Pass my food down, boys," he said demandingly, reaching out with both hands, and began stuffing the heavily buttered toast into his mouth as if he had not eaten in a month.

Twisting in his seat, Fred was pulling the curtain back for the umpteenth time when there was an ominous thud. An elaborate window display had been built for the forthcoming Easter celebrations. The large boxes of chocolates and chocolate Easter eggs in their colourful presentation boxes had been balanced on edge, one on top of the other, from sill to ceiling on either side of the alcove window. The centrepiece of the display was a huge basket of chocolate eggs that had stood, balanced delicately, on the largest box of chocolates. Somehow, Fred, in his previous visits to the window, had poked his head through the very centre of the display completely unscathed.

The first thud was followed by a sliding, slithering sound and then another heavier sounding thud. Fred froze for a split second, then jumped out of his chair to face the window and grabbed the curtains with both hands to yank them wide open. What he saw was twin towers of chocolates boxes tilting towards him as if he was a magnet. "Quick boys! Help me with this!" he cried out in panic.

Everyone at the table sat transfixed as the towers of chocolates began to tumble down on the luckless Fred. Valiantly, with both arms outstretched wide, he tried to prevent the disaster as they cascaded onto his unfortunate head. "Oh, boys bach," he moaned. "Just look what 'ave happened to me!"

The other four were in hysterics, rolling about in their chairs with laughter, tears of mirth streaming down their cheeks. "Just wait until they hear about this in the Plough tonight." Johnny was helpless from laughing and holding his sides as if in pain.

"Mrs Manageress! Come quick, some of your chocolates 'ave fell down!" At this sally, the others went into further peals of laughter.

"I only tried to help," Fred bleated to the Manageress, who arrived post haste on hearing the commotion from the confines of the alcove.

She looked as if she was about to explode as she surveyed the disaster scene. Her face went purple with rage and then turned to crimson with humiliation, while Fred's four companions, still sitting in their chairs, wiped the tears from their eyes with the backs of their hands like a crowd of little schoolboys who couldn't stop giggling.

"GET OUT! JUST – GET – OUT!" It was all she could trust herself to say at that moment.

"But, but, we 'aven't finished our food yet!" Fred stammered, having visions of paying for something he hadn't had yet. "And, and, we've still got tea! It's too hot to drink right away." He raised his hands in despair. "This is what you get, boys, for trying to help." He stood amidst the devastation with his hands on his hips as he looked appealingly at the others, who went into fits of giggling all over again at Fred's expression.

"HELP? WHAT HELP?" The poor woman's voice was climbing up the scale like a soprano trying to reach top C but not quite making it, as her voice broke in anger. "Help, you say?" she repeated tersely, now in full control of herself. "If you and your friends are not out of here in the next two minutes or less, I am sending for the police. Do you understand? That window display took my staff two days to put together and you have completely destroyed it in two seconds."

"Well, fair play," Fred replied with a silly lopsided grin creasing his face. "If none of the eggs 'ave broke you can still use them, can't you?" Johnny thought the Manageress was going to have a fit at Fred's seemingly logical statement.

"Here's your bill!" she said scribbling frantically and throwing it at Fred. "Now get out!"

They needed no second bidding and rose as one to beat a hasty retreat towards the exit as fast as their feet could carry them. Outside, they leaned weakly against the car to wait for Fred.

"Oh boys! What a start to the day," Johnny groaned, holding his sides where a stitch had suddenly developed.

Still in the hotel, Fred had taken a second look at the bill. "Hey, missus! Wait a minute here! This is a bit much, isn't it, for a few bits of toast and tea? Fifteen bob? I didn't want to buy the bluddy dishes too, you know!"

She glared balefully at him. "It's pay up or the police! Take it or leave it! Decide which you want, quick!"

"Okay, I'll pay it," he grumbled, putting a pound note on the table. As she turned away to get his change, he stuffed his pockets with all the spare toast he could lay his hands on and drained the milk jug in one gulp. Then grabbing his change off her outstretched hand, he ran through the lobby to the waiting car beyond, leaving behind a very startled woman.

"What do you think of 'er then, boys?" Fred demanded as he reached the car. "All that bluddy fuss over a few bits of chocolate. All that stuff will give you is toothache anyway," he said pensively, picking at his teeth with the end of a match stick. "What I should've done when it happened is grab her by the shoulders and give her a smacking kiss on the chops."

At this the others broke into peals of laughter again and were almost too weak to climb back into the car.

CHAPTER 8

Rabbiting in Llyswen

I T WAS SOMETHING of an event for Fred, arriving at Davies' Tŷ Mawr farm in a large highly polished black car, which rolled almost silently across the muddy, muck-strewn yard.

Fred jumped out of the front seat almost before the car had come to a halt. "Good morning, Mr Davies," he called out, his hand raised high in salutation.

Mr John Davies, tall and slightly stooped with a ruddy complexion from years of working on the land in all weathers, was at that moment coming out of one of the cowsheds. The jet-black sheepdog at his heels moved from side to side, never taking his eyes off Fred for a second, as he recited his favourite opener.

"Remember me, Mr Davies? I used to come here after rabbits years ago. How's Mrs Davies and the children?" he went on in a disarming manner, winking at the others, still sitting in the car.

Mr Davies walked slowly towards the car, where Fred was still standing beside the open door. He eyed each of them in turn a little suspiciously, as if committing their faces to memory for future reference. Then in soft tones he replied to Fred's query.

"Everybody is fine and I thank you for asking. So, what do you boys want here, then?"

"Well, Mr Davies, it's like this," Fred confided, raising his shoulders slightly and spreading his hands wide. "A couple of the boys here," he waves a hand nonchalantly towards the others, "'ave never been after rabbits in their life before and since I'm the best chap around these parts to show 'em how it's done," (at this point he puffed out his chest) "I said to them, we'll go over to Brecon and see my old friend Mr Davies at his farm in Llyswen. I said Mr Davies will be sure to let us on his land so I can show you the ropes, as it were." Smiling broadly, he added, "Cos he's always being bothered by them 'ol rabbits and will be only too pleased for us to get rid of a few of 'em for 'im."

"Oh, aye?" Mr Davies didn't appear particularly impressed with Fred's explanation as to why they were there, and stood rubbing the side of his head with his cap. "And who told you I was being bothered by rabbits, then? There's not much around here anymore, not since they put down that old Myxomatosis stuff down. It destroyed them by the thousands, so I haven't had any problem since."

"Well, I know that," Fred cut in quickly. "There used to be, but we cleared hundreds off your land and it was quite a while ago. You must remember me and my friend Georgie Mounts and our Colin. He was always with us as a boy." He pointed at his son who politely raised his cap to Mr Davies in acknowledgment to his sideways glance at him. "Come now, Mr Davies," Fred had conveniently forgotten Davies' question.

"Well, I must say, you do look a bit familiar but I don't know about letting you on my ground." He folded his arms, looking from one to the other. "I'm not too sure about this at all," he mused.

"Well really, Mr Davies, it's not too much to ask, mun. I only wanted to show these boys a few things, that is all," Fred persisted. "And it would only be for an hour or so. There should be enough time for me to demonstrate to them a few tricks of the trade." He laughed convincingly, ready to debate as long as it took to get his permission. "Mr Davies, I promise we will only use the gates to cross from one field to the next – and another thing, our dogs won't chase cattle or sheep. As an old farm boy myself, I know what you're concerned about." The lie rolled off his tongue like quicksilver down a slope.

"Is that so?" A slight flicker of interest showed briefly on his face, at which point he seemed to make up his mind. "Where was that, then – er, what did you say your name was?"

"Fred. My name is Fred. Fred Howells, we're from over Waun-gron way."

"Oh yes." Davies nodded and appeared a little uncertain exactly where Waun-gron was. "Well, all right then, but only on my top fields, mind. They are the ones above the road." He took out an old watch from his waistcoat pocket and pointedly looked at it, saying at the same time. "I'm pretty sure there is nothing up there, so you shouldn't be too long. Now remember. Only the top fields, up to the crest where the forestry starts."

He nodded to them all, then walked across the yard and into the house.

"Right you are, Mr Davies," Fred called out cheerfully. "Okay, boys, let's go. Take 'er up the hill, driver, onto the top road." He swung himself into the car slamming the door. "Right, we've got all day now! We can even go onto the next farmer's land."

"How's that, Fred? You just promised that man we would only go on his top fields," said Johnny. "We have to play the game you know!"

"I know that, but he didn't tell us where his boundaries were. Right? So, we can plead we didn't know." He started grinning as he pulled another piece of cold toast from his pocket. "You know what, boys?" he said through a mouthful of toast.

"What now?" Johnny said, sarcastically.

"It's a good thing he didn't remember me too clearly," he took another bite of toast, brushing the crumbs off his face.

"Fred, you're a bluddy animal," said Johnny glancing sideways.

"Aye. I know," he replied agreeably. "See, as I was saying. The last time me and Georgie Mounts was here, he wouldn't give us permission but we went on his ground anyway till he caught us, and the old so-and-so set his dogs on us to chase us off a bit sharpish. Anyhow, he forgot this time and now we've got his permission. Ya-hoo!" Fred startled everyone with his sudden yell.

"You crazy sod!" Jimmy growled, giving him a shove at the back of his head. "I think there's something wrong with you, mate!"

The big car climbed the hill effortlessly and the early morning sunlight slanting through the tall hedgerows of the narrow lane dappled the car with golden flashes of light. "Quick! Pull over there, right in front of that gate!" Fred pointed to a wide grass area. "That looks like a good place to start."

"Hey, Fred! Listen, give me a bit more warning next time you want me to stop. This car is not a magic carpet, you know, it can't move sideways." He braked hard and slipped it into reverse to ease the big car up onto the grass verge close to the tall hedge.

Fred jumped out of the car, stretched with arms above his head and took in a deep breath. "Aaah! Smell that fresh air boys!"

"Fresh cowshit is all I can smell – or is it bullshit, Fred?" Titch said, smiling.

Fred took another deep breath. "You don't know what fresh air is, mun." He stood, hand on hip, looking distantly up the sloping field, shading his eyes against the morning sun as he cast back and forth for any sign of movement. "Okay, boys, quick about it now. The dew is still on the grass, so if any rabbits are out and about they'll still be feeding."

Johnny went around to the back of the car to unlock the boot. Swinging the lid up, he reached in and picked up the guns and handed them out to eager waiting hands. Lifting the ferret cage with both hands he studied the little animal as it dashed excitedly back and forth, turning somersaults at each end in the confinement of the narrow wire cage.

"Fred, this little rascal could do with a bigger cage. Just look at him jumping around."

Fred glanced at him, grinning. "Nah! It keeps him supple like, don't you think? Colin, you watch the dogs. I'll have one of the shotguns and the rest of you get your guns. Johnny, if you don't mind, can you carry all these purse nets and the ferret?"

Jimmy and his brother Titch looked at each other. "Listen to 'im," said Jimmy.

"When were you in the bluddy army, Fred? You sound like a sergeant major about the place!"

"Now, now, boys! There will be no mutiny in the ranks." Johnny slammed the boot shut.

"That's right, Johnny! Make as much noise as you can. Wake everybody up, including the bluddy rabbits, with your nonsense."

"Oh! Sorry, Fred, I didn't think about it." He looked around sheepishly at the others.

"Well, okay, this time. From now on, boys, let's have a bit of hush, is it?" He leaned over the gate and stood the shotgun against the post on the other side then climbing onto the second rail of the gate, he again scanned the field, his hand shading his eyes as he looked for a likely place to start the hunt. "That looks like a good spot," he said quietly pointing to an area about fifty yards away. "Over there in front of those small bushes. It looks like the grass is cropped pretty short there." He swung his leg over the top rail and jumped down lightly on the other side. Once there, he picked up the shotgun, inserted two cartridges and closed the breech with a quick snap, making sure the safety catch was on. He tucked the gun under his arm and waited until everyone was over the gate, then led the way across the bottom of the field towards the area he had chosen to begin.

"Okay Colin, let the terriers loose but hold onto Fly." Fly was a huge grizzled cross Irish Wolfhound and greyhound, known as a lurcher. "I don't want her to run, unless it looks like a rabbit is getting away," he whispered to Johnny, who nodded his understanding. Colin held the big lurcher on a slip collar, ready to release her in a split second. The big hound stood stock still, eyes and ears alert for the slightest sign of movement, her muscular body trembling with the excitement of the hunt.

Fred, crouching down, was watching the actions of Judy, the tiny Jack Russell terrier, as she ran to and fro, quartering the ground, her short, stumpy tail waving from side to side. "If there's anything about, she'll find it. Stay behind the dogs, boys," he said quietly. "If anything rises, it will go away from us and the dogs, so be careful of the dogs when you fire, right?"

"Right!" Jimmy and Titch had formed a line diagonal to Fred's position.

Jimmy stood with his shotgun, barrels pointed skyward, eyes peeled in readiness for quick action. "Hey, look at that!" Fred whispered urgently, pointing a finger to where Judy had suddenly started running in small circles, her stump of a tail still waving like a flag but not a sound coming from her. "Wait now, boys," his tone of voice building up the excitement of the chase. "Quietly now, and stay behind the dogs. Wait for it!"

Rose, the other terrier, was now alongside Judy and working together, they closed in on the clumps of high grass near the bushes. Fly, the lurcher, watching them intently, was trembling violently, ready to run, when one of the terriers gave a yelp and two large rabbits raced away from them up the hill towards the sanctuary of the woods bordering the top of the field.

Jimmy and Titch both raised their guns but Colin had slipped the big dog's collar and in an instant she was in hot pursuit, rapidly gaining on her quarry with every stride, so they couldn't fire. The rabbits turned in different directions as they neared the safety of the woods but Fly chose one and changed direction with it, with Fred shouting encouragement as he ran up the field after the great beast.

The rabbit, meanwhile, was making a beeline for a tiny hole beneath the blackthorn hedge that bounded the woods. It got there a split second before the big dog crashed headlong into it, making a large hole and howling with pain as the sharp thorns plunged with force into her shoulders. All interest in the rabbit was lost in those few seconds as she tried desperately to extricate herself from the grip of the thorny bushes.

Fred came to a halt, out of breath, in front of the hedge. Head hanging down and his hands resting on his knees, he gasped. "Never mind Fly, boys. Get after those little sods that got away! I'll look after her. Well, there's something here, boys, whatever Davies said!" he puffed. "Look at Judy working!" He pointed back down the field where the little bitch was climbing up and down the bank separating the two fields.

"Look at Fly, Fred! Never mind the bluddy rabbits. Look at her!" Johnny, who had followed Fred to the top of the field, pointed to the big dog, limping along, trying to lick her wounds.

"Aye, all right! I know, just give me a minute." He grimaced a bit as he sat down, still out of breath. "I'm not as young as I used to be, Johnny. I could run all day once." Turning his attention to the injured dog, he called out, "Fly! Come here, gel." The poor dog, still pacing painfully, was going away from them until Fred called again softly, "C'mon, Fly. Come to me." She limped over to where he sat on the bank of the hedgerow. "Damn! Look at all those bluddy thorns!"

She stood quite still in front of him, head hanging down, the long thorns quite visible in her muscular shoulders. Fred got to his feet and swung his leg over her back so he was facing her head then holding her with his knees he carefully removed the thorns. She yelped softly each time and licked Fred's hand, recognising the fact that he was trying to help get rid of her discomfort. "Damn," he said morosely. "That's a bit of bad luck. She's had it for the rest of the day now. I'll bet she'll be limping for days after this," he said, patting her head affectionately.

"Lucky she didn't have her eyes out," said Johnny, as he looked closely for any further injury.

"Aye, that's true!" Fred looked back down the field. "Can you see where the other dogs are now?

"No, not I!" Johnny scanned the lower part of the field again, shading his eyes against the bright sunlight.

Fred raised his voice. "Colin! Can you see the dogs?" Colin rose, gun in hand, from a crouched position behind a bush, signalling to his father to come back quickly, pointing with his finger towards a dense clump of nearby bushes.

Jimmy and Titch were still walking along the boundary of the field, hoping for a glimpse of the two escapees.

"C'mon, Johnny, quick!" Fred started running back down the field, slipping and sliding on the wet grass.

Suddenly Colin stood up, snapping the gun to his shoulder. BANG! "I've got one, Fred!" he shouted back excitedly. "Judy is still working the bank but I don't know where Rose is." Colin picked up the rabbit and holding it at arms length he eyed it critically. "It's a bit small, innit? Then he grinned as he remembered. "This one is Trefor's, right?"

"Right, Colin! That one is his," Fred panted as he and Johnny and the others arrived at the scene. "Okay, spread out and look for bolt holes. You 'ave to search carefully cos they may have long grass covering 'em. Who's got the bluddy ferret and the nets?"

"I have!" Johnny laughed. "What's wrong with your memory, Fred? You gave them to me. Remember?"

"Okay! I can't remember everything. C'mon, quick now!" Eyes flashing and orders given in all directions, Fred called out, "Colin! Where's Colin?

"Down here! What do you want?" Colin shouted back from further down the hedge on the other side.

"Are the dogs still marking?

"Yes. Judy hasn't moved an inch from this hole. I'll stay down here."

There was a pause. "Hey, Fred! Rose is coming back towards you. What's happened to Fly? She's limping badly." The big hound was picking her way slowly down the field toward the hunters.

Impatiently Fred shouted back. "Don't worry about her, Colin. She's done for the day now. Just watch along the hedge. Now then, boys, I think we've got a few more in the bank." Fred laughed at his own joke. "Get it? A few more in the bank?" He looked round at the others and getting no response to his humour, began spreading the nets out on the ground. "Colin!" he shouted. "Can you see anything down there?"

"Not yet, but don't you worry, I am ready for them." He was enjoying himself now, standing with one foot on the slope, gun raised ready, looking along the grassy bank for anything that moved within his line of sight.

"Okay, boys. Each of you take a net and spread it out just like this." Fred demonstrated how to place it over the rabbit hole. "Okay? Then you get one of these tent pegs and put it through this loop here," he put his finger into the loop, "and drive the peg all the way into the ground. Johnny, pass me that big stone." He hammered on the peg until he was satisfied that it could not pull out when a bolting rabbit ran into the purse net and the drawstring closed it up tightly to trap the animal. "Just like that, boys, right? Simple, isn't it?"

Jimmy and his brother looked at each other and smiled. "Hey, Fred! This is not our first time after rabbits, mind."

Fred looked up, grinning. "I know that," nodding his head sideways towards Johnny. "Now, who's got the ferret?"

"I have," said Titch, handing the caged animal to him. The excitement surrounding the hunt seemed to be affecting him too, as he dashed in a frenzied manner up and down his cage.

Fred grinned. "See, boys! He knows what he has to do in the next couple of minutes. Okay, here's what I want you to do now. Put a net over every hole you can find, just like I showed you, except that one." He pointed to one just a yard or so away. "That one has had a lot of travelling in and out. See how the ground is packed smooth and hard. We'll put our little friend in there because I think this is their front door." He stood up from his squatting position. "What's happening, Colin?"

"Nothing. Judy is still marking in the same spot and she won't move. She's halfway into the bluddy hole."

"Let 'er be, then. We're in the money here, boys. And Davies said there was nothing on his land," he scoffed, taking a small leather muzzle from his pocket. He opened the cage and very gingerly caught the ferret by the scruff of its neck. The other three, after finishing setting the nets, watched Fred's performance with some amusement.

"You're not scared of him are you, Fred? I've seen Colin with that thing inside his shirt and running around when we were playing cards in the Plough just last week."

Jimmy laughed. "Just look at all those lovely sharp little teeth, mun."

The ferret, lips curled back, was trying to twist around in Fred's grasp in an attempt to sink his teeth into Fred's thumb.

"Aye. I know he won't bite our Colin. Listen, I've handled live foxes and badgers too, but to tell you the truth boys, I have to watch this little sod or he'll 'ave me."

"You know what they say, Fred. An animal won't bite the hand that feeds it. Do you want a hand with that?" Johnny stepped forward.

"Nah! I'll 'ave 'im now, in a minute." He had a grip on the ferret's neck with one hand, and the rest of his wriggling body he tried to squeeze between his knees. With his free hand he deftly shook the knots out of the muzzle straps. Having succeeded in this he deftly slipped it over the ferret's head pulling the drawstring tight on one side and then the other until if fitted snugly around his head. He finished by tying both straps together and then held the little animal aloft for them all to see. "There," he said triumphantly. "And that's how it's done, boys. Now he can't kill anything he chases in the hole. Okay then, boys, now spread out and watch the nets. Hey, Colin!" he shouted. I'm putting the ferret in now. Okay?"

"Right, Daddy. If anything comes down this way, I'll have it."

"Righto! Yere we go then." Fred pushed the little animal into the warren entrance and it came back out immediately. He grabbed it and shoved it back in but it ran out again. "You little sod," he said impatiently, grabbing it again and spinning it around in his hands.

"Put it in backwards Fred, P'raps it'll turn around for you and go in."

"You don't know a bluddy thing about rabbiting, Johnny, so bluddy shut up!" Fred was rapidly losing his temper. "Now then, you." He held the ferret up in the air and gave it a bit of a shake. "Get bluddy in there and do your job." He pushed it into the hole and stood with his boot over the entrance in the bank.

"Hey, Fred! Have you ever thought about taking up ballet?" Johnny tried his best to keep a straight face.

"No, why then?" Fred had a puzzled look on his face while the others broke up laughing at the sight of him, one boot in the ditch at the bottom of the bank while the other was more than halfway up the bank, making his legs appear at right angles to each other.

"Well, you look pretty good at it from here, doesn't he, boys?" Johnny turned to the others for confirmation.

"Aye, he do. I can see him now in one of those frilly outfits, kicking his heels up in the air." Jimmy was holding his sides in laughter.

"Aye. You can bluddy laugh," Fred grinned. "I'm still fitter than you boys, even at my age," he boasted. He took his boot off the entrance and, squinting, peered into the blackness. The ferret had disappeared into the depths of the warren.

"Right, he's in. Now then, listen for the sound of rabbits running about. They make a thumping sound like this, Johnny." He made a dull thudding sound by banging the side of his fist rapidly against the earthen bank. "Now we have to watch the nets." He placed the last net carefully over the entrance. "All we have to do is wait now." He sat back and took a packet of five Woodbines from his pocket. He shook it and looked in. "Sorry, boys, last one," he said, as he replaced the empty packet in his pocket. Johnny, a non-smoker, watched him do this with some interest, having seen him do it on other occasions.

Fred looked up. "Not to leave any litter for old Davies to complain about, see," answering the unspoken question as he lit up the cigarette with a sigh of satisfaction.

At that moment, Jimmy called out softly. "Hey Fred, the ferret is over here and he hasn't got the muzzle on now."

"Bluddy 'ell!" Fred was on his feet in an instant, throwing his cigarette on the ground.

"Catch 'im, quick," he shouted, running to where Jimmy was lifting the net.

"You're too late, Fred! He's gone back in."

"Damn! Damn it all!" In that brief moment of silence, a distinct thudding sound could be heard from within the bank.

"Get ready, boys," Fred was once again alert, eyes flashing from net to net. "Colin! There's something moving up here."

"It's still quiet down this end," came the quick reply.

There was another thudding sound that seemed to be right under Fred's feet. He stepped back a pace, staring intently at the ground, listening intently. "Any second now, keep your eyes peeled, boys."

Moments later a piercing scream came from deep inside the warren. "What was that, Fred?" Johnny asked in surprise.

"It's the end of our rabbit hunting here, that's what!" Fred's face showed his disgust. "That little rascal of a ferret has just killed a rabbit in there and we won't see anything of him now for God knows how long. Days, a week, longer – I don't know."

"So what can we do now, then?" Johnny asked, looking at the others.

"All we can do is to wait and see if something happens. P'raps another one will make a run," he paused, glancing at his watch. "Tell you what, boys, we'll give about half an hour and if nothing moves by then, we'll give it a try somewhere else with the dogs on open ground." They all murmured agreement to Fred's plan.

"Right then, that's settled. Colin! Come up here a minute. Is Judy still with you?"

"Yes. I can't get her to move from here. What do you want me to do?" He had heard the muffled scream and knew from experience what it meant.

"Nothing, leave her be for a spell and you come back here."

"What about the ferret, Fred?" Johnny wanted to know.

"Oh, you can forget about 'im," said Colin. "We won't get that one back, right, Daddy?" Fred nodded as he rummaged through his pockets for his pocket knife.

"So you're just going to leave him here? What about digging him out or something?" Johnny felt a bit irritated by Fred's indifference.

"Listen, Johnny, we can't do anything else. Just imagine, even if we had shovels, what Davies would say if we dug away half his hedge! And look at all the time we'd be wasting." He glanced at his watch again. "Well, boys, that's 25 minutes gone already. Pick up the nets and everything, careful not to tangle them. Well, we might as well take these back to the car." He looked at the big lurcher still licking her wounds. "Johnny! Would you mind taking all this stuff back to the car, please? It's no use to us now."

"Fred, I think you're a callous so-and-so to just leave him like this. He has been looked after all his life, and now what will happen to him?"

Fred stared at him for a few moments in silence, wondering if he was serious or not. "Listen to me for a minute, Johnny. That little animal you are so concerned about will spend the rest of his life doing what he likes doing more than anything else in the world, and that is killing small game just for the fun of it, all right?"

He turned his back on him and looked up the field for another likely spot to start the hunt again. Johnny sighed, shaking his head as he looked at Fred's rigid back. "Titch, can you give me a hand with this stuff, please? You carry the cage and the pegs."

Returning to where the others were waiting, they walked slowly up the field, with Fred continuing to whistle for Judy, but it appeared that she didn't want to leave her post at the rabbit hole. Finally, Colin went back down the hill, picked her up and tucked her under his arm to rejoin the others.

"Stubborn little sod, isn't she?" he grinned, stroking her head with some affection.

"Well, we've got one rabbit anyway," Johnny said brightly, pulling faces at Fred's back and winking to the others.

"Aye," said Colin, wanting to be part of the fun, "but that one belongs to Trefor, don't forget that."

"Colin, bluddy shut up!" Fred was getting more irritable by the second. "Don't you worry," he turned back to face them. "We'll have something else today. You mark my words!"

They tramped in silence up and across the top three fields until they came to a double wire fence protecting a new growth of hawthorn hedge. Fred leaned on the fence looking down. "It doesn't look like there's anything up here, boys," he remarked sourly.

"And how the heck do you know that, then?" Johnny leaned on the fence beside Fred but couldn't see what he could see.

"Because," Fred replied patiently, "there are no runs to be seen and none of the bottom twigs have been chewed off the hawthorn, that's why. Now there's a bit more for you to remember, Councillor. No charge." He smiled. "I'm the best there is at this game, remember. Okay boys, let's go!" Climbing the fence, they waited for the dogs to crawl through and then made their way across the hill until they could see the roof of a distant farm.

Johnny held up a large mushroom he had found. It was about the size of a large dinner plate. "Fred! You could feed a family of six on one of these."

"Aye, you're probably right," Fred replied, looking at his watch. "Listen, boys, we don't have much time. Let's go towards the next farm, perhaps we'll have more luck there."

"I thought it was skill we had come to see, not luck. A sure thing, you told us last night in the Plough," Jimmy interrupted, tongue in cheek, as the others stood grinning at Fred's discomfort.

"Listen, you clever sods," he hissed, rounding on them in temper. "Are you willing to onto the next farm or not? Cos if you're not we might as well go home right now!" They all looked at each other in silence for a few moments then nodded in agreement to follow Fred.

They crossed the low hedge easily, lifting the dogs and dropping them on the other side. The big hound became a problem as she wouldn't go to anyone, limping to and fro, still feeling the effects of the thorn hedge. Fred climbed back over and picking her up with his arms around her front and back legs, he placed her gently on the other side. He waited until the dogs were out of the way and put one hand on the fence post he vaulted over to land with a flourish. "Ta-dah!" he cried out, arms in the air and fingers splayed. "How about that, then!"

"C'mon, you bluddy clown," Colin growled disrespectfully. "The boys were right about you being a ballerina."

"Colin, I've told you before: I'm the oldest teenager around," he joked as he did a few spins in his impression of the Twist. They trudged slowly along the edge of the hayfield, guns at the ready and alert for any sudden movement, when a heavy-set, black-haired man on horseback came out in front of them from behind a stand of trees. Titch, who was a few yards in front, called out softly: "Look out, boys, here's trouble."

Fred, holding Fly on a shortened lead, turned immediately to face the horseman. "Leave this to me, boys," he said quietly from the side of his mouth. "Hey!" he shouted, striding towards the man. "What are you doing on Davies' land? You are not 'is son, cos I know 'im!"

The man reined in his horse abruptly, looking down sternly at Fred. "This is not Davies' land…"

"Oh yes, it is!" argued Fred, interrupting him.

"This is MY land and you lot are on it WITHOUT MY permission!" he said, deliberately.

Fred let his jaw drop in fake surprise, while turning and winking to the others grouped behind him. "Well, fancy that, boys! Listen," he said as he addressed the horseman. "We've never trespassed before cos we always ask permission. And that's the truth of it, mister."

He eyed each of them suspiciously and turned his attention back to Fred, who appeared to be the ringleader. "I'll have you know this is my land and I want you off it right now!"

"Now, look here," Fred cut in. "We're very sorry if we are trespassing on your land but since we are here and we haven't damaged anything can we do a bit of hunting for rabbits?" This was as far as he got.

"WHAT?" he roared. "NO! No, you can't do any hunting on my ground. So get off my land this very minute, the lot of you. You cheeky sod! I've a good mind to call the police."

"Okay, okay! We're going, but remember that we asked you politely, there's no need to be so funny about it. C'mon, boys, I can see we're not welcome here so we'll go somewhere where our help is appreciated." Collecting the dogs, they turned to go back the way they had come, but the farmer spurred his horse to get between them and Davies' land.

"Not that bluddy way!" he shouted, waving a fist in the air. "Go down the hill. There are no gates between my land and Davies'. Go down to the road!" He crowded his horse as close as possible to Fred, glaring down at him.

"Right you are, then!" Fred put on a brave front. "You just wait, mate, until the rabbits ruin your crops. You'll wish then that you'd let us catch them before they became too many. I'll tell you this for nothing, I wouldn't come back here if you paid me."

He stood up in his stirrups in anger and said through clenched teeth. "Get bluddy going!" He followed them closely right down to the gate and the road beyond. As he galloped away, Fred stood there grinning and making rude gestures at his retreating back.

"Well, Fred," Johnny said, grinning. "So much for today's adventures in trespassing."

"Aye, you're right," Fred chuckled. "Attack is the best form of defence, that's what I always say."

"Defence? He could 'ave had the cops on us, Fred! P'raps that's what he is doing right now," Jimmy looked back up the field. "Especially after what you said offends 'im."

"Nah! I don't think so. It would be too much trouble and in any case, a country area like this might only 'ave one policeman to look after a huge area. Boys, we're safe enough for the time being."

By then it was early afternoon, and having tramped all over the hills for most of the day in hot sunshine, all of them looked more than a little worse for wear and were in dire need of some form of sustenance.

"I for one am starving," Johnny declared. "What about you lads?"

"Me too," Colin agreed. "My stomach thinks my throat has been cut again. Although I should be used to being hungry, I'm not kidding you, boys. In our house you have to hunt for food, and I mean hunt! Fred hides everything, don't you, Daddy?"

"Aye, and you know what I said about that too! If you work regular, then you can eat regular, right! Well, let's get back to the car, then we'll decide what to do with the rest of the day."

It was a long walk down the narrow lane to where they had left Alan's car. The hot sun beat down on them in the stillness of the afternoon across the wide shallow valley. In the distance they could see the roof of Davies' farm as they made their way slowly downwards. Some of the hedgerows had been recently pleached: Colin was an expert in this art. The young trees had their stems almost cut through with a billhook, and then they were intertwined to form a growing barricade which would eventually become a thick, impenetrable hedge. The patchwork of red earth and different-coloured fields somehow made it look like a soft quilt in the middle distance across the other side of the valley.

As they continued down the lane, Fred took the catch of the day from his pocket and smoothed its damp fur. 'Good thing that bluddy farmer didn't see this little beauty. He might have thought we got it on his ground, called the police and we'd have lost it."

"Aye, and think of what Trefor Plough would have made of that story, Fred!" Johnny chuckled. "Your reputation as a hunter would have gone straight down the drain."

"Aye, the old so-and-so!" Fred shook the rabbit in mock anger. "But you are my little alibi, aren't you?" he said, stuffing it back in his pocket. Everybody, as if on cue, started laughing, holding onto each other for support. Fred looked from one to the other, bewildered. "What's so funny? What the 'ell are you laughing at now?"

"You! You *twp* so-and-so." Johnny replied, tears in his eyes. "You, telling that farmer off like that. I thought he was going to run you down with his horse."

"Aye. Sure to be!" Fred replied belligerently, his fists bunched. 'I'd 'ave shown 'im a thing or two." He puffed out his chest. "I'd 'ave 'ad 'im."

"Get away, Fred! You're too old now for that sort of thing."

"Am I? Am I, indeed?" He turned towards Jimmy, but Colin put his arm around his father's shoulders and said, "Fred, look at the funny side of it. I'll bet that farmer will be mad till next week after what you said to 'im. Especially that bit about not being welcome on 'is land."

"Aye!" Fred's voice softened and he started laughing with them. "Aye. I bluddy told 'im, didn't I?"

Arriving back at the car, Johnny unlocked the boot and the doors and opened them wide to let some of the intense heat, generated by the sun, escape. They sat around on the warm grass taking a well-earned rest. Johnny lay flat on his back alongside the car, shading his eyes with his arm as he looked up at Fred. Jimmy and Titch were leaning comfortably against the car wheels on each side of him.

"Aye," Colin said. "You'd 'ave had 'im like that over-man when you were a boy."

Fred started laughing, with Colin joining in. "Aye, I did, didn't I?"

"Okay, boys," Jimmy said, smiling. "Tell us the story, Fred, so we can all have a laugh, is it?"

Colin, smiling, looked at his father. "Go on, Daddy. Tell them the story."

Fred rubbed the side of his jaw. "Well, I was about 13 or 14 years old and I had not long started work at the Tower Colliery. Me and two other boys had to move all these pit props and other timber by hand from the railway wagons to stack them where they could easily load them onto the journeys going underground. It was not like today when machines do everything for you.

"My two brothers – well, they were not my real brothers, cos my mother married second time to their father – anyway, there was this over-man who was a 'butty' to them and he had seen them give me a clip now and then, and he thought he could do the same and knock me about when he felt like it. Well, anyway," Fred went on, "on this particular day, he shouted something at me, I can't remember what it was but I answered him back a bit sharpish.

"Well, boys, he came after me and gave me such a wallop on the side of my head it was ringing for ages. I vowed then I would 'ave 'im for that, and I did too. I watched and watched what he did and where he went at every minute of the day for about a week.

"Boys, every day, just before the hooter went to go home, he would go down to the little privy we used as a toilet. It was a little shed made of corrugated sheets built over a small stream, and had two planks with a gap for a seat. Well, this day I got some really dry gorse bushes and stuffed them under the planks. When he went in there, I got a piece of wood and piled some newspaper I had *cwtch*ed and set light to it and floated it down the stream. Boys, I ran like 'ell down the mountain to watch. He would've killed me if he found out it was me. Well, the gorse caught fire pretty quick and he came out of there like a bat out of 'ell, his trousers round his ankles and dancing up and down, trying to beat out the flames round his arse and shirt tails with both hands. I was laughing fit to bust.

"The trouble was, the planks caught fire, and I had to help to rebuild the whole shed." He looked at the others rolling round laughing and couldn't help joining in. He got to his feet and brushed himself down. He looked at his watch. "Hey, boys, it's after three o'clock. I don't think we'll see anything now. Why don't we make our way home or find somewhere to get something to eat?"

Everything was loaded into the boot and Johnny drove slowly down the hill to the main road.

CHAPTER 9

Fred's appetite in Talgarth

JOHNNY BROUGHT THE car to a halt at the bottom of the lane and looked up and down the main road. "So, which way do we go now, Fred – left or right? There's no signpost here." He sat drumming his fingers lightly on the steering wheel.

"I dunno! This place has changed a bit since I was here last." Fred got out of the car and walked across the road to climb up onto a five-barred gate to get his bearings. Jumping down, he ran back to the car and getting in, said, "Go right, Johnny! Talgarth is that way. That's the nearest place I can think of out here." He pushed himself down into the passenger seat and pulled his cap down over his eyes. "Wake me up when we get there."

"Right! Talgarth it is then." Johnny spun the wheel and pointed the car in the direction Fred had indicated.

Talgarth was a small market town that in medieval times had once been the capital of the Welsh Kingdom of Brycheiniog. It was roughly in the centre of the county of Brecon. During the week the town was fairly quiet but at weekends it bustled with activity, due in part, to the large hospital and sanatorium situated about half a mile outside the town in spacious well-kept grounds. This was, at the time, the main treatment centre for mid Wales in the treatment of people with tuberculosis, cancer and mental health problems. Each Saturday and Sunday special buses and private cars full of people visiting family and friends would converge on the town from the surrounding areas. Naturally, all the local businesses benefitted from the constant weekend influx, and the town thrived.

The car was warm and comfortable and everyone, with the exception of the driver, dozed or fell asleep after the day's escapades. It was very peaceful in that part of Breconshire and it seemed more like a Sunday than a Saturday until they arrived on the outskirts of Talgarth.

"WAKEY WAKEY!" Johnny called out loudly while blasting on the car horn, rousing everyone with the sudden noise.

"Bluddy 'ell," Fred yelped. "You daft sod. I thought there had been an accident or something." He rubbed the sleep from his eyes with his cap.

Johnny laughed. "It's about time somebody woke you up, you tired old so-and-so. Okay, boys, eyes peeled! Look for a tidy place to eat, one with a car park if possible, cos looking at the signs, there is no parking on the streets here. I'll drive as slow as I can, so watch for something." He took the car slowly down the main thoroughfare and was looking for a place to turn around to make a second pass when Fred pointed up the street. "There's one up there on the right."

"Okay. I can see it." Johnny accelerated slightly and the café came into full view. "It looks a bit posh to me. We don't want a repeat of this morning's performance, do we, Fred?"

"Hey! That wasn't my fault," he protested. "They shouldn't 'ave balanced all those bluddy chocolates like that..."

"And you shouldn't have touched them like that." Johnny finished for him.

"Now fair play, boys –" Fred pleaded, but Jimmy cut him off.

"Aw, shut up, Fred! I'm starving, so just behave yourself for a change, all right?"

"All right, all right! Don't keep on." He wiped his face again with his cap, and smoothed the stubble he had for hair with the flat of his hand.

Johnny parked Alan's car in the furthest part of the car park, where fortunately there was a large tree that offered some shade for the dogs and the car.

"Fred! Make sure you lock the doors and leave the windows open a bit for the dogs to have some fresh air." Johnny got out of the car, stretching to ease some of the stiffness out of his back as they made their way slowly across the yard while trying to make themselves look a bit more presentable, brushing down crumpled clothes and wiping their faces with handkerchiefs limp with moisture. Stuffing his cap in his side pocket, Johnny led the way, leaving Fred to make sure his dogs were okay. Looking up at the hand-painted sign over the entrance, Johnny read it out loud. "'Ye Olde Tea Shoppe'. I hope that silly so-and-so behaves himself in here, that's all."

Entering the cool, dim interior, they looked around for a suitable table. "There's a table for four over there, by the window," said Jimmy, "but what about Fred?"

"Don't you worry about Fred," Colin said quickly. "He'll soon find somewhere to sit, if I know him.' Accepting Colin's advice and without any further ado, they moved smartly across the room to grab a chair each and sat down. One end of the table was against the window and the other end was too close to the next table, which already had its full complement of hungry diners.

Fred entered the room and shading his eyes in the dimness, looked around for the rest of the group. Spotting them, he threaded his way through the tables and stood looking for a chair to sit with them.

"Where am I going to sit?" he demanded in a loud whisper.

"I don't know," Colin answered in a whisper, "but there's no room on this table."

"Like that, is it?" Fred replied fiercely.

"Hey! It's not like that at all and lower your voice, Fred!" said Johnny, trying to defuse the situation. "Other people are looking at us. We'll be chucked out."

Fred looked around the dining room and noticed a few diners staring at his scruffy appearance. Realising the sense in what Johnny had said, he nodded to the others and said.

"I'm going to sit over there, there's only two at that table." His usual grin appeared. "Watch this," he said, making his way across the dining room.

Pulling out a chair, he plonked himself down with an audible sigh and made a big show of seating himself comfortably on the hard wooden chair. It hadn't occurred to him to ask if the seat was vacant or that his intrusion on their dining would not be welcomed.

"Shomai!" he said, with a grin. Fred had chosen to sit opposite a large overdressed woman, in a long summer dress of blue, covered with large blue flowers. She also wore a large hat, under the brim of which she glared balefully at Fred's grinning face. The young boy with her was dressed in what appeared to be a school uniform of blue, with grey edging on his blazer and a grey cap perched on his head. He stared at Fred, who really looked a disreputable character at that moment, then poked his tongue out at him and resumed pushing food into his mouth as fast as he could manage.

Fred looked from one to the other as they concentrated on the meals in front of them. 'Aye,' he thought, 'a real pair of toffee-noses.' Aloud he said, winking across the room at his companions. "Lots of toffs about today," pointing deliberately at the other two occupants of the table.

"'Ell's bells," Colin groaned in a low voice, "'ere we go again."

"Ignore 'im," Jimmy advised. "Give him a minute or two. P'raps he'll calm down."

"Like 'ell he will. I'll tell you now," Colin went on. "It looks like they have upset 'im. You watch 'im upset them, just for fun."

"If we don't watch what he's doing, "Johnny whispered, "he won't have an audience."

"No chance, Johnny," Colin replied instantly. "Boys, I've seen 'im perform like this before. Just you wait and see."

"Hey, boys," Fred spoke in Welsh. "Watch me fix these two."

"There you are!" Colin raised his hands. "What did I just say, boys?" They all looked across at Fred, but he had already turned his attention back to his adversaries.

"Lovely day, ma'am," he said brightly. The woman paused in her attack on the meal in front of her, her fork halfway to her mouth. She glared at Fred and tried to stare him down. Fred immediately took up the challenge.

Settling himself at the table he faced the unfortunate woman with his elbows on the table and his chin resting in his cupped hands. He continued watching them eat, looking from one to the other each time a loaded fork was raised.

"Now there's funny," he remarked. "Every time you raise your fork your mouth opens." He grinned at them.

The woman deliberately put her fork down, stood up and looked around as if looking for someone in authority.

"Half a minute now," Fred said softly, "you don't want to cause a row or something do you? That would be embarrassing for everybody."

The woman pursed her lips, hands clenched on the table, glaring down at him.

"C'mon," Fred said soothingly. "Sit down, your food is getting cold."

"Shut up! You, you, pig!" she spat out, sitting down heavily. Turning to the boy with her, she said tersely. "Eat your food up quickly, John, so we can leave this horrible man."

"I like praise," Fred said conversationally, leaning on one elbow, his face in his hand. "Yes, c'mon sonny, eat your food so you can grow up to be a big boy like me." He turned his full attention now to the boy. "That's it. Take that nice piece of meat." He pointed at it. "Damn, that looks good."

The young lad turned to his mother for support. "Come along. Eat it quickly," she encouraged.

"Aye, listen to your mother," Fred added. "Eat up!"

"Mind your own damn business," she snapped at him.

"Hey, lady, I was only trying to help. It's a shame to waste good food." The poor woman was almost crying in anger by this time.

"Damn you! You scruffy man," she cried as she jabbed the meat on her plate, clearly wishing it was Fred.

"Carry on, you," Fred said calmly. 'I got all day."

This undoubtedly was the last straw. She jumped to her feet and grabbing the arm of her son, yanked him to his feet. "Hey, mam!" he yelped. "You're hurting my arm.!"

"I'm sorry, love," She immediately put her arm around him. "It's this nasty man here who caused that. We are leaving this minute, come along."

Fred looked up at the woman towering over him. "But you 'aven't finished your food."

"Oh yes, we have," she interrupted.

"I was only joking," he protested.

"Joking my foot," she replied, in a tight voice. "You are despicable! Yes, despicable!"

"I'm sorry," he said as she swept away, dragging her child with her towards the cash desk.

Johnny got up from his chair, came over and leaned over him, saying with suppressed anger, "Knock it off, Fred, or I will leave you here and you can walk home. Got it?"

Fred nodded and swivelled in his chair to follow their departure, alert for any complaints the woman might make about his behaviour at their table.

He glanced quickly around the dining room but no one appeared to be in the least concerned, except his travelling companions, who were shaking their heads in disbelief at his latest nonsense.

Smiling now, he looked at the two meals on the other side of the table. 'Damn,' he thought, 'they have hardly touched them.' He looked around the dining room and catching Colin's eye, pointed to the unfinished meals and rubbed his hands together, grinning all over his face.

Colin shook his head violently and mouthed the word NO!

TOO BAD! Fred mimed in reply.

Colin whispered urgently to the others what he thought his father was about to do.

"My God! He isn't. Is he?" Johnny turned in his seat. "And I've just warned him, too!"

The waitress had moved towards Fred's table, pushing a trolley, with the intention of clearing away the dishes left behind. He held up a hand and said, smiling. "Excuse me, miss. You can leave all that there. They've just gone to the toilet." He dropped his voice to a whisper. "It's the little boy, you know, he's not very strong."

"Oh, I am sorry," she said, her hand up to her face in sympathy.

"But since you are here, I would like to order a meal for myself. Is that okay?"

"Oh yes." She was still trying to absorb Fred's revelations, then taking out her order pad and with pencil poised, she whispered. "What would you like to order, sir?"

"Ah, yes!" He glanced at the other plates. "I think I'll have sausage, egg and chips, a cup of tea and a plate of bread and butter, please." He thought, 'That's different to what is over there.'

"Is there anything else, sir?"

"Er, no. That's okay, thanks."

A little bit mystified by Fred's whispered instructions, she pushed the trolley back towards the kitchen, at the same time looking over her shoulder at him.

Meanwhile, he was keeping his head down, not wanting to catch the eye of anyone as he surreptitiously began moving the plates and cups around until the woman's plate was in front of him. Casually he picked up his knife and fork and demolished the remains of her meal in less than two minutes. It didn't take him long to switch plates and polish off what was left of the lad's meal, as if he hadn't eaten in a week.

"He's just greedy, that's all, boys," Colin said. "He can make food disappear like magic."

Johnny looked at his watch. "By my reckoning, he cleared both plates in just over four minutes. That's incredible."

Fred looked around with a satisfied smirk as he put one plate on top of the other and started picking at his teeth with a grubby fingernail.

The waitress approached Fred, her hands full with plates of bread and butter. She looked at the devastation he had wreaked and placed one of the small plates to one side of him.

He looked up at the puzzled girl. "Ah, yes. They've been and gone and they've paid too," he added quickly. "I saw them myself. You can check at the desk!" The girl nodded dumbly, still surveying the mess, and turned to place the plates on the other table. On her return, she brought the meals for the five of them. While she was placing the meals in front of the others, Fred took his plate of bread and butter and put it out of sight on his lap under the tablecloth. Moments later, returning with the trolley to clear the table, Fred said, "Excuse me, miss. Where is my bread and butter?"

The girl looked around, bewildered. "But I brought it already!"

"No, you didn't. You brought theirs, not mine," he said, pointing to his son's table.

She checked the number of plates on the other table. "That's funny," she mused. "I could have sworn..." She looked intently at Fred.

He lifted his hands in the air, palms out and shoulders raised, his face a picture of feigned innocence.

"Well, all right. I'll get you a plate, then." She made her way back to the kitchen and told them of the funny goings on in the dining room. She collected the dirty dishes and loaded them on the trolley with many a glance at Fred, who was tucking into his meal as if it was the first food he'd had that day.

"Where's he putting it all, Colin?" Johnny was curious. "Has he got hollow legs or what?"

"This is nothing, boys. I remember we went down to my granny's one day and Fred ate a big bowl of stew. My grandmother had left a big tureen of spuds on the stove and he polished off most of them as well and, on top of everything else, he ate nearly a full plate of tart she had made for tea. Der, she was off! He's a greedy sod when he gets going, I'm telling you." He nodded his head. "Sometimes it's not safe to get up from the table if you've left something on your plate." He laughed.

"Get away! It can't be as bad as that!" Jimmy leaned across to get the vinegar.

"It's right enough, what I'm telling you! Look what he's doing now, then."

Furtively, Fred was bringing another piece of bread from under the table up to his mouth, grinning at the others watching him.

"You see that? The greedy sod, he ate those other two meals and his own but he just had to cheat to get those extra bits of bread and butter."

"He's not all that big, either." Johnny eyed Fred's spare frame. "I'll bet he's got a tapeworm."

"More like a bluddy python," said Colin as they all broke up laughing.

"Just wait until they hear about today's escapades in the Plough tonight."

"Aye, Fred's going to take some stick over today's nonsense, all right." said Jimmy.

"It will be like water off a duck's back. You watch what I'm saying." Colin was laughing and coughing at the same time and holding his sides as if in pain. "Boys, he's priceless, and especially when he's on form!"

"C'mon, boys, lets go. It's getting late and Alan will want his car back." Colin collected the correct amount off each of them and went over to the cash desk.

Jimmy gave him a nudge. "What about Fred's meal?

"He can pay his own," Colin whispered, not to draw his attention.

Fred was still cleaning up the last few crumbs of his meal as they all trooped out to the car in the bright sunshine.

Opening the doors to let the dogs out and the fresh air to pass through, Johnny leaned against the car. "You know, I find it hard to believe what I just witnessed in there. That Fred, without a doubt, is an animal," he said to Colin, and shook his head in disbelief.

Colin laughed, lighting a cigarette. "You watch 'im when he comes out, boys. He'll be bragging how much he got out of that café."

As if on cue, Fred came out into the sunlight. "Damn, you get a pretty good feed in there!" he said, belching loudly.

"The boys are right, Fred. You've got hollow legs. I've never seen anything like it in my life."

Fred chuckled. "Just like Mae West said: 'You ain't seen nothing yet'. Mind you, you don't get a chance like that every day," he said reflectively. He leaned in through the passenger door before getting into the car and said, "I don't know about you boys but I could do with a pint or two after that little lot." He belched again.

"My God, Fred. You're the bluddy limit!" Johnny exploded.

"Hey! What's wrong with you, Johnny? I was only asking!" Fred stared at him. "Let's go to a pub I know in Brecon. We'll just have a couple, then straight home, is it?"

"It's not that place where we were this morning, is it?" Johnny asked him straight-faced.

"No bluddy fear! I couldn't afford a glass of water in there after this morning. Driver, go to the Three Salmons. It's right on the main street at the bottom end of town."

Having given his directions, he settled back in the comfortable seat with his hands clasped over his bulging belly and cap down over his eyes. He drifted off into the land of nod, followed in minutes by Colin and the two brothers.

Arriving in the market town, all the pubs were closed following the normal afternoon session, which had ended at four o'clock. Johnny switched off the engine in the car park of the pub. All was quiet, except for the gentle snoring of his passengers.

"Hey, Fred!" Johnny gave him a hard shove. Fred stirred and looked around sleepily, blinking his eyes.

"Where are we?" he mumbled.

"Your pub! The Three Salmons, but they're closed because it is well after 5 o'clock." Johnny smiled at him.

"They'll open for me," he boasted, sitting more upright. "Watch this!"

"Aye, okay. We'll watch and wait until you come back. Right, boys?" Johnny turned to the others who were stretching and yawning in the back, "Aye, we'll wait right here," they chorused as one.

"Right then," Fred was out of the car like a flash. "Be right back," he called over his shoulder. He tried the front door first, but that was locked. He shrugged his shoulders with hands open at the others. So they politely waved back to him, Fred replied with a rude gesture, and walked around the side of the pub to the rear door that could be seen through the archway. From their seats in the car they could see him knocking on the closed door, then stepping back to look up at the windows above it.

"Hey, Col!" Johnny said, "why don't you go and give your father a bit of support".

"Not I," Colin chuckled, "He got chucked out of here last time for being drunk and bothering people with his stories."

"Why didn't you say something about it, then?" Johnny was puzzled.

"Why should I? If he can't remember, I'm not going to tell 'im, and anyway, p'raps the landlord has forgot by this time. It don't matter, he won't get in.' Colin finished. Settling back into the corner and pulling his cap over his eyes, he waited for his father's return.

Fred gave the back door a few more hard raps with his knuckles then stepped back as the window above opened. Fred started talking quickly, then stopped abruptly, mouth open. He stepped back a bit further, said something, made a gesture with his fingers and ran quickly back to the car. He swung the door open and jumped in, slamming the door behind him. "OK," he said breathlessly. "Let's go, quick!"

"Why?" asked Johnny, starting the engine.

"Never bluddy mind why, let's go – I'll tell you on the way," Fred was watching the front door. "C'mon, let's go, quick."

"I dunno about you, Fred. First you're in a rush to get here, and now you are in a rush to get away." Johnny swung the big car quickly out of the pub yard onto the road for home. "C'mon, Fred, what did you tell him?"

"Well, I asked, tidy like, if we could 'ave a few pints, that's all, then he said, 'You cheeky swine, I had to throw you out last time for causing a bluddy row here.' So I told 'im to stuff his beer and the glass up his back end!" he chuckled. "'I'll bluddy give you...' he said. So I ran," he laughed. "The beer there is not so good anyway. It's okay at a push," his voice tailed off, lost in thought. Suddenly he sat up. "Colin, you were with me last time," he accused him, angrily.

"I know," Colin's voice sounded muffled under the cap.

"Well, why didn't you say, then?"

Colin sighed, "Cos you wouldn't listen if I told you, you'd only say that it was somewhere else."

"Ah, well, that's as may be," Fred grumbled. "Let's go straight back to the Plough boys, we'll get a pint there for sure." He beamed at the others. "Don't forget we've got a rabbit for him."

"Is everybody in agreement?" Johnny asked over his shoulder.

"Aye, if only to have a bit of bluddy peace here," Titch said. "Now shut up Fred, I'm trying to have a nap."

The journey back over the mountains passed without incident or comment as Johnny's passengers slumbered. Arriving outside the Plough, Fred had returned to something like his old self, having finally slept off the effects of the enormous meals he had consumed.

CHAPTER 10

To the Plough
to relate...

JOHNNY PARKED ALAN's car in the open area at the side of the Plough and switched off the engine. There was complete silence for a few moments as if everyone was waiting for someone else to make the first move.

"Hey, Fred," Jimmy leaned forward and tapped him on the shoulder. "This morning you were bragging that you always like to buy the first round. Well, here we are at Trefor's pub, so here's your golden opportunity to show willing."

Everyone started laughing, with the exception of Fred, who grumbled, "All right, all right!" as he got out of the car. Standing outside, he brushed the fur of the little rabbit. Holding the dogs' leads in his other hand, he said, "So I'll go in first, then, is it?"

"Well yes, Daddy," Colin smiled with delight at his father's obvious discomfort.

Fred looked at the others for a moment without speaking then pushed his way through the door into the crowded bar and shouted above the noise. "Hey, landlord, we're back! And here's your share for now!" Fred dropped the sorry-looking rabbit on the bar, giving Trefor the impression that it was only the first part of a bountiful harvest from the day's hunt.

Trefor stared down at the limp body on the bar and said. "I think I would like to see the rest of your haul so I can pick out a better rabbit than this one, Fred!"

"You asked for the first one caught, Trefor, and that's it!" he replied quickly.

Trefor looked at Fred, suspicious of his sharp reply. "Driver, is that right?"

"Oh yes, Trefor. It is the first one all right." Johnny paused and then added, "And the last!"

"WHAT?" Trefor pounced on this snippet of information like a cat on a mouse. "Is this all The Great White Hunter could produce after hunting all day? After all his 'bounce' last night about him and Blucher being the best hunters around?" His tone was incredulous. "Well, well, well. What do you think of this turn-out, boys? The crowd around Fred close to the bar rocked with laughter, while Fred, trying to find a suitable retort, could only stand there with his hands on his hips, looking from one to the other in frustration.

"Right then, Trefor! Let's have the money for this then," pointing to the rabbit. "And I want five pints of best bitter and less of your lip too, cos we've had a hard day. A bluddy hard day." He leaned on the bar, head down, as if exhausted.

"Five pints, Fred?"

"Yes. I'm buying the first round." He looked over his shoulder at Jimmy, Colin, Titch and Johnny, who were grinning.

"Oh, is that right? I'd better put that one up on the board, Fred." Trefor turned to pick up the chalk and wrote the time and date on the small blackboard on the wall. 'Fred bought the first round of five pints'.

"Aye," said Jimmy, tongue in cheek. "We've had a 'ell of a day, haven't we, Fred?" He winked at the landlord as he spoke and Trefor, as perceptive as ever, could sense immediately there was more fun to be had here.

"Ooh. So what did you get up to today then, Fred," he asked innocently enough. "Tell us, boys, what happened?"

Jimmy nudged Fred, and he, remembering the morning's escapade in the Brecon Hotel, came out of his grumpy mood straight away and started laughing 'til tears streamed down his lined face, while the others, between laughing, tried to explain the rest of the day's events. Things calmed down after a while and the stories were repeated in more detail while Fred, true to form, now the centre of attention, strutted up and down the centre of the bar, pint in hand, coat thrown back, a hand on his hip, and saying to no one in particular, "There you are! What do you think of that then, boys? See, I'm the bluddy boy for them," until the whole day's events had been repeated more than a few times over with some exaggerated additions.

Later that evening Old John Shinkins came back into the bar to sit in his place on the settle, and hearing Fred repeating the tale of the chocolates once again, called him over. "Hey, Fred! You know, don't you, that old fox of yours has been seen around the council houses again."

"What are you bothering about, John, 'that old fox of mine'? How do you say it's my old fox?"

"It's that sort of tame one you sold to Jack Honeyman. The one with the broken tail."

"Aaah, get away! That thing was gone from here ages ago. Anyway it's got nothing to do with me now."

"No," John replied, not mincing his words. "Not after you caught him by selling him a wild animal. Pity he didn't know you like the rest of us do." Old John was out of breath from his tirade against Fred and began to thump his chest with the side of his fist, as if to get more air into his dust-damaged lungs.

"Well, he's moved away from yere now," Fred replied, as if that solved the problem.

"You just mark my words, Fred!" John said, waving his hand

to include everyone in the bar. "That old fox is going to do a lot of damage around here because he is not afraid of people or dogs. You just wait and see!"

Fred pulled a face and moved back to the bar to get away from Old John's heckling as Trefor rang the bell to end that night's fun.

CHAPTER 11

Jack Thomas' chickens

IT HAD BEEN fairly quiet in the Plough for the past few nights, but one evening Fred's neighbour, Danny Thomas, came into the bar calling for a pint. While digging deep in his pocket for money to pay for it, he stood there slowly shaking his head in a negative fashion as he said, "I don't know about that Fred!"

"So what's he done now, then?" Trefor asked, always ready to hear about Fred's antics.

"It's not what *he's* done is the problem. It's that fox cub that he raised and sold to Jack Honeyman. That's the bluddy problem."

He went on to say that his father, Old Jack Thomas, had lost nearly all his chickens and some ducks just the night before. "He went out the back just as it was getting dark, to lock them up for the night, when he saw more than half of them dead in the back yard, and that old scruffy fox of Fred's was sitting there as bold as anything with a bird still in his jaws. The old man, as you know, Trefor, can't walk too sharp now so he threw his walking stick at the damn thing, but he didn't flinch until he threw a stone at it and would you believe, it came right past him close enough to touch and out through the gate and trotted up the street with the bird still in his chops. The old man was as mad as 'ell." Danny started laughing as he related the last bit, which for some reason he had found amusing. "Just you wait, Trefor, until the old man catches up with Fred! There'll be a bluddy row. You can bet your life on that!"

Everyone within earshot, upon hearing Danny's story and knowing Old Jack's fiery temper, began speculating on the outcome of the confrontation when the two of them met.

It appeared that Fred was in the soup again without even trying!

"Don't you worry, boys, Old John Shinkins has already primed Fred about that ol' fox and he'll have all kind of excuses ready. He's got more flannel than a Witney blanket. He'll find a way to get out of it, I'm sure," Roy Childs predicted from the card table.

"Maybe, if he remembers. He had been drinking quite a bit when Old John told him off about the fox, mind," said Twm, looking over the top of the *Western Mail*. Then he smiled. "But on the bright side, Old Jack is such a fiery character even though he's near enough ninety; he will remind 'im pretty quick and might even give 'im a crack on the nut with that stick of his. I've seen 'im give a few youngsters a crack across the back of the legs just for giving him lip. Hey Danny! How old is your father now?"

"He'll be 89 next month. Why?"

"I was just saying, p'raps he'll give Fred a crack on the nut with his stick when he finds 'im." Twm replied, grinning.

"Don't be surprised at that," Danny laughed. "I've had a few clips from him myself over the years, and I'm not too old now, mind! He doesn't mess about. When he loses his temper, everybody within range can look out. I was just warning Trefor, in case he wanted to borrow a stretcher from St John's Ambulance for the night." He grinned at the landlord while raising his glass in salute to him, and moved towards the card table.

"So who's up for a game of crib then? C'mon, me and Dai Banwen will play Roy and you, Twm, for a pint a corner. Okay?"

"Aye, okay," Twm agreed, folding the newspaper and laying it on the end of the table in front of Old John. "You deal then, Roy."

"Wait a bluddy minute! Damn, you've got a poor memory, Twm. We always cut the cards for deal in here."

"No, I haven't, Dai," Twm smiled knowingly, "and there's nothing wrong with my memory."

"Well, p'raps you didn't think I'd notice then," he said in a mocking tone.

"Something like that," Twm grinned, taking no offence at Dai's remarks.

"Right," Danny said after shuffling the cards. "Ace is low, cut low!" He banged the pack back on the table and tapped on the top of it with his knuckles. Dai Banwen cut a picture card and Twm cut an ace.

"Like I said in the beginning, it's your deal, Roy." Twm smirked.

Dai Banwen just glared at him.

CHAPTER 12

Jack Thomas confronts Fred about a fox

O<small>N</small> S<small>ATURDAY</small> <small>NIGHT</small>, just as he said he would, Old Jack Thomas made his way into the bar of the Plough and sat on one of the settles facing the door. He made no attempt to buy or ask for a drink. Everyone in the room could see from the set of his jaw and the way his dark eyes flashed from under the brim of his cap each time the door opened, that he was there for a purpose and coming nicely to the boil as he waited.

It was now quite obvious to anyone in the room who had learned in previous days about the killing of Old Jack's chickens and ducks by an almost-tame fox, that he was there to have it out with Fred. But, as the evening wore on with the usual noisy Saturday night crowd and his two sons in attendance placing the occasional glass of ale in front of him, he appeared to mellow slightly, to the extent that he joined in some of the lively discussions going on around him and across the table. But to the keen observer, his attention was only fleeting.

It was once again near to closing time when Fred rolled in, having had more than a few drinks elsewhere.

"A pint of your best ale, landlord!" His familiar shout could be heard above the clamour the moment he entered the bar. It made no difference to Fred that there were several other customers already waiting at the bar. He always wanted to be served first, last and anywhere in between.

Old Jack spotted him the second he came into the room. He stood up, gripping his heavy walking stick tightly. "FRED! Hey, Fred!" he shouted at the top of his voice. "You are just the man I want to see! Come here, you!" he ordered. "What about that old fox of yours and my chickens and ducks he 'ave killed for me?"

The general noise in the bar dropped rapidly to almost a whisper.

"You owe me for them, Fred Howells!" His voice rose again in anger.

"And I want payment for them right away!" He was leaning over the table towards Fred, his eyes blazing as he raised his stick in his direction.

Brazenly Fred stared back at old Jack across the table and then with a hint of a grin, he said. "I don't know anything at all about it, Jack." (Despite having heard all about it some days before.)

"Oh, yes, you bluddy well do," Jack yelled.

There wasn't a sound from the rest of the room, not even a whisper, as everyone's attention was on the two protagonists.

"It's all your bluddy fault this has happened. Who's going to pay for my birds? I'm an old age pensioner, you know, and I can't afford any nonsense like this."

"Well," Fred replied calmly, rocking back and forth slightly on his heels. "If he didn't damage them too much, you could eat them yourselves or sell them off to the rest of the family at half price." He ended with a short laugh.

"Damn your eyes, Fred!" Jack lunged forward, swinging his stick at Fred's head. "Don't you dare say such things to me you, you, *gwalch*. If I was a bit younger I would knock your block off for that," he shouted, swinging the stick again, narrowly missing Fred as he stepped back smartly out of range.

"Aye? Sure to be, Jack! I'll bluddy give you for that!" Fred, thrusting his head forward, suddenly became belligerent towards the older man. "Right! I'll get you Jack Honeyman's address and you can take it up with him. That bluddy fox, if it is the same one, has got nothing to do with me. Nothing at all!"

Old Jack was absolutely livid with Fred's remarks and was still trying his best to hit him with his stick. Danny, Jack's oldest son, stood between them, trying to calm them both down. His father continued to glare angrily at Fred as he said, "You're to old to be potching about with fox cubs and things like that. It's time you bluddy grew up!" he said, stabbing an accusing finger at Fred.

"And it's about time you minded your own bluddy business about what I do!" Fred yelled back angrily.

'Things are heating up nicely,' thought Trefor, 'but I have to find a way to calm things down a bit.'

Fred started to get a bit more personal. He said, "Hey Jack! I'm willing to bet that you don't have any planning permission from the Council to keep livestock in your back garden too."

Jack stared at him, his mouth open for a split second, then he retaliated: "And what about all those bluddy dogs you've got? Keeping people awake at night with their howling because you half starve them?" Jack thrust his head forward to glare at Fred. "And another thing, I am willing to bet that you haven't got licences for all those dogs!" he said triumphantly, seeing the sudden change in expression on Fred's face. "I've a good mind to tell the police tomorrow that you've got half a dozen dogs and not a licence between them. That will cost you a pretty penny when you appear in court, I'll venture. They might even take them all off you, you cheeky sod. Think about that then, Fred!"

"Hey, listen, Jack!" Fred's tone of voice changed dramatically in seconds, as he had visions of fines and the possible loss of his precious dogs. "We can't argue like this when we've had a few drinks, is it? So what if I come and see you tomorrow and we'll talk about it, is it?"

Unspeaking, Jack continued to glare at him, still out of breath from shouting and straining against his son while trying to get at Fred.

"Now come on, Dad, let it go." Danny, his hand firmly on his father's shoulder, said. "You've had your say so let it drop for a while, is it."

Angrily, Jack shrugged off his son's hand, his eyes still on Fred's face. Slowly he got his temper under control, then turning away he picked up his glass, took a quick swig, then sat down heavily on the settle beside Old John Shinkins.

"That damn Fred! Did you hear his cheek to me? I'm old enough to be his father and he gives me lip like that! No fear!"

"Aye, I did. We all did, but he'll never change," John said quietly.

"Him change? Never," Jack said indignantly. "But he will have to do something about my chickens or I WILL report him, for sure."

The noise in the bar returned to its normal Saturday night level. Fred wandered over to watch the card game at the large kitchen table in front of the shuttered window. Fred had not the slightest interest in card games.

Roy looked up from his seat facing the room, his back to the shuttered window. "I see you managed to cause a row here tonight again, Fred! You're getting quite the expert at doing that, aren't you?"

"I've had a lot of practice, Roy," Fred smiled as he turned towards the bar. "A pint of best bitter, landlord." His forced smile was still firmly in place.

CHAPTER 13

To catch a fox

On the Sunday morning following Fred's confrontation with old Jack Thomas, the usual pre-lunchtime crowd had gathered in the main bar and the subject inevitably got around to the previous night's episode of the partly-tamed fox, the commotion it had caused, and if it could happen again.

Fred took all the insults and innuendoes in good part. One of his most redeeming attributes, perhaps the only one, was that he never held a grudge or ill feeling for any length of time no matter what was said or done. He would often say, "I'll have you for that", but nothing ever came of it and most of the time it was over and quickly forgotten. He could flare up like a match and moments later the flame had died.

When asked to comment about the row, all he said was, "Jack got a bit upset, that's all. It's only natural, isn't it?" He chuckled, then added, "I'll talk nice to him and everything will be okay." He sniffed optimistically.

Tyrone, one of the regular patrons of the Plough, pointedly asked him: "So, Fred, how did you come by that fox cub in the first place?"

"Well. Hrrr!" He cleared his throat. "Remember the last time a crowd of us boys walked over the mountain to Cwmdare?" This is a village about eight miles from Rhyd-y-groes. "Pity you couldn't have come with us. Der, boys, we had some fun, I can tell you. Anyway," he shrugged his shoulders. "We shot a vixen on that long peat bog up on the top *waun* across from Craig y Llyn. You know the place, from there you can see the Maerdy water."

"Aye, aye. Go on, I know the place."

"Well, the ground where we had her was well marked all over, so we thought she must have a litter of cubs somewhere around there. We looked all over, then our terrier Rose started yelping and digging like mad. Our Colin pulled her away and started pulling back the clumps of grass, when two cubs bolted out of the ground. Colin hit one with a piece of wood and I shot the other one." He paused to take a swig from his pint, a faraway look in his eyes, as if he was reliving that moment in time.

Tyrone gave him a nudge, breaking into that moment. "Go on, Fred."

"Oh. Where was I?"

"You shot the second cub."

"Oh, yeh! We were just getting ready to leave when Rose went back to that same spot and just stood there not making a sound at all. I said to our Colin, 'I'll bet you anything there's more cubs in there.' 'Hold on,' he said, pulling back the grass around the hole and there, would you believe, was another cub just curled up. I thought it was dead, so I grabbed it and I started to cut his tail off when it yelped. After all the noise we had made and the shotgun being fired, it was fast asleep in that den. Boys, I couldn't believe it…"

"Like you in work, then. Or so I've been told," said Willi, laughing.

"You're a cheeky sod, Willi Bray. I only get into a corner out of the draught for a couple of minutes at the most, that's all." Fred had his answer ready in an instant, to refute what was obviously a fact to everyone listening.

"Never mind 'im, Fred, and your sleeping habits." Tyrone poked him with a finger. "What about that fox cub?"

"Oh. As I said, I had picked 'im up to cut off his tail, when our Colin said 'Lets keep 'im for a while. He looks pretty quiet. Maybe we can tame 'im.' I thought he must have been bluddy deaf. So I stuffed 'im in my pocket, cut the tail off the vixen and the other two cubs, and brought it home. I used to take it out with a wide collar and a good strong lead on it. Remember? Well anyway, Jack Honeyman saw it with me one day and thought it was a bit of a novelty and wanted to buy it off me as a pet for his kids. They're from London you know, as if that explained everything. He kept on about buying it every time he saw me. So, in the end I sold it to him. If I remember right, I was a bit broke at the time."

"As usual." Twm turned around to look at Fred from his seat at the card table.

"Well, we can't all be rich property-owners like you," Fred shot back in an instant.

"I'm not rich, Fred. I'm just careful with my money and I have to work too, you know!" Twm's face coloured up at Fred's biting remark.

"Aye! So I've heard," Fred nodded, but not convinced.

"Catching cubs is one thing," said Bobby, another of the regulars at the card table. "but catching full-grown foxes alive is something else, at least that is what I've been told." Tongue in cheek, he winked at Twm.

Twm caught on at once. "You're right enough, Bobby. That would be a pretty good trick."

"I can do it! Don't you bother about that." Fred rose to the challenge like a salmon to a fly. "I can do that anytime I want to!"

"Hah! Well, I for one would like to see you do that," Bobby winked slyly in Twm's direction, drawing Fred deeper into a commitment.

"I can catch foxes live. Without a trap even. Just like Blucher did," he bragged, his tone of voice rising a few notches to emphasise the point.

"Oh-oh! We're back to him, are we?" Twm chimed in. "It's a wonder he doesn't turn over in his grave in shame at some of the things you've said about him, Fred!"

"It's all bluddy true, what I 'ave said about 'im," Fred said hotly. 'I was with 'im lots of times, remember!"

"As I recall it was hundreds, last time you mentioned Blucher." Twm was desperately trying to keep a straight face against Fred's bluster.

"Well, it was!" He looked quickly from one to the other, uncertain at that moment whether they were being serious or pulling his leg.

"Well, let's get some other opinions, is it? We don't want you to think that we are the only ones who have a little bit of doubt in what you are saying here today." Twm raised his voice. "Hey boys! Listen a minute! Fred here says, he can catch a full-grown fox anytime he wants to. Without spring traps…" He looked at Fred who nodded agreement. "Or guns?" Fred nodded again.

"Or dogs!" a voice shouted from across the bar.

"Or dogs," Fred agreed reluctantly. The muscles on his jaw tightened in anger as he realised he had once again been sucked into a bet as easily as a bee to a pot of honey.

"Right then, boys! Here's the bet!" Twm stood up, towering over Fred. "He says he can catch a full-grown fox, alive, mind you, anytime he wants to, without the use of spring traps, guns or dogs. So what do you think, boys?"

Shouts of 'impossible' and 'rubbish' came from all quarters, along with some coarser opinions on his ability as a hunter and trapper to complete the task.

"Now, wait a minute! Now, wait a bluddy minute here! Listen!" Fred shouted above the clamour. "Listen here! Okay, okay. I'll do what I said, with no traps, guns or dogs and I'll bring it in here alive. Okay?"

"When will that be?" asked Bobby, without a smile, his face cupped in his hand and elbow resting on the table.

"About this time next week. Saturday if you like!" he said recklessly. "So put your money down with the landlord and I will cover all bets, if you feel that brave. I've got my last ten shillings here.' He waved the banknote in the air as he challenged them with his eyes. 'This is my reputation,' he thought.

Aloud he said: "Come on you lot, let's see what you are made of! You 'ave challenged me, now I am challenging you." He looked appealingly at the landlord. "Can I give you my money, Trefor? I know it will be safe with you."

"Right you are, Fred. Give it here, then." Trefor held out his hand, with fingers wriggling, towards him. Reluctantly, Fred handed over every penny he had in the world.

Many of those coming up to the bar looking for a bet with Fred wanted to redeem some of their past losses to him, when he had conned them into betting on something he knew for certain he could not lose. So this time, thinking they were on a good thing, they lost no time in placing a few shillings with Trefor, which they felt certain would come back as a profit and not be lost to Fred's severe lapses of memory.

Fred watched keenly who was placing bets and suddenly called out, at the same time waving his arms in the air: "Okay, everybody! That's it! No more bets. This betting shop is now closed. Trefor, I would like you to keep a list for me and keep all that money safe. I'll pick up MY money next Saturday, Trefor," he said in a loud voice and then in a much quieter tone. "Hey Tref, can you give me a pint on the strength of my winnings, please?"

Trefor, in the same quiet tones, replied. "I think I would rather put the pint on your current account, if that's all right, Fred?"

"Oh, okay," Fred replied grudgingly, "but I know for sure I am going to win this bet."

"If, as you say, you are so sure of everything, how is it you are not rolling in cash from betting on the horses, then?" Trefor asked as he placed the brimming glass on the bar.

"Ah well. It's like…"

"Time, boys!" Trefor called out, ringing the bell and purposely ignoring Fred's excuses. "The bar is closed! Time to go home, boys."

"Hey! Wait a minute before you put that money away, Trefor! What odds are you giving on the bets, Fred?"

"No bluddy odds at all, boys. If I am taking on you lot, it's even money."

"If you are so sure you can do it, Fred, you can clean up with a few points." Twm tried his best to press him a bit more.

Fred hesitated momentarily. "Nah! A bet is a bet, boys. Even money and that's it."

CHAPTER 14

To catch a fox (continued)

D URING THE DAYS that followed, the usual crowd in the
Plough saw very little of Fred, who, so it was rumoured,
had been seen walking the mountain paths at all hours of the
day and night and on those rare occasions when he did come
into the bar, he was totally subdued and refused to be drawn
into any arguments or debates, no matter how hard some of his
cronies tried. Even those who considered themselves experts in
winding him up at the drop of a hat, such as Roy and Trefor,
failed miserably.

Saturday afternoon was the one time when most of the pub's
gambling fraternity, Fred included, gathered in the bar while
making use of the betting shop that adjoined the pub, a mere
fifty feet away. They all appeared to study form from the same
Racing Gazette, but none seemed to win with any regularity,
even though they offered all sorts of encouragement to their
selections (which were shown on the TV perched on the end
of the bar) while drinking a few pints to salve their momentary
disappointment.

Fred was one of the first to arrive at the Plough that afternoon
and went to sit in his usual spot on the wooden settle near the

stove with the inevitable pint of bitter ale close to hand. He had the *Racing Gazette* spread out on the table before him, but it appeared that he was more interested in seeing who came through the door than looking in the paper. The bar gradually filled up, as one by one his critics of the Sunday before came in and took up their chosen places around the bar.

Finally, Fred stood up, pint glass in hand as he stared pointedly at each of his critics in turn. At that moment Bobby, the last of his tormentors came into the bar. A satisfied look passed over Fred's features and he called out loudly: "Landlord! How much money do I need to cover all my bets from last Sunday?" He was trying desperately to suppress his inner excitement as he waited for Trefor's reply.

"Just a minute, Fred, I'll check it for you now." Trefor made a big show of counting the coins and consulting the list he had made, which was also in the box. He raised it up and gave it a good shake, the coins jingling impressively. "You will need exactly five pounds and ten shillings, Mr Howells."

"Thank you very much. I will be right back." Then sternly he ordered, "and Trefor, don't you hand that money to anyone else but ME!" He emptied the remains in his glass in one gulp and walked out through the door with a sense of achievement.

Trefor, still holding the box aloft, looked around the bar at the expressions of surprise on the faces of Fred's critics as the door closed slowly behind him. A buzz of speculation broke out as to whether Fred would make good on his bets that day. Bobby, taking the lead, voiced an opinion that Fred could always find a way around bets, whether in his favour or not; it depended on his very selective memory.

Two minutes later the door swung open and Fred stood in the opening, grinning from ear to ear. "Right then, Trefor! I'll take all that money now and you can keep the box for next time." Fred stood there in all his glory with a live fox, wearing a wide collar and leather lead. Its muzzle was bound shut with soft copper wire.

The frightened animal was desperately trying to get away but Fred held it tight and close to his knee for all in the bar to see. Suddenly a huge clamour broke out from the terriers and dogs that some of the patrons had brought with them. The stink of the fox, and its own scenting of fear, was driving them into a frenzy of barking and howling. Fred's re-entry with the fox in tow had turned the bar into a bedlam of noise.

"Here you are, boys!" Fred shouted above the din. "See! I'm the world champion in catching foxes. I'm the champion of this village and any other village in the county. I have done what I said I could do. So here you are, look at 'im. Isn't he a beauty?" He yanked on the leather lead lifting the fox's front paws off the ground as he spun him around. "Now then, do you believe me? I didn't travel these mountains with Blucher for nothing, you know!" Dragging the fox behind him, he moved to the corner of the room and tied the fox to the leg of the wooden bench furthest away from the dogs which were still howling and barking their heads off. The frightened fox immediately disappeared into the dark recess against the wall.

Fred, jubilant now, collected his winnings from Trefor and nonchalantly went over to the big card table to wave the money under the noses of his critics.

"Boys, this is lovely music to my ears," he chanted, rattling the coins in his hands. "I'll have a pint of your very best ale, Trefor, if you please." He sat back down on the bench and leaning against the wall, one hand on his knee, a pint of best bitter in the other, as he savoured his glorious moment of triumph.

The disgruntled punters looked on as he laughed at the slightest thing, and drank away some of the money they had thought would be easy pickings for them. One of them, at the card table, said in a voice loud enough for Fred to hear, "I think it's a tame fox. He's done it before, boys. You only have to remember Old Jack's chickens! I've got an old dog at home with no teeth and it could see that timid thing off."

"Is that so!" Fred was off like a match at this taunting remark. "Well, I'd like to see it, that's all!" Fortified with a few pints of best bitter, Fred was ready for any sort of challenge at the drop of a hat. "I'll have you know that I've got the only terrier around here that can kill a fox outright!" He jumped to his feet, head thrust forward belligerently as he glared towards the group at the card table, since he wasn't sure who had made the remark.

"Who says so?" Jimmy looked up from the card game. "I've got good terriers too, mind."

"Not like my Rose, you 'aven't!" Fred stated flatly. "I've got papers for her as long as your arm. They can't even sell these pups unless the parents are proven fox killers," adding as an afterthought. "She's a Glen of Imaal terrier, the best there is for fighting."

The broad statement from Fred created the loudest argument of the day, with everyone who owned or had ever owned a dog chipping in with the breed they thought was the best fighting dog around – at least, they thought they knew, and everyone wanted to shout Fred down, all at the same time.

"Wait a bluddy minute, Fred!" Twm shouted from across the bar. "What about a Kerry Blue? Now there's a fighting dog if I've ever seen one," he yelled above everyone. "Why, I've seen one of them take on three dogs at the same time and walk away unmarked."

Fred shook his head, pulling a face. "Not a bluddy chance."

"How about a Bedlington, a Sealyham or a Staffordshire Bull Terrier?" Names of different breeds were flying in all directions with everyone shouting out their fancies at the same time.

Through all this noise, Fred sat totally unconcerned. He'd had enough beer and now, bolstered by his winnings, he threw caution to the wind, stood up and went over to the card table. "Boys! Listen! Who'll bet me that my bitch, Rose, won't kill this fox?" He went back to the corner of the room and dragged out the poor fox, yanking it up by the collar for them all to see. The terriers, catching the scent of the fox once again, set up an even louder clamour of barking and howling than before.

Trefor looked up from filling a pint and shouted above the din, "Fred! That's enough! Get that thing out of here right away or I'll stop serving you beer for a week!"

Fred spun around and looked at the landlord in amazement, his mouth open, as he tried to cope with two situations at once. "Aye, okay." He shrugged his shoulders at Trefor's sudden irritability and turned his attention back to the crowd around the table. "Okay, what about it then boys? Do you want to bet or not?"

"Fred! I won't tell you again," Trefor shouted. "Get that fox out of here!"

Fred left the room, pulling the fox behind him. Minutes later he was back and standing over the card table. "Well?"

Jimmy looked around the table at the other players and received nods of approval. "Right, Fred. You're on. Same bets as before, is it?"

"Yeh! Same bets as before." He made his way through the crowd to the bar and handed Trefor a handful of coins. "This is my money for the same bets as last time with those over there," he pointed over his shoulder at the card players. "I'll pick up my winnings later tonight, okay?"

Trefor took the handful of coins off him and carefully counted them and put them in the box, shaking his head in exasperation at Fred and his antics, and then put the box under the bar. 'Still,' he thought, 'he's good for business when things are quiet.'

Returning to his seat, Fred said loudly to anyone who was

interested, "Come down to my place after stop tap and I'll show you a fighting dog. You'll be sorry you bet against me again." Fred was now full of confidence, but mostly beer.

Trefor duly closed the bar at four o'clock and Fred, sitting on the stone windowsill outside the pub, was holding tightly onto the fox, which was constantly seeking some avenue of escape as the betting crowd gathered around him. Fred stood up and glanced around, checking their all-too-familiar faces. "Is everyone here? Right then, let's go," he ordered roughly. Those who had a bet on the result of Fred's bragging formed up in a casual group straggling behind him as they went down the lane towards the backyard of his home on the council housing site. Arriving there, Fred's dogs set up a clamour at the sight of the fox, which only boosted Fred's ego a little more.

"Are you sure, boys, that's all you want to bet?" he asked, tongue in cheek. "Or do you want to raise the odds a bit?" He grinned when the punters shook their heads.

"C'mon then! Let's get this over with. I for one want to get home for my tea," said Twm, in not too kindly tones.

"Right, here's what we'll do," Fred announced. "I'll use the biggest kennel because it has a screen mesh window for you to see what goes on, if you want to that is. I'll put the fox in first and then put my Rose in there, and then you'll see what I am talking about." He started to hum 'I'm in the money', as he stumbled, laughing and slightly drunk across the yard to the kennel. He forced the fox in backwards and while holding it tightly by the scruff of its neck he carefully removed the collar, then, he unwound the soft copper wire from its muzzle and quickly pushed it further in. The fox moved into the darkest part of the kennel, snapping his jaws at Fred looking through the mesh. Turning away and getting to his feet with some satisfaction he said, "Now then, boys, where's my dog?"

Rose was a stocky well-built terrier, quite large for a true terrier, weighing in at more that 20 pounds and far outweighing the poor fox.

Fred gently picked her up and speaking softly and coaxingly in her ear, he opened the door of the kennel and quickly thrust her in with the fox. Bedlam reigned for about a minute of fighting then there was silence, except for a quiet whimpering from behind the door. The punters were pushing and shoving to get a view of what was going on as they peered through the mesh into the darkness. They could only see the fox, his rear end pushed tight into the corner and his jaws open ready to attack. There was no sign of Fred's champion fox-killer. The crowd looked at each other as they heard a soft scratching on the kennel door.

Fred, on his knees, opened the door gingerly and as the crack widened, Rose, the champion terrier, slammed it open and scrambled out, almost knocking him over. Without a backward glance she disappeared up the garden in a cloud of dust, accompanied by the jeers and cheers of the onlookers.

Fred was absolutely furious at this turn of events and when all the punters began poking fun at him and his constant bragging, all coupled with the disappearance of his champion dog, his ego fell to the ground with a thump that could almost be felt.

"They caught me when they sold me that bluddy dog," he complained angrily. "I'll take them to court over this," he said, clambering to his feet and brushing himself down, and staggering slightly from the belated effects of best bitter. He looked around as the laughter from his critics gained strength.

"You can laugh," he growled, "but I'm going to fix that bluddy fox!" He picked up a small heavy iron shovel and opened the kennel door and reaching in to arms length he hit the fox on the head. It yelped once and fell in a heap in the corner. Fred retreated and closed the door.

The others stopped laughing. Bobby said, "Hey Fred! Leave

it there, mun. Why don't you let the poor thing go, you've had your fun and we've had fun at your expense."

Fred looked at the dismay on their faces and said, "Well, that's the end of him."

Twm looked through the wire mesh. "Fred, he's not dead. He's just laying there, that's all. You just watch yourself, Fred, I think he's only pretending."

"What are you bothering about, Twm? You don't know foxes like I do."

Jimmy motioned to Twm to move over. He shaded his eyes to the dimness of the kennel. "I think Twm is right," he announced. "He is just shamming, that's all, so watch out or he'll 'ave you with those sharp teeth." He laughed and stepped back. Fred stood there looking from one to the other, the shovel still in his hand. "You all saw the belt I gave 'im. When I hit 'em, they've 'ad it."

"Never mind what you say, Fred, I'm saying he's NOT dead, right!" Twm repeated.

"We'll see about that right now!" Fred's jaw was tight with anger at this point. "I'll pull 'im out of there this minute, just to show you what I'm talking about. Take it from me, he's bluddy dead! I don't mess around with these things. I've handled live badgers before now, never mind foxes." As he spoke he opened the door of the kennel as wide as possible and began to crawl in. It was a bit of a squeeze for him due to the width of his shoulders.

They all moved forward to get a closer view to see if Twm Mawr's prediction was right.

Just as Fred stretched out his hand to grab the fox it suddenly came alive and lunged at him, teeth snapping together like a steel trap. Fortunately for him, he was wearing an old cloth cap which the fox snatched off his head, shaking it like a rat. Fred's speed in reverse out through the narrow kennel door was remarkable for a man his age, and had to be seen to be believed.

Everyone there began cheering. Fred landed in a sitting position and the wily fox, taking full advantage of the open door, jumped onto and over Fred to streak down the garden and through the hedge to freedom, and back to the mountain, with the gleeful punters cheering it on its way knowing that their bets were now safe and the fox had indeed won the day for them.

Fred, looking up at the ring of jubilant faces above him, turned his anger toward those 'rotten liars' who had sold him that bitch with papers under false pretences. "They caught me when they sold her to me," he bleated, looking from one to the other, expecting but not receiving any sympathy at all.

"It's about time somebody caught you for a change," Twm said, laughing at the sight of Fred still sitting on the hard ground. "You have caught a lot of people, one way or another, over the years." Fred was speechless, and just sat, fuming.

"Hey, Fred! You don't need to pay us out right away," Bobby called out. "We can get what you owe us from Trefor in the Plough tonight."

Fred watched them leave and turned his attention to the mountain behind his house. "I'll bet you anything that bluddy fox is laughing at me too," he muttered, his arms wrapped around his knees. 'There is one good thing to come out of this,' he thought, with something of his good humour returning. 'I'm glad they didn't take me up on increasing their bets.'

CHAPTER 15

The fox of Treherbert Road

Later on that Saturday, Fred sat alone in the Plough and appeared totally downcast. Trefor, the landlord, had not seen him this low for a very long time. Fred was deep in thought as he reviewed the day's events, in which he had come off second best, much to the delight of his detractors. In his mind, at that moment, there were two reasons for this. In the first place he had no cash left, and, after celebrating far too much on the strength of winning all his bets for catching a fox alive, as he had said he would do, he had then lost everything through his childish boasting about the ability of his 'killer' Glen of Imaal terrier, and later her failure to live up to his expectations when it had mattered most. The most galling part of the whole episode was that bluddy dog. 'Because of her I am being held up for ridicule by everyone in the Plough and no doubt elsewhere too,' he thought glumly. On top of all that, there was Trefor Plough, asking all innocent like, "Is that right what I hear, that you have a 'real fighting dog', with papers, for sale?" and when I said something a bit sharpish back to him, he said, "I am only repeating what I heard in here earlier, Mr Howells."

"Bluddy cheek I call it," Fred muttered under his breath.

Thinking of all that now, and of all the ribbing he had taken from some of the regulars from the moment he had set foot in the Plough, made him seethe inside. 'I've got to find a way to get some money or my life in here won't be worth living – and without cash I can't go elsewhere for a pint either,' he thought angrily, staring down moodily into the remains of his first and only half-finished pint, which he had been nursing for the best part of an hour. It was in danger at the moment of going flat.

George Teale sat down heavily beside Fred, interrupting his miserable train of thoughts. George lived in a large village in the valley some 1,200 feet below Rhyd-y-groes. He was a heavy-set man of six feet, but inclined to be more chubby than muscular. He had a dark, ruddy complexion, black close-cropped hair, and almost black eyes above a small button nose. He owned a couple of Jack Russell terriers who were more like pets than true working dogs. With these in tow, he occasionally joined Fred and his cronies on some of their hunting expeditions across the mountains above the Rhondda Valleys. George's main hobby, however, was breeding and selling pedigree Welsh Springer Spaniels, at which he achieved much success. "I've just come over the mountain road from the Rhondda, Fred," he whispered, his mouth close to Fred's ear.

"Oh, 'ave you?" Fred replied without any of his usual inquisitiveness.

"Aye, that's right," George continued, still keeping his voice low, "and I saw this big dog fox lying at the side of the road, up by that mountain gate. You know the place. It's right by that little stream that crosses the road into the forestry. I stopped the car to take a good look and it looked to me as if it had just been knocked over too but there wasn't a mark on him. Damn, he's a big one and I mean big, really BIG!" He stretched his arms sideways to demonstrate. "You should see it, Fred. Beautiful thick red coat. No doubt preparing for next winter I suppose."

Hearing all these details in complete confidence from George, Fred came alive inside. "Oh, is that so?" he replied, as casually as he could muster. He didn't want George to think that he had any more than a passing interest in the information he had just provided. "By the mountain gate, you said, is it?" His calculating mind was already scheming how he could turn this valuable knowledge to his advantage, moneywise. He glanced up briefly at the clock on the wall behind the bar, noting that it was still early evening.

"So how's things then, George? How's the family? Everybody in good health, are they?" Fred desperately wanted to change the subject of the fox on the mountain road, just in case George might mention it to someone else in the bar. He cast a glance quickly around the room but there was no one there, at the moment, who might be even remotely interested in a dead fox up on the mountain behind the Plough.

"Oh, fine, Fred. Everybody is fine, and thank you for asking." George looked intently at him. He was surprised at Fred's sudden good humour – a change from just a few minutes before – and the interest he had shown in the well-being of his family. In all the years he had known him, he couldn't recall him ever asking him that before.

Moments later, Fred rose from his seat. "Wait here a minute, George, I've got to go out the back to the toilet." He shot a pointed look at Colin, who was playing cards at the big table then inclined his head slightly in the direction of the outside toilets at the rear of the pub.

"I'll be right back, George," he called over his shoulder as he moved across the room, casting another meaningful glance at his son as he went out through the door.

Trefor, having a quiet night, was leaning with his elbow on the bar, chin cupped in his hand watching this brief interchange between the two of them; he also noticed Fred's sudden change in demeanour with more than a little curiosity. What is he up to now, I wonder?

Colin then got up from his seat at the game and called out to George, "Hey, George! Can you play my hand until I come back? I've got to go out the back for a minute," pointing in the direction Fred had taken.

Gladly George moved into Colin's seat and played a few hands of crib for him – and scored a lot of points for him – and when he resumed his seat George now watched the game with a greater interest, pointing to the scoreboard with a broad grin. Unspeaking, Colin nodded his thanks.

More than an hour had slipped away and the remains of Fred's pint still stood on the table where he had been sitting at the other end of the room. Old John Shinkins, sitting in his chosen spot on the wooden settle beside the stove, looked around the room.

"Where's Fred, then?" he said, to no one in particular. It wasn't like Fred to leave even an egg-cupful of beer unattended, much less almost half a pint.

Colin looked up quickly from the card game. 'He had to go back down the house for a minute. He'll be right back." Then he added sharply. "So why don't you mind your own business where he is, John!"

Old John stared at Colin in some surprise at the sharpness in his voice. Immediately sensing something fishy, he looked at him a second time. 'There's something going on here,' he thought. There's one thing about Colin, he always has respect for older people and women. That bluddy Fred must be up to his old tricks again, that's for sure, otherwise, Colin wouldn't have snapped at me like that. Mind you, when you think about it, they have both been a bit touchy since Annie left them on their own. He looked up to see Trefor looking directly at him, smiling and nodding his head. 'Aha!' he thought, 'Trefor has seen it too.'

Fred didn't return until more than another hour had passed. He gave a brief nod to Colin as he came through the door into the bar, then, picking up the remains of his almost flat beer, downed it in one go. "Drink up, Colin. Let's have a few pints, is it?" he said, smiling broadly. His good humour had returned – or so it appeared.

Trefor, pulling Fred a fresh pint, murmured. "I thought you were flat broke, Fred?"

Fred just smiled, and said, as he lifted the brimming pint to his lips, "Not really."

It was a couple of weeks before any of the regulars in the Plough Inn were able to find out some of what Fred had been up to that Saturday night.

Arwyn, the owner of Tŷ Uchaf farm, was playing a game of four-handed cribbage with some of the other local farmers. As it happened, they were the only customers in the bar at that time, otherwise the subject may not have come up. It was fairly quiet, with the volume on the TV turned low, and Trefor busying himself stacking bottles under the bar for the following day's business, when one of the farmers with land adjoining Arwyn's farm came in and sat watching them play. At some time during the course of general gossip, Fred's name had been mentioned and how he had caught a fox live, up on the mountain somewhere and they all had a good laugh at the outcome of his betting antics with some of the local boys.

"He's 'ell of a boy, mind," said Arwyn, laughing. "He'll have a bet on anything. But tell me, boys. This fox he caught. Was it a huge one? I'll tell you why I'm asking. He came to my place fairly late, it was dark anyway. Week last Saturday night I think it was. Anyway, he had this really big dog fox with him. He told me some story that he had trapped it on my land up by the forestry road. I didn't know whether to believe him or not but I couldn't think where else he could have got it so I gave him the benefit of the doubt and I paid him the usual three quid."

"What's that! Week last Saturday you said, right?" interrupted one of the other farmers. Leaning across the table he said in low tones. "Boys, I'm willing to bet you anything you like, it's the same bluddy fox he showed me, by damn! The crafty sod came to my place week last Sunday morning, gun under his arm, saying he had shot it up by the forestry so I paid him three pounds right away. It was such a beautiful fox too. It's a pity they have to be killed, but they kill so many sheep and lambs for me that I'm glad to see them gone. Another thing! He cut off the tail in front of me so he can now take that to the Foxing Club and get another three quid from there too. So, nine quid in all from one fox. No wonder he was smiling when he took the carcase with him as he left my place."

"Well, there you are then. I paid him for the same one as well." Arwyn leaned back in his chair, looking under his spectacles, as he raised them to look at his neighbour. "Just wait until I catch up with the bluddy schemer."

Arwyn's playing partner, dealing the cards, said, "I've heard quite a few stories about Fred over the years. He's always been the same, trying to get something for nothing or trying to find a way to put something over on somebody, and when he's found out, he just laughs and makes a joke out of it. He doesn't mean any harm. It's just the way he is. From what I hear from some of the old folks about him, he had a rough time growing up."

"Wait on a minute!" Will Mawr cut in. "I've been thinking about this, while we are all here together, right. We need to find out the truth of what he's done or not done before we can nail him for it. Now listen, boys, let's keep all this quiet and just between us few, is it?"

They all looked at each other around the table before nodding agreement to Will Mawr's plan. "Another thing, boys," he said quietly. "Knowing Fred as we all do, he won't be able to keep this to himself for very long, and when we know for sure, we can decide then what we can do about it. Agreed?"

"Aye. That's all right by me – but I have another idea." Arwyn leaned forward. "For the time being, let him think he has got away with it and when he comes to work for me at shearing time, I'll just deduct what I have paid him from his pay. If I know Fred, he'll have a good laugh out of it too."

"Better still," Will Mawr chuckled, "deduct my £3 at the same time and I'll get it back off you, cos if Fred finds out, he won't come to work for me!"

"Okay. I can do that. I can't wait to see the look on his chops when I do that. Now, boys, don't forget. Mum's the word!"

Fred had been feeling pleased with himself for the past little while. He had managed to put one over on two of the local farmers. The only thing was, he couldn't say anything to anyone about how clever he had been in turning things around in his favour, for fear of reprisals, such as not getting any work on those farms when he badly needed money.

Unfortunately for him, he had confided in his son, Colin, who was not bound by any loyalty to his father to keep silent about his little schemes (or Fred to Colin in anything he said or did, for that matter).

It was one night a few weeks later that Colin, who had been drinking for most of the day at the sheep sales near the Red Lion (a pub within walking distance in the next parish), and had continued into the evening, began to relate to one of the local lads the details of his father's money-making scheme with the dead fox.

Jimmy, one of Fred's rivals in the hunting arena, just happened to be sitting just a couple of tables away from where Colin was holding forth. It so happened that Jimmy's sister was married to the brother of one of the farmers Fred had bilked out of £3 for a fox he had found and not shot. Jimmy's ears had pricked up when he had heard his relative's name mentioned. It appeared that Fred, having heard about the dead fox on the mountain road, had left the Plough unseen, by the back door, and had made his way across the forestry in near total darkness, some two and a half miles as the crow flies. There he had found the fox and carried it down to Arwyn's farm to claim he had trapped it on his land. Arwyn paid him the bounty and he disappeared into the darkness, carrying the dead fox.

"Next day he shows up at Will Mawr's Beilli Uchaf farm with the dead fox and claimed to him that he had shot it on his land too. So Will pays him £3 more. My father can be a cheeky sod, mind," Colin had said laughing.

If Fred had only known that the beans had already been spilt by none other than his own son, he wouldn't have felt so pleased with himself as he raised the pint to his lips...

CHAPTER 16

Trefor and the door frame

A FEW DAYS after Fred's episode with the dead fox on Treherbert Road, Johnny was sitting in one of the large stuffed armchairs in Alan's house beside the brightly burning fire, waiting patiently for him to finish his tea. He picked up an edition of the local newspaper from the rack beside him, and was idly leafing through the pages when his attention was drawn to a column of news from Rhyd-y-groes. He straightened up in the chair and read the item again.

"Hey, Al! Did you see this item about the post office?"

"Do you mean the article about him being granted an off-licence?"

"Yes, that's the one. I'm thinking this will cause a bit of a commotion with Trefor Plough, don't you think?" He looked up from the newspaper, a smile wreathing his face.

"That news is history now," Alan replied grinning. "Look at the date! That is last week's paper. I'm told he has the shop down there all stocked up with every brand of booze. You name it, he's got it on the shelf and he's been advertising for some time now."

"Has he now?" Johnny sounded surprised at the news. "Well, I didn't know about that, look."

Alan laughed. "Well, all I can say is, you must be going around with your eyes closed, and you a councillor too. His shop is right across the road from where you live."

"To tell you the truth, Al, I don't go anywhere near the place if I can avoid it. Unless of course, I'm in need of some postage stamps or a postal order. That place was okay when those old ladies had it. They kept it all in order, but now...?" he shrugged his shoulders, pulling a face at the same time.

Alan stretched his arms over his head at the living room table and pushed his empty plate to one side. "Damn, that was good," he said, with a deep sigh of satisfaction, sucking at his teeth. "Fancy going up to the Plough for an hour? We might be able to find out from Trefor what the latest news is. You can bet he's keeping a close eye on it."

"That sounds like a good idea, Al," he replied, getting up from the armchair, stretching and yawning at the same time. "Yes, let's do something," he mumbled through the yawn, "before I fall asleep. It's too bluddy warm in here."

"It's lovely," Alan replied, thumping him playfully on the shoulder. "What's wrong with you, then? You must have ice for blood!"

"There's nothing wrong with me!" Johnny, quick to anger, replied sharply.

"Right then, if you're ready, let's go." Alan picked up his coat off the chair, and slinging it over his shoulder, went out through the front door with Johnny trailing along behind him down the steep hill.

Entering the bar, they slowly eased their way through the crowd to their usual station at the far end of the long room. For them it was a natural place to be. From there they could survey all the goings-on around the room in an instant. They could also find out from the landlord about any local issues which might concern them as councillors, and deal with them before they got out of hand. Trefor seemed to spend a lot of time at that end washing and drying fresh glasses for his many customers, which made it easier to talk.

Johnny leaned slightly over the bar and said quietly to the landlord, "Sorry, Trefor, I don't know how I missed it but I only saw the news in the paper tonight about an off-licence opening up in the post office shop."

Trefor replied with a slight smile as he filled a pint glass for each of them. "And you a councillor too," he murmured.

"Ah, well! You know that's nothing to do with the parish council, don't you?" He looked to Alan for support. "Licences for pubs, clubs and all private functions are dealt with by the local magistrates' court."

"Yes I know that," Trefor smiled. "I had to go there to voice my objection to him having a licence." He cast his eyes up to the ceiling, raising his chin at the same time.

"I'll bet that him getting a licence to sell beer and other booze will affect your business quite a lot, especially if he decides to knock a few pennies off the bottled beer."

"I dunno about that. He's too mean to even think of that," laughed Trefor.

"Well, there's one thing for sure," Johnny said thoughtfully, "he will be open more daytime hours – normal hours, that is," he amended quickly, "than you are, and he's right on the doorstep, as it were, for a lot of the narrow-minded people who like to have a drink or two on the sly without the chapel knowing about it. Mind you, there also quite a lot of them from the old village who couldn't care less who knows they like a few drinks."

"Aye," Alan cut in, "especially if someone else is paying." They all laughed, nodding in agreement.

"Seriously, though," said Trefor quietly. "I went to court to oppose him getting the licence. In my objection I said I was dependent on custom from the village for my livelihood now that the opencast site behind the Plough was just about finished, and that any loss of trade, however small, would mean I would find it very hard to make a living wage..."

"Get away from yere, Trefor! There's nobody around here as rich as you. You could give away free beer for a whole year and not even notice it," Johnny grinned at him.

"That's not the point, Councillor," the landlord said modestly, a slow smile creeping across his round features. "Anyway, listen a minute. The magistrates thought that the normal licensing hours were perhaps too restrictive on this particular community, since the main part of the village was a long way off the main road and it meant that people from the village would have to catch a bus into the nearest town – and because of the poor bus service through the village, it meant, if they wanted something, they would have to walk all the way up here and back, which might be too much for some of the older members of the community! Have you ever heard such nonsense in your life before?"

Trefor jabbed the air with his finger. "I'm telling you now, some of those people on the magistrates' bench should have been pensioned off years ago! Then, on top of all that, the chairman said that they had also taken into consideration the petition. 'What petition?' I asked. 'What petition? Oh, didn't I mention it?' Then he said, 'It's the one presented to the court by the applicant listing the reasons why he *should* be granted this licence to operate an off-licence in his shop'. I tell you boys, I was stunned. I looked across the court and there he was with his mother, laughing at me, right there in the courtroom. Then the Chairman said, 'Licence granted' before I had time to think of something to say in my defence. It was then I remembered that one of Gwilym's relatives had once sat on the bench as a magistrate with this lot!

"I'll tell you what, though. I will have my own back on him one of these days for laughing at me in court. Can you imagine? The cunning sod had a damn petition ready." He shook his head in disbelief.

"Well, Trefor, if you are going to lose that much business, you might as well put the Plough sign outside the post office." Johnny's casual remark caused the three of them to break into peals of laughter.

Trefor suddenly stopped laughing, his eyes bright with mischief. "Now there's an idea for some fun, boys, and a way to get back at him. I've got the very thing." He beamed. "Thank you for reminding me, councillor!"

"Oh-oh! What's that then? What did I say? Or better still, what are you up to now, then, Trefor Plough? I can always tell when you are scheming something." Johnny straightened up from his leaning position on the bar. "C'mon, out with it! Let's hear it, then."

"Shhh a minute. Keep your voice down a bit," Trefor cautioned. "I don't want anybody else to hear. Now, come a bit closer, boys," he gestured with his hands towards himself, "and I'll tell you what I want you to do." The three heads came together and Trefor, frequently casting furtive glances around the room, began to explain his latest idea in quiet tones.

Old John Shinkins, from his usual seat on the settle by the stove, watched the conspirators intently. He couldn't hear any of what was being said but his eyes told him that somebody was in for it, especially when those three put their heads together. 'Aha!' he thought. 'That Trefor is cooking up some scheme again.' I can feel it now. So, who's in for a bit of ribbing then? Can't be Fred, he's been a bit too quiet lately. (At that point in time, neither Old John nor anyone else was aware of the trick he had pulled on the local farmers!)

Alan and Johnny always seemed to be pretty near the landlord when a good, well-thought-out, harmless practical joke landed on someone's doorstep, and they gave as good as they received, all in good humour.

Old John glanced sideways without turning his head, as he pretended to watch the game of cards on the big table in front of him. Even from across the room, he could plainly see their shoulders lifting in silent laughter. 'Aye,' he thought again, 'whatever it is, it's bound to be a good one, for sure.'

"Now then, boys," Trefor's voice was barely above a whisper. "What I would like you to do is this. Out the back, near the coal *cwtch*, leaning against the outside wall, is the complete door frame. Remember, I had it taken out in one piece when they put in a new front door for me."

"Oh aye. I remember seeing it. It's a great big thing and I'll bet its bluddy heavy too," Alan murmured in a dubious tone.

"Of course it is. It's a really solid oak frame, but the best part about it is this. It's got Plough Inn on the glass above the lintel and the name of the old proprietor on the board and I'll bet you any money you like it will fit right in that wide door of the post office."

At this, all three were desperately trying to control their laughter while looking away from each other. Trefor still smiling, looked over their heads around the rest of the room and noticed that Old John was the only one who appeared to be looking in their direction, nodding his head knowingly.

"Okay, boys, let's break it up for now," Trefor said quickly. "Old John over there is keeping an eye on us. Will you two stay behind until everyone has left? Then we can get things going, okay?"

"Who says we're going to do anything? It's a great idea, but we are both on the Council, remember. Can you imagine the stink it would raise if we were seen, or even worse, if we were caught red-handed, so to speak."

"C'mon, boys, it's only for a bit of fun." Trefor, just at the very thought of his latest practical joke, was grinning like a Cheshire cat.

"Johnny's right," said Alan. "We could get caught going down the road with it. What could we say? You know what this new cop is like. Any little thing and he is on it like one of Fred's terriers. No wonder they call him 'Bookum' Jones. That's Dai Bandit's name for him, by the way. He told Barney the other day, when he was dusting his car for fingerprints after it was broken into, that he loves his job – especially when he knows one of his cases is going to court to plead guilty. Barney told me he made a 'ell of a mess in his car with that powder they use. It was everywhere with him."

"You could say, if anyone wants to know, that I have given it to you for firewood," Trefor interrupted. "What could be fairer than that, boys?" He raised his shoulders with his palms facing up to emphasise the point.

"Oh aye! That's fair all right, then we'll have all the fault if anything comes out of it, and you're in the clear," Alan said quietly, motioning with his thumb between himself and his brother-in-law.

"Listen, boys, where's the harm in it if someone sees you carrying some timber?" Trefor asked persuasively. "Like I said, this is only for a bit of fun…"

They all looked at each other in silence for a few moments then Johnny, looking at the other two with mischief in his eyes, said impulsively, "Aye, you're right, Tref. It's only for a bit of a laugh. C'mon Al, let's have some fun."

"Right then, boys! I'm sure there's nobody about now but I think it might be better if you wait for half hour or so to let all the stragglers get safely home. You know how some of them love to stop and chat, because they can't walk and talk at the same time."

They stood at the bar discussing some of the local issues that had come up in their capacity as parish councillors. Council work was something they both took quite seriously, and they related to Trefor one of the problems they had recently solved, without any need for court action for the damage that had been done.

After many complaints from their parishioners regarding the poor state of the cemetery, they had encouraged the parish council to invest in a motorised lawn mower, which they looked after and maintained, and had spent many hours of their own time getting the grounds of the cemetery once more into a reasonable condition. They arrived there one day only to find that someone had been there and had driven across the lawn in a vehicle and had badly churned up the grass. The marks were quite distinctive from a set of mismatched tyres: three smooth and one with a heavy Town and Country tread.

Johnny said, "I jumped out of the car and said 'Who the 'ell has done this? I'll knock his block off'. After all the work we've done down there, Trefor, it was beyond belief. I drove all over the village looking at every car and van in sight but there was no sign of it – until one night when I was looking for Alan, and I saw this small van in the car park of the New Inn. Well, there it was, as large as life, with that one odd tyre. I got Alan to confirm it, and was ready to go after whoever the owner was..."

"Same as usual," Alan said, grinning. "Just like a stick of dynamite."

"Well, you know me!" Johnny smiled. "Yes, Alan said to calm down and we'll find out who it is. So, we went into the bar and had a drink while we looked around for whoever it might be. Eventually it was coming up for stop tap and you know how keen they are over there, being right on the main road. Alan said, let's have a stroll through the other rooms, we might spot who it could be. Well, down in the long room were a couple playing darts. We knew her, Jean Davies from Pant-y-waun farm, but the chap with her was a stranger.

"'I think that might be our culprit,' Alan said, and I said 'I'm going to tell him right now', but Alan is a bit calmer and said 'I'm going to ask them if they want a game of darts, and when I say something you just follow on from there, okay?' So I said, 'What are you going to say?' And he said something similar to the trick you told me about fish hooks."

Trefor looked up in surprise. "Fish hooks? What fish hooks?"

"Oh, I'll tell you about that one after." Johnny grinned, remembering. "Anyway, Alan goes over and asks them if they wanted to have a game. Alan and me against those two. He said okay.

"'Just one game,' Alan told him, 'because it's almost closing time.'

"'There's nothing on the game, is there?' this young chap wanted to know.

"Alan told him no, it was just a game. So they threw first then Alan threw and with his last dart got a double. Then as he was turning away from the board he asked casually, if I had seen the tyre marks on the lawn in the cemetery. Well, it was as much as I could do to hold my tongue before I answered, 'Yes, I said, and what a bluddy mess. Just wait until the police catch up with him, whoever it is, he'll have a heavy fine for that and he'll have to pay for the repair of the lawn.'

"'Right enough,' said Alan, 'but what a place to go courting. In a bluddy cemetery, of all places.' Alan then raised his glass to the other two in mock salute. We saw them take a quick glance at each other without any comment. Then Alan said, 'I know how we'll catch him, though.'

"And I said, 'Putting some nails all over the grass?'

"'No, no! Listen. We're around the place all hours of the day and night so all we have to do is get a chain and padlock and when he goes in there again we'll take the padlock and with that high pointed iron fence we'll chain both gates together and they won't be able to get out, until we call the police the next day after they have spent the night with the ghosts!' We had a good laugh about that, especially when I reminded Alan about Joe Baker. He would rather walk the four miles around the village than pass the cemetery in the dark to get to his house, which was only about 300 yards or so past the cemetery gates. Jean and her boyfriend looked at each of us suspiciously when I said, 'It's not the dead ones you have to worry about, it's the live ones all around you.'

"This young chap said, 'Hey, boys, thanks for the game, but it is getting late and we have to go. C'mon, Jean, drink up, let's go.'"

After they had related this story, Trefor asked mildly, "Has there been any trouble down there since?"

"Not a thing," Alan replied, smiling broadly. "I'm willing to believe we put the fear of God into them that night."

"I'm sure you did," Trefor said dryly. "Now then, boys, the last bus from Waun-gron has just gone through without stopping, so there won't be anyone else knocking on my door for a pint after hours." He came from behind the bar and began collecting glasses and placing them on top of the counter. He then banked up the fire in the stove for the night by putting moistened small coal on top of the still bright coals, then turning the damper down, he turned towards them and called out. "Right, then, boys. I'll go and get my flashlight."

Outside, Johnny and Alan stood still, listening intently. There was not a breath of wind or sound anywhere in the dark, almost moonless night, with just the slim crescent of a waning moon in a clear sky. Moving quietly around the side of the pub into the car park, Trefor flashed his light across the large wooden door frame and concentrated the beam on the words: "Plough Inn" on the glass panel, and "W. J. Jones. Prop." still clearly visible on the wooden centre board above the lintel.

"Now then, boys! What do you think?" His mischievous grin could just be seen in the gleam of his flashlight.

"It looks bluddy great," Johnny replied, keeping his voice low, "but I bet it's too heavy for two men to carry any distance and it's more than a mile to the post office. Besides, it might fall apart on the way. Did you think of that?"

"Nah, it won't, and two strong boys like you should be able to handle that easy," said Trefor confidently.

"C'mon then, let's see if we can handle it first, before we start debating what we can or can't do," said Alan, moving forward and pulling the frame off the wall. "Hey! You're right enough, this thing is bluddy heavy."

"Well, of course it is. There's a lot of good wood in that. The best oak from about a hundred years ago, and its been out in all weathers for all those years and not a spot of rot anywhere. Okay, boys! Lie it down first," he instructed quietly. "Now then, one on each side with the top facing front..."

"Hey, Trefor," Johnny said, slightly irritated. "Do you think this is the first time we have moved something?"

"Shhh! Someone might hear – the farmhouse is just b'there!" Alan hissed. "Okay then, up with it. One, two, three." They stood up, both on the outside of the heavy frame, holding it in balance, and with a brief nod to the landlord they set off. The post office was just over a mile away down the winding lane. Swaying from side to side with their ungainly load, they were forced to make frequent stops to rest and get their breath back, giggling weakly as each, in his own way, imagined Gwilym's reaction upon finding the Plough Inn sign literally on his doorstep.

The frame seemed to get heavier the closer they got to their destination. Eventually they arrived outside the post office without seeing a soul (and, hopefully, without anyone seeing them). They carefully laid the frame on the ground directly in front of the shop and stood back in the shadows for a few minutes to recover from their efforts, all the while listening for any sound from inside the shop. There was none.

The post office was a converted dwelling house. The original corner bay window had been removed and converted into a double doorway, provided with a wide flagstone step.

Together they eyed the height of the doorway and compared it to the frame laying at their feet. Alan gave the thumbs up sign that he thought it would fit under the overhanging bay window of the upstairs bedroom.

Trefor was right again. It looked like a perfect fit in the dim light of the street lamp more than 100 yards or so away.

"Right! Let's do it. Put the top end in the doorway," Alan whispered. Lifting the frame slowly, they tried the frame for width. 'Okay. Let's move it back out. Now put the bottom end in first. How does it look?" Alan was holding the full weight of the frame against the doorway while Johnny stepped back to check the position of the frame.

"Bluddy marvellous, Al."

He carefully lowered it to the ground. "Right then. Here we go. We'll put the top end in first and lift it up slowly to tuck the lintel under the overhanging roof." Together they lifted, pushed and manoeuvred the frame in complete silence into the doorway of the shop, pausing frequently and listening intently for the slightest sound from inside. Not a sound was heard, except the sudden release of pent-up breath as they struggled in silence to complete Trefor's scheme.

Finally the frame was in place. The lintel fitted snugly right under the overhang, so as not to fall on anyone opening the shop door. Fortunately the shop door opened inwards; consequently anyone coming from inside the shop wouldn't know anything about it until his first customer entered and said something about it.

Breathless, the two conspirators stood back to admire their handiwork in the dim light of the distant street lamp.

"It looks great," Alan whispered, forming his hands in the shape of a camera viewer.

"Aye. It does too! Trefor will be proud of us. Pity we can't take a picture of it!"

Clapping each other lightly on the back, they ran off in different directions into the darkness to await the fallout on the following day.

CHAPTER 17

Gwilym the Siop and the door frame

THE FOLLOWING MORNING being a Saturday and no work, Dai Banwen was outside the post office before 9 o'clock, in the phone box ringing his son, when he noticed the newly installed addition to the shop doorway. He immediately recognised it as a brilliant practical joke.

At that moment, Gwilym Williams – 'Gwilym the Siop' – unlocked the door of the shop and came out to stand on the wide stone step, right in the centre of the additional door frame. He was, as usual, wearing a soiled white apron which hung loosely from his thin shoulders, whilst the apron strings were drawn tightly across his bony hips.

Dai poked his head around the edge of the telephone box and called out, "A pint please, Trefor!" laughing at his own joke.

Gwilym the Siop looked at him in puzzlement for a moment. "Is there something wrong with you, Dai Banwen?" he asked in his high-pitched nasal voice.

"Not with me," Dai replied, still laughing. "It's you! You don't look a bit like Trefor Plough."

Dai, still standing half-in and half-outside the phone box, could see that Gwilym the Siop, as yet, had not noticed the addition to his shop doorway. He said to his son on the other end of the line. "Listen, there's something really hilarious going on here at the post office. I'll call you right back." He put the phone back in the cradle and stepped outside to get a better view of Gwilym the Siop's reaction when he realised that a monumental practical joke had been played on him.

Suddenly Gwilym the Siop, despite his poor eyesight through the heavy lenses, saw something was different with the doorway. He turned, then stepped back into the open area in front of the shop to get a better look at the addition, and just stood there, transfixed, his jaw hanging, as he gazed up at the sign which read: "Plough Inn. W. J. Jones Prop."

Dai Banwen, weak from laughing, leaned against the wall, holding his sides.

"It's that bluddy Trefor Plough again!" Gwilym the Siop shouted at the top of his voice, suddenly coming to life. "I'm calling the police right away!"

"What do you want to do that for?" Dai asked him weakly, still trying to control his laughter. "Look, there's no damage to be seen, and besides, you don't know for sure if it was Trefor Plough. Anyway, think about it! He couldn't have done this on his own, could he? Don't be so bluddy daft!"

"Well, I'm going to phone that bluddy Trefor, then." Gwilym the Siop was obviously determined to phone someone. He went back into the shop, shouting as loud as he could. "Hey, Mam! Come and look at this, will you!"

His mother, hearing the sound of panic in his tone, came rushing out to the front of the shop and turned to look at what he was pointing to. Moments later, when she had got over the initial shock of seeing "Plough Inn" over the door, she began shouting and screaming Trefor Plough's name and what they were going to do to him. She was working herself into a frenzy by shouting at the top of her voice, "That Trefor Plough! That bluddy Trefor!" She turned to Dai Banwen. "Did you know he tried his best to stop us having the off-licence?"

Dai watched her performance with growing alarm as her features began to turn blue with temper.

"Now, now, Mam, wait. Wait a minute, Mam," Gwilym the Siop had a crafty look on his face as he looked closely at the large oaken frame. "There's a lot of good wood in this," he announced, standing with hands on hips, 'and I know what we'll do with it too. I'll cut it up for firewood and sell it. Yes, that's what I'll do and then I'll tell that Trefor Plough and see how he likes that!" His mother stopped shouting; nodding her head in agreement, she clapped her hands in approval at her son's solution.

"Hey, Trefor will be off, if you do that," Dai warned him. "I'm willing to bet he doesn't even know it is here!"

"And I don't care, right!" Gwilym the Siop raised his voice in temper. "He shouldn't have done this to us in the first place, should he?" he shouted, as he pulled and pushed the frame out of the doorway, letting it fall with a crash that broke it into three pieces.

"Now you've bluddy done it!" said Dai, jumping back out of danger as it fell.

"It doesn't matter! I'm going to cut it up right away and then I'll phone 'im and complain," Gwilym the Siop replied, out of breath with temper and the exertion of moving the heavy frame by himself.

"Well," Dai said, as he turned to walk away. "There's going to be trouble over this, you mark my words!" Looking back over his shoulder, he saw Gwilym the Siop dragging one of the sides of the frame around the corner of the house. "Silly so-and-so," he muttered. "He won't best Trefor Plough."

Just before midday, the phone rang in the Plough. Trefor put down his cup of tea. "Waun-gron 252. Who's speaking, please?"

"Trefor! This is Gwilym Williams!"

"Oh, hello, Gwilym. What can I do for you today, then? Have you run out of bottled beer?" he said, tongue in cheek. "I can lend you a few cases to help you out, if you like."

"No, I haven't! I am calling to complain about what you did to us yesterday, well, last night anyway..."

"Complain? Complain about what? Excuse me, Gwilym, but what on earth are you talking about?" Trefor interrupted. "I certainly didn't do anything to anybody last night or yesterday, or any other time for that matter. In fact I haven't been from here for a couple of days and I have witnesses to prove that. So what are you bothering about?"

"Oh, yes, you did!" Gwilym the Siop got angrier by the second as he thought of Dai Banwen laughing at him and no doubt telling everyone he knew about the Plough Inn sign over the Siop doorway.

"Well, tell me then, Gwilym," Trefor cut in again. "What is it that I'm supposed to have done to make you so angry?"

"You put that old door frame of the Plough in my doorway, making me a laughing stock in front of everyone, that's what you did!"

"No, I didn't," Trefor replied in innocent tones. "And another thing, that old frame is still out the back in my car park. I saw it there yesterday," he said truthfully.

"No, it isn't! I've got it down here!" Gwilym the Siop was shouting his replies down the phone.

Trefor held the phone away from his ear and said, "Well, Gwilym, if my door frame is down there with you, I'll come down and get it right away."

"You can't have it back now," Gwilym the Siop interrupted. "Cos I've already cut it up for firewood!"

"WHAT! You've done what?" Trefor raised his voice in pretended anger. "Listen to me, Gwilym. You can't do that..."

"I've already done it,' Gwilym the Siop replied triumphantly, starting to feel good for the first time that morning.

"I don't care what you say you've already done. You have no right to cut up or damage other people's property without them knowing anything about it. Now get off the phone this instant. I am going to call the police and have you taken in charge. I'll give you, cutting up my property indeed. Damn you, Gwilym!"

"Wait a minute, Trefor!" Gwilym the Siop's stomach turned over in sudden panic at the thought of what he might do. "You are responsible for this..."

"Oh no, I'm not!" Trefor cut him off. "Somebody must have taken that frame from here and I'm saying it was YOU, and you just made up this cock-and-bull story to cover yourself. Now, get off the phone so I can call the police."

"I didn't do it," Gwilym the Siop bleated, "It wasn't me, Trefor, honest to God. I never took it."

Trefor sat back in his chair, a meaty hand across the mouthpiece of the phone, laughing out loud. Fighting for control, he said in a calm voice, "Well, all I can say to you is this, Gwilym. You are in possession of stolen property. You told me yourself it is now damaged beyond repair, and you have also admitted to me that you have cut up my property for firewood. That is disgraceful, Gwilym." Trefor didn't think for one minute that his prank would turn out quite like this, but he was enjoying himself as he heaped as much misfortune on Gwilym the Siop's head as he could muster. "You do realise that you could be fined heavily for your actions today," he paused, listening intently. There was no sound from the other end. "Hello? Hello? Are you still there, Gwilym?

"Yes, Trefor. I am still here." His reply was subdued.

"Well, I don't really know what is best to do," Trefor went on slowly, rubbing a bit more salt into the wound. "I should go to the police, by right, and tell them that the local postmaster is in possession of stolen property. That doesn't sound good at all, does it?"

"No, Trefor, but..."

"Think of the shame, Gwilym," he went on. "I can see the headlines in the paper now." He affected a stentorian pulpit voice: "POSTMASTER SELLS STOLEN PROPERTY FOR FIREWOOD! And what about the Postmaster General? What do you think he would have to say about it, Gwilym?"

Gwilym the Siop's toes curled at the very thought. Dai Banwen was right. 'He said there would be trouble,' he thought miserably. Sighing audibly, Gwilym the Siop said quietly. "Well, what do YOU want to do about it, Trefor?"

"Ah, well now." He knew in that instant that he had Gwilym the Siop in the palm of his hand. "Let me think about this for a minute." His agile brain had already decided what to do but he wanted Gwilym the Siop to feel a bit more pressure first. "You said you have already cut it up?"

"Yes, I have," Gwilym the Siop replied in a miserable voice.

"And no doubt you have got it all ready to sell."

"Yes."

"Well, I'll tell you what, Gwilym. If you can bring me say £5 for the value of the wood and I will promise not to go to the police. How does that sound to you?" A distinct sound of relief came through the phone.

"Okay, Trefor, but £5 is a bit much, isn't it?" A little bit of fire crept back into his voice.

"Well, how much do you think is fair then, Gwilym?" Trefor asked, blandly.

Gwilym the Siop was desperately trying to calculate how much he could sell each bundle for and how much his own labour was worth. Divide the bundles by...

"Hello! Hello, Gwilym?"

"Yes Trefor. I'm still here. How about £3?" he said timidly.

"Come off it, Gwilym!" Trefor said sternly, "that's a lot of wood, and good stuff too, remember!"

Gwilym the Siop made a valiant effort to bargain further. "Right then, no more than £4, Trefor. That's my limit!"

Trefor paused for a full minute before replying. He could sense from the silence at the other end of the line that Gwilym the Siop was bitterly regretting making this phone call to complain.

"Right you are, then, Gwilym. Four pounds it is, That's settled then."

"I'll be there right away with the cash!" The phone clicked into silence.

Trefor sat back in his chair laughing and holding his sides until he was weak. "Oh *Duw*!" he gasped. "Oh *Duw*!"

Not more than a few minutes had passed when there was a knock on the front door. Rising from his seat he unbolted the various locks and opened it to find Gwilym the Siop standing there, with four £1 notes in his hand.

"Here you are, Trefor: £4 as agreed, right?"

"Thank you, Gwilym." Trefor took the proffered notes graciously. Then, folding them carefully, he placed them in his pocket. 'Do you want a Bill of Sale, Gwilym?" he asked softly.

"No, that's okay." Gwilym the Siop thrust out his hand, "Let's shake on it instead, is it?" Trefor shook his limp hand, and Gwilym the Siop turned away, shoulders slumped, and climbed wearily into his van. He sat there for a moment. All that work for nothing and I had to pay him too, what a lousy start to my day. He started the engine and drove slowly away, all the time wishing he had listened to Dai Banwen's advice that morning.

Trefor watched him drive away. Leaning against the door jamb, he started laughing all over again as he said aloud, "Oh, boys bach. Wait until those two come in tonight, we'll have some laughs over this!"

The afternoon passed far too slowly and quietly for Trefor the landlord, as he waited impatiently for the evening crowd to arrive so that he could relate the morning's events with Gwilym the Siop.

That evening, as the regular crowd began to gather in the long bar, Old John Shinkins, in his usual spot on the settle alongside the stove, kept a close eye on the landlord. Instinctively he could tell from the way Trefor was acting that something had happened to keep him in such good spirits this early in the evening. He seemed to have a permanent grin on his face, and each time the door to the bar opened, he would turn quickly to see who had entered. 'Yes,' Old John thought, 'he's been up to something, for sure.'

About nine o'clock, in strolled Dai Banwen and he was all smiles as he bellied up to the bar.

"Pint bottle, please, Trefor." He began grinning like a Cheshire cat as the bottle was uncapped and the sparkling liquid was poured into his glass. "That was a good one this morning, Tref." He continued grinning at the landlord.

"Oooh? What was that then, Dai?" Trefor was all innocence when he posed the question.

"C'mon, Trefor. You bluddy well know what I'm talking about!"

"No, I don't, honest!" he protested.

"Well, I'm saying that you had Gwilym the Siop with a good one this morning. I was there, mun!" He began pointing an accusing finger at the landlord and himself, jabbing it back and forth to emphasise each point.

"Dai," Trefor said patiently. "I haven't been from yere all day and that's the gospel truth."

"Aye, aye! I know. I'm only saying, that's all. It was I who told 'im too, cos he didn't notice a thing. His eyesight must be getting really bad, that's all I can say," said Dai, nodding confirmation.

"And what's that, then?" Trefor still didn't let on what he knew. The time for all that would come later.

"Der! You're a 'ell of a boy, Tref." Dai walked slowly away from the bar sipping his beer. At that moment he felt more than a little deflated. He had come to the Plough with the sole intention of relating the events of the morning outside Siop Gwilym Williams, but his hints at finding out more about it had fallen on stony ground for the moment.

He sat down beside Old John. "So, what was all that about then, Dai?" he asked from behind his hand.

"Oh. You remember when they put a new door on the front? Well, that old door frame with the Plough sign on it ended up being jammed into the doorway of Gwilym the Siop's place this morning!" he laughed, "I just tried to find out from Trefor how that happened but he wouldn't let on. I'm pretty sure he knows all about it, though."

'Now then! I know very well who the culprits are in this,' Old John thought. Aloud he said, "And what did Gwilym the Siop have to say about it, then?"

"Ooh, the silly so-and-so was going to get the police and was blaming Trefor for it, but I told 'im he'd never prove anything against 'im. He's too clever by far for any of that. So in the end I don't think he called the police. Now, that Trefor is denying having anything at all to do with it, but we know 'im and his practical jokes. Nobody is safe if he wants to get back at you, mind."

Before Old John could think of a reply, the bar door opened slowly and Alan and Johnny stepped into the room and stood together near the door, each with a broad grin of expectation on their faces.

"Here you are, boys. A pint each, on the house." Trefor's round features were wreathed in smiles as he put the foaming pints on the bar in front of them.

"Did you see that, Dai?" Old John nudged him with his elbow. "They didn't even have to ask for a drink! It was there for them. Well, I'm damned!"

"Aye, I did!" Dai studied the pair intently. "Trying to act all innocent, is it, boys?" he called out, grinning with them.

"Whatever do you mean, Dai?" Johnny asked politely.

"You two are as bad as 'im," Old John said knowingly, nodding his head sideways towards the smiling landlord. "I saw the three of you together last night, remember. I knew then you were cooking something up."

"Not *as bad as*, Mr Shinkins. *As good as*," Johnny replied politely to him also, ignoring the blatant accusation.

"Well, you know very well what I mean! You two were up to your tricks again last night!"

"Not us, John," Alan smiled at him. "We were good boys last night, like we always are."

"I'll bluddy believe that when I see it!" Dai chipped in loudly.

"Shhh! Not so loud. Don't attract attention, Dai, or you'll spoil everything. Hang on a minute and I'll tell you all about it." Trefor motioned sideways with his head. "Come over here."

Dai helped Old John to his feet. "This ought to be good, John," Dai said, as they made their way from the settle to the bar.

Trefor glanced around the room and saw that things appeared, for the moment, pretty quiet. The inevitable card game, complete with referees and onlookers was, as usual, taking place on the large farmhouse table in front of the shuttered front window, while Alan and Johnny, nursing their free beer, stood in silence, also watching the progress of the game.

"Well, now then, boys. Last night someone took that old door frame from my car park."

"And I know who!" Old John interrupted, casting a quick glance over his shoulder at the two councillors across the room.

"No, you don't, John, so shut up for just one minute. Anyhow, they, whoever they are, managed to somehow shove it right into the doorway of Siop Gwilym, or so I hear, anyway. Dai by yere had to tell Gwilym about it. Come on, Dai, tell us what he said after you told him."

Dai Banwen, now the centre of attention, cleared his throat. "Well, it was so funny. First of all, he was going to call the police and blame you for doing it," he pointed an accusing finger at Trefor. "I told 'im straight away you can't prove that, Gwilym. So then he pushed it out of the doorway and it smashed into three pieces, so he said he was going to cut it up for firewood and sell it in the shop. I don't know if he did, mind. I also told 'im that it belonged to you, Trefor, and he could get into trouble. And that's all I know, but I couldn't stop laughing and the more I laughed, the angrier he got. Yes, it was a good start to the day, I must say."

Trevor, his face beaming, said, "Let me tell you what happened up here. You won't believe it, boys, but just before opening time this morning I got a phone call from Gwilym the Siop to complain and blame me for my old door frame being in the doorway of his place. I told him since it was mine, I would come down for it right away and bring it back where it belonged. Then he said to me, 'You can't have it back because I have already cut it up for firewood and I'm going to sell all of it in my shop'.

"I shouted a bit at him and told him he was in possession of stolen property and p'raps it was me who should be calling the police and get him taken in for theft."

Despite their quiet tones, it soon became evident to the councillors that something was going on at the other end of the bar. Johnny nudged Alan and they turned away from the card game to move closer to hear the story being related by the landlord. Soon, almost everyone in the room had gathered around the bar to listen as Trefor went on. "I told him that for a postmaster to be charged with theft wouldn't look good at all. I said to him, 'Think of the shame, Gwilym.' To tell you the truth, boys, I had a 'ell of a job just talking to him, I was laughing so much inside. In the end I said, if you are going to sell all that wood then I want £5 from you and I promise I won't go to the police.' We argued a bit over the amount but I finally got £4 out of him…"

Trefor's audience roared with laughter at that, because Gwilym the Siop had always been pretty tight-fisted when it came to money. Some started to drift away, until Trefor raised his voice. "Hey, wait a minute! I haven't finished yet! A couple of minutes after he had put the phone down there was a knock on my front door and there he was, reluctantly holding out the four £1 notes. I took them off him, but I had a job to keep a straight face, I can tell you. In the end we just shook hands and he left. I'll tell you boys, whoever did that with that old frame, did a good job." He broke into peals of laughter and tears of mirth ran down his cheeks. "And best of all, I wanted to get rid of that old frame anyway and now I've got paid for it too." He held his aching sides as he leaned against the bar for support.

Alan, a broad smile creasing his face, said: "You shouldn't have taken his £4, Tref."

"And why not?" the landlord asked, wiping tears from his eyes.

"You should have asked him to bring all that wood back here, already cut up into firewood for your own use. Then he would have worked up a sweat for nothing at all." Alan wilted against the bar and laughed until his eyes brimmed.

The smile left Trefor's face for just a second or two. "Nah! That timber wasn't worth four quid anyway! Oooh, what a place this is! Drink up, boys."

Alan and Johnny swiftly placed their empty glasses in front of Trefor, which he refilled in double-quick time, saying. "There's no charge for these, boys, Gwilym the Siop is paying this round.

C'mon, John, and you, Dai. This beer will taste the best of all because Gwilym the Siop doesn't buy too many pints. Oh boys bach! I am weak from laughing."

"That's the penalty for your tricks," said Alan, smacking his lips.

"Damn, you're right enough, Tref. This is a good pint!" He raised his glass. "My very best to you, Gwilym!"

Over time, bits and pieces of the practical joke got back to Gwilym the Siop, who was absolutely furious at being bested by Trefor Plough once again. "I'll get him for this," he vowed. "Somehow, I've got to get him back."

CHAPTER 18

Gwilym the Siop's revenge

IN THE WEEKS that followed his confrontation with Trefor Plough and total humiliation at Trefor's hands as the story of the door frame became public knowledge, Gwilym the Siop's temper would come quickly to the boil each time a customer came into his shop. Nothing was ever said, but he sensed each and every one was laughing at him every time they spoke or asked for some item in his capacity as postmaster. And so, every spare moment was consumed by thoughts of revenge on Trefor Plough.

Gwilym Williams didn't display any of the refinements usually expected of a man in his position. Thin and stooped in stature, his usual daytime apparel included a soiled 'white' apron pulled tightly across his skinny hips, and his heavy-framed spectacles were topped by an unruly crop of lank black hair which didn't appear to have had the benefit of treatment by a comb for some time.

Late one night, as he was returning from visiting a relative in the valley below, he decided to take the road home across the back of the mountain, which eventually connected with the road through Cwm Du, and would pass directly in front of the

Plough Inn. He glanced at the time on the dashboard clock as he drove up hill: twelve fifteen, and the lights are still on and cars parked all over the place. He slowed right down as he drove past and attempted to look inside, but the wooden shutters inside the window were tightly closed.

On the spur of the moment he turned his van into the parking area adjoining the pub. He sat for a few minutes while deciding what to do. Shall I call the police and come back to watch? He discarded that thought: it might be a private party and Trefor would be within the law and Gwilym would look foolish again. He pondered what to do as the minutes passed, drumming his fingers on the steering wheel, then said aloud, "Hey, c'mon, Gwilym. This is your chance to get even. This is exactly what you have been waiting for!" He climbed out of the van and went into the Plough. Entering the bar he looked around the noisy smoke-filled room. It was crowded, as usual, with many of the nearby village patrons, many of whom he recognised by sight. He felt his gorge rising in excitement. 'I've got him now,' he thought triumphantly. His beady little eyes glinted behind his glasses as he turned towards the bar and asked for half a pint of draft ale.

Trefor looked up in surprise and greeted him like a long-lost friend, which couldn't have been further from the truth. "Well, good evening, Gwilym. How nice to see you here in such a social capacity."

"Hello, Trefor." Gwilym's reply was surly as he nodded in a perfunctory manner. Placing the correct amount of money on the bar, he turned away without another word and sipped his beer as he looked around the crowded room, making a mental note of the time showing on the large clock on the wall behind the bar, and the number of customers still drinking beer.

Twm, sitting at the card table, glanced up. "Well, look who's here, boys! Are you lost, Gwilym?"

"No, I am not lost, Twm!" Gwilym was immediately on the

defensive. "It's a free country isn't it?" His strident nasal voice had an edge to it in his sharp reply.

Twm grinned back at him. "What about free speech then, Gwilym?"

Gwilym turned away and stood with his back to Twm as he continued to plot how to have his revenge on Trefor and some of these people. He could see a few sitting there drinking who had openly made fun of him within earshot.

Twm played a few more cards when a sudden thought crossed his mind. "Hey, Roy!" he whispered across the table to his playing partner.

"What do you think that sly sod is doing in here at this time of night? I wouldn't trust 'im any further than I could throw that!" He nodded his head sideways at the piano in the corner of the room.

Roy turned in his seat to look at Gwilym Williams, who had moved further down the bar, away from the card table, to stand alone in the centre of the room. "I notice he is not talking to anyone and I'm willing to bet he's not here for anyone's benefit, that's for sure." He turned back to the game. "Is it my deal?"

Gwilym Williams, with a final look around the bar, made a mental note that nobody, despite the lateness of the hour, appeared to be in any rush to leave. He finished his drink and placed the empty glass on the nearest table. Nodding briefly to Willi Bray, he pulled the bar door towards him and left the room. Outside, he hurried to his van and starting it up, drove back to his house as quickly as he could. In the downstairs hallway at home he picked up the phone and dialled the number for the main police station.

"Er. Good evening – or is it morning? Could I speak to the Inspector in charge, please? Oh, okay. I'll speak to the duty sergeant, then." He waited impatiently, moving his weight from one foot to the other. He didn't want everyone to leave the Plough before the police arrived and caught them in the act. "Ah, yes. I want to report some drinking after hours that is taking place at the Plough Inn in Cwm Du. Yes, that's near Rhyd-y-groes. Who am I? My name is Gwilym Williams and I'm the postmaster at Rhyd-y-groes.

"Oh yes. I am very sure. I drove past there just a few minutes ago and I happened to see a crowd in there through the front window," he lied. "Yes, that's right, at a quarter past twelve. Yes. Thank you. You're welcome, and thank you." He hung up the phone and rubbed his hands together gleefully with a feeling of complete satisfaction. Aloud he muttered, "I'll bet this is going to cost you a lot more than the four quid you got out of me, Trefor Plough."

Gwilym laughed as he went up the stairs to his bedroom to sit in the window facing the road and watch for any sign of the police passing through on their way to the Plough. He looked at his watch. It was more than twenty minutes since he had made his call. Perhaps they had not taken his complaint seriously enough; if that was the case, then Trefor would have got away with something again. He was just about to get up and go to bed, disappointed, when a police van drove past in the direction of the Plough. He clapped his hands in delight and did a little dance of triumph, secure in the knowledge that he'd got one over on Trefor Plough. "Just wait until I tell Mam about this in the morning."

The police van stopped directly in front of the open front door of the Plough on the opposite side of the road. The duty inspector and two constables climbed out and made note of the number of cars parked in front of them and also in the parking area at the side of the pub.

Willi Bray, on his way back to the bar from the outside toilet, saw the police van come to a stop and immediately ran into the bar shouting that the police were outside. As one, everybody with a glass in front of him swallowed their beer as quickly as possible. Some, unable to drink as quickly as others, hid their glasses under the nearest convenient seat or bench. Trefor, moving quickly, ducked under the hatch to try and delay things as long as possible, but he was too late: the Inspector was already opening the door into the bar. By the time he had entered the room, most of the men in there had empty glasses in front of them and could not now be charged with drinking after hours. The four playing cards at the table appeared unconcerned with the sudden appearance of the police because they had stopped drinking some time before; they carried on with their game.

"Everyone is to remain where they are!" he commanded in a loud voice. "And I will need everyone's name and address!" He looked down at the card players – for some unknown reason, their playing on seemed to irritate him. He approached the table and stood over them frowning, as he said in a heavy tone, "Gentlemen, do you mind?" Everyone in the room sat silent as the two constables wrote down their particulars. Finally the name-taking was completed.

The Inspector stood by the door and looked across the room at Trefor, calling out in a loud voice so that everyone in the bar was aware.

"Mr Trefor Williams! As landlord of this establishment you are being charged with serving alcoholic drinks after hours and in contravention of the licensing laws. Those persons who also had alcoholic drinks in their possession at the time we, the police, came in here, will be charged for drinking outside the designated hours of this establishment. I would therefore suggest, Mr Williams, that you clear this establishment as quickly and quietly as possible. Goodnight – or should I say, good morning."

As soon as the police left, everybody started talking at once.

Willi Bray said it was a good thing Fred wasn't there at the time otherwise they might have all got arrested. Everyone laughed, which broke the tension of the moment.

Meanwhile, Trefor followed the policemen outside. "Excuse me, Inspector," he asked quietly. "Was this raid a spot check?"

The Inspector looked steadily at him for a moment. "As a matter of fact it was not," he replied candidly. "We received a phone call a short while ago complaining about after-hours drinking here, but that is neither here nor there now, is it?"

"Not really," Trefor replied dryly. "I was quite late opening, mind. I couldn't get back here in time to open at six o'clock due to a previous commitment at our family farm over by Llwydcoed, so I added the time on at this end. You know how it is."

"If I may say so, Mr Williams, that is not a good defence to present in court." He touched his cap to him as he climbed into the van and drove away.

Trefor stood in the darkness watching the lights of the van disappear over the hill. "Well, I'm damned. A phone call, eh? I wonder," he murmured into the night. He went back through the door and into the bar.

"Okay, boys, everybody out!" He looked around the room at the mess he would have to clean up before he went to bed, a thoughtful expression on his round features.

Twm and Roy stood up from the card table. "Hey, Trefor," Roy said speculatively. "That was a 'ell of a coincidence if you ask me. That bluddy Gwilym Williams the Siop was in here just a short while ago and then the police arrive? Makes you wonder, don't it?"

"Now, it's funny you should say that, Roy. I was just thinking the same thing myself," Trefor replied, his eyebrows raised. "The Inspector told me they came here following a phone call they received a short while ago. I know I can't prove anything, but I wouldn't lose any money if I bet it was him, the vindictive sod."

"Then it's up to us to get him back for this," Twm said angrily.

"No, no! Don't you do anything! There's not a shred of proof, so we can't be certain it was him. Don't worry, I'll look after it, okay? Promise me now, boys, you won't do anything."

Twm and Roy looked at each other then nodded their agreement. Trefor turned to the stragglers still there. "Listen, boys! How many of you had a drink in front of them when the cops came in?" Some hands went up. "Just the three of you, is it? Well, I'll cover your fines when we go to court, as I'm sure we will, all right? I don't think it will be much for a first offence, so don't you worry yourselves about it, okay?"

Later, Trefor sat alone in his kitchen, thinking about the night's events and what must be Gwilym Williams's part in it.

Trefor was busy out in the yard the following day, stacking empty crates of bottles and barrels in preparation for collection and making room for new deliveries, when the local newsagent Jim Dimot, who delivered his paper on a daily basis, stopped his van in front of Trefor, holding out his *Western Mail*.

"How's things going, Tref?" he called out cheerily. 'How's business?"

"Oh, I can't complain, I suppose, except for last night!"

"Ooh. What happened?" Jim laughed. "Did you forget to charge someone, or what?"

"No, mun! The police were here pretty late. I was a bit late getting here so I added some of the time on the other end. You know how it is."

"Aye, I know," Jim chuckled. "Well, that was a bit of bad luck, then."

"Luck had nothing to do with it," Trefor replied angrily. "I think it was that bluddy Gwilym Williams the Siop. He phoned the police as sure as I am standing here. The sly little sod was in here having a drink after hours too, can you believe that?"

"I'd believe anything about him," Jim replied, bitterness in his voice. "Do you know what the so-and-so tried to do to my business? As you must know, he's got a van similar to mine – same colour anyway." Jim's newsagent's business in the village was not enough to support his growing family, so to supplement his meagre income he drove from factory to factory on the nearby large industrial estate selling, from the back of his van, anything he could make a few extra shillings on: cigarettes, cigars, chocolates, pies, pasties, newspapers, magazines; in fact anything that the factory workers asked him to supply on his rounds.

"That sly little sod went to the factories down there about 20 minutes before I got there, selling the same bluddy stuff as me. I couldn't make out for a few days why I wasn't getting any trade at all, until someone at one of the factories told me about this other chap. He said they thought I was ill and I had sent someone else in my place. When they described what this other chap looked like, I knew straight away who it was. Can you imagine what a scheming sod he is?"

Trefor stood shaking his head in amazement at Gwilym Williams's trickery. "So what did you do?"

"Well, when I found out what he had been up to, I went straight to his shop and told him, in front of his customers, 'If you try and pull that stunt again, I'll come back in here and knock your bluddy block off!' Anyway, he hasn't been down there since. That's my living he was trying to take away, the greedy sod! He's already got the siop, the post office and now the bluddy off-licence, too. What more does he want?" Trefor's eyes narrowed at the mention of the off-licence.

"I'll still have to watch him, though," Jim went on. "That industrial site is where I make most of my money. There's about 4,000 people working in just one place down there, and then there's all the other small places. I also found out that he had been into the offices of the largest factory trying to get some of my other business. Using my warehouse card I can offer some pretty good prices on a lot of stuff. Especially at Christmas. Somebody told me he had been seen chatting to Bert Tomlinson: he's the assistant manager down there and he's in charge of all their social events, office parties and so on. Damned if I know how Gwilym got hold of his name but apparently he asked if he could supply all the booze for any upcoming parties. He's a cheeky sod, Tref.

"Anyway, I've got to go, I'm late already. Gwilym the Siop will be in there." He climbed back into his van, at the same time advising, "You watch him, Trefor," before driving off in a cloud of dust.

"Yes, I will. Thanks," Trefor replied absently to the departing Jim Dimot. His mind at that moment was busy with certain thoughts involving Gwilym the Siop.

CHAPTER 19

Fred and the gravedigging contract

ALAN AND JOHNNY were in Alan's car on the way to the petrol station when they spotted Bill Thomas, the Clerk of the Parish Council, plodding slowly up the steep hill in the same direction. Coming to a stop just in front of him, Alan called out politely: "Good evening, Mr Thomas. Are you out on your evening constitutional?" Then he noticed that the Clerk was hugging his overstuffed briefcase to his chest with both arms.

He smiled at Alan's question. "No such luck, I'm afraid. I am on my way to an appointment with Fred Howells in the Plough and I am optimistic that this evening I can get him to sign a new gravedigging contract for the next twelve months. If you remember, boys, we discussed this at last month's ordinary meeting of the parish council. I must apologise for the length of time it has taken to convene this meeting, but you know Fred – it's very difficult to pin him down to a date and time to do anything at all, and especially to get him to sign anything, but we must still live in hope."

"You have our commiserations, Bill," Johnny, leaning

forward, called out. "Jump in. We'll give you a lift the rest of the way."

Gratefully, Bill Thomas climbed into the back of the car with a sigh of relief. "Thank you, boys – my old feet are killing me." He thanked them again profusely as he got out of the car at the door of the Plough, waving further thanks as they drove away.

Bill Thomas had done his share of walking and marching during his experiences in the wastes of the Libyan deserts during the last war, which, from time to time, had left him with bouts of unexplained illness. On his return to civilian life he had persevered in his profession as an accountant and eventually became head of department with the District Authority, his current full-time employer.

Fred and his son Colin were the gravediggers for the parish council. Officially Fred was under written contract to do the job and had Colin as his unpaid assistant. The re-signing of the contract, which was shortly due to expire, became something of an event for Fred. He had taken up the position after much haggling, following the demise of Jim Cronin, the previous signee. The signing procedure usually went on for some weeks, somewhat like a protracted trade union negotiation. On this occasion, if Fred stayed true to form, there was unlikely to be any change for the better.

On the one hand, the Clerk of the Parish Council, being a gentle and quiet-spoken man, was trying to out-manoeuvre Fred, who was full of bluster, bombast and threats, into signing the contract for another year. It was at times like this that Fred was (in Fred's mind anyway) 'cock of the walk', and he would say: "Remember, boys! Everyone one of you is depending on ME! And, if the council don't watch out, I won't sign and then you've had it cos nobody else would want this lousy job!"

All these long-winded negotiations revolved around the

signing-on fee. The lump sum payment for his signature was a £40 retainer. For Fred, whose weekly pay packet for his job as a rat-catcher (sorry, rodent operative) in the local coal mines never exceeded £8, this was a princely sum. Nevertheless, he would hold out for as long as possible in the forlorn hope that the Parish Council would see their way clear to add a little bit more to his already lucrative signing-on retainer fee.

However, unbeknown to Fred, the Clerk, who was getting used to his shenanigans as the time of signing came around, would try and find out his financial situation before coming to any agreement for a final negotiation date. It so happened on this occasion that Fred had built up quite a substantial amount of debt with the landlord; upon inquiry, Trefor had suggested that now might be a good time for Bill to approach Fred. He had smiled as he said, "If you can get him to sign, Bill, and he gets his retainer cheque, there's a good chance I will get my money from him too."

That evening, the Clerk, as arranged, met with Fred and told him that it was time to discuss his new contract. Fred started to bluster until the Clerk, as a gesture of goodwill, offered to buy him a pint of best bitter while they negotiated.

Fred, fresh pint in hand, led the way into a side room where it was quieter and closed the door. He sat down, slowly sipping the sparkling free ale, as he waited for the Clerk's opening parley.

"Well, Fred bach. It's that time of the year again. I have been instructed by the parish council to ask you if you will be good enough to continue as our official gravedigger. The duration of the contract, as you know from previous occasions, is for a period of 12 months from the date of your signature on the contract. For this, I am also instructed by the Parish Council to issue a cheque to you in the sum of £40 as a retainer for the service you provide.

"If this is to your satisfaction, then I have also been instructed to request your signature on these other documents, which are binding by law, as you are also aware. Do you understand everything I have said?" Not getting any argument from Fred, he looked up from his paperwork to see him still sipping his free beer. For some reason, known only to himself, he had sat in silence throughout the Clerk's official procedure and explanation.

"Yes, yes! I understand," he said quietly.

The Clerk, surprised at Fred's tone, looked up again from the documents scattered across the table. "Er, what was that, Mr Howells?"

"I said, yes! I understand," Fred repeated, his tone becoming surly. "So where do I sign? And can I have the cheque tonight? I mean, right away!"

"Of course, of course, right away, Mr Howells, and thank you." Bill was both relieved and delighted that Fred had capitulated so easily this time around. He turned the documents to face Fred, pointing out the various areas that needed his signature, and then turned his attention to issuing the cheque that Fred appeared so anxious to receive. He completed the paperwork and Fred impatiently signed witness as requested.

"Seems like a lot more paperwork this time," he commented gruffly. Unspeaking, the Clerk handed Fred the cheque. They shook hands on the completion and Fred left the room without a backward glance. The Clerk slowly repacked the documents into his briefcase, thankful that this ordeal was finally over for another year.

In the long room, Fred swaggered up to the bar, waving the cheque to and fro in the air to attract the landlord's attention. Trefor glanced up from pulling a pint as Fred called out, "I'd like to exchange this bit of paper for cash, please." He paused momentarily, then said with some reluctance, "I suppose I'd better settle up with you, too." A slight grin appeared on his thin lips and disappeared in an instant.

"Now, that *is* a good idea, Fred." Trefor smiled slowly as he approached him. "Pay up now and maybe – I'm saying, *maybe* – you can do it again. Fair enough?"

For a moment Fred looked at him in utter shock, until he realised he was just pulling his leg. Silently, he signed the back of the cheque and looked down in dismay at what remained of it when Trefor placed some notes and small change on the bar. Stuffing it all in his pocket, Fred turned from the bar with an audible sigh. Not much to play with, and our Colin will have to have a share of this too. He looked across the room to where the Clerk and Trefor stood talking with their heads close together. Instinctively he knew at once they were talking about him and the cheque he had just received for signing so quickly this time. 'Aye,' he thought, 'if I didn't owe Trefor all that money…' His thoughts stopped abruptly. 'Hey, wait a bluddy minute. If I could get out of that contract... Nah!' He discarded the idea before it formed. He needed that bit of extra cash when a job came up for him and Colin to do. His thoughts went off on a different tack. What if Colin...? "Now there's an idea worth following up with our Colin," he muttered under his breath. He glanced from under the brim of his cap in Trefor's direction. He was now laughing at some joke with the Clerk. Think you've outsmarted me, boys, is it? You just wait a bit.

Fred's spirits rose, buoyed by the germination of another scheme to get some extra money out of the Parish Council. He rose from his seat and sauntered over to the bar.

"A pint of best bitter, please, Mr Williams," he grinned. Their conversation ceased as he spoke. 'Aye,' he thought, 'I was bluddy right, me you were talking about. Okay, boys, I know what to do now.' He sat back down on the settle near the stove and, ignoring the constant noise in the bar, he concentrated on his new strategy.

He had come to the conclusion that if he resigned his position as the official gravedigger, they would need to sign someone else. So why not our Colin? He could sign up easy and we would have another £40 to split between us – that's if I can persuade him to take it on. Right, that's it.

He rubbed his hands together as, smiling inwardly, he looked around the crowded room. His eyes came to rest on Old John Shinkins, who was studying him closely from the other end of the settle.

"What's wrong with you, John? You look as though you have just discovered something important!"

"No, Fred, I don't think I have done that, but there is something going on with you. I know you of old, mind, and I know when you are scheming something."

Fred smiled, staring up at the ceiling. "Not me, John. Not me!"

Before Old John could think of a suitable reply, the door of the bar opened and Alan and Johnny stood in the opening, surveying the crowd in the room.

"Hello, boys! Two pints is it?" Trefor's round features broke into a broad smile.

"More than that, Tref," Johnny nodded a greeting. "Good evening again, Mr Thomas. A pint of whatever the Clerk is drinking, if you please, and a pint for Old John over there."

Fred stared at both of them, his face expressionless.

Johnny stared back at him, then suddenly grinned and said. "You'd better pull a pint for this old rascal too, Trefor," pointing at Fred, "before he goes around telling everyone that the Councillor is mean."

Fred's sombre features lit up in a big smile. "Thank you,

Johnny. All donations are gratefully accepted – as long as it's beer and money," he added, laughing.

Alan was talking to the Clerk and Trefor when Fred joined them at the end of the bar. He was just in time to hear the landlord say, "Yes, I've got to be in court early in the morning. That bluddy Gwilym Williams the Siop did this. It's about me serving a few drinks after hours. Remember that?"

"Have you got a solicitor, Tref? You might need one if Gwilym Williams is going to be a witness for the police."

Alan thought about his own question for a second or two, then he said. "What's wrong with me? He can't be a witness for the cops because he was in here himself drinking after hours. You could get no end of people to swear he was in here having a drink with everybody else. C'mon, Tref."

"I know. I served him myself," he shrugged. "Well, I'm not going to lose any sleep over it. What's done is done, and I can't prove a thing against him. No doubt it's going to cost me a fair bit of money but I will have him for that. Just you wait and see."

"The courts haven't given you much time, have they? It only seems like a few days ago the police were in here, and only yesterday you get the notice to appear." Johnny looked from one to the other.

"Listen, boys," Trefor chipped in. "It doesn't really matter how much notice they gave, does it? I was open late and serving drinks. I was caught in the act, as they say. No. I am going there to plead guilty and that's that." He smiled. "Don't any of you boys worry about a thing. It will be okay."

CHAPTER 20

Trefor's day in court

TREFOR WAS UP and about much earlier than usual the following morning. Living alone had its disadvantages when everything had to be made ready for the afternoon opening of the Plough, but today, because of Gwilym Williams's sneakiness and vindictive nature, everything had to be done in double-quick time. It hadn't improved the situation that the notice and request for his presence in court that morning had arrived at his door only the day before. He had wondered fleetingly if Gwilym Williams, as postmaster, had had anything to do with the delay in its arrival, but that would be a criminal offence and he didn't think even Gwilym would stoop that low. He rushed through his long list of jobs, changing barrels, washing and stacking glasses under the bar, replacing fresh bottles in the racks on the shelves; all the other little time-consuming jobs which seemed to take forever to complete.

He arrived at the courthouse in Aberdare just five minutes before the appointed time of eleven o'clock. He scanned the courtroom and made his way quickly to where the other three men charged were sitting together. "Hello, boys," he whispered. "Have they said anything yet?

"No! Not yet, but I think we are on next," Tyrone replied softly as the other two nodded agreement.

"Now listen, boys. Is this your first offence?" Trefor looked at each of them in turn for confirmation.

"Yes, it is," they replied in unison.

"Wait a minute!" Tyrone held up his hand. "I got fined once for not having a dog licence."

"I don't think that will matter in this case, Tyrone. Now then," Trefor said quietly. "It will probably cost each of you about five quid for this, but don't worry about that. I will pay the Clerk of the Court on your behalf after it's all over. Okay?"

"Well, that's great, Trefor," Tyrone said gratefully. 'Thanks a lot, we appreciate that, don't we, boys?" The others nodded agreement. "We've had to lose a shift to come here today because our foreman wouldn't let us switch shifts, the miserable sod."

"I can't pay you for that, mind,' Trefor grinned. "Your foreman must be related to Gwilym the Siop. He's the cause of all this!"

"Can you prove that, Tref?" Tyrone was on it like one of Fred's terriers. "Cos if you can..." He left the rest of his thoughts unspoken.

"No, I can't. Not yet, anyway."

"What I'm saying, Tref, is this. We are just grateful for what you are doing for us, that's all. Innit, boys?" Tyrone whispered. The other two nodded.

Trefor stood up and removed his raincoat, which he folded and placed on the seat beside him.

"Damn," said Billy, looking him up and down. "You look like that minister from Nebo chapel in that suit!"

Trefor, when he worked around the farm and in the Plough, usually wore the same old dark green woollen jumper that had seem more than its share of summers and had been patched many times over. The hand-knitted patches were of various shades and colours which didn't always match the original hue.

As Fred once said, 'He looks like Joseph in his coat of many colours'. Trefor looked down at himself. "Makes quite a change from my old woolly jumper, don't it?" He looked resplendent in his Sunday best dark pinstripe suit, white shirt and dark military-style tie. Even though he had not served in the last war, his shoes, which were polished like glass, would have made any serving man proud.

"Got to make a bit of an impression, see." He was looking carefully around the courtroom and spotted Gwilym Williams, right at the back of the room, just inside the main door. "That bluddy Gwilym Williams is here!" he whispered fiercely to the others. They turned, as one, to look for him and as Trefor pointed him out, Gwilym pretended he hadn't seen them and sidled behind a group of court officials.

At that moment, the Clerk of the Court stood up and, clearing his throat, called out, "Mr Trefor Williams. Publican. Plough Inn. Cwm Du. Rhyd-y-groes. Please stand up!" He looked around the room.

Trefor stood up, wiping his moist hands on the leg of his trousers. "I am here, sir," he replied loudly.

"Come forward, please," the Clerk instructed. 'Do you have anyone to represent you, Mr Williams?"

"No, I do not, but…"

"Then please get into the dock, Mr Williams. Take the Bible in your right hand and repeat after me, 'I swear by Almighty God to tell the truth, the whole truth and nothing but the truth.'"

Trefor dutifully repeated the oath, then stood facing the Bench where the three magistrates were seated. The Chairman looked Trefor up and down over his half-spectacles. "Mr Williams!" He shuffled through the papers in front of him. "You have been charged with serving alcoholic drinks after the designated closing time. Is that correct?"

"Yes, sir," Trefor replied meekly.

"Do you have anything to say in your defence before I call for police evidence?"

"Yes, sir," Trefor brightened up in the dock. 'Well, sir. I live alone in the Plough Inn but I also work on my family farm over in Llwydcoed on any bit of spare time I can fit in. I was over there on that day and unfortunately I couldn't get away from there, so I was a bit late in getting back to the Plough to open on time. So, I thought I would add the missing time to the other end of the designated licence hours, sir. And that is exactly what happened, your honour," he finished lamely.

"Hmmm!" Again he looked Trefor up and down, over his spectacles.

"Tell me, Mr Williams – how long have you been the landlord of the Plough Inn?" He looked down and shuffled through the papers again.

"Almost twenty years, sir," Trefor answered promptly.

"Then you should know the licencing laws off by heart, don't you think?" the Chairman said drily.

"Yes, sir." Trefor's face went slightly red.

Abruptly the Chairman turned to the Clerk of the Court and asked: "Who is bringing this charge?"

"Deputy Inspector Jones, Aberdare station, sir."

"Call him to the witness box then!" he waved his hand impatiently.

"You are Inspector Jones of the Aberdare station?"

"Yes, sir."

"Please take the oath."

He solemnly took it, and was asked by the Clerk: "Are you prepared to give evidence on the charges as laid out in this case?

"I am," the officer replied, taking out his notebook and facing the Bench. "On the night in question, it was about two weeks ago..." He looked up at the Chairman. "It was the twenty-second of May, sir, when my duty sergeant received a phone call at 12.20 in the morning. The person on the other end of the line was calling in to complain. He alleged that the landlord of the Plough Inn in Cwm Du, Rhyd-y-groes, was still serving beer and spirits to customers at 12.15. It had been witnessed by the person calling in, who claimed he had looked in through the front window as he was driving past."

"Was this witness prepared to give his name? It was a male caller, was it?" One of the other magistrates asked.

"Oh, yes, sir. The complainant gave his name as Gwilym Williams, postmaster at Rhyd-y-groes. Upon receiving assurances from this gentleman that there was still a crowd of people in the Plough Inn, I proceeded with my duty and dispatched a vehicle with myself and two constables to investigate the complaint and lay charges if required." He referred again to his notebook. "Arriving at the Plough Inn, we entered the bar and found the room fairly crowded, with approximately twenty men in the main bar, but only three of them had any drink in their possession. Those three men are present here today, sir.

"I then issued the statutory warning and charged the landlord, Mr Trefor Williams, and the three other defendants."

Trefor, in anger at the revelation of the informant, turned in the dock to glare at Gwilym Williams at the back of the court who, seeing his anger, sidled once again behind some people near the door.

"Thank you Inspector for your most comprehensive evidence. You may step down. Now then, Mr Williams, do you have anything further you would like to add in mitigation to the charges you are facing?"

"Yes, sir. If you please," Trefor's voice was suddenly strong. "The witness, Gwilym Williams, is lying when he said he looked through the window. He could not have done that because the wooden shutters on the inside are always closed because of the noise from the opencast lorries passing every day from morning to night. And further to that, he himself was drinking in the bar at fifteen minutes past twelve! I know that for a fact because I served him with a glass of ale myself at that time. He has done this out of pure spite because I objected, in this very court, to him having an off licence in his shop. And there he is!" Trefor's clenched fist thumped the rail so hard it shook, as he pointed an accusing finger at Gwilym Williams, skulking at the back of the room.

The Chairman raised his hand towards Trefor. "Now, now, Mr Williams. If what you are saying is true..."

"I am under oath, sir," Trefor interrupted.

"Yes, yes!" he said testily. "As I was about to say, if what you are stating is correct, then we might have to consider some mitigating circumstances in this case. However, you are the one being charged with an offence in contravention of the law, and not the postmaster. You are the person holding the licence and you also knew full well the statutory hours of opening and more to the point the statutory hours of closing. Now then, gentlemen." He turned away to confer with the other two magistrates.

A full five minutes passed before they reached a consensus. The Chairman cleared his throat. "Hrrr! Mr Williams. We find you guilty of the offence as charged and fine you £25 plus court costs." Addressing the Clerk of the Court, he said. "There is no need for the other three men, also defendants in this case, to enter the dock. As this is their first offence, we find them guilty as charged and impose a fine of £2 each."

Trefor nodded his acceptance to the Magistrates' Bench and said quietly, "Thank you, sir. This won't happen again."

"I hope not indeed!" the Chairman replied shortly. "I do not want to see you back in here again, Mr Williams. The penalty may be much higher!"

Trefor climbed down the two steps from the dock and

approached the Clerk's desk. "I would like to pay for everything in cash, if that's acceptable. I would also like to pay the fines for these other three chaps," he added, pointing to the men standing beside him.

"No problem, Mr Williams. In total, that will be £41." The Clerk turned to his secretary. "Sheila, could you please make out a receipt for the full amount for this gentleman right away. Thank you."

In the Plough later that night, Trefor was recounting to Alan and Johnny the details of his day in court.

"Well, I think you got off pretty light considering the crowd that was in here that night," said Johnny.

"Aye, I know that well enough," Trefor agreed nodding his head. "I've been thinking a lot about that since I came back here. It could be a couple of things. Gwilym Williams was in there just to gloat over me being there in Court, and I pointed him out to the Magistrate. Or it could be that one of those chaps on the Bench thought about giving me a bit of fair play for Gwilym being so vindictive. I really don't know. One of those chaps on the Bench used to come in here sometimes in the summer but now I come to think of it, he hasn't been in for a while now."

"What did Gwilym Williams do when you pointed him out to the court?" Alan wanted to know.

"Oh, him? He went to hide behind some people and then he left with his tail between his legs before we came out of the Courthouse. I'll have to watch out for him now. He might try to do something else to make things awkward for me!"

"I wouldn't think so," Alan murmured. "Not now that you know who it was that called the police. I think he is going to be on pins just waiting for you to do something to get him back. I'll bet you anything he won't sleep much tonight or any night this week for worrying." He laughed out loud, the others standing there joining in.

"I never thought of that," Trefor beamed and said, while holding his sides, laughing, "Then that fine I paid today is well worth the money if it keeps him awake at night."

CHAPTER 21

Fred and the blasting powder

JOHNNY AND ALAN were standing at the far end of the bar chuckling at Trefor's scathing remarks about Gwilym Williams the Siop and his day in court when the bar door opened and Bill Thomas, Clerk of the Parish Council, poked his head around the edge. He peered short-sightedly around the crowded smoke-filled room.

"Hello, Bill," Johnny called out. "You look a bit agitated. Come on in and have a drink with us."

Bill smiled briefly but ignored the offer. "Has anyone seen Fred or Colin tonight?"

Johnny, sensing something amiss, replied immediately. 'I know Fred is here somewhere. I saw him just a short time ago and I can't imagine him leaving here before closing time. I'll find him for you. What's the rush?"

"Thank you," Bill replied gratefully. "We have a real problem on our hands tonight!"

Without questioning him any further, Johnny quickly looked in the other rooms without success.

He went outside, and saw a figure standing near the farm in the dim glow of the street light across the road. It was Fred, leaning on the top of the gate and staring off into the distance towards the Brecon Beacons. He was visibly startled and spun around quickly when Johnny called out, "What are you doing out here, Fred?"

"Oh, it's you, Johnny. I was just dreaming a bit," he replied sheepishly. "I don't have enough money for another pint and I don't want to put any more money on my slate with Trefor. Not until I can pay off what I owe him already. You know how it is. So, I thought I would have a bit of a spell by yere then walk home."

"You'd better come back into the Plough then. The Clerk of the Parish Council is looking for you. C'mon. It's a wonder you didn't see him on his way in. He must have passed right by you in the dark!"

Fred straightened up. "Oh, he is, is he? I'll bet he's got a job for me. Right you are. Let's get going then!" His step was quick and light as he hurried back towards the pub.

"You wanted to see me, Bill?"

"Yes, Fred! Thank goodness I've found you. Now, listen, we've got a bit of a rush job for you," he paused, then went on. "It's for a grave to be dug," he paused again, holding his hands tightly together. 'I'm sorry, Fred, but the funeral is tomorrow afternoon. I am sorry it is at such short notice but I was only informed about it by the undertaker earlier this evening. They said they had forgotten to let us know and I don't have any further details at the moment except that it is plot number 87. These people are from away, up in Birmingham somewhere, and they will be setting out first thing in the morning to be down here by the afternoon."

"Bluddy 'ell! That's too much work to complete in a morning, Bill, even if I started it at first light." Fred puffed out his cheeks.

"Yes, I realise that, but what else can we do?" They all stared back at the Clerk as he looked anxiously from one to the other, as if looking for inspiration. Alan and Johnny motioned to the Clerk to follow them over to the corner of the room and out of Fred's earshot.

"Listen, Bill. You are quite right. We have to do something and as Chairman of the Parish Council I am going to propose that we pay Fred *and* Colin, because he'll have to have help, an extra £5 each for doing this job in such a rush. Agreed? What do you think, Alan?"

"I agree totally. These extra payments can be squared up at the next meeting. The undertaker can sort it out with the family. They should be understanding of the situation, because it is at very short notice! Agreed?"

Bill nodded his acceptance. "I'll put it to Fred right away!" He turned towards the expectant Fred, who had watched the brief meeting with eager anticipation and knew at that moment that he was, for once, in the driver's seat.

"Fred, we've had a bit of a discussion regarding this situation and it has been decided that we, the Parish Council that is, will pay you and Colin, some extra money for doing this rush job."

Fred's eyes lit up for a second but his face showed no change of expression. "How much are we talking about then? And when are we going to get paid for this 'rush job'?" He grinned slightly, just enough to let the Clerk and everyone else know that they were all depending on him.

"Well." The Clerk glanced briefly at Johnny and Alan. "It is fairly substantial." He was reluctant to give Fred too much of a hold on the situation as he knew he would grab every opportunity to get that extra penny.

"Hmmm," he said slowly. "I'll tell you what, Bill. If the money is right, I'll find our Colin and we'll make a start on it tonight," he said, tongue in cheek.

"Tonight? Well, that's a great idea, Fred, and it will be a tremendous help. We were discussing offering you and Colin an extra five pounds." He paused, watching Fred's expression closely.

Fred sniffed. "Five pounds you say? For a rush job?" He pulled a long face.

"Oh, I meant for each of you, Fred," the Clerk replied quickly, realising that Fred could change his mind and might not follow through on his idea of starting the gravedigging job that night.

Fred's face lit up with a beaming smile. "Oooh! Each is it? Now you're talking." He spun on his heel and looked towards the councillors and from his expression it was obvious what had been going through his mind. He said: "Would one of you two gentlemen be good enough to take me to look for our Colin, so we can make a start tonight. I know we've got some storm lamps in the building at the cemetery that we can use."

"I'll take him," Johnny said to Alan. "C'mon, Fred!"

"Wait a minute! What about the cheque before we start?"

"To tell the truth, Fred, I only have one blank cheque with me at the moment. I can make this out to you for £10 and give you another one for £20 tomorrow. They have to be separate, see, because one comes out of the burial account and the other from the undertaker, you understand."

"That'll do." Fred didn't care where the money came from just as long as he could get his hands on it. "Landlord! Can you turn this into cash for me, please." All the current negotiations had taken place at the end of the bar where the landlord, Trefor, had listened to everything that was said.

"Certainly, Mr Howells. Just sign the back and the money is yours," he replied, smiling at Fred's jubilation.

Outside, Fred stepped jauntily towards Johnny's car, humming his favourite tune, 'I'm in the money'. "Stop at our house first. He might still be home," he instructed. He was all business now. They found Colin fast asleep in the chair beside an almost dead fire. "Hey, Colin! C'mon, wake up! We've got a job to do, starting right away. Here's a fiver to start with."

Colin sat up, rubbing the sleep from his eyes. "What time is it, then?"

"It's seven o'clock, but never mind that now! We've got to start digging a new grave right away."

"Bluddy 'ell, that's ridiculous," Colin protested. "At this time of night? That's nuts."

"No, it isn't. Tell 'im Johnny!"

"It's right enough, Col. There's a funeral tomorrow afternoon for someone in Birmingham. They left it a bit late to let us know so we have to get it done right away, and that's all we know about it."

Colin got up out of the chair with a sigh and put his coat on. "Come on then, let's get it over and done with."

Johnny dropped them off at the cemetery and returned to the Plough. "Everything is under control," he reported. "They have already started digging."

"Thank goodness for that, boys," Bill said, the relief he felt showing through. "I can sleep in peace tonight."

"Tell you what, though," Johnny said thoughtfully. "I think Fred is scheming something. It was something he said quietly to Colin about 'see how we can work things out for you, Col. It's easy money'. He is under a written contract, isn't he, Bill?"

"Oh, most definitely. I signed him up quite a while ago for the next twelve months and as you know, as a Parish Council we are responsible by law for all burials within our boundaries. We are also empowered to increase the annual rate to cover costs and for various other functions of local government. Everything is in writing, boys."

Fred and Colin returned to the Plough just before closing time, covered in mud and clay.

"Hey!" Trefor said sharply. "Go and kick the mud off your boots outside or no beer for you. You can use the sink in the kitchen to clean yourselves up if you want to. Now go!"

Coming back into the room a little later, in some semblance of order, they found two pints of best bitter waiting for them in the bar. "On the house, lads, for being such good boys tonight and there's two more waiting when you have finished, paid for by the councillors." Trefor nodded his head sideways in the direction of Johnny and Alan.

"Thanks, boys." Fred acknowledged them, his face beaming. "Aaah! This tastes great," he said, after taking a long swallow. He sat down with a sigh. "We've been busy tonight, boys. We are down about three feet already. Bill didn't say how big the coffin is so we measured for an average size and added quite a bit more all round. It should be okay," he added optimistically. "C'mon, Colin, drink up, cos Trefor closes on time now."

"Less of your lip, Fred," said Trefor with a grin. "It's the law, you know."

On the day of the funeral, Fred and Colin were down in the cemetery at first light, digging furiously. They were almost at the right depth when they encountered a huge boulder in the side wall. It was sticking out into the grave by about nine inches. They sat on the piled earth for a few minutes weighing up what to do next.

Colin said, "We can't go to the other side any more or we'll be into the next grave, unless it is a very small coffin in there, or a very shallow grave. We'll never know what Old Jim Cronin did down here." Jim Cronin had been the previous gravedigger – a hard-working man, now passed on, of little education and with no head for figures, which accounted for the problem of the spacing they were now faced with.

Frantically they dug into the side opposite the boulder until they could see the edge of the next coffin. They had just put the planks on each side and covered the mound of earth and clay with artificial grass when the cortege entered the gates of the cemetery.

"Just in time, Colin," Fred murmured breathlessly. They moved away from the grave area. Respectfully standing some distance away from the proceedings, Colin nudged Fred as the coffin was removed from the hearse.

"Look at that, will you! That looks a lot bigger than average to me!"

"Damn it all," Fred muttered. "Now we're in trouble."

The graveside service commenced, prayers were said and finally hymns were sung by the small group of mourners. The coffin was lifted carefully by the bearers and lowered into the grave. Suddenly the ropes went slack and the bearers pulled on the ropes to lift it out again. Fred and Colin inched closer. The bearers tried a second time and again it got stuck. The undertaker looked around and came across quickly to where Fred and Colin stood.

"What have you done here – or more to the point what have you NOT done here?" he whispered, fiercely.

"Well, to tell you the truth," Fred stammered. "We weren't told this was such a big coffin and we couldn't go any wider on the grave because the ones on each side are too close."

"This is the grave plot that he bought years and years ago," the undertaker hissed in anger.

"Well, it's not our fault the others are too close, is it? We're the new gravediggers for this parish. And another thing, we didn't know about this till late last night. We've also got a big boulder stuck in the side and top end which we didn't know about!"

The undertaker raised his hands in frustration. "All right! All right! We'll sort this out later," he said, keeping his voice low. He went back to the graveside and instructed the bearers to put the coffin back into the grave and keep it as level as possible.

He did his best to placate the family, apologising profusely for the fiasco. The family and friends paid their last respects as they filed past the grave, each pausing momentarily before making their way slowly to the waiting cars.

The undertaker came back up the path towards them. Colin nudged Fred, breaking into his train of thought; he hadn't as yet seen the approaching storm. "Now then, you two!" His pent-up anger showed through. "This has been the worst-organised funeral I have ever officiated at and I will be in touch with your Clerk of the Council to complain. It has been an utter disgrace and both of you should be ashamed of yourselves."

"Excuse me, sir." Fred was holding tight onto his temper. "I have already explained to you. It is not our fault. This plot was already too narrow to start with and we didn't know anything about this funeral until late last night because somebody didn't let our Clerk know about it. We started digging this," he waved his hand in the direction of the grave, "at 7.30 last night, by the light of storm lamps, mind, and we started again at first light this morning. I think that me and my son have done the best we can under the circumstances." He and Colin nodded to each other in agreement. "And another thing, we are not getting much extra for this either. There's that big boulder in there which we have to get out yet. I don't know how you expected us to know that was in there!"

"Oh." Somewhat mollified by Fred's tight-lipped explanation he said, "Well, perhaps we were a little hasty. You have to understand, it's a very difficult time for people to have things go wrong. What remains now is to put things right as soon as possible, isn't it?"

"Well, yes, I know that," Fred agreed softly. "What would you like us to do?"

"I'd like the coffin taken out and the boulder removed, then put the coffin back in and make everything neat and tidy as soon as possible. The family is returning to Birmingham tomorrow, see, so they will want to come here in the morning. Do you think you can sort all this out today?"

Fred took off his cap and wiped the sweat off his face with it and puffed out his cheeks. "That's a lot of work for the two of us, we usually have a couple of days to do all that." He winked slyly at Colin. The undertaker looked from one to the other. "I'll give you an extra £5 if you can finish it all by morning," he said pleadingly, holding out the £5 note to Fred. Fred looked at it speculatively but made no attempt to take it. "Okay, boys," the undertaker said reluctantly. "I've only got another £2 on me. If I give you that too, will that be enough?"

"Of course it is," Fred assured him smiling. "Don't you worry. Everything with be ready for tomorrow morning." He took the proffered money and stuffed it in his top pocket.

As the undertaker walked quickly back to his car Fred grinned at Colin. "Hey, partner, we haven't done too bad out of this one, have we? £20 for the job, £10 for the extra rush, and now seven quid to put things right for the morning!"

"Mmm!" said Colin, unconvinced. "We still have a lot of work to do, mind."

Between then, using the planks and ropes, they managed to get the coffin out and resting on the side of the grave. "Lucky for us they didn't take the ropes out," panted Fred on his hands and knees.

Colin got the short ladder and climbed down into the hole. "Fred, we'll never get this damned boulder out of here!" His voice was muffled as he sat on the bottom rung of the ladder studying the problem. "It'll take a stick of dynamite to get that out of here before those people from Birmingham come back! This is a bad job, Fred." He looked up at his father squatting on the edge of the hole.

"Colin, that's a brilliant idea, and I know just the place where I can get a pill of black powder and a fuse to go with it."

"Are you nuts or what? The police station is only 300 yards away and we are right on the main road too." He stared up at his father in amazement.

"Listen to me a minute," Fred said excitedly, the idea now firmly implanted in his mind. "It's underground almost six feet and if it is a small charge we can put the planks over the top to muffle the sound. People around here are used to hearing them blasting on the opencast site everyday so it won't be that noticeable."

"You don't know anything about explosives, fuses or black powder, and neither do I."

"It's easy," Fred said convincingly. "I've seen the boys underground do it hundreds of times." In his capacity as a rat catcher (sorry, rodent operative) in the local coal mines, he was able to go anywhere throughout the system and had no doubt witnessed the setting of explosive charges by experts… but that did not make him an expert, by any means. "You just have to dig a hole under it, stick the powder in, pack it with clay to seal it, light the fuse and up she goes. Simple."

"Well, I don't like it, simple or not." Colin shook his head. "Sorry I said anything now."

"You dig a hole under it with your knife and I'll go and see if I can get some from Twm Mawr. He'll give me some if I ask 'im nice. I'll be back in about an hour." Fred strode out of the cemetery and across the fields towards Twm's small mine.

"This is stupid," Colin muttered to himself as he lay on his stomach at the bottom of the grave and began scratching away with his sheath knife under the boulder, which lay almost in the corner and half across the end and into the side of the grave. "He's bluddy crazy!" he shouted out loud to the open sky. "It will save a lot of time though," he grinned. "Unless we do time for it.

NO BEER THEN, FRED!" he shouted again to the sky, but Fred was already half a mile away.

Fred talked Twm into letting him have a charge of black powder with a long fuse but he never explained what he wanted it for. Twm wrongly assumed he wanted it to get rid of a fox's den, since Fred was the local expert in that area. He just said: "Remember, you didn't get this from me, right?"

"Fair enough," Fred replied straight-faced. "Your secret will go to the grave with me." He hurried back across the fields, giggling hysterically at his own joke. Out of breath, he peered down at his son. "I've got it, Colin, and a good length of fuse too. Is everything ready?"

"Well, I've dug a hole about as deep as my arm, if that's what you mean by ready." Wearily he climbed out of the grave. "Now its up to you, you daft sod!"

"Don't you worry, it will be okay." Fred swung his legs over the edge onto the short ladder and knelt down beside the boulder. He took the sack of black powder, in its waterproof packaging, from his pocket, pushed it tightly into the hole, and behind it he packed the loose clay and small stones that Colin had dug out.

Unwinding the long fuse, which was already attached to the powder, Fred carried it up the ladder and put a large stone on top of it to hold it in place. He then pulled up the ladder and threw it on one side. Then they placed the planks across the open grave. "I still think this is nuts, Fred. We could get into a lot of trouble over this." Colin stood to one side shaking his head.

Fred only laughed. "Where's your sense of adventure, Colin. We'll be quids in after this."

"There's going to be one 'ell of a bang with that much powder, I know that much," Colin forecast. "Just you mark my words."

"Nah! It's not that much and it's a big boulder remember. Well, here we go!" Fred lit a match and touched it to the end of the fuse. "Quick," he shouted, "get behind the building!" He ran for all he was worth down the path. Colin passed him at a high rate of knots before he had gone ten feet, and disappeared behind the protection of the concrete building.

Breathless, they crouched down tight against the wall, their hands over their ears. Suddenly, the ground and the building shook, followed by a tremendous boom that totally overwhelmed them. Colin tumbled to the ground. Fred staggered to his feet and looked around the corner of the building.

"Bluddy 'ell," he muttered, his ears still ringing from the blast. A huge cloud of white smoke was drifting towards them and through it he could see the coffin. It lay on its side some twenty feet or more from where they had left it. The grave itself was now a gaping hole, almost round and not the rectangular shape it should have been. They walked slowly up the path towards the scene of devastation, stopping only to turn the coffin the right way up.

"Look at the dents in this, Fred," Colin said in hushed tones. "Those small stones must have been like shrapnel flying around."

Fred shrugged, still holding his hands over his ears as he tried to look down into the gaping hole, but the smoke, which hadn't yet cleared, obscured his view.

"Climb down and 'ave a look, Col."

"No bluddy fear! If you want to have a look, you go yourself, you crazy sod."

"Well, there's one thing about it." Fred was holding his sides, laughing like a fool. "If that poor soul," he nodded towards the coffin, "wasn't dead, that bluddy bang would have woken 'im up for sure."

Colin couldn't help laughing, more with relief than anything else. "Fred, you're a bluddy nutcase," he gasped.

When Fred had recovered his breath, he replaced the ladder and clambered down into the hole. "What a bluddy mess," he muttered, wafting his cap to clear the remaining black powder fumes. The heavy charge had indeed removed the boulder, there was not a sign of it or any pieces from it laying around. The remains of old coffins on either side were now quite visible and shattered.

"Sorry if I disturbed you, boys," Fred said irreverently.

"Hey, Daddy! Be serious, will you! You shouldn't talk like that." Colin glared down at his father.

"Aye! You're right enough, Colin. I shouldn't say things like that." Fred doffed his cap to each side.

Colin looked around for the planks. "Hey, Fred! The planks are in bits! How are you going to explain that to the council?"

"'ell, Colin, I don't know! Let me think for a minute... I've got it!" he said. "Vandals! Remember Alan and Johnny talking in the Plough last week about the mess they found down here with tyre tracks and things knocked over? Vandals, that's it."

Colin shrugged his shoulders. "I hope God forgives you for all this, Fred. You can look out too, if Alan and Johnny find out, you can bet on it."

"Don't be silly, Colin. I don't mean any harm by it. Come on, let's get this mess cleaned up before someone sees it."

Working non-stop, they cleared the debris and manhandled the coffin back into the grave. Shovelling like mad, they rapidly filled the grave and packed it down. Finally, everything had been cleaned up and the area looked neat and tidy once more. Collecting the remains of the planks, they hid them behind the storage building. Casting a final look around, Fred said, "Well, Colin, it worked didn't it?"

"Aye, it did. We were lucky the opencast is always blasting or we would have had the police here by now. I can still smell the fumes of that powder."

Fred grinned. "Never mind, Col. Let's go and have a few pints, is it? We'd better not say anything about all this," he waved his hand in the direction of the neatly mounded grave. "Agreed?" Now that it was all over, Colin just nodded, trying not to smile.

Brushing themselves down as they went out through the gates they suddenly stopped dead in their tracks. There was the boulder, as large as life, on the other side of the main road and barely on the edge of the grass verge. "Bluddy 'ell. Look at that, will you?"

Colin looked back up the cemetery to the grave and back to the boulder. "Fred, that's about 150 yards! That could have killed somebody, you bluddy head case!" His tone was incredulous. "You're absolutely nuts. I'm sure of that now. That must have been that whoow, whoow sound I heard right after the explosion. It came right over the top of us!"

"Well, it didn't do any damage, did it?"

"No, and you're very lucky it didn't."

"C'mon, give us a hand to roll it away from the road," Fred said, trying to push it with his boot. Between them, they somehow managed to roll it away onto the grass slope leading down to Llew Thomas's hayfield. Fred wiped his hands on the grass and said. "C'mon, Colin, we deserve a few pints after all this work today."

They were standing there momentarily surveying their handiwork when the boulder started to roll down the slope, gaining speed until it crashed right through the wooden five-bar gate, eventually coming to rest about 70 feet into the hayfield. They looked at each other in amazement.

Fred was the first to move. "Hey, Colin! Let's get away from yere before somebody sees us and we get the blame for this." Together they quickly crossed the road and cut across the fields in the direction of the Plough.

CHAPTER 22

Fred resigns as gravedigger

FRED CLIMBED SLOWLY and painfully over the stile onto the road opposite Siop John. He looked at his battered watch and said: "Colin, I think it is too late to go up to the Plough, it's getting on for four o'clock and Trefor closes on time now, since Gwilym the Siop reported him to the police. There's some of the boys coming down the lane now!" In the distance they could see half a dozen or so of the usual afternoon patrons strolling towards them.

"I don't know about you, Fred," Colin replied as he sat on the bottom step of the stile, "but I'm tired enough to go to bed right away. That was bluddy hard work down there today, especially after the mess you made with that black stuff." He looked around to see if anyone was near enough to hear his comment.

Fred gave short laugh. "It worked, though."

Colin gave him a sideways look and then got to his feet to walk slowly up the steep hill to the house they called home, with Fred trailing a few yards behind him.

"Aye. You're right enough," Fred panted, holding onto a garden fence for support while he got his breath back. "I've said it before, but this bluddy hill is going to kill me one of these days. Lets 'ave a nice cup of tea when we get in and a couple of pints in the Plough after, is it?"

"Okay by me." Colin straightened up from leaning on the fence. "I just hope there's not too many jobs like that one. C'mon, Fred, let's go home."

Colin was the first to wake up. Exhausted from their extra work earlier in the day, both men had fallen into a deep sleep the moment they had sat down in the rickety chairs on either side of the fireplace.

"Hey, Fred! C'mon, wake up! It's getting late!" Colin climbed stiffly to his feet and groaned aloud as he stretched his aching back. "I should 'ave gone to bed for an hour, like I said," he moaned. "That bluddy chair is not a bit comfortable."

"You can say that again," Fred muttered, echoing his sentiment. "I'm going to have a swill in the sink and go up to Trefor's for a couple of pints. I still have that extra money the undertaker gave me."

"Gave US you mean! We're Partners, remember?" Colin looked at his father, a grin on his face.

"Aye, you're right enough, Colin. I just forgot about it, that's all."

"Don't worry, Daddy! That's why I'm here, to remind you." Ten minutes later they were walking swiftly down the hill en route to the Plough. Fred was the first one through the door with the now familiar order: "Couple of pints, landlord!"

"Wait your turn, Fred!" Trefor replied without looking up to see who it was. Eventually he worked his way along the bar to where Fred was impatiently waiting to be served.

"Now then, Mr Howells, a couple of pints, you said! Is that best bitter or just draught beer?"

"Well, best of course! I – we – have got the money to buy best tonight." He cast a quick sideways glance as he said it. Colin grinned back at him, at the same time holding out his hand for his share of the undertaker's extra tip.

"Oh, aye, the money!" Fred took the crumpled notes from his pocket and smoothed them out on the bar. "Now then, Trefor. Take for the two pints out of this one," he said, handing the £5 note to him. Receiving the change, he divided it equally on the bar and then added a single pound note to Colin's share from the extra £2 he had also received.

"Don't I get something extra for making the deal, then?"

"No bluddy fear! We're Partners, remember?"

They moved away from the bar to the other side of the room, away from anyone who could listen in as they quietly discussed Fred's scheme for switching the gravedigging contract. Trefor, watching them from behind the bar, knew instinctively that Fred was up to something and was dragging his unwilling son into it, whatever it was.

It was about 10 o'clock when Fred saw the Clerk of the Parish Council looking through the hatch into the bar and motioning with his hand for him to join him. Fred nodded agreement and turned to Colin. "Looks like Bill Thomas 'ave got our other cheque. I'll be right back!" He finished his pint in one gulp and followed him into the quiet of the side room.

"Shomai, Bill. Got my other cheque, 'ave you?"

"Yes, I have, as a matter of fact, but first I have something to say to you."

Fred raised his eyebrows. "Ooh? Got another job for me, 'ave you?

"No. I'm afraid it is not anything like that at all. Sit down a minute, because this is serious." Fred sat down, a puzzled expression on his face. "Now then, Fred! I have received a very serious complaint from the undertaker. He came to see me this evening and complained about the shoddy work you did…"

"Hey! Now just hold on a bluddy minute there!" Fred's beer-charged temper was coming rapidly to the boil.

"Fred! Let me finish first and then you can have your say. As Clerk of the Council, it is my duty to see that affairs are conducted in a proper manner. I will not have the good name of the Council sullied in this way. At least, not while I'm in office, it won't. What happened today, by all accounts, was an utter disgrace and the family is very upset about it, I can tell you. Furthermore, against my better judgement, I allowed Alan and the Chairman to sway me into giving you and Colin that extra money for this job. Now, I want your solemn promise that nothing like this will ever happen again. There, I have said my piece. What have you got to say in your defence regarding this complaint?"

Fred, mouth open, was scarlet with temper as he glared at his accuser. "Right! Right you!" he replied angrily. His voice going up in tone each time he spoke. "Now then, I'll tell YOU what really happened down there today, just as I told that bluddy lying sod of an undertaker! Hang on a minute!" He jumped to his feet and strode across to the door. Turning, he shouted as he left the room, "I'll be right back and don't you bluddy move from there!" The Clerk watched Fred's departure with some alarm.

Fred poked his head around the edge of the door into the bar. "Colin!" he shouted across the room. "C'mere a minute!"

Trefor looked up in surprise at the angry tone of Fred's voice and knew at once that something was going badly wrong in the other room. He glanced through the hatch but the door was already closing behind Colin.

Once inside the room, Fred turned to his son. "Colin, after all we did yesterday at the cemetery, that bluddy undertaker has complained to the Council – well, to Bill here – that we did shoddy work down there. After all we did at night and in a 'ell of a rush too, and on top of all that, all the extra work we did for him to try and make things right." He glared at the Clerk. "Did he tell you how much bigger the bluddy coffin was? No? I didn't think he would tell you about that. Did he tell you we found a bluddy huge boulder at the bottom of the grave? No! He didn't tell you anything about that either did he? On top of all that, he wanted everything filled in and put tidy because the bluddy family is going to be there in the morning before they go back to Birmingham tomorrow. We usually have a couple of days to put things tidy. I'm willing to bet he never said a word to you about that either, did he?" The Clerk sat open-mouthed throughout Fred's tirade.

"What he's saying is right enough, Bill," Colin cut in. "Me and my father worked really hard down there to get it all done, and on short notice too, remember. That undertaker must take a lot of blame for not giving us the right information or enough notice in the first place, and we only got an extra fiver from the Council for all that – and now he is trying to put all the blame on us! That's not fair, Bill!"

"Well, I am very sorry about this, boys," the Clerk said, red-faced with embarrassment.

"SORRY? You didn't bluddy even ask either, did you?" Fred said bitterly. "You just thought, like everyone else in here. Oh aye, Fred is up to his old tricks again. They're only old working boys, so the undertaker must be right!"

"No, no, Fred! That's unfair!"

"Un-bluddy-fair!" Fred shouted. "I'll tell you what's not bluddy fair. It's not fair to us, that's what! I think you should have a letter of complaint from us about the lack of information from him, the old sod. You just wait until I see Johnny and Alan. I'm going to tell them all about this and lodge a complaint ourselves. How about that, then, Bill?" He banged on the table hard with the side of his clenched fist.

"Well, Fred. I am sorry that you feel that way about it but, if that is your wish, then you have every right as a parishioner to do so." He clasped his hands together as if in prayer that Fred would not go down that road.

"Then I will bluddy well do it, then!" Fred got up from his chair and began pacing back and forth, muttering to himself.

"Fred! I've got a cheque here for £20 made payable to you," the Clerk said softly.

"What's that? A cheque? Oh aye, my cheque!" he repeated, his thoughts obviously elsewhere at that moment.

"It's twenty quid, Fred!" He waved it back and forth slowly to attract his attention. Fred stopped pacing and sat back down and said abruptly. "Okay, let's have it then!" He reached across the table for the slip of paper.

"About the other thing, Fred, I have to tell you that any word of mouth complaints or reports are not acceptable. Everything needs to be in writing and addressed specifically to me as Clerk of the Council. I will then add it to the agenda to be discussed at the next full parish council meeting."

"Right you are, then, Bill! I will bluddy well do that! C'mon Colin, let's go and change this into spending money." He stood up, waving the cheque under his son's nose. Back in the bar, Fred was still livid with temper. "I'm telling you now, Colin! I'll 'ave him for this. Not Bill – that undertaker, the old sod. I'm going to complain about 'im right away, and then I'm going to resign too!"

"Now, Daddy, don't be too hasty in doing that. Remember you've had a few pints, mind."

"I don't care,' Fred said angrily, still smarting from Bill's comments. "We were going to do this anyway and this nonsense has given me a good excuse to resign, then you can take over and we'll have another forty quid to split between us. That'll teach them a lesson to listen to that bluddy man and put all the blame on us."

"Well, that's up to you, if that's what you want to do. All I am saying is this: I think you should sleep on it first and we can talk about it in the morning."

"NO! Now is the time, Colin!" He stood up and strode, full of temper, to the bar. "Trefor! Do you have some writing paper and a pen I could borrow?"

"Writing paper, Fred? Borrow?" Trefor's eyebrows raised up in surprise. "What do you mean 'borrow'? Yes, I've got some you can have at no charge. Are you writing love letters or is this going to be your last will and testament?"

"Don't talk daft, Tref. Have you got some that I can borrow or not?"

"Well yes, of course, Fred." Trefor disappeared into the back kitchen and returned with a small lined writing pad and a ballpoint pen. "Here you are, Fred. As I said, no charge." He smiled as he handed it to him.

"Thanks Tref." Fred suddenly grinned as he asked. "Is the Clerk of the Council still here?"

"Oh yes. He's sitting in the side room. Why?"

"Oh, nothing. I just wanted to know, that's all," Fred said nonchalantly. He went across the room to sit alongside his son and lost no time in putting pen to paper:

'To the Clerk of the Parish Council

I am writing to complain about the treatment my son and me got from the undertaker at that funeral from away. He said lies to Bill about us and we got the fault for the mix-up. We did our best but he didn't give us the proper information too.

Yours truly,

Fred Howells.

PS I also resign from gravedigger right away too.'

He signed his name with a flourish. "There!" he said aloud. "That's it, by damn!" He picked up the pad and pen and dropped it on the bar. "Thanks, Tref." He left the bar and went in search of the Clerk, and found him still in the side room nursing a small glass of ale as he thought about the complaint lodged by the undertaker. It now appeared to Bill, from Fred's reaction, that things were not exactly as he had claimed.

He looked up as Fred approached his table and handed him the single sheet of paper. He quickly read the note and looked up at Fred standing threateningly over him. This was a disturbing turn of events indeed. He knew at once that he would have to call an extraordinary meeting as soon as possible to discuss Fred's decision to quit his position. It was unthinkable to be without an official gravedigger. He looked up again at the set of Fred's face and knew at once there would be no changing him tonight, especially as he had a few pints in his belly.

"I'm sorry, Bill but I can't go on with the job at the cemetery, not after this complaint about our work." He pointed to his letter of resignation. "There's my answer to that undertaker's complaint – but I have managed to persuade our Colin to take the job instead of me. Of course, you will now have to sign him up to take it on, won't you?"

'Well, I'm damned,' Bill thought. 'Johnny was right about Fred scheming something. The wily old so-and-so is trying to catch us out. It has nothing to do with the complaint from the undertaker: it's more money he's after, and he only signed up about five or six months ago.' He cleared his throat. "Well, Fred, this is a pretty serious decision you have taken here and I have to tell you that now I have it in writing from you, I will have to put this matter before a full parish council meeting at the earliest opportunity, and declare this as a vacancy. Before I do, though, I think you should know that I am empowered to advertise in the press for applications from within the parish, and also to consider all applications from outside the district, too. We can even consider putting it out to contract to the Borough Council. I seem to recall they have a small machine that can do the job in a quarter of the time it takes by hand. We'll just have to wait and see what comes out of this." He pointed to Fred's note, then picking it up, carefully folded it and placed it in his briefcase.

Fred's jaw dropped, and it was quite obvious from his look of incredulity that he hadn't thought of any other option but Colin being given the job out of hand.

Bill Thomas smiled inwardly, secretly pleased with the way he had handled a tricky situation. 'That will give him something to think about tonight, I'll bet,' he thought, rising from his seat. "I hope you realise, Fred, that I cannot change anything that has transpired tonight. It's the law, you know, and now we have nothing further to discuss, I'll wish you a good night."

Fred turned away from the Clerk. He went back into the bar totally subdued, and a lot more sober than when he had gone into the other room brandishing his letter of resignation. Sitting down beside his son he said: "Well, Colin. It looks like I have made a real cawl potch of things again."

"There you are! I bluddy well told you, didn't I? I told you to sleep on it but no, not you. What did he say, then?"

"Only that the parish council will have to advertise for somebody else to do my job now. What it means, Colin, is this: if you want that gravedigger's job, you will now have to apply in writing to the Clerk of the Council. I think you had better do that right away before somebody else gets it." Fred felt totally deflated now that his grand scheme had failed so miserably.

"Fred! You're a menace. If you had any brains, you'd be dangerous and that's a fact."

"Hey! Come on, Colin. That's not fair. I thought we'd be okay on this."

"You thought! You don't think like everybody else, that's the problem." Exasperated, Colin sighed, got up and went over to the bar. "Trefor, can I borrow that writing pad again and a pen, please."

"What's wrong, boys? Are you two not speaking and have to write to each other instead?" Trefor now knew full well what had been going on between the Clerk and Fred in the other room.

"Nah! It's nothing like that, Tref. I've just got to get Fred out of another mess again, that's all." He tilted his eyes and head up to the ceiling. Sitting down beside his father he wrote:

'To the Parish Council

Dear Sir.

I would like to apply for the gravedigger's job with the Council, that my father just left.

Yours truly

Colin Howells.'

Colin approached the Clerk just as he was about to leave the Plough.

"Excuse me, Bill. Is it okay if I give you this now?" He held out the slip of notepaper. "That Fred is a nutter. I told 'im to sleep on it, but no! You know what he's like when he's had a few pints."

"Yes. Unfortunately I do indeed." He read the few lines of Colin's application. "Hmm. Well, Colin, the best I can do at this juncture is to offer you the job on a temporary basis. This means that the job is yours until I can convene an extraordinary meeting of the full Council to discuss tonight's events and of course your father's complaints. You may also be called as a witness to what actually happened at the cemetery yesterday. So, let's leave it at that, then. Oh," he said, as an afterthought. "Please let your father know there will be no signing-on fee until everything is sorted out, that is IF you are awarded the position of official gravedigger. Goodnight." He opened the front door and went out into the night, leaving Colin standing in silence in the passageway.

"Well, Fred!" Colin sat down heavily on the settle next to his father and picked up his beer, which had gone flat. "I've got the job BUT it is only on a temporary basis AND there is NO signing-on fee! I bluddy told you to think first!"

"I'm sorry, Colin. When I've had a few I do silly things," Fred mumbled.

"Only when you've had a few pints? Hah! Don't make me laugh, Fred! Anyway, if I get it, I get it. Let's leave it like that, is it? C'mon, drink up, it's almost closing time."

CHAPTER 23

Colin signs
the contract

JOHNNY AND ALAN were on their way home from watching a rugby game in nearby Neath when Alan, who was driving, turned off the main A465 road to follow the long way around the village. They passed the Plough and then carried on down the narrow lane to the main housing area of Rhyd-y-groes. Then they saw the tall, stooped figure of the Clerk of the Council walking slowly up the long hill in the direction of the Plough. Alan turned the big car around and came to a stop beside him.

Out of breath, Bill held onto the window sill of the car, clutching his heavy briefcase to his chest. "Hello, boys! Are you going in my direction?" he asked optimistically.

"It depends. Where are you going, Bill?" Alan replied, smiling.

"As a matter of fact, I'm on my way to the Plough to look for Colin. I need him to sign the gravedigging contract. As you are both aware, I gave the letter of confirmation to Fred for Colin more than a week ago, but I haven't heard anything from him yet, which is a bit mystifying, because there is a signing-on cheque involved and if he doesn't sign, technically we won't have an official gravedigger.

"Here's another item of concern. I've been informed that old Tom Williams is pretty low, so we must be prepared, either with Colin, or I'll have to contract the gravedigging job to the District Council."

"Jump in the back, Bill. We'll give you a lift right to the front door." Alan waited until the Clerk had settled himself, then drove slowly up the long hill between the tall hawthorn hedgerows.

Entering the bar he found Colin playing a game of four-handed cribbage on the large table in front of the shuttered window. Colin looked up with a smile. "Hello, Bill. Long time no see. How are you?"

Bill nodded politely and replied, "I am well, and thank you for asking. When you have a minute to spare, Colin, I need to speak with you. It's about you signing a new contract with the Parish Council. I take it you have received my letter about it?"

"Yes, Bill. Fred gave it to me last night."

"Last night! I gave it to him for you, in here, more than a week ago. Damn it all." He sighed in frustration. "Okay, Colin, when you are ready I'll be in one of the side rooms." He went over to the bar and got a small glass of ale, before finding a seat at an empty table to await Colin's arrival.

Opening his briefcase, he spread out on the table the necessary documents in readiness for Colin's signature, took a sip of the pale ale and looked up to see Colin standing there. "Oh, Colin! Please take a seat." He turned the contract on the table to face him. "This is the same contract your father signed some months ago. The terms are laid out step by step. If you are satisfied with them as shown, then all you have to do is sign on the dotted line at the bottom and this document, as the law specifies, is then in force for a period of twelve months, for any work that is required within the cemetery boundary. For this I am empowered to issue a signing-on fee of £40 in your name. Do you have any questions?"

"No, Bill. It all looks pretty straightforward to me. If there was any fault with it, I'm sure my father would have found it and let you know. Hand me your pen and I'll sign it right away."

Visibly relieved, Bill handed Colin his pen. Colin signed, then returned to his game of cards with no mention of when or how he would receive the retainer cheque, which surprised Bill no end. Without any more ado he packed up his briefcase and left the Plough for the long walk home, in a much happier frame of mind than when he had arrived.

Two days later, as predicted, old Tom Williams passed away and the Clerk notified Colin, via Fred, which plot number he needed to prepare for the upcoming funeral.

Colin and Fred had worked out a partnership for all future burials. Fred would start digging the grave and clear all around the site, then Colin would complete the grave after he had come home from the early shift at work. They would both be in attendance on the day of the funeral or at least be on hand for any contingency that might arise. Later, Fred would start back-filling the grave and Colin would be there, after work, to complete the job and tidy up the site, just in case any of the family should want to come back to the cemetery. In theory, this appeared to be a well thought-out working system. In practice it was an absolute disaster.

Initially, Fred had done his part in preparing the site and digging down a few feet and Colin continued with it after work. Fred went down later to join him, and they completed the job together by the light of storm lamps in the drizzle. Satisfied that everything was in order for the following day, they called back into the Plough for a few pints on the strength of the cheque to come.

They sat together on the settle next to Old John Shinkins and Fred said, "Don't worry about tomorrow, Col. I'll be down there early to make sure everything is okay. Bill said it's an early funeral so I'll have all day to tidy up. Anyway, I've got a rest day from work, so I can do that pretty quick."

"Fair enough," Colin said agreeably. "Thank you, Daddy." The following day when he came home from work, he found the house empty. There was no sign of Fred, the fire was out and had been for quite a while – the cold feel of the oven was proof enough of that. Consequently there was no hot meal for Colin.

"The lazy so-and-so," he muttered. "He's home first… No, wait a minute! He's got a rest day! I'll bet he's gone to pick up his pay from the office at the Tower Colliery. I wonder if he's been down to the cemetery to finish that back-filling job? I'd better check that first." His voice echoed eerily in the almost-empty house.

Arriving at the cemetery, he found that Fred hadn't done anything he had promised. The funeral had been and gone and the coffin was lying at an awkward angle in the bottom of the grave. Colin shook his head in frustration and walked back down to the entrance gate where he stood for a few moments deciding what was best to do now. He turned to the left and went up the hill to the New Inn pub. In his mind, he thought that would be the most likely place to find his father.

"I'll bluddy tell 'im too! If you think you're going to get half the cheque money and not do your share of the work, think again, Fred," he muttered angrily. Arriving at the pub he quickly looked in every room without seeing any sign of Fred.

"Has my father been in here today, Mrs Lewis?"

"Not today, Colin," She smiled pleasantly. Then sensing his irritability, she asked, "What would you like to drink, then?"

"I'll have a pint of best bitter if you please, Mrs Lewis," deftly hiding his inner anger. By the end of the afternoon, he was more than a little tipsy. He had had no food since about five am, so the beer he had consumed had a greater effect on him than usual.

Leaving the pub, he stood outside in the drizzle while deciding what to do next.

"I'll go and finish the bluddy job myself," he said aloud. "To 'ell with Fred and his 'work sharing' scheme. I'll keep the money myself. That should teach the lazy sod a lesson, not to break a promise to me."

Meanwhile, Fred, as Colin had suspected, had collected his pay from the Colliery office in Waun-gron, and while waiting for the bus to Rhyd-y-groes had decided to walk the extra few yards out of the rain and into the Globe for one pint. The one became a few and the few became a few more until finally he wasn't in a much better state than his son. When he got off the bus at the bottom of the hill he walked a little unsteadily towards the cemetery and the work he had promised to complete that morning.

There was no sign of Colin near the grave, and the mound of clay and dirt was still there on the sheets of tarpaulin. Fred gathered up the shovels and tools he would need from the concrete block building and made his way towards the grave. Looking down the hole, he got the shock of his life. There, lying stretched out on top of the coffin, arms folded on his chest, was Colin, fast asleep.

After he got over his momentary shock and could see his son was still alive, Fred shouted, rapidly sobering up, "COLIN! You bluddy fool. For a minute I thought you were bluddy dead! What do you think you are bluddy doing down there? What if one of the family came back or someone saw you down there like that? Damn it all, Colin. Have a bit of respect, mun."

Colin, in his slightly tipsy state, had returned to the cemetery and walked up to the graveside, and seeing the coffin lying at an angle he had straddled the grave to try and make it level, but the clay sides of the grave were quite slippery from the steady rain and he had fallen almost head first into it, and had landed heavily onto the coffin almost knocking himself out. He had attempted a few times to climb out but was unable to get a grip on the clay sides, and had fallen backwards and promptly gone to sleep.

"Gimme a hand to get out, Daddy, please," he mumbled. With Fred's assistance and one of the planks laid across the open grave, he climbed sheepishly out of the hole. "I was only going to put the coffin a bit more level," he said with a lopsided grin. "It wasn't properly level and I fell in and I must have fallen asleep after it," he said lamely.

"Oh aye," said his father. "That's a likely story. Tell me, who the 'ell is going to check if it is level or not with this bluddy pile of dirt and clay on top of it?" Fred pointed to the huge pile of clay on one side of the grave. "The one in the box is past caring. Hah! Fell asleep by damn! Fell in half-drunk is more like it!" he shouted accusingly at his son.

"No more than you are, you lazy sod. All this should have been done by now! You promised me too, last night in the Plough, in front of Old John. I'm in work and you on a rest day, and no food ready when I came home, too!"

"All right! All right! Colin! You don't have to rub it in. I know exactly what I said in front of Old John," Fred muttered. "Let's get on with it as quick as we can. I haven't had any food too, remember! We can go to that café at the top of the hill opposite the pub after."

Still angry at him for not doing as he had promised, Colin glared at his father. He raised his voice. "Don't think you are going to get a full bluddy share of the money for this job when I am doing a lot more work than you, right!"

"We'll see," Fred replied shovelling the clay into the hole like a man possessed.

Together they shovelled as quickly as possible, in complete silence, all the while exchanging angry glances at each other.

Finally completing the job, they tidied up the area by the light of the storm lamps, gathered up the tools and stored them in the concrete shed, and closing the iron gates behind them, left the cemetery to walk in silence up the hill to the café. Not a word passed between them during the meal or on the long walk around the village towards the Plough Inn. As they walked in silence, Fred was smiling to himself as he thought about his son's latest bit of silly old nonsense. 'I can think of quite a few better places to have forty winks than lying on top of a bluddy coffin in the rain. The daft so-and-so.' He glanced sideways at his son, who ignored the look and stared straight ahead.

Later, entering the bar together, they each bought their own beer and sat broodingly well apart from each other. It didn't take long for some of the regulars to pick up on the Partners' obvious annoyance with each other, and asking Colin a few indelicate questions was like pouring a drop of petrol on a smouldering fire.

Colin began by telling Twm in a loud voice across the bar that Fred was dodging the previously agreed amount of work for the share of the gravedigging money! "And now he expects to get paid for it. Some bluddy hopes!"

At the other end of the crowded room Fred jumped to his feet and shouted angrily, "Work! That bluddy Colin won't go to work regular and there's me, almost an old age pensioner, keeping him in food and shelter!"

"What! Keeping me in food? Like 'ell you are. Boys, you've got to hunt for food in our house and I mean HUNT. He hides stuff all over the place. Some he buried in the back garden under the cabbage by the dogs kennels. He thinks I don't know. Last week he put some tinned cans in the toilet tank and the labels came off so I didn't know what I was opening. Then he hid the saucepan so I used the electric kettle…"

"Aye," Fred interrupted, "and when I went to make a cup of tea, bits of carrots and peas ended up in my bluddy tea."

The bar erupted with laughter with some of them banging their hands on the card table. Trefor, drying glasses behind the bar, was absolutely beaming with delight; such revelations of their life together were making his night. Fred looked around the room at the sea of faces looking at him. "And I will still hide my food from you, Colin. As I've told you before, if you don't work, you don't eat! Not my food, anyway," he shouted above the noise.

Colin was warming to his task now. "Hey, boys, you want to know what sort of bloke this is? I'll tell you! Trefor, ask him where he was all afternoon instead of doing the work down at the cemetery he promised to do while I was in work. Isn't that right John?"

Old John Shinkins, sitting on the settle beside the stove, began waving his arms at Colin. "Don't you go bringing me into your old row. I don't have anything to do with either of you!"

"Well," Colin went on, his face red with temper. "I'll tell you where he was. He was in the Globe in Waun-gron drinking away money he could have been paying you, Trefor, for what he owes you over the bar. Go on, Tref, ask him where he was!"

Trefor, just to keep the pot boiling, looked across at Fred and asked politely. "Is this true, Fred?"

"Colin! Never mind about me and what I owe Trefor. You need to go to work to pay off what *you* owe him, which is a damn sight more than I'll ever owe him!"

Before Colin could say any more, the Clerk of the Parish Council poked his head around the edge of the door and peered short-sightedly around the crowded, smoke-filled bar. "Boys, I'm looking for the parish gravedigger!"

Fred jumped to his feet. "Over yere, Bill," he called out, making his way across the room. He had, in the heat of the moment, forgotten he was no longer the gravedigger, just a helper now.

"Just a bluddy minute, Fred! No you bluddy don't!" Colin shouted from his seat on the window sill behind the card table. "I'm the bluddy official parish gravedigger now, not you!"

"Oh, aye," Fred mumbled and sat back down, his eyes still on the flimsy piece of paper being waved by the Clerk. "Sorry, Colin. We've both been a bit hasty today, haven't we? C'mon, Col. Let's have a few pints, is it?"

Colin ignored his father and made his way to where the Clerk was waiting. He graciously took the cheque, thanked Bill, and placed it on the bar.

Trefor walked over and stared down at the cheque without saying a word, then picked it up very deliberately, looked at against the light above his head, "This is a genuine parish council cheque is it, Bill?"

"Oh yes, Mr Williams. It's as good as gold," the Clerk replied, playing along with Trefor's teasing.

Colin looked from one to the other then grinned as he realised Trefor's intent. Fred finished his pint in one gulp and came up to the bar. Colin stared silently at his father, then at Trefor and said, "Could you turn this into cash for me, please, Trefor?"

"If you sign the back, Colin, it is as good as done." Trefor reached into his trouser pocket and took out a thick roll of bank notes.

Accepting the money, Colin placed a single pound note on the bar and grudgingly said: "Give my father a pint of best bitter out of that, please."

Fred quickly came around the end of the bar and put his arm around his son's thin shoulders. "Thank you, Colin. I really appreciate this." He turned to Trefor. "See, he really looks after me!"

A few of the locals began to cheer, knowing the Partners,

whatever their differences, were back together again. As the old saying goes: blood is thicker than water.

Trefor looked at the banknotes in Colin's hands and said softly, "I think most of that belongs to me to clear up some of your IOUs, Colin. Shall we attend to that now to avoid any confusion later on tonight?"

Colin looked down at the money and put it back on the bar. "Right you are, Tref, just leave me enough to have a couple of pints tonight, that's all."

The Clerk, standing behind Colin and Fred, coughed politely. Leaning forward, he said in soft tones to Colin, "If I could have a moment of your time in private, I would be most obliged." Colin followed him into a side room to sit at one of the small tables. Bill looked at Colin and said: "If you can recall, last week you signed the contract for the official job of gravedigger for the parish." Colin nodded in agreement. "Well," the Clerk went on. "I have here a cheque for the £40 which is the retainer fee you are entitled to. If you would be so kind as to sign this document to the effect that you have received this sum made out in your name, I would be more than pleased to give it to you now."

Colin's eyes lit up at the prospect of receiving more money than he had seen in quite a while, and he said: "Bluddy 'ell. Where do I sign, Bill?" He quickly scribbled his name as requested, grabbed the cheque, and with his thin face wreathed in smiles, disappeared in the direction of the bar.

"Trefor!" he called out above the noise. "Can you change this other cheque for me, too?" He floated it in the air and it landed softly on the bar. Trefor looked across the room at Fred, who was now sitting bolt upright as the piece of paper landed on the red plastic surface. Laughing, Colin turned towards him, "Hey, Fred, I've got twenty quid here for you. How about that, then?"

"Bluddy great," Fred breathed. "That's bluddy great, Colin." He finished the remaining beer in one gulp. "My turn, Col," he said in delight. "I'll have two pints of best bitter for my Partner and me."

When Johnny and Alan came in some time later they could immediately sense that something had been happening. They moved down the bar to their usual vantage spot and Trefor, placing drinks in front of them, couldn't wait to tell them of the goings-on with Colin and Fred.

"You should have seen it, boys. It was like being at Wimbledon. Everyone in the bar would turn to face Fred when he was shouting, and when Colin started shouting back, everyone would turn to face him. Even the card game stopped to watch the pair of them going at it. Fred was this end, on his feet by the dartboard, and Colin at the back of the table by the window, shouting insults at each other over the gravedigging work they were supposed to share. They were beyond."

Johnny looked at them sitting close together, toasting and drinking to each other's health. "Well, they seem to be okay now."

"Now they are, yes. That's because Bill, our Parish Clerk, came in and gave Colin a cheque for old Tom William's burial and a minute or so later gave him the £40 retainer cheque as the official gravedigger. It was like pouring oil on troubled waters – or in this case, best bitter beer."

Later that night the Partners left the Plough arm in arm, walking down the lane singing their favourite songs all the way home.

Fred went to bed immediately while Colin, half-drunk, slumbered in his chair beside the open fire. After a while he began to feel hungry and stirred himself enough to search around the kitchen in all the usual places, but he couldn't find anything eatable until he looked in a corner cupboard and noticed a pile of rags on the bottom shelf.

"Now then, boys," he said in a whisper, "what are you doing

in there?" He felt underneath the rags and his features broke into a smile as his fingertips touched something solid. "I've got you again, Fred," he murmured, looking up at the ceiling as he pulled out a large tin of vegetable soup. He opened the tin and looked around without success for their small saucepan to heat it up. "Where the 'ell has he hidden it this time?" he muttered in frustration while trying not to make any sound which might alert his father to what he was doing. "Shhh!" he said softly, giggling to himself. "He'll give you what for if he wakes up, mind." He looked at the old battered kettle, which Fred had picked up somewhere on his travels, a second time. His eyes went from that to the open tin of soup and back again to the kettle.

"Ahh! What the 'ell, it can't do any harm, can it. He's still alive after the last time I used it, isn't he?" he said, convincing himself that what he was about to do was okay. He began giggling again as he poured the whole tin into the kettle and plugged it in. Minutes later he had a piping hot bowl of soup. His hunger satisfied, he made his way contentedly to bed.

Fred was up early the following morning nursing a pounding headache from his over-indulgence of the night before.

"I think I'd better have a cup of tea before I do anything this morning." He groaned as he filled the kettle, squinting his eyes in the brightness of the morning sun streaming through the curtainless kitchen window. He sat down beside the now dead fire and held his head in his hands while trying to calculate, in his mind, how much of the £20 that Colin had given him the night before he had left to last him the rest of the week. Giving up on the mathematics of his financial situation, he rose to his feet, rinsed out the teapot and put in a couple of generous spoonfuls of loose tea leaves.

The water in the kettle was now boiling merrily as he poured it onto the tea leaves. Suddenly he stopped pouring in disbelief as a flood of peas and bits of carrot shot out of the spout and into the teapot. He put the kettle down on the rickety table and removed the lid to peer inside through the steam and there, floating around the heating element, were the remains of his hidden tin of vegetable soup.

"What the 'ell ...." he started to say. "It's that bluddy Colin again!" He ran to the bottom of the stairs, his pounding headache for the moment forgotten, until he shouted. "Colin! You bluddy monkey! Come down here right away!" His voice echoed eerily up the empty stairwell as he yelled.

"COLIN! Come down here!" Colin sat up in bed with a start, trying to get his fuddled brain back on track.

"COLIN!" Fred shouted again, angrier this time.

"Yes, Daddy?" Colin grinned, remembering the soup in the kettle from the night before.

"You bluddy clown," Fred yelled again. "Come down here!"

"I'll be right there!" he yelled back, holding his head. He lay back down on his bed. He knew full well that if he went downstairs now, Fred would be raging but if he waited a little while, Fred's temper would be almost flat and he would see the funny side of it. He waited another five minutes or so then got out of bed, dressed and went slowly down the stairs to face his father.

"Yes, Daddy? What do you want at this time on a Sunday morning?" he asked, as if butter wouldn't melt in his mouth.

Fred looked at him open-mouthed. "What do I want? You bluddy clown! You know exactly what I'm talking about!' He pointed to the kettle. "You've eaten my bluddy tin of vegetable soup again, that's what! I didn't think you would be daft enough to do it again after I said about it in front of everyone in the Plough last night but here we are!" His voice had now become a croak from shouting.

Colin, trying to keep a straight face, lifted the lid and peered into the kettle. "Oh, that," he said casually. "I couldn't find our saucepan, Daddy. By the way, where is it?"

Fred's mouth fell open in surprise. "Our bluddy saucepan?" he repeated weakly. "They are all right up there, on the shelf above the kitchen door." He pointed to the narrow shelf he had installed when they, as a family, had first moved in all those years ago. "Don't give me that! I know very well what it was, don't I? The bluddy fire was out so you used the kettle to boil it up! That's why!"

"Well," Colin replied, with a shadow of a grin. "That too, I suppose."

"For God's sake, Colin. Use a bit of common sense, mun! You've made me spoil a full pot of tea, look! You'd better get all this mess cleaned up right away from out of the kettle and the bluddy teapot too." His previous anger had all but disappeared.

"There was no harm in it, Fred," Colin replied, openly grinning now. "Sometimes I've seen you have a cup of tea right after you've had a bowl of soup. This way you can save time and have them both together!" He laughed out loud at his own joke.

"Get away from yere, you cheeky sod!" Fred raised the back of his hand towards him, feigning to give him a clip. "I don't know about you, Colin. You do some *twp* things when you've had too much beer. Go on, clean up that mess out of there so we can have a nice cup of tea, is it?

Later, their dispute forgotten, Fred and Colin washed up and made their way up to the Plough.

Fred's roast chicken: Part 1

O N THIS PARTICULAR Saturday evening, after Fred had done his meagre bit of shopping down in Waun-gron, he found he did not have enough money left in his pocket to spend the night in the Plough. Drinking in the Plough had its advantages in the same way that bills are run up with a credit card, except that Trefor never applied any exorbitant interest charges, but Fred, as he told himself, didn't want to add any more to his already heavy bill with the landlord. He had no radio or TV to entertain him – they had both disappeared on the same day that his wife left him and Colin for greener pastures – and so he sat in lonely silence and enjoyed the warmth of the glowing coal fire. He stared into the dancing flames wondering what to do next, when a singular thought struck him. 'I'll prepare that little chicken for tomorrow's dinner.' Turning his thoughts into action, he began cleaning the scrawny bird. When he was finished, he looked at it with some disdain and recalled how long it had taken him to persuade the butcher, who had known him for so many years, to drop the price by a few shillings and throw in a couple of sheep's heads, 'for the dogs'.

The only highlight of the day, for him anyway, had been

seeing his boyhood teacher, Miss Edmunds, from the school he had attended so many years ago, walking towards him. He had gone up to her, introduced himself and thanked her for teaching him, shaken her by the hand and for some unknown reason he had kissed her smack on the lips and walked quickly away to get on the waiting bus to Rhyd-y-groes, while she had stood there transfixed until the bus had departed.

'Damn,' he thought, 'now why the 'ell did I do that?'

He busied himself building up the fire for the combination fireplace and oven. "No electric stove for us Partners!" he had bragged on a number of occasions. "We do things the old fashioned way, it tastes better." He never explained where their electric stove had gone.

When he thought he had enough heat in the oven, he placed the chicken, wrapped in foil, in a small roasting pan and into the oven and sat back in his dilapidated chair to await the results of his labours. Picking up a week-old *News of the World,* he re-read some of the stale news. Eventually tiring of his own company, he decided to climb the wooden hill to the solitude of his bed, as the aroma of the roasting chicken began to permeate every room in the house. He lay in bed day-dreaming of an almost Christmas-like dinner for the morrow as he drifted off into sleep.

Meanwhile Colin, who was in the Plough, drinking to his heart's content and rapidly building up a substantial debt in IOU's, with Trefor's consent, wondered from time to time where Fred was. Saturday night in the Plough without him making a fuss over something or other was pretty tame, to say the least. He looked up at the heavy framed photograph of his father high up on the wall behind the bar. It showed Fred in shirtsleeves, many years before, holding across his arms the body of an enormous otter which he had killed with a single blow of his shovel while defending himself from its attack on his legs. This had occurred at one of Waun-gron's former beauty spots, where he had been clearing out a blocked waterway into one of the two large ponds which had been constructed in the nineteenth century to provide a constant water supply to the now-defunct ironworks. The local coal mine's washery had spoiled this area as a beauty spot forever, as the tailings and slurry from the mine gradually displaced the clear mountain water.

'Damn,' he thought, with a feeling of pride, 'he's a 'ell of a boy, mind, Good thing we have our rows in front of everybody, otherwise there might have been a murder in the family by now.' His thoughts were rudely interrupted by the card player opposite him.

"Oy! Are you playing or sleeping over there?"

"I'm playing," Colin replied a bit sheepishly and thought, 'I must be getting sentimental in my old age.' He tried to concentrate on the game in front of him.

Leaving the Plough later, with a bellyful of 'milk of amnesia', as he liked to call Trefor's best bitter, he climbed slowly and a little unsteadily up the steep hill to where they lived. He glanced up; the house was in darkness.

'Fred must be still out drinking somewhere,' he thought, then remembered that Fred had already told him he had no money to go out. 'He could have come with me, though, cos my credit is still good with Trefor.' He opened the back door and stood for a moment, swaying slightly in the doorway, only to be met by the tempting aroma of the still-roasting chicken. "Oh-oh! He's already in bed," he whispered, "and there's a chicken in the oven. I'm sure you won't miss just little bit, will you, Daddy?" he said in a low voice, looking up at the ceiling and saluting.

Careful not to make any noise which would bring Fred down the stairs in a hurry, he opened the oven door and took out the roasting tray to place it on the hearth near his chair. Slowly he peeled back the foil wrapping. "Oh! you look so beautiful," he whispered to the little bird. "I'll be back in a minute to see what you taste like!" Little by little he began to demolish his father's anticipated Sunday dinner until only the carcase lay in its foil cradle. He looked at the devastation he had just created and thought about Fred's first reaction when he found out in the morning what he, Colin, had done while he slept. He sat back in sudden panic and tried to think of a way out of the mess he had made. There was no excuse he could think of at that moment to salvage the situation, so he wrapped up the remains in the foil as he had found it, and put it and the roasting tray back in the oven, washed the tell-tale smell of the chicken off his hands, and on bare feet climbed without a sound up the stairs to his bed.

The following morning when Fred came downstairs, Colin was already up and about, washed and dressed and the fire already burning brightly and the kettle boiling merrily at the side of the fire. Fred looked him up and down, a puzzled frown creasing his forehead. "You're up early! What's wrong?" He looked carefully around the sparse furniture in the room. He was immediately suspicious of Colin's motive. He was never, ever, up this early, and more especially on a Sunday, too.

"Nothing's wrong, Fred. Nothing at all," Colin shrugged his shoulders, raising his hands, palms open in protest at his father's tone of voice. "I just felt like getting up early for a change and I was starving too. What's for breakfast?" he added with as innocent face as he could manage.

"Same as bluddy usual." Fred grunted in a surly tone, not convinced by his son's platitudes.

Same as usual meant two slices of dry bread with a scrape of margarine and a cup of tea.

"Okay, then. I'll make some tea for us, is it?"

This again was unusual. Colin never volunteered to do anything around the house. Fred's eyes swept the room once more and what he could see of the kitchen from his chair alongside the fireplace.

'My bluddy chicken,' he thought, in sudden panic! 'I wonder...' Getting out of his chair quickly and quietly while Colin had his head in the little pantry, Fred opened the oven door an inch and peered in to see his bundle of foil still sitting in the roasting tray. 'Well, it looks just as I left it last night. Sorry, Colin.' Closing the door without a sound, he got back quickly to his chair and returned to his suspicions about Colin and why he was up at this time on a Sunday morning. Something was definitely wrong, he could feel it, but couldn't put a finger on what it was. He just knew it, and his instincts had never let him down before.

At that moment, Colin came back into the living room carrying the pot of tea, which he placed on the hob to finish brewing. He sat down and picked up the outdated *News of the World* and pretended to be completely immersed in the ancient news portrayed in its yellowing pages.

Fred tried unsuccessfully, to start a conversation with him. "So where did you go last night then?"

"The Plough," Colin grunted from behind the newspaper.

"So, who was there then?"

"All the boys."

"Did you 'ave a good night?"

"Yes, I did!"

"Where did you get the dough for a night out, then?"

"Strap!"

"Colin! Where's your sense, boy? Drinking on strap and not working regular..."

"Hah! You can bluddy talk!" Colin snapped back at him, struggling with his rapidly growing hangover. "How much do *you* owe Trefor? I'm willing to bet it's a lot more than me!" Throwing aside the newspaper he got up from the chair to pour himself a much-needed cup of tea.

"Have we got any more of those aspirins in the house?" he asked gruffly, looking at his father over his shoulder.

"No, we haven't. We haven't got much of anything, come to that!" Fred got to his feet and made his way to the small rickety table they shared.

"Duw, Colin, you're stinking of booze!" In passing he had caught a whiff of his son's breath. "Mind you," he went on, "they say the best cure for a hangover is to stay drunk!"

"That's not funny, Fred." Colin groaned, holding his head in his hands.

Fred, still sitting at the table, holding his cup of weak tea with both hands and studying his son over the rim, said quietly, "I think I had better start peeling some spuds ready for dinner. Time is getting on!"

Colin was bounced out of his self-pity in an instant by Fred's casual remark. Hells bells, he's going to find out pretty quick what I did to his chicken last night.

"I think you're right, Fred. About staying drunk I mean. I'll bet you any money, if I had a pint right now instead of tea, I would be as right as rain!" He made his way to the sink and briefly swilled his face under ice cold water from the tap and while drying his face vigorously he mumbled to his father. "I'm going to take a stroll up to the Plough, Fred. By the time I get there it will be almost open tap. See you after, then." He turned and moved as casually as possible towards the open back door. Once around the corner of the house, he ran for all he was worth down the hill in the direction of the pub. On his way down the steep hill he flew past Alan and Johnny as if he had sprouted wings. Alan, guessing where he was going, called out, "Hey Colin! He won't be open for another hour!"

Out of breath, Colin came to a stop and held onto a nearby garden fence for support. "I know!"

Coming to a halt, Alan asked. "So what's all the rush about then, Col?"

Colin, his face twisted into a lopsided grin replied. "That Fred is going to kill me when he finds out that I ate nearly all of the chicken he roasted last night for today's dinner. I'd had a few in the Plough last night and when I came home I was starving and all I could smell was his chicken. He knows what I'm like when I've had a few pints!" He looked back up the hill. "I'd better get moving, it won't be long now before he finds out!" Suiting words to action, he set off at a trot towards the Plough.

Further down the hill Alan waved to Norman 'corner house', standing by his gate holding himself upright with a pair of walking sticks. "I wonder what happened to him?" he said under his breath to Johnny, walking beside him.

"I'll tell you in a minute, Al," Johnny replied from behind his hand. "I was talking to him earlier about those sticks before I came to see you. Last night, he was walking home late from Waun-gron after a few pints and you know that area where there are no street lights, just round the corner by Jonah Roberts' house. Well, he thought he saw something coming towards him in the dark, like two people on bikes, so he thought he would give them a bit of a scare and jumped between them, shouting at the same time. It turned out it was an Austin A35 car. You know the one, it's got those tiny little sidelights on top of the wings. He had jumped right onto the bonnet. Luckily, the driver had quick reflexes to stop, otherwise he might have gone right under the bluddy car. As it was, he landed on his knees, so the silly so-and-so is hobbling around today on sticks. D'you know, if I had done something as *twp* as that, I would never in this world tell anyone what I had done," he said, coming to a stop and laughing out loud.

Arriving at the Plough, they found Colin sitting on the bench outside, relating the story of Fred's chicken to some of the regulars, who were all waiting patiently for a few thirst-quenchers before lunch. His tale drew laughter from some, while a couple of the others, knowing Fred of old, predicted what he would do to Colin if he could get his hands on him.

"Well," said Colin, with a touch of bravado, "he shouldn't tempt me with such a lovely smell of roast chicken when I come home. He knows what I'm like," he laughed, but it had an unconvincing hollow ring to it.

Fred, meanwhile, was not in any hurry to follow Colin to the Plough since he was still flat broke, so he went into the garden to dig up a few spuds and cut a cabbage in readiness for their afternoon meal. When everything was prepared to his satisfaction, he opened the oven to take out the roasting tray to use the stock to make gravy. He liked to make a lot of gravy because any scraps of bread went into it when they were finished, to feed their dogs. He picked up the foil-wrapped bird and thought, as he hefted it in his hands, 'Damn, this feels a bit light.' All sorts of thoughts raced through his mind as he quickly unwrapped what was left of his anticipated dinner. Disbelief poured over him like a bucket of ice water as he surveyed the pile of bones and scraps of meat stuck to the bottom layer of foil. He stood, momentarily stunned by what he saw. "SO, THAT'S WHAT HE WAS UP TO ALL ALONG!" he shouted. "I'LL BLUDDY KILL 'IM! I'll bluddy kill 'im! I will! I'll bluddy kill 'im. Just wait until I get my bluddy 'ands on 'im," he yelled, throwing the remains of the bird back in the tray. "Oh, the little swine! No night out, no beer and now no bluddy dinner! Oh, that bluddy boy!" he ranted, as he went from room to room clenching his fists and yelling what he was going to do to Colin when he caught up with him.

Jinny Thomas, his next-door neighbour, must have thought that some sort of fight was in progress between the Partners, until a short while later she witnessed Fred running down the hill, waving a clenched fist in the air as he went and shouting to anyone he knew, "That bluddy Colin 'ave eaten my chicken!"

The lane up to the Plough was not by any means steep, but in his temper, running and shouting at the same time, Fred was completely out of breath by the time he was in sight of his destination. He clung almost exhausted to the farm gate and contemplated what he was going to do to his son if he could get to the Plough.

"Oh, just you bluddy wait, Colin!" Minutes passed as he struggled to regain his strength and breath and then he walked as quickly as he could up the remainder of the hill.

In the meantime, Colin, who knew exactly what was coming, had placed himself strategically behind the card players and spectators at the big card table and sat down on the window sill with his back to the heavily shuttered window. He was flanked on each side by two more players and other spectators. 'Discretion is the better part of valour,' he thought.

Suddenly the door into the bar was flung open and a red-faced, out-of-breath Fred stood panting in the doorway. The usual noise in the bar petered out to silence.

"Where is he?" he yelled, casting his eyes from one end of the room to the other, searching in the dim light for any sign of Colin, while his eyes adjusted from the bright sunlight outside.

"Daddy, let me explain…" He didn't get any further with his explanation. Fred was across the room in a flash and tried to launch himself across the table, reaching for Colin with both hands, at the same time knocking over pints of beer across the card table, doing nothing to endear him to those sitting at the table whose card game he had just destroyed. The men on each side grabbed him and dragged him away from the table, while Fred was just as determined in his struggle to grab Colin by any means at his disposal, all the while shouting what he was going to do when he did get hold of him.

Colin was only adding to the commotion by apologising at the top of his voice. That was until Trefor came from behind the bar to join in the fast-developing bedlam, grabbed Fred by the collar and dragged him over to the bar, where he handed him a pint of best bitter.

The change that came over Fred was nothing short of miraculous. Free beer could calm Fred in an instant; he guzzled half of the drink in one swallow. "Well okay, Trefor, I'm all right now! But I'll bluddy 'ave 'im, just you wait and see. I 'spect he's been telling you all about 'im eating my chicken last night, 'ave he? The swine!"

"We've heard a bit about it AND we don't want to hear any more. You can say you'll have him, but NOT IN YERE!" Trefor's voice went up as he shouted Fred down.

Draining the pint glass, Fred put it on the bar in front of the landlord. "Well, can I have another pint then?"

"Last one then," Trefor replied, winking at the others standing at the bar, as he handed Fred the first pint of the day, which he had drawn to clear the pipes at opening time. "No charge, Fred."

"About time too, that you looked after your best customer!" Fred stood in the centre of the room in his usual pose, the skirt of his coat thrown back and one hand on his hip, pint in the other as he surveyed the mess he had created just minutes before.

"Best customer, is it?" Trefor said dryly. "It wouldn't be so bad if you paid me in cash as a best customer!"

In a lull in the general noise, Colin once again tried to justify his actions of the night before. "Daddy, you know what I'm like…"

"Colin! Shut up before I come over there and belt you one."

"Aww. C'mon, Daddy. Will you…"

"I said…"

"I think you've bluddy said enough, Fred!" one of the card players stood up and glared down at Fred.

There was a moment of complete silence in the room, then Colin called out. "Trefor! Give my father a couple of pints of best bitter and add them to my IOUs, okay?"

Fred's eyes glittered momentarily "Make that *three* pints of best, Trefor." The landlord looked across the room at Colin, eyebrows raised in question.

Colin, from his position of safety behind the card table, looked across the room at his father for a moment, then nodded agreement to the landlord. "Aye, okay. Three pints it is."

Fred raised his glass in salute and downed the remains in a flash without comment, or even noticing anything was wrong with the quality of the beer.

"Okay, Tref!" he said triumphantly. "Fill 'er up!"

CHAPTER 25

Fred's roast chicken: Part 2

A FULL WEEK had passed since the previous Sunday morning's confrontation in the Plough over Colin scoffing all his father's roast chicken. The bar door was pushed wide open and Fred swaggered in, grinning from ear to ear. He moved to the centre of the room and slowly began turning around for all and sundry to take notice of him. He didn't say a word but stood there beaming, just waiting for someone to ask the question.

Trefor, in his usual place behind the bar, looked up from pulling a pint of foaming amber ale for a customer and, as perceptive as always, immediately put the pint on the bar and called out: "Here you are, Fred! Quick! Tell us all what you've been up to now! I can tell from that smile on your face you've been up to some mischief or other and you've just come in here to brag about it! That's right, isn't it?" Trefor began waving his arms upwards in encouragement to the rest of the room. "C'mon, boys, let's give him a bit of support, is it!" Fred stood with the skirt of his jacket thrown back, one hand on his hip and holding the remains of his free pint aloft, savouring this brief moment of glory as he became the centre of attention in the crowded room.

"C'mon, Fred," Trefor called out again. "Let's have it! What sort of mess have you got into again? Don't just stand there gloating, mun!"

From the other side of the bar, Willi Bray shouted out, "His wife has come home to stay!"

This brought Fred back down to earth with a bang. He spun around to glare at Willi. "Like 'ell she 'ave or bluddy will, mate! No boys, that's not it at all. Remember last Sunday morning when I found out what our Colin had done and I said I would 'ave 'im for that? Well, I bluddy had 'im last night. I really had 'im this time, and it drove 'im mad."

"So what did you do this time? Lock him out all night?" Bobby jeered from the card table.

"Nope! Nothing like that at all, boys, I bought another chicken down in Waun-gron and cooked it last night for today's dinner while he was out somewhere. When our Colin came home all he could smell all over the house was roast chicken. I was in bed listening to him trying to be quiet as he searched all over the place. Boys, I have to say it smelled lovely too, with sage and onion stuffing and everything. I couldn't stop laughing. He even looked around the edge of the door into my bedroom but I pretended to be fast asleep, so he went back downstairs for another look around. It was great, boys. I'd got my own back on him! And when I got up this morning, he was still looking for it.

"In the end he said: 'C'mon, Daddy, I give up! I know there's a cooked chicken here somewhere. Did you give it to Mrs Thomas next door to keep safe, or what?' So I said, 'No,' and I had 'im going for quite a while guessing different hiding places until he got really angry, so I went upstairs to fetch it." Some of his now captive audience were listening intently to his story and dying to know exactly where Fred had hidden the roast chicken. Finally he said, "Seeing that look on his face was well worth the wait, especially when I dangled it in front of his nose. My revenge was even better. It felt great!"

"Well? Where was it?" Willi shouted out impatiently. "Did you hide it in the toilet with the tinned stuff from last week?" Everybody in the room laughed at that one, remembering Colin relating stories of his hunt for food at home and the consequences of having no labels on the tins.

"Nah! It was nothing like that," Fred replied, laughing. "I just tied it up with string and hung it on the springs under my bed. I was bluddy sleeping on top of it all night, while he was searching the rest of the house for it."

Everyone in the room was roaring with laughter, just as the butt of their hilarity came through the door into the bar. Colin looked around the room at the sea of smiling faces and said grumpily. "I 'spect 'e've told you, 'ave he?" which was a bit of an understatement. "Well, boys! I have to say this. He really had me this time!" He bowed his head in his father's direction and began to grin, joining in the fun they were having at his expense. "My turn next, Fred!" he said, as Trefor handed him a free pint of best.

In the landlord's eyes, an occasional free pint to the Partners was well worth the marginal expense when he considered the fun that was had by all in the Plough from some of their antics and escapades in and outside of the bar.

Chapter 26

The butcher in the Plough

Saturday afternoons during the flat racing season was when most of the horse racing crowd descended on the Plough as soon as it opened for business, *Racing Gazettes* and *Racing Guides* spread across the table and a pint within reach.

The TV at the end of the long bar was tuned into whichever of the thirty-odd venues, from Ayr in Scotland to Epsom in the south of England, was being favoured on that day. The volume, set near maximum, seemed to compete with the raised voices of the punters as they called out their selections to each other, creating a bedlam of sound. Throughout all this noise, Trefor appeared unperturbed as he plied the crowd with pint after pint of beer. Fred, seated in his favourite spot on the settle, lopsided granny glasses perched near the end of his nose, had the *Racing Gazette* spread out in front of him as he scribbled his 'picks' on tiny scraps of paper, and went next door to place his bets.

He came back into the bar, grinning from ear to ear and sat back down beside David Samuel Noel Goliath Jones, known to everyone locally as Dai Bandit. "Guess who I just saw in the betting shop?"

"I haven't the slightest idea," Bandit replied.

"Dai Morris, that's who! Der, what a rugby player he was. Played for Wales 35 times!"

"No, he didn't, Fred!" Bandit contradicted instantly.

"I'll bet you any money you like that he did! I saw his record of number of games ages ago!" Fred blustered, his tone of voice going up a few notches.

"I'm telling you that you'd lose money on that bet. Dai played for Wales 34 times. He may have been picked for the thirty-fifth game but he got injured playing for Neath against Ponty, didn't he? I'm willing to swear on a stack of Bibles I'm right."

"How do you know that then?" Fred asked, raising his voice.

"How do I know? Well, when I am in clink in Swansea, I have my own 'trustee' job in the library and I've got all the time in the world to read up on sports records for everything. As I said, he played 34 times, scored six tries between 1967 and 1974. He played in one Grand Slam and two Triple Crowns. How many rugby internationals do you know who come from Rhyd-y-groes, Fred? Two! Dai and Glyn Shaw, loosehead prop. Both played for Neath."

"Oh," said Fred, somewhat mollified by Bandit's sporting knowledge. "Okay then, clever clogs. I know this one cos I read it just the other day! Who won the Epsom Derby in 1946, then?"

"That's going back a bit, Fred!" Bandit thought for a few moments then replied, "It was a three year old called Airborne, a big grey horse."

"Bluddy 'ell, Bandit, that was a good one to pull out of the hat. Anyway, I said 'Shomai, Dai,' and he said 'Shomai, Fred,' back to me. That's all!"

At that moment David Samuel Noel Goliath Jones looked a bit overdressed in a light blue pin-striped double-breasted suit, white shirt and military-style tie amongst the nondescript apparel worn by the majority of the working men and retired miners in the bar.

Bandit had served all his time inside for recurring debt. He knew from past experience that when he appeared in court he would be given no more than 28 days. Once there he would be given his 'trustee' brown armband and his job in the library and what he laughingly called his 'home from home' cell, from where he could watch all of Swansea's home games as a bonus. On his release he would be provided with brand new clothes from the skin out and a few pounds spending money in his pocket. He often said he found it hard to understand a system which put him inside for debt where he would have no chance at all of earning any money to pay off what he owed, while his long-suffering wife and five kids would be struggling to make ends meet and relying on government help and local assistance to survive while he was 'away'.

The door to the bar opened slowly and Johnny and Alan entered the room. Johnny immediately came over to where Bandit and Fred were seated. He nodded to Fred and shook hands with Bandit. "How the devil are you? I see you've been to see your tailor in Swansea."

"Yes, sir. I got out of nick just this morning. In fact I haven't been home yet to see the old pullet." (his pet name for his wife)

Johnny looked towards the bar and catching the landlord's eye, he called out, "Trefor! Put a pint over for this gentleman, if you please." Trefor, still busily serving others, just nodded. Fred, never one to miss an opportunity, turned quickly in his seat and looked up expectantly at Johnny with his almost-empty glass in his hand. Johnny grinned and nodded sideways to his brother-in-law. "He doesn't miss a trick, does he, Al? Tref, when you have a minute, you'd better put a pint over for this old rascal too, otherwise he'll tell everybody what mean people we are."

Fred drained his glass in an instant and stood up with a slight bow in Johnny's direction. "Thank you, councillor. Thank you very much. I won't forget this."

"Not until the next time, I'm sure, Fred!" Johnny laughed and moved away from him to the other end of the bar, where Alan was paying for their drinks. "So what's new, then, Tref?"

"Oooh, nothing much, except that damn butcher has started calling me up on the phone at all hours. This morning it was about 3 a.m. and I have no idea why he does it. I can't for the life of me think why."

"Why don't you report him to the police for harassment?" said Alan. "I would."

"It wouldn't work," Trefor replied, keeping his voice low, not that anyone could hear what was being said in the noise all around them. "Even though I know very well who it is, I really can't accuse him without some definite proof."

"But surely the post office telephone people can trace the call from him to here if they know the time of the call and everything, can't they?"

"I suppose that's possible, but he could say anything he liked about why he called me and it would still be my word against his. You boys know the law. You have to have proof of intent. Don't worry, I'll find a way to get him back for all the aggravation."

Alan and Johnny looked at each other and grinned. In unison they said, "There's a practical joke coming here somewhere!"

Over a period of many years there had developed, in and around the village, a system of door-to-door roundsmen. Some delivered daily, while others were on a weekly, biweekly or monthly basis – whichever system suited their business needs the best.

Trefor, a confirmed bachelor, lived alone in the Plough Inn so this system suited his needs to perfection. His milk, bread and newspaper were delivered daily. The greengrocer arrived twice a week, as did the van driven by the local butcher. It was also customary for the landlord to settle all his bills at the end of each week or month as requested by the various tradespeople, so aspects of day-to-day life became fairly routine. The only fly in the ointment of a peaceful existence, as far as Trefor was concerned anyway, was the owner of the local butcher's shop.

Rhys Rees was a large, overweight, bombastic man, with florid, almost flat features and his close-set black eyes were separated by a large hooked nose. His straight wiry black hair was cropped short with a middle parting and brushed down close to his skull. He strutted around with short steps for a tall man and looked down with arrogance at everyone. It was his open opinion that everyone in the village and beyond was beneath him, and when he was 'in his cups', which was fairly frequently, not many people escaped his efforts to belittle them.

On this particular night he came into the bar with some of his friends. It was obvious to everyone in the room he'd had more than a couple of drinks elsewhere. Unceremoniously he pushed his way to the bar, loudly demanding service right away.

Trefor, being his usual placid self, glanced up at the order but continued to serve his other customers waiting patiently at the bar. This did not suit the butcher at all, who started raising his voice above the general noise and being abusive by proclaiming loudly, 'This isn't a pub! It's more like a bluddy stable!"

Trefor still made no move to serve him or even acknowledge he was there by answering him. This infuriated the butcher even further, and more especially in front of his friends. He expected attention when he called for it: he and his family were old village people and deserved respect! He continued to rant and be abusive to Trefor, loudly enough for people in the next room to hear. "You are not fit to be in here! You have no idea how to run a proper pub, not like my friend over there! What do you think of this bluddy dump, Twm? It's like a bluddy stable, isn't it?"

"Well, it does look a little bit shabby," Twm Mawr smiled weakly, more than a little embarrassed but still going along with the butcher's tirade. "Perhaps a coat of paint or something," he continued, looking around the bar before shrugging his shoulders with a sort of silly grin at Trefor's impassive face, until he turned away, red-faced with embarrassment.

Trefor still hadn't made any move to serve the butcher or any of the others. This appeared to anger Rhys Rees even more than before, and he became more personal in his verbal attack. Raising his voice, he shouted. "Why haven't you paid your meat bill? You owe me a lot of money. It's people like you that keep me waiting for weeks to get paid and that's not right," he added scathingly. Out of breath, he glared at the landlord. Looking up at him across the bar with a straight face, Trefor replied in a mild tone but loud enough for everyone in the bar to hear, "Then why don't you deliver the top quality meat you charge me for? You're always charging me top prices for the rubbish you send here!"

The butcher's mouth fell open but no sound came out. He stood there speechless for almost a minute while his face turned beet red. Finally he shouted at the top of his voice, "Damn you, Trefor Plough! Don't you dare say that to me! In front of all these people, too!" His arm swept the room in anger.

"It's right enough! Only rubbish you send here, mostly scrag ends, and I don't care who knows it." Trefor spoke in level, quiet tones.

"You shouldn't be in charge of a pub," Rhys yelled at the top of his voice. "Just look at this filthy place! You wouldn't know how to run a proper pub," he shouted, repeating himself and wiping the spittle of temper from his lips with the back of his hand. "Look at what Twm Mawr has done with his pub! Now *that's* a pub. We've had newspaper people there and pictures in the press. We had the Hunt there and all the *crachach* of the valley in attendance. They wouldn't come near this stinking hole!"

While all this shouting from the butcher was going on, the rest of the people in the bar watched in silence as the big man began to completely lose control of himself, punching a fist into the palm of his other hand in temper. Trefor stood motionless, with only the width of the bar between them.

"Is that so?" he smiled pleasantly and said in quiet tones, "Well, why don't you go down there now then and take your friends with you, because neither you nor they will get served with any drink in here tonight."

The butcher was flabbergasted, his mouth opening and closing like a fish in a bowl as he struggled to find something nasty to say in reply. In the end he stuttered. "What about my bluddy money?"

"Aye, okay, I'll pay you right away, but don't you ever bring any of your rubbish or any of your meat here again!" Trefor took out a large roll of money from his trouser pocket and slowly peeled off four £1 notes, which he placed one by one on the bar. "You can keep the change," he said, offhandedly.

The butcher stared down at the bank notes as he tried to think of something vindictive to say, then suddenly he crumpled the notes in his fist and pushed away from the bar to disappear through the door, slamming it behind him.

The room remained silent as Twm Mawr and the other two stood alone for a moment or two in confusion at the butcher's outburst, then in quick succession they almost ran after him out of the bar, followed by a chorus of cheers and laughter and shouts of "Well said, Trefor!" and "He deserved that!"

Trefor was all smiles following these accolades, but his eyes had that sort of distant look in them which, to those who knew him well, was a sure sign he would be looking for a way to get his revenge for the insults thrown at him tonight.

"Does anybody know what he was on about? The big opening do down in the Bont?"

"Aye, I do," said Fred, coming up to the bar with an empty pint glass in his hand.

Trefor reached for Fred's pint glass, filled it and placed it on the bar in front of him. "Go on then, Fred," he said encouragingly. "Let's hear all about it, then!"

Fred picked up the glass and took a sip, but made no attempt to pay for it and the landlord never asked. "Well," he squared his shoulders and cleared his throat. For a moment he was in charge. "They had a Grand Opening of the Lamb in the Bont last Saturday cos it is now under new management. Twm Mawr, who was in yere tonight with the butcher, invited all these big shots in the district for free drinks and food, you know – sandwiches and things like that. So I was told." He took another swig from his pint. "Aaah!" he said approvingly. "Free beer always tastes the best." He grinned at Trefor.

The landlord ignored the slight dig and rested his arms, folded, on the bar top. "Go on Fred! Let's have all of the story, is it?"

"Oh aye. They all had their ladies there too, dressed in posh frocks and big, big hats," he spread his hands above his head to demonstrate. "It was all pretty fancy. I was outside in a bit of a garden sitting on a bench having a free pint or two. There were photographers all over the place. By the look of them there were big shots from the Council, all with fancy chains across their shoulders. The Banwen Hunt was there too in their red jackets sitting on some fine horses, and with a large pack of hounds. Nice dogs too! Anyway, it was all pretty posh for the Bont."

"So how do you know all this, Fred?" asked Old John Shinkins from his place on the settle.

Fred turned to face the room, his elbows resting on the bar behind him. "I just told you, mun. I was there. I was there in that bit of garden with everybody else."

"That sounds about right! If anything is going for free, Fred will find his way in there. You can lay money on it," Roy laughed, some of the others joining in.

"Well, anyway," Fred grinned agreeably, "It was a good do. Oh, I forgot. There were lots of pictures of it in the Neath papers this week." He lifted his glass to finish it off with a flourish. "Same again, Trefor, if you please." Trefor dutifully refilled the glass, then turned away to serve someone else. Fred, never one to look a gift horse in the mouth, as the saying goes, turned quickly away from the bar lest the landlord remembered he had not paid for the previous pint either.

"That's all very interesting, Fred," murmured Trefor. "A very posh affair, you say!"

"Aye, it was," Fred replied as he went back to sit beside Old John on the settle. He wiped his mouth with the back of his hand and winked at Old John.

Behind the bar, Trefor busied himself opening and pouring two bottles of ale for Tommy John Fforch y Garon. "That will be four shillings, if you please."

Old John and Fred were closely watching his movements behind the bar and it was quite obvious that he was now deep in thought. They looked at each other and grinned, nodding their heads.

"I know that look," Old John murmured quietly behind his hand. "He's already scheming something."

"Oh, I expect he is," Fred agreed. "All I hope is, John bach, that he doesn't drag me into it after what I told 'im. Somehow, he's always having a bit of fun at my expense."

"Well, Fred, there are times when you deserve it too, for some of the nonsense you get into,' John said, laughing.

"Aye, you're right enough there, John," he chuckled. "But I nearly always get a free pint or two out of it, anyway. So I really don't mind." Lifting the pint glass over his head he intoned, "Here's good health to you, Trefor. I'm not saying it too loud, John," he whispered, "because I haven't paid for these last two pints."

"I know! I've been watching the pair of you," said Old John, "so there must be a very good reason for that, I'm sure."

CHAPTER 27

Fred and the funny money

ONE MONDAY AFTERNOON, Johnny was on his way back after a particularly hectic District Council meeting when he decided to call in the Plough for a quiet pint before going home for his tea. Only two other people were in the bar, which was unusual for that time of the day. He acknowledged the other two men with a nod of greeting and raised his shoulders, hands open, in an unspoken question. Trefor answered him in an instant.

"No horse racing today, and the couple of boys that were in earlier have gone home for their tea."

"Then I'll have a pint please, with a drop of pop in it. Would you two boys like a drink? I'm buying," he said, addressing Twm and Roy.

"No, thanks," they said in unison and started laughing spontaneously at the similarity of thought.

Trefor looked momentarily from one to the other, then reached under the bar and placed two bundles of what appeared to be bank notes on the bar top in front of them. They all, as one, moved closer to examine the notes without touching them.

"What's this then, Trefor?" Roy said with a broad smile spreading across his face. "Now what are you up to, then?"

Johnny leaned on the bar with his elbows. "I'm beginning to sense something naughty here. Where in the world did you get these from, Tref? They can't be real, though, are they?"

"Not at all boys," he replied. "My brother found a huge bundle of them washed up on a beach in Kent and brought some of them down last week because he thought they were a bit of a novelty and that we might have a bit of fun with them." His round features beamed in anticipation.

"Well, he's brought them to the right place, then, hasn't he?" Roy said with a short laugh. He looked closer at the top note in the first bundle. "It says, 'Confederate'. Of course, the American Civil War. This is just funny money, Trefor."

"I know that," Trefor replied innocently.

"How much money is there anyway?"

"I don't know exactly." He picked up one of the bundles and weighed it in his hand. "My brother said it could be as much as 150,000 dollars. The paper wrappers are still in place, look."

"Hello," Johnny chipped in. "Is it just a coincidence that Fred's daughter is working in the United States as we speak? I understand she went over there just before his wife left him, to work for a family in California – as a nanny, perhaps? I don't know."

Trefor smiled. Then he said, "What if we sent them to Fred and Colin for a bit of fun?"

"And what sort of excuse could we use to do that?" asked Roy.

Twm replied. "Excuse the pun, but Fred would smell a rat right away. He would know that you are having him on!"

"Not if they came to him in the post or something like that. You know, Special Delivery!"

"I know how we can do it!" said Roy. "How old is his daughter?"

"Not sure, but she must be about 19 or 20, somewhere in that region. Why?" Johnny replied.

"Good, that's close enough." Roy grinned. "As I understand it, under American law, she would have to be over 21 to claim."

"Claim what?" asked Trefor.

"Winnings on the horses! We could say she had won a big prize on the Kentucky Derby or something like that, and that she couldn't claim on the ticket because she was too young, but Fred, as her father, could do it in her name."

Trefor was all smiles. "Now you're talking. That sounds like a bit of fun to me. He would get some laughs out of it too. I like it. Okay, let's put it all together then. Right! Who's got the best handwriting? That's got to be you, Roy!"

Trefor went back into the kitchen and returned with a writing pad and fountain pen.

And so it began.

'Re Shirley G Howells
To the Parent or Guardian of the aforementioned.

Dear Sir,

I have been given to understand that you are the parent of the above-named Minor. I beg to inform you that she has been fortunate enough to purchase a winning ticket in the Kentucky Derby which has resulted in her winning a large sum of money, as enclosed, in prize money.

Unfortunately, due to the fact that by American law she is a Minor (under 21 years old), you, as the parent or guardian, have now become the administrator of her now substantial estate, to take care of or put into a trust fund on her behalf until she reaches majority at 21 years.

Would you therefore be good enough to present this large sum in American Dollars to a bank of your choice at your earliest convenience to exchange these bank notes for Pounds Sterling.

Phone confirmation of receipt of this money, 002 625 1778.

I remain, Yours truly

J W McGillicuddy

Attorney to US State Department'

Roy signed it with a flourish. "Now then, Mr Landlord," he said grinning like a Cheshire cat. "How are we going to deliver this, then?"

"Hang on a minute, I've still got the large envelope they came in so I will post them to Fred. Wait a minute, Roy, you have to write his name and address in the same hand." He was back in seconds with the large buff coloured envelope. "I'll take this down to Cardiff and post it from there so he won't know any different – and if I don't put enough postage on it, the postman will have to knock on his door so he can't say he didn't receive it. Right?"

"That's pretty clever, Tref," said Johnny, nodding slowly at Trefor's ingenuity. 'Let's hope this doesn't get out of hand. We all know what Fred is like."

Trefor shrugged. "It's only for a bit of fun." They all laughed, each with their own thoughts about how this prank would be received by Fred.

They didn't have long to wait. On the Thursday morning a couple of women were waiting for the postman at the front gates of their houses, on the opposite side of the street to where Fred and Colin lived. They could see him making his way slowly up the steep hill. He paused outside Fred's house and re-read the address. He needed to be sure, for this house never received any post, but it appeared there was a surcharge to be paid for this particular delivery.

"Is anyone living in this house? It looks empty to me!" he called across the street to the two women.

"There should be. I don't think they are in work this week but you might have to knock really hard," came the prompt reply.

The postman nodded his thanks and began banging on the door with the side of his fist. This went on for more than a minute, and he was about to walk away when Fred appeared at the door wearing just his vest. The postman looked him up and down in disgust. Fred looked down at himself, grinned and said "Oops, sorry," and disappeared to return moments later in his working trousers.

The postman informed Fred: "There's a surcharge on this letter, if you want it!"

"What is it?" Fred asked, eyeing the thick envelope suspiciously. He thought it might be a solicitor's letter from his departed wife.

"I don't know, do I? Listen, if you don't want it I can take it back to the depot." He was getting a bit irritated with the time he was wasting trying to deliver this letter and Fred's surliness wasn't making it any easier.

"How much is the surcharge?" Fred was still a bit wary.

"It's only a shilling!"

"Oh. A shilling, is it? Wait a minute," Fred ordered. "I'll have to go next door cos I don't have any money." He came out of the house barefooted and jumped spritely over the intervening fence to knock on Danny Thomas' door.

"Oh, good morning, Mrs Thomas. Could you please lend me a shilling to pay the postman?"

She poked her head out and looked at the postman waiting

impatiently for Fred to return. She dipped her hand into her apron pocket for her purse and handed Fred a shilling, with the reminder: "I want this back tomorrow, mind!"

Fred nodded his agreement and his thanks and jumped back over the fence.

"You will have to sign for this first." The postman held out the log book to sign his name, and then handed Fred the large buff-coloured envelope.

He stood on the doorstep, weighing the envelope in his hands, while he debated with himself on the contents. Finally making up his mind, he ripped the end of it open and a bundle of dollar bills fell out on the ground at his feet. He stared at the 'money' open mouthed and then at the postman, then back at the 'money'. Suddenly, he yelled up the stairs.

"Colin! COLIN! Come down yere quick! We've hit the bluddy jackpot." He began dancing around the bewildered postman and shouting to the women on the gate across the street. "HEY! We've hit the bluddy jackpot this time!" he waved the 'money' and the letter around his head like a banner.

The two women from across the street hurried over to get a closer look at the reason for Fred's excitement. He held out the bundle of 'money' for them to see and then began dancing around them too.

Colin peered from around the front door at his father's antics. He was still running back and forth on the street calling on everyone to witness his good fortune. "Hey, Fred!" he yelled. "What the 'ell are you up to now? Have you gone mad?"

"No, no. I haven't. Come and look at this, will you!"

Colin pulled on his boots and walked over to where Fred was still walking barefoot on the street. He handed the cover letter to Colin, who read through it quickly. "Daddy, this is about our Shirley. She 'ave won this money on the Kentucky Derby and you are to look after it for her."

Fred stopped dead in his tracks. 'What do you mean look after it for her? This money is ours.'

"No, it isn't. This letter says you 'ave to change these dollars into British money and keep it in trust for her at a bank. This is not ours."

"Isn't it, by damn?" Fred said, his temper rising rapidly. "We'll see about that! She's living a long way from yere, remember." A moment later he said, "I know, we'll go and see Trefor Plough. He'll know what to do. C'mon, let's get dressed and go and see 'im. P'raps we can get 'im to take us to Aberdare to the bank because we've got no money to catch a bus."

"What bank? We don't have a bluddy bank!"

"Well, we'll find one. Gimme that letter, let's see what it says."

They both turned as one and went back into the house, leaving their neighbours dumbstruck by all this activity and excitement so early in the morning. Fred washed and shaved as quick as he could, then he waited impatiently while Colin counted the dollars.

"How much is there, Colin?"

"Well, I've counted it twice and I think we've got $185,000."

"What! That's a bluddy fortune. Well done, our Shirley. She always was a lucky girl," Fred grinned. "We can buy a few things for ourselves out of this. Some new guns for a start, and maybe a new Jack Russell. Our Judy is getting a bit past it now. Shirl can give us that for keeping it safe for her." He picked up the letter again and read through it. "It says to keep it in trust for her. Well, she can trust me. We should be able to get a car out of this too."

"Aye," said Colin. "Trust you? No, by damn, she can't, not the Fred I know. C'mon, let's go and see Trefor Plough." Colin stuffed all the dollar bills into the side pockets of his jacket and went down the hill, almost at a run, in the direction of the Plough, with Fred scurrying about 20 yards behind him.

Arriving at the front door of the Plough, Fred banged on it

with the side of his fist. Trefor, sitting down at the table in the back kitchen having his breakfast, glanced at the clock on the wall and instinctively knew it was Fred. He didn't get up right away, slowly lifting the cup of tea to his lips then waiting until Fred had banged on the door a few more times. "Who's there?" he shouted, knowing full well who it was.

"It's me, Trefor." The sound was a bit muffled. Fred must have had his mouth right up against the door panels.

"What do you want that's so important at this time of the morning?" Trefor was grinning to himself as he leaned his weight against the door.

"I need to go to the bank. It's very important."

"The bank?" Trefor called back. "What bank are you talking about? They are not open yet, it's much too early. Anyway, I didn't know you had a bank."

"I don't," Fred bleated, "but I need one now. Can you please open the door?"

"Wait a minute, then!" said Trefor. He slowly unlocked the numerous locks on the front door and listened to Fred mumbling something to Colin. "Now then, Fred, what's going on here then?"

"Trefor, look at this lot, then," they said in unison as they held out the bundles of bank notes for him to see.

"*Arglwydd Mawr*! Come inside quick, before someone sees you!" Trefor stepped quickly to one side to let them in, and walked back to the kitchen and sat down to finish his tea. "So tell me, where in the world did all this come from, then?" Trefor, asked, his voice almost in a whisper.

"From America," Fred whispered back.

"How much have you got there?" Trefor asked in the same low voice.

"Our Colin and the letter says we've got 185,000 in American money," Fred whispered in reply.

"What the 'ell are you two whispering about?" demanded Colin, looking from one to the other.

"Oh aye," Fred grinned. "There's nobody about out there, Tref."

Trefor smiled. "I've got a bit of a sore throat, that's all. So, what are you doing here, then, Fred? I'm not taking any old Yankee money to clear your debts and that goes for the both of you…"

"No, no," Fred cut in quickly. "We want you to take us to Aberdare to the bank. You tell 'im, Colin."

"Trefor, my father got this letter in the post this morning and when he opened it two bundles of American dollars fell out of it. Our Shirley, you know she's out in America, well, she won a pile of money on a ticket she've bought in the Kentucky Derby and the Yanks 'ave sent it all to Fred," he nodded in his father's direction, "to look after for her…"

Trefor started laughing as he repeated, "Fred to look after it for her? You must be joking, Colin."

"Trefor, be serious." Colin began pulling bundles of banknotes from his side pockets and stacked them on the table. "Just look at what we've got!"

"Oh, I see," Trefor stood up and leaned on the table to look down at the stacks of banknotes. "So what do you want me to do about all this, then? I suppose it is real, is it? You know what some American conmen's tricks are like!"

"Of course it is! It came in the post and as I asked you before, Trefor," Fred's tone now was one of pleading, "all we want you to do is take us to Aberdare, so we can find a bank to change all this," he pointed to the stack of notes, "to British pounds." He paused, then said lamely. "So we can keep it safe and look after it for our Shirley."

"What bank?"

"I don't care what bank. Any bank will do. Read this letter." Fred pulled the slightly crumpled letter from his inside pocket and handed it to Trefor. "Our Shirley has hit the jackpot for us out in America, see!"

Trefor slowly read the terms of the letter out loud and said: "Wait a minute, Fred! This money isn't really yours, you know!"

"Yes, it is!" Fred raised his voice to emphasise his right to claim it.

"Okay. Let me read the letter again, then!" Fred tried to retrieve the letter, but Trefor avoided his outstretched fingers easily by moving slowly around the kitchen table, all the while reading the letter out loud, with Fred trailing no more than two feet behind him. He was playing Fred like a fly fisherman with a good catch on the end of his line. He came to a sudden halt. Turning to face Fred, Trefor said, in the sternest voice he could muster, "Fred, if you use any of this money for your own use to buy anything at all, I think it would be very dishonest of you, because all of this belongs to your daughter."

"Trefor! Never you mind about all that!" Fred shouted. "She is my daughter and it's my family. You look after yours and I'll look after mine!"

"Right, you! Out you go, boys, this very minute!" Trefor shouted, giving him a sharp push, knowing full well that Fred would immediately change his attitude.

"Aaw! C'mon, Tref," Fred's tone was now pleading. "All we want is for you to take us Aberdare." After a moment he added, "Please."

Trefor was beginning to think it might be a good idea to try and put Fred off with this bank business, just in case. "It's still not right! Tell him, Colin! It all belongs to your sister. For goodness' sake, boys! It just isn't the honest thing to do."

"I don't think she'll mind, Tref. We heard she's having a good time out there and we don't know when we'll see her, so what's the difference?"

"Well, I don't want to be a party to any of this. You know I'm an honest businessman and I can't afford to be involved in any fraudulent dealings, like this is."

Fred looked across the table at Colin and winked. "Listen, Tref. You want mine and Colin's IOUs cleared up, don't you?"

"Well, yes. They have been going on for quite a spell now and yes, I would really like them to be paid up as soon as possible."

"Okay, then! We'll pay your petrol to Aberdare and back and then you are not involved because we 'ave only asked you to give us a lift there and back. Okay?" Trefor nodded and seemed lost in thought for a few moments, as if weighing up the pros and cons of the situation, when in fact he was almost bursting with laughter inside as he looked at the comical expressions on their faces while they waited impatiently for his decision.

"Well," he paused momentarily. "Okay, but you'll have to wait until I wash and shave, have a cup of tea and clear away all my breakfast things, then we'll go, right?"

Fred pulled a face and looked askance at his son, but Colin was busy on the other side of the table counting and recounting the stacks of dollar notes over and over while muttering to himself, "Bluddy marvellous, bluddy marvellous."

"Can't all that wait?" Fred was more anxious than ever to get going, now that Colin was busy cramming the bank notes back into his side pockets.

Trefor ignored Fred's pleas and asked Colin, "How much in dollars did you say you have?"

Colin, grinning all over his face with delight, replied. "At the last count we've got 185,000 dollars, Tref!"

"That's a tidy sum, I must admit. Right you are, then. I'll go and shave first. I'll be back in a minute." Ten minutes later he came back into the kitchen. "Oh, wait a minute. I forgot," and began to clear the food off the table and back into the cupboards. By this time Fred was biting his nails in frustration at Trefor's apparent delaying tactics and said as politely as he could manage, "Time is getting on, Trefor."

"I won't be a minute, Fred, and then we can be on our way." They went out through the front door, with Fred leading the way as Trefor carefully locked up and walked slowly to the car park at the side of the pub. He started up his van and with Fred in the front seat and Colin sitting on a small wooden box right behind him, they set off down the lane.

"I'll have to stop in Waun-gron for petrol on our way down the valley to Aberdare," Trefor announced brightly. "We don't want to be stuck on the road on such an important mission, do we? Especially with all that money you boys have." Fred was about to say something in reply when Colin put his hand on his father's shoulder and Fred bit back whatever it was he had thought to say.

Trefor, being a very cautious driver, drove right on the speed limit, all the while chattering about any old rubbish he could think of.

Meanwhile, Fred was on pins to get into the town at the bottom of the valley as quickly as possible, but when they finally arrived, Trefor found a parking space as far away from the centre of town and the banks as he could, and said it might be better if they walked the rest of the way.

"Do you have a bank in mind, Fred?"

"I don't know anything about any bluddy banks," Fred growled as they walked through the top end of town. Colin meanwhile was marching step for step behind Trefor's bulk, hands deep in the pockets where the money was, eyes casting from side to side as they went past a row of shops which were just starting to open up. Eventually they arrived at the front door of the Midway Bank, just as the main doors were being opened for that day's business.

"There you are, boys! See, I got you here bang on time, despite all the fuss you were making, Fred!" He smiled. "Well, gentlemen, shall we go in?"

Fred pushed his way through the glass swing doors and looked around with a kind of awe at the highly polished woodwork and the gleaming glass of the partitions on the wide counter. The young lady behind the glass smiled at Fred and asked him if she could be of assistance. Fred stepped forward smartly with Colin right on his heels, and said in a whisper, "We want to see the Manager, please." She smiled again, then asked Fred if he had an appointment.

"No," said Fred. 'We don't have an appointment."

"Then I'm sorry, sir, but you cannot see the Manager without a time and a date."

Fred looked at her in utter disbelief. "Hey! Wait a minute here," he whispered fiercely, leaning forward on the counter. "We've got all this stuff to put into the bank! Show 'er, Col!" Colin pushed his way past his father and planted a handful of the dollars on the counter in front of her.

"See!" whispered Fred. "We've got a lot more of this sort of money so it's important that we see the manager about it as soon as possible."

The sight of such a large number of bank notes caused her to consult the tall supervisor standing close behind her, who in turn looked over her shoulder at the pile of notes, and disappeared in a hurry through the glass door at the end of the counter without a word to Fred. The supervisor had opened his mouth to say something, but no sound had come out.

Fred and Colin just stood there, fretting at the delay, looking at each other, not realising that that there was a protocol to be observed as per the bank's rules of business. Finally the glass door at the end of the long counter half opened and the supervisor's head poked around the edge. He beckoned to them to come through.

Colin swept up the bank notes in an instant and followed Fred through the door with the landlord close behind him. They found themselves in a sort of anteroom with chairs along one wall and three doors leading off the other walls. One of them had the impressive title 'Manager' in large gold lettering on the upper panel. The tall supervisor pointed to it, nodding his head slowly with an air of reverence.

"Okay," Fred replied in a whisper, totally overawed by the silence in the small room. "Can we go in and see him now?" The supervisor, who still hadn't uttered a single word to either Fred, Colin or Trefor, knocked softly on the door and waited a moment, before opening it and ushering the three of them into the manager's inner sanctum.

The manager, resplendent in a black pinstripe three-piece suit and with a small red flower in his lapel, was ensconced behind the most enormous desk they had ever seen. Fred stopped dead in his tracks, his mouth opening and closing like that of a goldfish as he stared at the bank manager as if he was some sort of demigod from another world.

"Excuse me, sir," Fred still spoke in a whisper. "We've got a lot of money..." He paused and then, as if the very sound of the word 'money' had given him a boost of adrenaline and galvanised him into action, he regained his normal voice and said, "Quick Colin, grab those chairs and follow me!" They quickly moved the chairs across the room to place them right up to the front of the manager's desk.

The manager appeared quite unconcerned with this rearrangement of the office furniture and sat quietly, his hands fingertips steepled and barely touching, with an expression of mild interest as Colin pulled bundles of banknotes from his pockets and stacked them in order on the polished surface of his desk, delving into each pocket in turn to make sure he hadn't anything left. There was still no sound in the office except the rustling of paper as Colin separated the notes into their various denominations. Finally, Fred settled himself on the chair and addressed the manager.

"Sir, I have in my possession a letter from the office of the American State Department to say my daughter has won a lot of money on their Kentucky Derby and I'm to look after it for her." He took the crumpled letter from his pocket and pushed it across the desk towards the manager. "Now then, what do you think of that, then, eh?" He looked around the room with a smirk on his face and nodded to Trefor who was sitting against the far wall, enjoying a grandstand view of the whole proceedings, which in his heart he knew had now got completely out of hand and as a practical joke would be very difficult to explain, once the truth came out.

"Hmm!" said the manager, uttering the first sound they had heard since entering the room. He said "Hmm!" again while he adjusted his gold-rimmed spectacles to glance through the letter Fred had given him. He looked up at his supervisor, who was standing almost at attention slightly to one side of the manager. "Would you be good enough to obtain this number in Cardiff? I wish to speak with this gentleman," he said in soft tones, as he pointed to the signature at the bottom of the page.

The supervisor disappeared in an instant through the door to the outer office and was back alongside his manager before Fred had time to blink, or so it seemed. He looked up at him and his face was a picture of suspicion as he leaned forward to whisper something urgently in his manager's ear. The manager looked up in alarm and glanced quickly at Fred and then at the pile of banknotes.

Fred's instincts for survival came to life in a split second and his stomach turned over. In that instant he knew, beyond all doubt, that something was very wrong. He looked quickly from one to the other in the room, his gaze resting a just split second longer on the landlord, who was sitting quite still, hands clasped together across his ample middle, without any expression at all on his round face.

Fred swung round to face the desk and picked one of the banknotes off the pile in front of his son and scrutinised it carefully. 'It looks okay to me,' he thought. The bank manager looked from Fred to Colin and back again without moving his chair. Fred's stomach began churning again as the deathly silence continued. Meanwhile Colin, unaware of Fred's feeling of doom was carefully stacking and re-stacking the pile of banknotes.

The manager picked up the letter and read through it again and then a second time, glancing at Fred at the end of each reading. Fred was getting more and more uneasy at the continued silence. "Hmm, and how did you say you came by this large sum of money, Mr Howells?" the manager asked politely, in a soft voice.

"Well, it was my daughter, see! I mean she's in America and, I mean, it came by post to me today!" Fred was getting confused by everything at that moment because his instinct was telling him he was in some sort of trouble but he didn't know why.

"It is your money though, Mr Howells, isn't it?"

"Well, yes. Well I mean it's, it's, well, it belongs to the family and I'm in charge of it! Isn't that right, Colin?"

Colin was staring open-mouthed at his father. He had never seen him in such a state before. "Yes, daddy. Mr Manager, he's in charge for our Shirley."

"Oh, I see. So you're in charge of this money and completely responsible for it. Am I correct in assuming that, Mr Howells?"

"Yes, you are, sir," Fred replied, feeling more and more that he was up to his neck in something he didn't quite understand.

There was a long pause and then the manager asked Fred, "Could you hand me one of those banknotes, Mr Howells, please. Any one will do. It doesn't matter which."

Reluctantly Fred selected a hundred dollar banknote off one of the stacks in front of Colin and slid it across the desk with his finger tips toward the bank manager.

He didn't immediately pick it up but leaned forward and adjusted his spectacles to carefully scrutinise it, then he just as carefully turned it over to study the reverse side of the note. He looked up at Fred and asked in a mild tone, "So how much did you say you have in your possession, Mr Howells?"

"$185,000, sir." Fred beamed. 'This was more like it,' he thought. 'There can't be anything wrong with it now,' remembering Trefor's earlier warning about American conmen.

"I see," said the manager, then turning to his supervisor, he said in much harder tone of voice, "Would you be kind enough to call in the local police for these two gentlemen because these banknotes are counterfeit in every respect and I would say that what has been attempted here is tantamount to fraud on a grand scale!"

Fred was thunderstruck. His face went white in a second as he collapsed in his chair gasping for air, but he had the presence of mind to cry out weakly: "I am innocent of the charge, sir. I've been had!"

Colin sat motionless with his mouth hanging open, clutching a handful of banknotes.

The manager, looking quickly from one to the other, could see in an instant that the intrepid pair were obviously the innocent dupes of a very unkind practical joke. "Hughes, fetch this man a glass of water and some aspirin right away before he faints."

Trefor watched all this with some trepidation. It hadn't been meant to go this far at all. Johnny had said it could go wrong, especially with Fred in the middle of it. Mentally he shrugged. It will have to run its course now; but he reassured himself, hopefully nothing much will come of it.

Fred was wringing his hands and practically in tears as he

repeated almost to himself. "Oh *Duw*! Oh *Duw*! How could they do this to me?" he lamented, looking at each of them in turn. "And me on Security with the NCB wages van too. What am I going to do now, Colin? What can we do now?"

"Just calm down a minute," said the manager. "These so-called 'bank notes' you have brought in here are printed as 'confederate' money to commemorate the American Civil War and are worthless at this time, or any other time, for that matter, Mr Howells. However," he said heavily, "there will have to be an inquiry on what has transpired here today, and the police, whom Hughes here has already called, will need to interview you in this regard!"

Fred clung to the sides of his chair and mumbled over and over. "Oh *Duw*! I'm too old to go to jail!"

The manager looked across the room at Trefor, who was still sitting with his hands clasped across his ample midriff, calmly watching what was going on. "And you, sir! What do you know about all this nonsense?"

"Not a thing, sir," he replied blandly. "They knocked on my door early this morning and asked me to bring them here so they could pay off their debts to me. Isn't that right, Fred?"

Fred pulled himself together momentarily to reply to Trefor's question. "Oh yes. That's quite true. Oh *Duw*! What am I going to do?" and promptly slumped back into the chair waving his arms weakly to and fro muttering almost to himself. "I've had such bad luck. My wife has left me, I'm flat broke and my rent is going up and now this and I'll most likely lose my security job with the NCB."

The manager looked up at his supervisor and then at Fred and Colin and shook his head. "Well, let's get this all sorted out right away. Could you check if the policeman has arrived to take some statements from these two gentlemen, and of course the other gentleman over there."

Fred looked as if he was about to wet himself at that. Moments later a constable walked into the office and saw Fred slumped in the chair in front of the desk. He said in some surprise, "Hello, Fred! What have you been up to, then?"

The manager looked at the constable in some surprise. "You know these men?"

The constable gave a short laugh. "Oh yes. We come from the same village, Waun-gron, and I've known these boys for years. So what's the problem?"

The manager went on to explain what had occurred and his claim of attempted fraud against Fred and Colin, with both Fred and Colin nodding vigorously at every step in his narration. Later when statements from everyone had been taken, the manager took the constable to one side and spoke quietly to him for some minutes with frequent sideways glances at Fred and Colin.

When at last the preliminary investigation was complete and statements taken from each of them, he approached Fred, who looked as though he was ready to break into tears again, and informed them they were free to leave pending further investigation into whether other charges could be laid against them, apart from the charge of attempted fraud. Meanwhile all the banknotes, envelope and covering letter would be forensically examined and used as evidence against them if and when their case came to court.

Fred's thanks at this information was overwhelming now that he knew he wasn't going to be taken to a cell in the police station. He thanked the manager, his assistant and of course the constable, and also Trefor the landlord, and anybody else in the bank.

"You are not out of the woods yet, Fred – er, Mr Howells," the constable reminded him sternly. "What has gone on here today is very serious, very serious indeed. My advice to you both would be, be very careful what you say from now on."

"Oh, I know!" Fred bleated. "But I am innocent, George, and our Colin is, too!" he added, wringing his hands.

Moments later, Fred, Colin and the landlord were ushered out of the manager's office and into the brightness of the morning sunshine on the street outside.

Pale-faced, Fred leaned against the wall of the bank and muttered to the others, "Well, boys," he said weakly, "we're in it now, right up to our bluddy necks. Who would do such a thing to me? What a dirty trick to play on someone!" Then in the very next breath he said, "Damn, I could do with a pint or two to put me right after all that fuss in there." He nodded his head sideways in the direction of the bank.

Trefor's face lit up with a broad smile as he caught onto Fred's arm. "And I know the very place! C'mon boys, it's almost opening time and I know a pub just a few yards up the road from where we're standing." Suiting action to words he turned and led the way towards a large pub he could see in the distance, on the corner of the town square.

At this, Fred brightened up. He had the uncanny ability to bounce back from almost any devastating situation on the promise of a free pint. This maxim appeared to work even when he was extremely sick: a pint would always put him back on his feet.

Colin throughout the debacle in the bank hadn't spoken a single word, except to give his version of the events to the constable, and now stood unmoving alongside his father with a dazed expression on his thin features.

Fred came to life as soon as Trefor began walking away and, grabbing his son by the arm, pulled him along the street in Trefor's wake. Eventually they reached the gloomy-looking pub, and Trefor made his way quickly to the bar. "I would like three large whiskies right away, and then two pints of best bitter to follow," he ordered, with a smile at the buxom barmaid.

The barmaid looked from one to the other, making a mental note of the pale complexion on the other two, standing, as if uncertain what to do, in the centre of the room. She moved smoothly to the line of optics on the wall behind the bar and placed a double whisky in front of each of them in quick succession.

Fred grabbed the glass in front of him with both hands and shakily raised it to finish the drink in one gulp, pulling a wry face as he did so, not being used to drinking the fiery liquid, much less gulping it down in one go. Colin, following his father's lead, did the same thing.

"Aaah," said Fred, swishing his tongue around his mouth. "I'll have that pint now, if you please." The barmaid lost no time in pulling a foaming pint of best bitter for him and placing it on the bar in front of him. Fred had his hand on the glass almost before she could let go of it and raising the glass, he drained it to within an inch of the bottom in one movement. Before Colin could reach for his pint, Fred finished his own and was already calling for a refill.

"I'm glad you two are not regulars in here," the barmaid said with a short laugh, "or I wouldn't have time to serve anybody else."

"Well, you haven't been through what has happened to us, remember! What do you say, boys?"

"Oh? What's that then?" The barmaid's curiosity was aroused by their vague remark.

"Never you mind, but I'll tell you this. It was a bluddy let down, and a 'ell of a fright for us into the bargain!"

The landlord sat quietly a few chairs away from the Partners, nursing his drink and watching Fred regain his normal ebullience.

"Yes!" Fred started again. "We thought we were rich, and I mean really rich!" He stopped speaking to look at his son, all the while nodding his head as if in confirmation.

"Well, go on then!" she prompted, determined to get some of the story out of him.

"Nah! It's a bit of a secret really and we might get into trouble, right, Col?"

"Right," echoed Colin, finishing his second pint. "Fill 'er up, please."

"C'mon, boys, what's the real story, then? She had a burning desire to know what had transpired earlier that morning. "Tell you what," she paused momentarily. "I'll buy each of you a pint, okay? But I want the full story," she said, looking towards Trefor, who appeared to be lost in thought and was taking no part in the discussion. Turning back to Fred, she added.

"Look, there's nobody else in here except us few, so come on, what happened to you boys this morning, then?"

"Well," Fred said expansively, squaring his shoulders. "We had a lot of money sent to us in the post – $185,000 and I had to borrow a shilling to get it because there wasn't enough stamps on the envelope, right, Col?"

"Right, Daddy," he replied, pushing his empty glass towards the barmaid.

"And, we went to change them at this bank, right, Col?"

"Right enough, daddy," Colin picked up the foaming pint and looked at it speculatively against the light over the bar while the barmaid, without taking her eyes off Fred, pulled another foaming pint and placed it front of him. Fred suddenly realised that here was a golden chance to turn misfortune into a money-spinner, or, in this case, a free beer spinner.

"Sooo, we had all this money. Yankee money it was and..." he was searching for the right words and repeated... "We had all this money and we went to change it into pounds and then they found out it was counterfeit Confederate banknotes…"

"Tell 'er how you fainted when they said they were not real." Colin grinned at his father's shocked expression,

"Hey! Colin. I didn't faint, okay!"

"So why did they have to bring you a few glasses of water and some aspirin to bring you around, then?"

"But you're not crooks, though, are you?" she cut in, breaking up the budding dispute about what actually happened in the bank manager's office.

"Nah! We're just a couple of old working boys. Have you ever seen a couple of crooks looking like us two?" Fred grinned and the landlord, who was now watching his antics, knew he was back on form. It always amazed him the transformation a few pints could work on him in times of adversity.

"I wouldn't know a crook if I saw one," she replied, giving a short laugh.

"So anyway," Fred went on, "the manager said they were forgeries and sent for the police. So there you are! Now the police have got our money and we might be charged with attempted fraud." His face began to show signs of self-pity again as he thought about his current problems and those that might yet be on the horizon from this morning's escapade.

Seeing this, Trefor roused himself from his seat and called out to him, "C'mon, Fred. Last pint, boys, then we'll have to go. I have to open up my own pub and we're late already."

"Well, in that case, we'll come back with you to the Plough, and you can give us a pint while we try to think who would pull such a dirty trick on us."

"You can come back with me all right but you can forget any idea of me giving you free pint, that's a non-starter. You've already had a double whisky and four free pints out of this morning's nonsense, so leave it there!"

"Aye, you're right enough, Tref," Fred said agreeably. He was back to good spirits. The morning's fright was rapidly dimming in his memory.

"Yes, boys! From now on I'm going to be called the Dollar Boy, and not Fred Rats."

They all laughed out loud at this sally as he bowed towards the barmaid and thanked her for the free beer. She in turn, laughed at his attempted gallantry and thanked him for the story of their early morning escapades. She knew it would make for a good yarn to relate in her bar later that day.

Outside, Fred, Colin and the landlord made their way back up the High Street in a very different mood to when they had passed that way earlier in the day. Fred and Colin, their dreams shattered, had come back to earth with an almighty bang, from being newly rich to their former state of being close to poverty.

Meanwhile, Trefor was alone with his thoughts of what might happen to himself and the other conspirators when the truth finally came out via the projected police investigation. His stomach churned at the very thought and he sighed. It had been a good practical joke. Unfortunately it had sort of got out of hand because Fred had not done what was expected of him. Damn, but what a story to tell in the Plough tonight. 'I wouldn't mind betting there'll be 'ell of a place there when this tale gets around. Fred is in fine form as it is, with free beer under his belt and no breakfast. It's probably worth the inquiry for the fun we'll have.' He turned to look back at the pair of them window shopping. They would give anyone the impression that this was the first time they had ever been in a town this large.

At that moment, Fred had paused in front of a jeweller's to point out some expensive watches to his son, and speaking just loud enough for him to hear, he said: "Der, Colin, just look at those beauties. We could 'ave bought us one each, but it wasn't to be, was it?" With frequent stops at a variety of shop windows, it took some time to get back to where Trefor had left his van. They piled in and made their way back up the valley road to Rhyd-y-groes, with all the talk centring on the money, and who it could be that had created their current misfortune.

"I'll bluddy 'ave them, Fred said grimly, "whoever they are."

"What about the police then? If they can't find out, we won't have much chance, will we?"

"I dunno," Fred replied, his anger a bit deflated by the prospect of not knowing or finding out for sure. "Oh, to 'ell with them. We 'aven't really cheated anybody, 'ave we, Tref?"

"I don't think so," he replied, without taking his eyes off the road ahead. Moments later they arrived at the Plough, where a few of his staunchest customers were sitting on the wooden bench opposite the front door of the pub.

"About time you got here!" they shouted in unison. "We've been waiting almost an hour already."

Fred was the first out of the van. "Mind your own bluddy business," he shouted back at them "We've been away on special business, so be quiet!"

"Oh aye, we've all heard about some of your nonsense from the Bryn this morning," Mock said, laughing. "Had a bit of a pull, 'ave you?"

"Listen yere, Mock," Fred started but Colin caught him by the arm and whispered, "Don't say anything yet, Daddy. Wait till later when there's a crowd."

Fred's mouth closed like a steel trap and the two of them followed Trefor into the gloom of the pub and into the back kitchen and sat down.

"Hey, you two," Trefor raised his voice to a shout. "Go out into the bar right away. You've got no business being in yere!"

"Hey, wait a bluddy minute," Fred replied snappily. "We're both starving. How about you giving us a piece of bread and butter, then?" He pleaded his case so pitifully that Trefor relented and allowed them to sit at his table, where they helped themselves to a couple of slices of bread and butter whilst he went through to the bar to serve his already impatient customers. Minutes later when he returned to the kitchen, he stopped dead in his tracks in the doorway.

Fred, ever the opportunist, had found that the landlord had put a pound of pork sausages in a roasting pan in the oven on the side of the fireplace, and in his absence they had gently cooked to perfection. He had also found a couple of plates, and had already dished up a generous helping of the landlord's dinner for each of them.

"Damn you, Fred Howells! You're a cheeky sod and no mistake! Get from my table and out of here right now!"

"Aw, Come on, Trefor!" Fred mumbled, his mouth full of sausage. "You're going to make a lot of money from me and our Colin over this morning's escapade, so what's a couple of bangers and a bit of bread and butter between friends? Not very much."

Trefor, for once, was at a loss for words and was beginning to regret ever getting involved in this practical joke, which was starting to prove a costly venture. Fred hadn't as yet got into his full stride. That was yet to come – Trefor could feel it in his bones.

"Right then, boys! Finish up and be quick about it and get out there into the bar with no more nonsense!"

Ten minutes later in the bar, Fred became the centre of attention, as the story of him dancing barefoot in the street had become public knowledge. "Well, c'mon then, Fred! What's been happening today, then?" Bobby was more than curious since for the past hour Trefor had been dropping hints that Fred and Colin had been involved in something big and they were the only ones able to relate the story.

Fred refused to be drawn into any discussion at first, but as the beer began to loosen his tongue, he began strutting to and fro, one hand on his hip in his usual style when he wanted to be noticed. Finally, after many prompts from his audience, he was ready to spill the beans with a touch of pride.

"Well boys, today me and our Colin 'ave had a 'ell of a time…"

"Oh aye. We've heard a bit about it already," Jimmy interrupted "I heard you've had a bit of a windfall, haven't you?"

"Well, you could say that," Fred replied, smirking. He was now in his element, strutting back and forth and the centre of attention.

"Let me tell you, boys. You don't know the half of it, do they Col?"

"No, Daddy, they don't," Colin was slurring his words by this time. "If they only knew half the truth…" He started laughing.

"Okay then, Fred! How much money did you win?" Bobby asked from his seat at the card table.

"Win? I didn't win anything. Our Shirley did out in America. That's where all this started," he said with just a touch of bragging.

"How much then, Fred?"

"$185,000, if you must know. How about that, then?" Fred had decided to brazen it out for a while just to see how much capital he could make out of the day's misfortunes.

"$185,000? I don't believe that for one minute," Jimmy said, derisively.

"Nor me too," Old John added from his seat on the settle alongside the stove. "Never! *Byth*!"

"Trefor!" Willi Bray called out from across the bar. "Did you see that much money with Fred at any time today?"

"Well, since you've asked me I would have to say yes, I did see Fred with a lot of paper money that looked like American dollars."

"Aha! Looked like dollars! That's what you said, 'looked like dollars' – but were they? And if they were, where are they now? C'mon Fred, show us."

Despite his best efforts to avoid telling everyone the truth, Fred had painted himself into a corner and he knew there was no way out now.

"You can't see them at the moment," he paused and took a deep breath, then added, "because the police are holding on to them at the moment until they have an investigation."

He looked at the shocked faces around the bar as everyone said, "The police?"

"Hey, Fred! Did you rob a bluddy bank or something?" Jimmy was holding his sides in laughter.

"Hey, boys! What's the name of that famous American bank robber? Something Nelson, wasn't it?" Roy said joining in the laughter.

Mock, sitting on the tall stool at the bar, turned around and said, "Okay, Fred! I'll buy you a pint of best bitter to spill the beans on the whole story."

"Only one pint? Boys, this story is worth more than one bluddy pint. Any more offers for an almost old age pensioner?"

"I'm in for another pint, Fred," said Alan, smiling at Fred's expectant face.

"Well, okay. This morning first thing I got this big envelope in the post, but I couldn't have it until I paid a shilling because there was not enough stamps on it." He grinned. "Boys, I didn't have any money so I had to borrow a shilling from next door. Well, I opened the package and two bundles of bank notes fell on my feet. Der! I had a shock. It was all dollars, more than I had ever seen in one place before. So we went to this bank…"

"Hey, Fred!" Colin called out from his seat to one side of the card players. "Go back before that!"

"What are you talking about, Colin?"

"Before, we went to the bank, Daddy. Trefor, you had better tell the story because you are sober, not like us," he grinned in a lopsided manner. "And you sat in the bank manager's office with us when everything went nuts."

Trefor looked up from pulling a pint, his round features beaming. "Well, I can only say what I saw and heard this morning, if that's what you want me to do."

"C'mon, Tref, tell us in your own words," Alan prompted him.

"Well, I can only say what I know. You all appear to know the first part when Fred got the money in the post. Next thing, I hear a hammering on my front door and it was early, like. Turned out it was Fred and Colin, and they wanted me to take them down the valley to Aberdare to look for a bank. I wanted to know why, and then Colin showed me all these dollars. I didn't look too close at them; for Fred's sake, I wish I had now. Anyway, we found a bank that was just opening and Fred asked to see the manager, nobody else would do, mind, and the young lady behind the counter asked him if he had an appointment. You should have seen the look he gave her!"

At this point Fred was strutting up and down the room in his normal pose, one hand on his hip, a pint in his free hand and nodding agreement with everything that Trefor related.

"Things began to move a bit quick after Colin pulled out a handful of banknotes and plonked them on the counter. The tall chap, standing behind her, disappeared like a flash through the glass door at the end of the counter and next thing we were being taken in to see the manager, who was sitting behind this huge desk. Fred and Colin dragged some chairs across the office right up to the front of the boss's desk. While this was going on I was sitting on a chair right by the door, but I could see and hear everything that was going on. Then Colin took all the cash from his pocket and stacked it on the manager's desk, and Fred gave him the letter that had come with the money. The manager read it through a couple of times, and asked his chap, Hughes, to call the number in Cardiff.

"It was then they found out it was fake. The manager asked Fred to pass him one of the banknotes and that, boys, was when they found out the money was all phony stuff. He told Fred in a stern voice. 'This is a job for the police,' and Fred fainted."

Fred stopped strutting in mid stride. "Hey! I didn't bluddy faint! That's a lie, Trefor."

Colin stood up, swaying slightly, and through a haze of beer fumes, said, "Oh yes, you did, Daddy!" Which caused more fits of laughter.

"Yes, Fred," Trefor went on. "I'm sorry to say it in front of everyone here but you did, and that is why the manager ordered his chap to fetch you a glass of water and some headache pills. By this time you were almost flat out in the chair. Boys, he was as limp as a wet sock..." Everybody in the room broke up at that. Even Fred couldn't help joining in at the description of that defining moment.

"And when he came round a little bit, he started waving his arms around and calling out, 'I'm innocent of all charges, Mr Manager', and then he said, 'How could anyone do this to me? I'm on Security with the NCB!' With that, in comes a policeman, and straight away he says, 'Hello Fred!' Even the manager was surprised and asked him how he knew Fred. 'Oh,' he said, 'we grew up in the same village, Waun-gron, and I've known him for years. He's harmless enough.' Fred just sat there with his mouth opening and closing, but no sounds came out..."

"Hey, Fred, did he put handcuffs on you?" Jimmy shouted out, interrupting Trefor's story.

"No, by damn, it was nothing like that!" Fred shouted back in an instant.

"Hey, Jimmy!" Alan called out from his spot at the end of the bar. "Stop interrupting and let Trefor finish his story, mun. This is a good laugh and I've paid for a pint to hear it."

"What letter, Fred?" Jimmy interrupted again.

"Hey, Jimmy, be quiet like Alan says," Fred told him, impatiently. "This is my bluddy story…"

"Mine too," Colin mumbled, in the advanced state of alcoholic appreciation.

"Colin, be quiet for a minute." Fred was desperately trying to gather his thoughts. Draining his glass, he ordered the landlord to "Fill 'er up." Fresh pint in hand and standing in the centre of the room, he looked around at his captive audience. "Right you are, boys. Now where was I? Oh yeh! This Hughes chap phones the number in Cardiff and tells the manager it's no good. So he looks at the bank note and says they are counterfeit and this was tanta… this was tanta… What was it, Col?"

"Tantamount to fraud." Colin's reply was a little slurred.

"Yes, that's right, on a grand something…"

"Fair play to you, Fred, you don't do anything by halves, do you?" Willi Bray cut in, laughing at Fred's expression as he tried to remember the manager's exact words.

Trefor, his round face beaming, called out. "This is what he said to you, Fred. 'This is tantamount to fraud on a grand scale,' and I'm willing to swear to that on a stack of Bibles."

Fred looked stunned for a split second, then he said, with a touch of excitement in his voice. "Hear that, boys? He accused me of fraud on a 'grand scale'. To tell the truth, I almost bluddy fainted…"

"You did bluddy faint!" Colin cut in, laughing at his father and holding his sides in pain.

"No, I didn't! I was only pretending," Fred shouted back across the room.

"Well, it didn't look like pretending to me. Isn't that right, Tref?"

"Yes, Colin," Trefor replied, laughing. "And for a moment, I thought he was going to wet himself." The crowd in the bar roared again as Fred stood in the middle of the floor with his mouth hanging open.

"Hey, you rotten sods, listen to me. LISTEN!" he shouted above the noise. "It's my bluddy story and I'm the one to say what happened…"

"Me too," Colin shouted, grinning lopsidedly at his father. The bar was again in an uproar and Trefor thought, 'This practical joke on Fred was worth it after all.'

"Okay!" Fred shouted above the noise. "Okay, if you don't want to know…"

"HEY! I paid a pint for this story, so come on Fred. Out with it or pay me the pint back." Alan cried, then called out: "ORDER IN THE BAR!" The noise abated just a little.

"Anyhow," Fred went on. "When I was better the manager sent for the cops and the constable, George Williams, who is from Waun-gron, took our statements…"

"Don't you mean confessions?" Roy, turning in his chair, looked directly at him.

Fred just glared at his tormentor. "No, I bluddy don't." He sucked in a deep breath and went on. "He said we might be charged with fraud but we don't really know what will happen next and the police have got all the money too," he finished lamely.

"Well, here's to Bonnie and Clyde," shouted Alan, raising his glass to make a toast to the Partners.

Fred likewise raised his glass, and asked in a mystified voice, "Who's Bonnie and Clyde, then?"

"Oh they were just a couple of bank robbers in the United States," laughed Alan.

"Well, I'll tell you this, boys," he said, trying to adopt a serious tone, "After today's escapade I'm going to be called 'Dollar Boy', and not 'Fred Rats'!" This drew another wave of laughter from the crowd.

During the weeks that followed, whilst the police were still pursuing their investigations, Fred made full use of the escapade at the bank by offering to regale patrons visiting the Plough with the 'true version' of that day, and unless the customer was absolutely deaf, they ended up buying him a pint or even two pints of best bitter before he would depart in search of some other unsuspecting visitor. His usual opening gambit was to ask, "I bet you don't know who I am?"

Invariably whoever it was he approached wouldn't know him from Adam and would reply in the negative. This was Fred's cue to say: "Well, I'm the Dollar Boy, and if you've got a couple of minutes to spare I'll tell you a great story of how I got my nickname!" This pestering of the landlord's customers went on for some time until the novelty of it wore a bit thin and he was told not to bother the patrons of the pub anymore. Trefor told Fred, in no uncertain terms, that because of him, he had lost a good paying customer who had come there once a week until Fred had started bothering him and his friends with his outlandish stories.

"This nonsense has to stop, and I mean right now, Fred." Fred finally took the hint, but it wouldn't take much more than a single word to set him off on another story.

CHAPTER 28

The dog show and Fred's terrier

IT WAS FRIDAY, a few days after Fred's brush with the law over the funny money, and being payday, the usual noisy crowd were in the bar of the Plough. Colin and Fred were enjoying the last few shillings that remained from Colin's gravedigger retainer fee cheque when George Teale came into the bar. He took a roll of posters from his pocket and asked Trefor if he could have permission to put one on the notice board on the wall above the piano.

"What is this all about, first?" the landlord asked, while pulling a pint.

"Oh, it's for a working dog and terrier show in Treherbert next Saturday – not tomorrow, the week after. And I'm judging one of the pedigree classes," George announced with pride.

"In that case, by all means pin the poster up there." Trefor smiled when he saw the look of disdain Fred, who was listening in, gave George.

George Teale, as Fred and some of his cronies knew, hadn't had much to do with dog shows, but he had successfully entered and won some trophies with his own Welsh Springer Spaniels, and had had even more success in breeding them and selling them all over the country. But he was a relative newcomer in the world of terriers and working dogs other than spaniels.

"What do you know about working dogs, Georgie?" Fred asked, in a challenging tone. "You haven't had dogs more than five bluddy minutes. I've had dogs all my life and I've had the best, too!" he added.

"Enter them in the show then, if they are that good," George replied sharply. He turned his back to Fred, ignoring him completely as he pinned the poster to the board.

Fred was a man who didn't like being ignored or left out of anything that was going on. He edged closer to the poster to get a better look, pint in hand and the skirt of his jacket thrown back as he leaned forward to read the small print. He studied the different classes carefully. "Hey, Colin! Come and have a look at this, will you!"

"Aye, aye. I know all about it," Colin replied from his seat at the game of four-handed cribbage, not wanting to miss anything in the cards being played. He and his partner were at that point in the game when they were almost within reach of winning a pint each from their opponents and he didn't want to be bothered with his father's opinions on a dog show right then.

"We could enter that new dog of ours," Fred continued, as if his son hadn't spoken. "He's a good-looking dog, too." Fred had found enough money to buy a young Border Terrier a few weeks before, and took it with him everywhere. "Look at this one!" He looked round at George Teale. "How about this, then, for a champion terrier?" Fred had lifted his dog and stood him on top of the piano, where the poor animal looked too afraid to move. It appeared to be too gentle a dog to be owned by someone of Fred's nature. Some Border Terriers had a natural mournful expression; this one might have sensed what life under Fred's control would be like.

"That bluddy dog doesn't look much good from where I'm

standing," George said, disdainfully. "Look at the way his ribs are sticking out. He could do with a bellyful of grub, if you ask me!" He shook his head slowly from side to side, his bottom lip pushed out. "I think he's too frail to enter a show like this." He pointed to the poster. "Perhaps when he grows up a bit he might have a chance."

Fred stood there, his mouth open in shock at George's critical remarks. "And who the 'ell are you to say things like that about my dog, Georgie Teale? You don't know a bluddy thing about dogs. Colin! We'll enter 'im, right?" Fred's voice had gone up a few decibels. His irritation at George's unkind and unfounded remarks brought his temper to the boil in an instant.

"Right you are, Daddy," Colin replied from the card table without showing very much interest in his father's dispute with George Teale.

"And," Fred paused, "we'll bet you five pints, right, Colin?"

"Right!" Colin replied, wearily. He had had enough of arguments for one week.

"Okay, George. Five pints it is."

"On what? Five pints on what, Fred?" George raised his hands despairingly. "On what, Fred?"

"That we will win over there with our Border Terrier, of course!" Fred's eyes were bright with challenge, his jaw thrust out belligerently.

"I'll tell you what then, Fred!" George paused, thinking for a few moments, wondering if he had left any loopholes through which Fred could escape. "I'll bet you five pints that you don't get through the first round of judging, and then I'll bet you another five pints you don't win anything at all, excluding the booby prize for showing up!" Sure in his mind that he had covered everything that might go wrong, he said, "Well? What about it, Fred?"

"Right. You're on, mate!" Fred replied triumphantly, looking round the bar. "Well, you all heard what the bets are, boys. Wait till next Saturday night. Then we'll see who's right about our Border Terrier. Yes, by damn, then we'll see who knows best."

"So who's going to take us over there, Fred? There's no buses running over the mountain anymore." Colin posed the question without looking up from his game of crib.

"Oh 'ell, I forgot about that." Fred's eyes cast about the room looking for a volunteer. Suddenly his eyes lit up "Hey, Georgie, you're going over there to do some of the judging aren't you? Can you give us a lift?"

"NO! Not bluddy likely. You're a cheeky sod – after all you said to me just now! Anyway, I've got to be there really early in the morning and it wouldn't look right for one of the judges to bring a contestant to the show."

"C'mon, George. Who's going to know," Fred coaxed. "Anyway, you are judging in one of the pedigree classes, aren't you?"

"You're right enough, Fred and that little thing of yours doesn't come anyway near to being a pedigree of any sort." George laughed, with contempt in his tone.

The dog still stood on the piano where Fred had placed him, head hanging down and looking thoroughly forlorn and sorry for itself. George looked sceptically at the Border Terrier. "One of my pedigree Springers would lift his leg over a pup like that. I'm not kidding, Fred." He grinned as he patted Fred on the shoulder.

George's scurrilous statement regarding the quality of Fred's young dog brought howls of laughter from some of the listeners, who were always ready to join in the fun at Fred's expense. Fred was about to reply with some insult, but thought better of it since he wanted to be taken to the show in George's car. "Look, George," he said, his tone of voice conciliatory. "We'll be up early, ready to go, I can promise you that, and we'll get out of your car before we get to the show. If you stop on the mountain road above Treherbert we'll walk down from there. If it's not raining," he added as an afterthought. "No point in getting my dog wet, is there? It wouldn't look too good like that, would it? We'll also pay your petrol there and back. Think of the beer you'll win if we lose!" he added, dangling the final carrot. "C'mon, George."

"Well, okay, Fred," George replied reluctantly, after some of the locals started jeering or encouraging him, depending on their support or not for Fred's request.

"Now don't forget, and I'm saying this in front of everyone here : you be ready to go early or I'm going without you, right?"

"Right!" Fred made his way to the bar, a smirk on his face.

"Just wait 'til Saturday, boys. Pint, landlord," he said to the grinning Trefor. "I'll 'ave 'im, don't you worry," he promised, nodding his head in confirmation.

The day of the show came around quickly and Fred, as he had promised, was up bright and early. He and Colin had spruced themselves up like two new pins. Fred was standing, carefully grooming the prospective champ as it stood on the rickety table amid the bread and butter and other items which were scattered across the table top. He stood back and held the dog's head and tail up in the recommended position.

"What do you think, Col? How does he look?"

"He looks bluddy great to me, Daddy," came Colin's prompt reply. "A real champion!"

Meanwhile, the dog was making a valiant but unsuccessful attempt to grab a nearby crust off the table. Fred lifted the dog, who was still casting wistful eyes at the dry crust, off the table, to stand alone in the centre of the living room in the morning sunlight streaming though the curtain-less window. At that moment, there was a loud bang on the door and George Teale walked in, resplendent in a dark pinstripe suit, white shirt and red tie. "Are you ready, boys?" he asked, looking at Fred's Border

Terrier with critical eyes. "I think you're wasting your time and money on that, Fred!"

"Georgie!" Fred scowled at him. "You take the bluddy biscuit, you do." His temper rose to near boiling point in an instant.

"You 'aven't been in this game more than five bluddy minutes and listen to you, going on about dogs. You couldn't tip ashes, never mind champions. C'mon, let's go before I lose my temper with you."

They walked out to George's car with Fred carrying the Border in his arms and Colin trailing behind, with the blanket off Fred's bed neatly folded for the dog to sit on in the back of the car.

"Making a bit of a fuss, ain't you?" George looked over his shoulder at Colin with his arm around the Border terrier.

"Oh, shut up and drive," Fred muttered, settling himself in the front seat.

George drove up the winding mountain road at a leisurely pace and Fred had time to reflect and reminisce on some of his haunts of years past across the huge expanse of countryside offered, from the Brecon Beacons in the distance to the Craig above and below him, and the thousands of acres of dark green conifers, now a haven for the wily fox that he hunted at every opportunity. As they drove towards the gate leading down into the forestry road Fred suddenly shouted. "Hey! Colin!" startling the life out of his son, who had almost fallen asleep while holding the young dog on the blanket. Fred was pointing to a large clump of bushes near the wooden gate. "Isn't that where you shot that huge dog fox last year?" George brought the car to a stop to get a better view of the site.

"Looks like the place, Daddy. It was almost dark, mind. That fox was the size of an Alsatian bitch, with a bright red coat. It took two shots to knock 'im down too."

"Aye," Fred chipped in, "and he got his name and picture in the paper for that."

"Right enough," Colin cut in, laughing, "but I only got the same £3 from the Foxing Club or the local farmers, as if it was a little vixen."

"Foxing Club? What's that?"

"The proper name for it is the Fox Destruction Society, and we both belong to it. We meet once a month in the Croesbychan pub on Merthyr road, at the bottom of Merthyr mountain. Anyone can go there if they've got a fox tail and they will pay you £3 for an adult fox and a pound for a cub's tail. George, do me a favour. When we get to the top of the Craig, can you stop for a minute in the layby? I want to show you something."

George drove the car into the layby to face the Brecon Beacons and got out. Fred stood beside him and pointed to the mountains in the distance. "Me and Blucher walked every inch of all that land and we lived off what we could find." He pointed west to face the crest of the mountain they were standing on. "See that pile of stones right over there? Well, that's the highest point in Glamorgan, and from there, on a clear day, you can see the West Country in England."

George looked at his watch. "Thanks for the geography lesson, Fred, but like I said, I've got to be at the Show early."

Going down the mountain, each was silent and deep in thought as the car followed the winding road down into the Rhondda Valley and the town of Treherbert. George brought the car to a stop two streets away from the venue, letting Colin and Fred walk the rest of the way to the Show. Fred carried the little dog in his arms so that he wouldn't have a hair out of place before the judging of his class began. Minutes later, they arrived at the hall. Fred paused outside the entrance to study the details of the Show on the notice board.

Owners/Contestants: Free admission. Ten shillings registration fee for each dog. "Right, Colin! If anybody asks, we are joint owners, remember."

Fred never missed an opportunity to get out of paying anything, if he could help it, even if it was only a penny.

Once inside, he made his way to the organiser's table, while Colin brushed the dog's coat yet again. He looked up at Colin as if wondering what all the attention was about.

Fred duly registered his Border Terrier in his class and paid the requested fee of ten shillings. In return he received a lapel sticker which read: 'Owner/Contestant'. "I'll have another one of these, if you don't mind, for my son. We are joint owners, see." Receiving the second sticker, he handed it to Colin as he studied the other contestants and their dogs scattered around the large hall. He made a mental note of the trestle table for judging the smaller dogs, and then he stood for a moment looking at the blue cloth-covered table with all the rosettes, ribbons and medals lined up in neat rows for the winners of each group or class. The overall Champions Cup for Best in Show stood in the centre of the array. 'That's for me,' he thought. 'Then let's see what Georgie Teale will say about that!' He went back to the organiser's table and waved his arm to encompass the hall. "Is this everybody who is competing today?"

"Well, there can't be many more to come. You only got here just before closing time for all entries." The man looked at his pocket watch. "Yes, another ten minutes and the list of entries for this Show will be closed!"

"Damn, we were lucky then." He left the official's table and crossed the hall to where Colin was still grooming their dog. He took another look round the hall, all the while nodding to himself. "Colin! We're in with a chance," he whispered excitedly. "There's not a lot to beat in the terrier class. Look around, mun. There's only about a dozen that look anything like terriers and ours is the best of the bunch. In my mind he is, anyway," he added, grinning like a Cheshire cat. "Besides, the entry book closes in less than ten minutes. Yes, we're in,

Colin. There's not much to beat." Gleefully, he rubbed his hands together.

"Well, let's hope you're right. Ten pints is a lot to lose, mind!"

"Don't bother, Colin, we're not going to lose ten pints, believe me!" 'Aye,' thought Colin, scratching the side of his head, cap in hand, 'you'll find a way around it somehow.'

The judging of the different breeds was soon under way and their Border Terrier got through the preliminary rounds with little difficulty. Each time any dog was eliminated from the terrier class, Fred's expectations for his dog rose accordingly. Finally it was announced that three dogs had been selected for Best in Class. Two of them were registered Jack Russells, which didn't appear to have had any obedience training at all, and the other was Fred's Border Terrier, who was either too weak or too timid to move from the spot where he stood for the judges to examine. At this point it was Fred who was doing his best to stand still while the judging was taking place. His eyes flashed back and forth between the two judges as if willing them to look with favour upon his dog.

Fred held his breath as the two men conferred quietly to one side, viewing the three dogs from every angle. Finally the senior judge stepped forward and pointed his finger at the Border Terrier and declared him the Best in Class for the terrier group!

Fred was absolutely delighted. He jumped around, swinging his son to and fro by the shoulders. "Heh, heh, heh!" he cackled. "Where's that George? I want to see that George's face. That's five pints we're in, so we can't lose now. Where is he?"

"Hey! Wait a minute, Fred!" He grabbed his father's arm. "Don't you go bluddy near him now or at any time. He's a bluddy judge here and you could get disqualified or something. Are you listening to me?"

"Bluddy 'ell, yes. You're right enough, Colin, but I'd still like to see his face all the same." They sat impatiently with the Border

Terrier on Fred's lap while the judging of the other groups took place, late into the afternoon. It was then announced that the Best in Show competition would begin in fifteen minutes. All Champions of their group would assemble in the main hall. Fred told Colin that this would be a lot more complicated for judging and they would be using a different judge. "I think the last judge liked Border Terriers." He shrugged his shoulders. "Well, if we don't win, we haven't lost anything cos we won our class."

Fred had groomed his dog again and again until he had every single hair in place. He walked into the arena head held high, as he took his dog through the routine requested by the judge. The final test was total obedience. Fred told his dog to sit, then he turned his back on the dog and walked away some distance to the other side of the ring, without the dog following him or moving an inch from where he had been told to sit. He waited the mandatory period of time and called the dog to him; then he gave the order to sit. The dog's and Fred's performance were faultless.

Fred left the ring and went to sit with Colin as they waited for the other competitors to go through the same procedure.

The group of judges began comparing notes, each with their slips of paper marking the salient points for each contestant. They conferred quietly, until the independent judge took out his pen and signed the register, followed in turn by each of the other judges. He crossed to the other table and picked up the rosette for the Best in Show. The sounds in the hall died away to a whisper as the contestants and spectators alike waited with bated breath to know who was going to receive the winner's trophy, with all the attention usually reserved for a champion at Crufts.

Finally, with one last word to the other judges, the senior judge walked straight across the ring to Fred and announced, "This is the overall Best in Show Champion. Congratulations!"

Amid the immediate applause, Fred and Colin stood stock still, mouths agape in total surprise, but only for a few seconds.

"We've bluddy done it! We've done it, Colin! I told you we had a chance. Yippee!" Fred began leaping around like a lamb in springtime. Colin picked up the Champion and held him in his arms as Fred, belying his age, jumped up and down, waving his arms in the air. The judges moved closer together, bemused by Fred's antics as he jumped back and forth across the arena. Colin, with a broad smile on his face, moved to one side of the judges' table, still holding the Champion, who appeared unconcerned at all the fuss Fred was making.

Minutes later, after Fred had calmed down a little, totally out of breath, he walked towards the judges' table to accept the Silver Cup and Challenge Certificate for Best in Show. Proudly he raised the Cup over his head, to another round of applause from the spectators, as he managed to say, "Thanks to everyone. It has been a great Show and we'll be back next year to defend the title of Best in Show. Thanks again." He made his way slowly through the ritual of handshaking and congratulations from the other competitors, to where Colin, still holding the dog in his arms, stood smiling broadly.

"Now then, Col, let's have a few pints to celebrate, is it?"

"Nothing better," Colin replied agreeably.

At that moment George appeared, hand outstretched. "Congratulations, Fred and Colin. I've got to admit, you did it, like you said. Good luck to you both. I suppose I owe you a few pints, too," he added grudgingly, with a slight grin.

"Come on, George, no hard feelings for what you said before about my dog." Fred put his arm around George's shoulder. "Let's all go together and have a few drinks, is it?" His broad features beaming with delight, he led the way to the nearest pub, where he filled the Cup with beer and passed it around everyone nearby to have a swig, amid congratulations from all sides. Meanwhile the Champion was tied unceremoniously to the leg of the bench near the door, where Fred sat as he proceeded to put away as many pints as he could before the pub closed. After a while Fred looked up at his son and said, "Colin, our dog is now a Show Champion and I'm thinking of making some money from this. We can put him out to stud. We can advertise in the papers and dog books that he is a Show Champion and Cup winner. With the money we make from that we can buy a Champion bitch and start our own champion line! What do you think?"

"There's no holding him now," George said, smiling.

"You're right enough, George," Colin replied, slurring slightly, doing his best to look serious.

Fred's money-making mind was racing ahead of everyone with plans for his new-found status of Champion dog owner. 'Damn, this was a good trip over the mountain,' he thought delightedly, a bit tipsy and half drunk, but happy.

"Well, boys, I think it's time to go from yere and let everyone in the Plough see what we've done over here today." Fred bent down to untie his Champion – but when he looked under the bench all he found was the lead still tied to the leg of the bench. The dog was nowhere to be seen.

Fred jumped to his feet, sober in an instant. "Quick, boys! Our bluddy dog has gone from under there!" he shouted, pointing to the bench. "Colin, look outside quick. P'raps he's just wandered off somewhere!" Fred began to panic, all his visions of wealth and status dashed to the ground in an instant.

"HEY! Hold it, everybody!" he shouted above the noise. "Has anybody seen my Champion dog? He's a Border Terrier!"

An immediate chorus of "No" greeted his inquiry. Fred sat down, an expression of total shock on his face. What was to be done now? All these people with dogs and all those without dogs. Lots of dogs look alike too. Who could he ask? He looked helplessly around the crowded room, seeing only a sea of unfamiliar faces. Somebody had stolen his Champion dog, that was now a certainty. 'I'll go to the police, that's it,' he thought. 'The police will find him for me.' He got to his feet in a daze and wandered out into the street, calling his dog's name in vain. He returned to the bench where he had tied up his dog and sat down, the misery of the moment bowing his shoulders. George and Colin came back in and sat beside him and informed Fred that as yet they hadn't found any trace of him.

"We'd better go to the police then," Fred said. "I can only hope that they will find him for us!" He raised his hands and shoulders in despair. "Who would do such a thing?" he mumbled. "And me almost a pensioner!"

Together they entered the local police station and reported their sorry tale to the sergeant on duty, who in turn took down all the relevant details and a description of the missing Champion. He was very sympathetic to Fred's plight but as he pointed out, the chances of getting his dog returned to him were very slim indeed. As he understood it, there were entries from all over the Valleys, both near and far, and of course there were the dog-fancier spectators to consider, who could have come from anywhere, or any local could have taken him. In a nutshell, he said, the situation is a bit hopeless. Anyone in the crowd there could have also taken a fancy to the Show Champion. He was most apologetic and promised they would do their best, "But at this moment we have very little to go on."

He looked at the three of them and said, "You were all there when it was stolen and not one of you saw it being taken! Right from under your noses, so to speak. So you can imagine the problem we now have. I'm really sorry, but as I said, we will do what we can for you. Here's our telephone number, Mr Howells. Give me a call tomorrow for any news."

Fred was almost in tears by this time, not only from the loss of his champion dog but at the thought of having to go back to the Plough and the humiliation of having to tell them all in what had happened while he was having a few pints. He could well imagine some of the comments: that he had lost his Champion dog while he was drinking with complete strangers, having left his dog on his own and tied up near the open door. If he didn't tell them now, someone would find out one way or another. When he had won, he had lost no time at all in phoning the Plough with the news of what he and his dog had achieved, but now they were going back to a big welcome with just the silver cup and a piece of bluddy paper to show for all his bragging. 'Damn it all! They are going to have a field day poking fun at me after all I said about my Border Terrier. If I could only get my bluddy hands on him or them – but where?' he thought angrily.

"C'mon then, boys, if you've finished here." George was ready to leave. "We'll call in the Plough if you like, but only if you want to, Fred," he paused. "It's up to you!" Secretly he couldn't wait to see the reaction to Fred's misfortune in the main bar.

Fred stared at him for a long moment as he realised George's real reason for going back to the Plough right away. Turning back to the desk he then thanked the sergeant and asked him if he would be kind enough to phone the Plough if he had any news of the whereabouts of his Champion. He then wrote down the number of the police station on a scrap of paper and stuffed it in his top pocket.

"Come on then, boys," he said, looking pointedly at George. "Don't think I'm *twp* and don't know why you want to go back to Trefor's so bluddy quick. When we get back there, don't you say a bluddy word about all this. I'm going to tell the boys the story myself. Right?"

"Right enough, Fred! I am really sorry you 'ave lost your dog. It's a crying shame!" George tried to make amends for his previous thoughts.

"Well, whoever took him, I hope he gets all the bad luck in the world, the rotten sod," Fred said, bitterly. He nodded his thanks to the sergeant and said, "Okay, boys, let's go!"

Meanwhile, in the Plough, Trefor was full of enthusiasm for Fred's success at the dog show and told everyone who came in, in both Welsh and English, that Fred's Border Terrier had been named the Best in Show and won the Cup. "There'll be a place in yere tonight, you can bet on it. I'll have a job to get him out of here at stop tap, he'll be singing all night if I know him. Now we'll have some fun," he said, laughing at the prospect.

On the drive back over the mountain the three men sat in silence, each with his own thoughts on how this calamity had come about. Arriving at the Plough, George turned the car slowly into the yard at the side of the pub and switched off the engine, and they sat in silence for a few moments. As if by one thought, George and Colin glanced briefly at each other and waited for Fred to make the first move to get out of the car.

"Well, boys, this is it!" Fred said, tersely. "Come on, let's get it over with!" He turned toward them as they climbed stiffly out of the car, rubbing the circulation back into their legs. "Remember! I'm to say first, mind."

Entering the pub Fred held the cup in front of him as he pushed open the door into the bar. "Hooray!" shouted Trefor across the room. "Here's the Champs, boys! Show us the cup, Fred!" Everybody in the room turned to look at him, cheering as he stood in the centre of the room holding the Silver Cup above his head for all to see. His eyes glistened but there was barely a smile on his face.

Trefor, as perceptive as ever, suddenly realised there was something very wrong with what he was seeing. He glanced quickly at each of the three men in turn then called out, "So where is the Champion dog then, Fred?"

Fred's features immediately became a picture of misery, all

thoughts of enjoying the moment lost in a split second. "Well, Trefor, since you have just asked me, I have just come from the police station in Treherbert. Some rotten sod stole my dog from where I was sitting and I was only away from there less than a minute or so!"

A sudden silence descended on the bar. No matter how much fun and sometimes ridicule was had at Fred's expense, everyone at that moment had a feeling of total sympathy for him.

"No!" said Trefor, in a shocked tone. "I can't believe it!" He looked towards Colin for confirmation, who nodded.

"It's right enough, Tref," he said, his voice on the edge of breaking.

"My Champion dog was stolen from me, and right under my bluddy nose too." Fred's features were a picture of dismay as he looked around the room for some support.

"Aww, Fred. That's terrible!" Trefor said sympathetically. "One thing for sure though: you and your little dog won at the Show and you've still got the Cup to prove it! Come on, Fred," he said encouragingly. "Come and have a couple of pints of best bitter on me. I think you'll feel a bit better then."

"Aye, maybe you're right." Fred turned towards Trefor. "Hey, wait a minute. I've got something else to prove what we did over there – I've got a certificate too." He took the gold-edged scroll from his inside pocket and held it up for everyone to see.

"Look at this, boys! See what it says here: Open Champion. Best in Show and my name in the middle. Fred Howells. Owner."

He handed it over the bar to Trefor. "Keep this safe for me, Tref, please. Just in case I lose it somewhere. You know what I'm like." Characteristically, he squared his shoulders and hitched up his trousers with the sides of his arms, his loss now being somewhat tempered by the thought of some free beer coming his way for what he had done in the Show, and Trefor's promise of a couple too. "Aah! I 'ave to think positive that the police will find him for me. So we'll wait and see, is it?" His features broke into a smile.

"C'mon Colin, George still owes us ten pints! How about it then, George?"

George managed a weak smile, at the same time taking out his wallet to place enough money on the bar to cover the ten pints owed to Fred and Colin. "Here you are, Tref. Ten pints' credit as per our bet last week." He raised his glass in salute as he said, "Good luck to you, Fred, in getting your little dog back."

"Thank you, George." Without further ado, Fred had the Cup filled with beer and was soon passing it around the room as if nothing had happened. The crowd in the bar, which had for the most part been silent during the telling of the happenings at the Dog Show, began to return to the normal Saturday night revelry, and the plight of Fred and his stolen Champion soon faded into the background.

By the end of the evening, Fred and Colin had everyone singing all the popular Welsh folk songs. Fred's chagrin of the hours before and his loss were cast from his mind with the enjoyment of the free beer and the singing. It must be said that Fred and Colin, when they chose to, could have the stage to themselves with their rendition of 'Myfanwy', complemented by some other favourites, which could bring a tear to the eye of the most hardened person. 'Cartref' or 'It's The Ring Your Mother Wore' were particularly poignant.

That night they stood arm in arm singing to each other and acknowledging the applause at the end of each song by bowing to all and sundry, their faces beaming with pride. Such a night had not been seen in the Plough for a very long time and Trefor, the landlord, was delighted that everyone seemed to have made an effort to cheer Fred up. It was well after midnight when he finally got everyone out of the Plough and leaned wearily against the locked and bolted front door.

CHAPTER 29

Ode to a Champion

O N THE TUESDAY of the following week, the telephone rang in Trefor's kitchen. He left the bar to answer it, and a voice said, "I would like to speak to Mr Fred Howells, please."

"Um, he's not here at the moment. Can I take a message for him? I'm the landlord here," Trefor said helpfully.

"Well, yes, I suppose you could. It's about his Border Terrier. This is Sergeant Thomas at the Treherbert police station."

"Yes, sergeant, please go on. We know all about his dog's disappearance here. Fred has told everyone in sight about the theft of his Champion."

"Right! I'm afraid we haven't had much success with our inquiries in locating or tracing where the dog is at this point in time. We did, however, receive a story – or rumour, if you like – that a dog answering the general description of the missing dog was sold the same night in a village some 20 miles down the valley from here. We have done our best to establish how or where this story came from, but unfortunately we have reached a dead end on that one. Please convey to Mr Howells our regret at not being able to do any more at this time. However, we will not close this file, just in case we get another lead to follow up. Thank you, sir and goodnight."

Trefor returned to the bar in a thoughtful mood as he mulled over the information the police had given him and what he was going to pass on to Fred. He looked quickly around the crowd in the room, just in case, but there was no sign of him tonight.

Old John Shinkins was standing looking at a sheet of paper pinned to the noticeboard next to the Dog Show poster. He looked sideways in the landlord's direction, pointing a finger at the same time to the board.

Trefor just shrugged, thereby denying any connection with it. John came over to the bar and began to whisper something. Trefor leaned forward. "What was that, John?"

Old John looked around to see if anyone was listening in to his conversation, then said, "Has anyone else said anything about that?" He pointed with a finger across his chest towards the notice board.

"I don't know what you mean, John bach," Trefor replied, wearing his innocent, nothing-to-do-with-me look.

"Come off it, Trefor! You must know something about it. It's about Fred's bluddy dog."

"Show me, John!" He came from behind the bar and into the room to stand beside Old John in front of the notice board as he pointed to the ode to Fred's dog. Trefor read it through and began laughing. Moments later everyone in the bar was standing behind him as he read it aloud.

Ode to a Border Champion

Fred and Colin with hearts aglow
Entered their dog in a terrier show
And by the efforts of this handsome pup
Fred was awarded the Champion's Cup
With spirits high and joyful still
The Cup with ale they both did fill
Around and around they both did chat
No chance of ale then getting flat

The Champion dog meanwhile in fright
Was tied up under the bench so tight
Fred then without thought or care
Drank his health but did not share
Some person viewed with envious eyes
Then carefully the dog unties
Excitement! Yet the dog forlorn
Fred looked round too late. Doggone
They searched on high and then down low
Did anyone see my Border go?
No answer was the stern reply
Still you have the Cup to know him by
Fred dismayed by someone's sin
Returned sadly to the Bryn
Without a trace of Champion hound
Perhaps a better home he'd found.

"This will cause one 'ell of a row when Fred sees it!" John said with a gruff laugh. "I'd like to be here when he comes in."

Fred came into the bar the following night with his usual cry of: "Pint of your best, landlord!" While Trefor was pulling Fred's pint, he passed on the information provided by the Treherbert police the night before.

"WHAT! They sold my Champion dog? They bluddy sold 'im!" he fumed. "Damn it all, Tref! That was a really good dog, too." Pulling a face, he turned away from the bar, the pint glass to his lips, while looking around the room.

Old John Shinkins, in his usual spot on the settle beside the stove, waved a hand to attract Fred's attention to come and sit beside him. His opening words were, "Have you seen that poem, Fred?" He pointed to the sheet of paper pinned on the noticeboard.

"No! What's it about then?" Fred asked, squinting his eyes slightly to see what Old John was on about.

"Go and have a look for yourself, I can't read it from yere," Old John replied, grinning.

Fred put his glass down on the table beside Old John and walked over to the board, taking out his granny spectacles to look closer at the notice in the dim light.

"Wait for it," Trefor said quietly to Johnny, at the same time waving his arms to attract the attention of the other patrons in the room, and pointing a finger towards Fred. The general noise in the room slowly abated as Fred quickly read the poem.

He looked over his shoulder at the sea of faces looking in his direction, then ripped the paper off the board and spun around in anger. "You're a rotten lot. Making fun of me again, is it? Just wait until I find out who did this, he'll be sorry – there'll be a bluddy row. You can bet on it!" With angry eyes, he looked around the room, but no one was laughing. "I'm going to burn this bluddy thing," he said, scrunching the paper into a ball in his hand.

"Go right ahead," Trefor called from behind the bar. "I got a lot more copies of that."

"Come on, Fred," said Johnny. "It's not poking fun at you, if you read it properly. It's exactly what happened to your Champion in rhyme, just as you told us all in here. There's no lies at all in it. It's what you said! Read it again slowly, mun."

Fred's anger started slipping away. "Well, I would like to get my hands round the neck of the sod who stole my dog, that's all," he growled, redirecting his bitterness as he smoothed out the crumpled paper. He read the ode to his dog again, this time slowly. Then be began to laugh, "Whoever did this has got all the details right…"

Johnny called out quietly to Trefor. "Put a pint over for Fred on me."

"What was that, Johnny?" Fred's hearing was as sharp as the foxes he hunted.

"I said I'll put a pint over for you, Fred, you nosy so-and-so. You don't miss much, do you?"

"Not if it's for free," Fred chuckled. "It's the free ones I really enjoy."

CHAPTER 30

Fred's ferrets loose in the Legion

L EAVING THE HOUSE, Fred strolled slowly down the hill, stopping occasionally to admire a garden or pass the time briefly with a passer-by. He sat for a while on the sill of Shop John while he rolled himself a cigarette with mixture taken from a battered OXO tin half full of new tobacco and old cigarette ends. When he had it burning to his satisfaction, he got to his feet and continued his slow progress up the lane towards the Plough, until he came to the stone bridge over the small stream that made its way down from the mountain behind the council estate. He sat for a while on the wall, staring down into its crystal clear waters, as he thought about his latest run of bad luck. He sighed heavily and told himself that he would buy a new Border Terrier at the first opportunity, and a new ferret too. He took off his ratting cap to scratch the back of his head and grimaced as he stood up. "Damn," he said aloud. "My old legs are a bit stiff. I think it's time to walk the mountains a bit more often."

Entering the pub, he found he was the only one in there. "Pint, Tref," he grunted to the landlord.

"Hello, Fred! You're up early. How's the head? You had quite a few on last night, if you can remember!" Trefor's cheery greeting was a stark reminder of the night before.

"Aye, you're right enough. We all did, didn't we?" Fred grinned sheepishly. "Maybe a pint now will do me the world of good. You know what they say, 'hair of the dog', and all that."

"Mmmm!" Trefor didn't look all that convinced by the old adage as a solution to hangovers, but it didn't deter him, either, from selling as much beer as possible to the likes of Fred and his cronies when the opportunity arose.

Fred, sipping from the foaming pint, moved slowly across the bar to sit in Old John Shinkins' appointed seat on the wooden settle alongside the stove. He carefully placed his glass within reach and opened the daily paper to the racing page.

"I see you've got your name in the *Aberdare Leader*, Fred!" Trefor called out.

"Oh, what was that, then?" Fred was immediately on the alert. Was it something to do with that 'funny money' escapade?

"Oh, it was something to do with you catching a vixen and cubs up on Craig y Llyn mountain. You did do that, didn't you?"

"Oh, that!" Fred tried to be a bit offhand about the report but his chest puffed out, just a little bit, with pride, at being recognised for doing something which had been recorded in the local paper. "Aye, somebody was sent out from the *Leader* to interview me a couple of weeks ago. I don't know how they found out about it, mind. Me and Jimmy were walking back from Cwmdare past Padell y Bwlch when we raised a big dog fox. It took us ages to track it down with the terriers, but we finally got it above the Llyn." He gestured with his thumb towards the back of the Plough.

"That was the long way back from Cwmdare, Fred."

"Aye, it was and it was almost dark too. I'm telling you, Tref, I had a bluddy shock too when I crawled through to the edge of the drop and looked over. I thought, in the dark, there was a lamb on the ledge, so I reached down and grabbed it by the scruff, but it was a bluddy vixen, mun! It was fighting like 'ell to get away but I hung onto it and eventually bumped it off. I had another look over the edge and saw there were some cubs there too. So, Jimmy and me, we had them too."

"Get away from yere, Fred! How is it we haven't heard about this before now, then?"

"Well, I didn't want to say too much about it 'til it came out in the paper," he said, tongue in cheek. "See, there some are people around yere who don't believe anything I say. So I thought, if it is in the paper, p'raps they'll take notice of that and can't argue it's not true."

"Oh aye? That's not like you, Fred!"

"Now, there you are, Trefor!" Fred slapped his knee in frustration. "See! You read it in the paper and still you don't believe. Okay, ask Jimmy when he comes in and he'll say the same as I'm telling you now. Anyway, I don't care if you don't believe me. I killed that vixen and between us, Jimmy and me, we had the five cubs off the ledge too."

Before Trefor could reply, the door to the bar opened and George Teale came into the room. He grinned at Fred, nodding his head. "Pint, Fred? And a pint of best bitter for me, Tref."

"Pint of best for me, too," Fred said quickly, smiling at the alarmed expression on George's face. "Don't worry, George, I've got money. It's a good thing you have just come in, George. I was just telling Trefor about that vixen I caught on that ledge up on Craig y Llyn a few weeks back."

"It's right enough, Trefor. Jimmy told me all about it last week. He said he thought Fred was going to be pulled over the edge because he had the vixen by the neck and she was fighting like mad to get loose, and if he hadn't put his weight on Fred's legs, he would have gone over for sure."

"*Duw, Duw*, Fred!" Trefor turned to Fred with admiration in his voice. As a farmer himself, he knew the devastation a fox with cubs could cause among a flock with newborn lambs.

Fred, a stranger to praise, sat a bit more upright in his seat and a soft smile of pride wreathed his face. "Yes, I'm the bluddy boy for these foxes," he said immodestly. "Blucher taught me a lot when I was a young man, but I don't brag about it."

"No, Fred! Fair play, you don't brag about it." Together George and Trefor laughed out loud at the expression of puzzlement on Fred's face.

After a while, when they were on their second pint, Fred said, as nonchalantly as possible, "Hey, George! Do you fancy a trip down to Penderyn Road in Waun-gron? I want to buy another ferret. I lost a good one over in Llyswen a few weeks back."

"Aye, so I heard, mun," George grinned. "I also heard about the café in Talgarth."

Fred grinned in remembrance. "Well, you know me – and it was a restaurant, not a café. Well, what about it, then? Shall we go and see Old Dai Abbott about buying one of his ferrets, and call in somewhere on the way back for a few pints, is it?

"Aye, okay then, but I want to do a few likkle bets first."

Later that afternoon they arrived at Dai Abbott's house and Fred rapped on the back door then sat on the low wall looking with admiration at the neatly laid out garden. The back door opened slowly and Dai Abbott came out to stand on the top step.

"Fred, mun! How's things? I saw your name in the paper this week."

"Aye," Fred grinned. "We got lucky, that's all. Listen, have you got any ferrets ready for sale?"

"Got a few you can pick from," Dai replied, with a smile. "Come on down the garden and I'll show you what I've got ready." He led the way down the paved path to a small shed at the bottom of the garden. He took out a bunch of keys, selected one and unlocked the door. "Can't be too careful," he said, over his shoulder. "Too many petty thieves about the place nowadays. Now then, boys, let's see. At the moment, I've got three ready to go right away. Two are jills and one a big dog! It's supposed to be called a hob, but..."

"Nah! I don't want any females," Fred shook his head. "Let's have a look at the dog ferret, then."

"Oh, he's a beauty too, Fred," Dai said, enthusiastically. "He's a big polecat and he's pretty quiet too."

"Ah! Now that's exactly what I'm looking for, something that's quiet." Fred grinned at George. "These little sods have sharp little teeth. Damn!" he said in admiration. "Now that's a good-looking ferret!"

With both hands, Dai was holding the huge polecat ferret towards Fred, who reached out gingerly towards the animal with the back of his hand and it in turn sniffed his skin. Fred turned his head slightly in George's direction. "When you turn your hand like this," he explained, "they can't bite you cos the skin is too tight if your wrist is bent a bit."

George just nodded and watched the ferret.

"How much, Dai?"

"To you, Fred, thirty bob!"

"Too pricy for me! I haven't got that much to spend! I thought about a pound." He looked at the ferret again and knew it was a good buy at the price offered.

"Thirty bob is fair, Fred!" Dai's tone of voice was firm.

"Can't be done, Dai," Fred turned away, winking at George.

"Now, a female I can see at that price because there's always a chance I can breed from her, but I don't want a female."

There was silence in the small shed as they eyed each other, as if waiting to see who would give in first.

"Tell you what, then," said Dai. "I'll give you this old female and the polecat dog for thirty bob. Yes, she's old but I'm pretty sure she should last you at least a couple of seasons. You'd be helping me out, because I need the extra space for these young ones coming along. How about it?"

Fred shook his head in refusal until George nudged him hard in the back and made him think again.

"C'mon Fred! This is a good deal! I wouldn't offer this to anyone else, but I know you will look after them," Dai said seriously.

Fred cast a sly look at the female. She was almost as big as the male. "Well," he paused. "Let me see if I've got that much on me," he said, reluctance in his tone. He searched from pocket to pocket, pooling the coins he found on the nearby bench. He counted out the money into a separate pile and announced, "Well, that's all I've got. 29 shillings, take it or leave it, Dai!" He grinned as he exchanged glances with George.

"It's near enough, I suppose. There you are then, Fred," he said, handing him the big female. "I'll get the other one for you now. Have you got cages to put them in? I can lend you a couple, so long as I get them back by next week."

"Nah! I'll just put them in my coat pockets. I can button the flaps down so they'll be safe enough in there. Thanks a lot, Dai. I'll see you again, then."

Fred walked jauntily back to the car. "That was a good deal for me, George," he muttered from the side of his mouth.

"Aye, I could see that," George replied. "But you've got more money than that, haven't you?"

"Oh, yeh! I've got ten quid in my back pocket. That shilling I saved is better off in my pocket than in his. Besides, that extra bob is worth two bets on the horses for me. Who knows? I might be lucky enough to win more than a shilling," he laughed. "I know, let's call in the Legion on the way back, is it? It's early, so we might be in time for a game of bingo. P'raps we'll be lucky there too."

George parked his car just in front of the main entrance into the Legion and locked the doors. He stood for a moment looking at Fred. "What about them ferrets, Fred? Do you want me to lock them in the boot? They'll be safe there."

"Nah! They'll be just as safe with me. See, they're as quiet as mice in my pockets." He hefted his coat pockets to demonstrate.

"Well," said George dubiously. "If you really think so, we'll go in, then."

"C'mon then, George! Let's go and have a couple of pints." Fred glanced at his battered watch. "I think the bingo starts in half an hour," he said, as he hurried through the door. They purchased tickets and sat in the main hall to wait for the game to start.

"We're only playing six houses, mind, and if we win, we'll split it fifty-fifty, okay? Then we'll go back to the Plough, is it, Fred?" George picked up his glass and drained it.

"Aye, okay! We can drop these off at our house on the way." He lightly touched both pockets to confirm they were still there.

They were in the middle of the third game when Fred dropped his marker and stood up sharply. He quickly looked under the seat and along the bench they were sitting on. "George!" he whispered fiercely, "the bluddy ferrets 'ave got out somehow!"

"WHAT!" George looked up startled. "What are you bothering about?"

"Shh!" somebody on the next table said, then repeated, "I said shhh!"

The numbers were still being called when there was a piercing scream from halfway down the hall, followed by another scream – louder this time – and the sound of breaking glass as a table went over onto the wooden dance floor.

"Quick, George! They're down that end of the room!" Fred dropped everything and ran towards the stage. Then another woman started screaming at the other end of the hall. Fred spun around, only to see some women climbing on chairs and tables to get out of reach of the little animals, while others just stood there in total fear, crying their eyes out. Pandemonium reigned briefly as officials ran back and forth trying to bring some sort of order to the chaos.

Meanwhile, Fred was on his hands and knees under one of the tables, his hand reaching under the bench and holding onto one of the ferrets. Suddenly the woman on the bench started beating Fred about the head and screaming out loud, "This man is looking up my skirt!"

"No, I'm not!" Fred protested, holding up the ferret. "I just noticed that you've got nice legs, that's all."

"You dirty old so-and-so. Get up from there! I'm going to report you for that!" she shouted, as she continued to thump on his unprotected back. Fred managed to get to his feet without losing control of the big ferret. He looked around for George, but he and some of the other men were rolling around laughing at the antics of the women and Fred. The officials were running up and down, trying their best to bring some sort of calm, and all the while the bingo caller, up on the stage at the far end of the room, was still trying to call out the numbers, until an official called a halt to the proceedings. One of the other officials grabbed Fred by the scruff of his neck and began pushing him towards the door.

Fred was resisting for all he was worth, while at the same time shouting: "Wait a bluddy minute. I've got another ferret in here somewhere. Don't you open that door!"

Suddenly, a tall blonde woman jumped up on the table right in front of them and pulled her skirt up over her thighs. Everybody stopped what they were doing as she stood there, with everything on view, screaming loud enough to break windows.

Fred's mouth fell open. "Bluddy 'ell, what a sight!" He broke free of the official's grip and ran towards the woman. He dived under the seat to grab his other ferret, while taking full advantage of a close-up view for the second time.

"Hey you, Fred!" the official grabbed him by the scruff of his collar once again, spinning him around. "Out you go this bluddy minute!"

"Hey! Wait a bluddy minute yourself!" Fred shouted, belligerently. "We've only played three houses and we've got three more to play!"

"No, you bluddy haven't. You and these bluddy ferrets have caused enough trouble in here today, so out you go!"

"What about a refund, then?" Fred tried his best to turn and face the angry official but he held him in a vice-like grip and propelled him rapidly toward the open door.

Meanwhile, George was talking quietly to the cashier. "Hey, listen, all this was nothing to do with me. I just happened to be sitting next to him, that's all. So, can I please have my money back for these tickets?" He held up six tickets.

"Well, I expect so. Give them to me." He looked at the unmarked tickets and dropped them in the tray, at the same time giving George a full refund. He leaned forward and in a whisper said, "If I was you, I'd get out of here as quick as you can. The Chairman is on his way here."

"Thanks for the tip," George said gratefully. "I'm on my way." Once outside he leaned against the wall and laughed until he was out of breath. Fred was standing nearby glaring indignantly at the door of the Legion that he had been unceremoniously pushed through. "Those rotten sods," he fumed. "We might have won something on those tickets. Now somebody else might use them and win!"

"Don't bluddy bother, Fred. I got all the money back for the six tickets. We'll split it between us in the Plough, okay? Now we'd better scram from yere because the Chairman of the Legion is on his way here!"

Fred's face broke into a wide smile as he hurried around the car to get in. George started the engine, backed out, and turned the car towards Rhyd-y-groes.

"That was a bit of fun while it lasted, wasn't it?" said Fred laughing. "Der, did you see what she had on view?"

"Fred, you're the bluddy limit," George laughed. "That poor woman was afraid of your ferrets. Bet she had never seen one of them in her life before. She looked as if she knew you, too!"

"I don't suppose she has," Fred laughed, "and yeh! I sort of knew her many years ago before I was married and living at home in Waun-gron. I said all along she wasn't a real blonde all those years ago, and I was right!"

"C'mon. Let's drop those bluddy ferrets off at your house and go to the Plough."

Entering the Plough, George related to Trefor what had happened in the Legion in Waun-gron earlier, while Fred stood in the centre of the room as proud as punch as the story of his latest escapade unfolded.

Trefor didn't appear to be at all impressed or sympathetic when the story was told. "Well, Fred, I'll tell you this. You can cause a row wherever you go without even trying. I'm willing to bet, here and now, that you will get banned from the Legion in Waun-gron for a very long time. Believe me!" he said with a short laugh.

"Oh, no, Trefor! You are wrong there," Fred replied, pulling a face. "As a matter of fact, they are pretty good down there. There 'ave been loads of fights in there when there's been a dance, and those boys involved still go there. I know, because I know some of those boys. C'mon George, let's 'ave a few pints, is it?" He dug deep into his back pocket and brought out a £5 note. "Two pints of best bitter out of that, Trefor, if you please," he said with a broad grin, dismissing the landlord's prediction with a flick of his hand.

A few days after Fred's enforced removal from the Legion he received a letter by Special Delivery, to advise him of the result of the emergency meeting regarding his escapade with the two ferrets on the previous Friday afternoon. It informed him that he was being banned for a minimum period of two years, which included any dances or private functions put on by any private party. The secretary's letter also advised him that a fine for his misconduct had also been considered but had been left in abeyance for the time being.

Angrily he stuffed the letter in his coat pocket and made his way to the Plough. He was the first one through the front door moments after Trefor ducked under the hatch of the counter to stand behind the bar.

"Look at this bluddy nonsense, Tref!" he said, throwing the letter onto the bar.

Trefor read the letter through a second time. "Well, I did say you could get banned, didn't I? What you did was pretty serious," he said, laughing at Fred's hurt expression.

"But, but, look what it says about dances! I can dance the bluddy legs off any of them down there. I've known most of that committee for years and years! Especially that bluddy committee man who grabbed me by my coat collar and chucked me outside, and I couldn't do a bluddy thing about it cos I had a ferret in each hand! But, I'll 'ave 'im. Just you wait and see!"

Fred never 'had him' as he had threatened, at that time or any other time, and he never rejoined the Legion as a member, either.

CHAPTER 31

Trefor and the butcher: Part 2

M ORE THAN TWO weeks had passed since the episode with the butcher, and apart from the report and loss of Fred's Champion dog and his hilarious escapade with the ferrets in the Legion, life in and around the Plough, on the surface anyway, seemed fairly normal, with the exception of the butcher's silliness. It was Monday morning. Trefor, the landlord, had once again been woken up by the shrill ringing of the phone at 3.00 a.m., and despite the caller's feeble attempts to muffle and disguise his identity, Trefor knew exactly who it was when he said "Did I wake you?", after which the phone went silent.

It had already happened four times in the past week, and now again this morning. It was enough to try any man's patience, or, as Fred once said, 'It's enough to make a Pope swear'. Irritated by the call, and unable to go back to sleep, Trefor sat in the easy chair beside the warmth of the open door of his AGA stove, and thought about ways to get even with the butcher and his current bit of nonsense. He discarded one idea after another in his quest to make the bombastic man and his friends pay for all the insults and humiliation he had been subjected to in front of all his customers and friends two weeks before. Finally, he rose to his feet, smiling to himself as he made a cup of tea for breakfast.

Later, he sat at the littered kitchen table with his second cup of tea and the telephone directory open in front of him as he dialled a number.

"Yes. Good morning! I'm a representative of the Publicity Department of the major brewery you are currently dealing with – or should I say, frequently dealing with." Trefor adopted a different way of speaking, but he doubted very much if Twm Mawr's wife Mary would recognise his voice anyway, since he couldn't recall ever seeing or speaking to her.

He said he had seen glowing reports of the pub's grand opening of roughly three weeks before and had thought at the time that it had been a tremendous way to promote the establishment and was good also for the brewery and their particular brand of beers.

"The point I am getting to here," he went on, "is that our brewery has its own publicity department, of which I am a part, and we produce a magazine with a very large circulation. Perhaps it would have been very beneficial to your pub if we had known the exact date and time that you had your grand opening so that we, the brewery, could have sent some society people along with our official photographer. I'm sure you know the drill!"

Mary listened intently as he went on, at the same time signalling with her hand to Twm Mawr, standing at the other end of the room.

"The fact of the matter is, the president of the company himself has got wind of the event and called me into his office…"

"The president?" she said, weakly.

"Yes. The president! As I said, he had got hold of the story and wondered, if it would be at all possible…" he paused, "if it would be at all possible to do a repeat opening on say, Friday of this coming week?"

"Well, it's very nice of you to mention our grand opening and ask if we could do it again, but I'm not all that sure we could repeat that at such short notice. Friday is just four days away! It took us ages to arrange the first event," she said in confusion. "We might be able to manage it in two weeks' time?"

"Ah! That could present a problem. You see, that might not be possible because the chairman of the board and the president have such a lot of commitments for the next few months, and to be truthful, I don't want to be the one who tells them it cannot be done. Please look at the problem from my point of view."

Twm Mawr was now standing close to his wife, listening as best he could to what was being said by the man on the other end of the line. "I am sorry to spring this on you at such short notice but it appears that this coming Friday is the only available date open." Again Trefor paused.

Twm Mawr nodded to his wife, signalling with a thumbs up that it would be okay to go ahead.

"Oh, I see. Well, we could do our best to get everything done the same as before," she replied, looking at her husband, who was nodding vigorously in agreement.

"Thank you very much. Oh, by the way, there is one other thing I forgot to mention. We would be inviting a Welsh international rugby player to attend the event with us, but I am not at liberty to say who it is at the moment. We would also be inviting one of the touring New Zealand players to join him in signing autographs and so on. We will, of course, be giving these players major publicity in our magazine in photographs at your pub on that day. Now, to the cost of all this. All expenses will be taken care of by the Publicity Department of the brewery. Hopefully this will be acceptable to you, if only for the inconvenience it will cause."

"Oh yes, yes. That will be quite acceptable," she replied,

looking toward her husband again. Twm Mawr nodded, his head spinning with the information provided by the faceless voice on the phone, and all the organising they would have to do now to recreate the event as before. Rugby internationals, eh!

"Well, sir. I think that under the circumstances you have described, we can do it! Yes, I am sure we can do it," she said firmly.

"Good. That's very good indeed. I want you to know that I am very pleased that we have come to a suitable arrangement. It makes my job so much easier. Thank you so very much," Trefor said graciously. "So, to recap. We will look forward to meeting your guests this coming Friday at, say, 1.30 p.m.?"

"Right you are, sir," Mary replied. "1.30 p.m. it is."

The phone went dead. Twm Mawr took it and replaced it on the cradle, his face beaming. "Damn it all, Mary! It looks like we'll have another good day with everyone here again. If this business carries on like this, we'll be able to retire earlier than we thought." He did a little jig around her. "Think of it, with this kind of publicity we could well be millionaires in ten years or less. You'd better get out that list of people we had in here for the grand opening and start inviting them to come back this week for a second helping. Only pick the best, mind. There were a few the last time I wasn't all that sure about." He paused, "I meant to ask you at the time but I forgot. How did that older chap with wellies and a cap on one side of his head get in here last time? You know the one I mean. He was the one sitting on the bench in the garden drinking our free beer like it was his last pint on earth. Funny, too, I thought at the time that I had seen him up in Rhyd-y-groes when I was out with a couple of the boys and our butcher friend."

"Oh, I don't know, do I? I thought he was one of the locals having a free pint or two. We have to depend on them in the future, you know. It doesn't matter now, does it?"

"Okay, okay! I just wondered, that's all, cos he seemed a bit out of place. Now, who was the chap on the phone?"

"I don't really know." She looked a little bit flustered by the question. "I didn't catch his name, but he sounded genuine enough to me and he knew all about our grand opening event too. You heard him yourself when he was explaining the situation…"

"Okay, okay, that's good enough for me." He put his hand on her arm in reassurance. "Let's sit down now and make up a list of the people we want to be here from the other list, is it?"

Turning words into action as the excitement of another social event took hold of them, each took turns on the phone to inform 'suitable' guests of the upcoming free buffet that coming Friday at 1.30 p.m. for photographs taken by the publicity team from the brewery.

"Which brewery was it?" Twm Mawr asked, as he added the last name to the list of guests.

"He didn't say directly, only that we deal with them on a pretty frequent basis. He knows all about us, Twm, so there's no need to worry."

"Aye, okay!"

Rhys Rees, the butcher, being a close friend, was the first one on the list to be informed about the free do at the Lamb. "I'll put an order in right away to get some top quality roast beef and ham for the sandwiches," he said, thinking at the same time that he could make some good money at the brewery's expense on this bash. Rees wasted no time in dialling the number for his step-brother. His secretary answered in an instant and apologised that he would be out of the office for the rest of the day.

"Well, give him this message! There is a free do at the Lamb in the Bont this coming Friday at 1.30 p.m. It is being put on by one of the breweries and there will be some rugby internationals at the bash. Tell him his brother said he should be there! Have you got all that? Be sure to tell him. Okay, thanks."

The butcher sat for a few minutes planning what to do next. He picked up the phone and called his cooked meat supplier and told him the quantities he would need in beef and hams, and that he wanted them in this coming Thursday's delivery.

"This is a bit short notice, isn't it?"

"Yes, I know, but I have only just received notice myself, and I don't want to let them down. They are very good customers and personal friends, you know how it is. Anyway, how much will that set me back? Hey! Wait a minute. That's a bit much isn't it?"

"Well, it's a big order and on top of that you want me to deliver it all by Thursday, right?"

"Aye, okay. I'll just have to pass the cost on. Thanks, Joe." He smiled to himself as he put the phone down: well, the brewery will.

Twm Mawr leaned back in his chair, thumbs hooked in his braces. "Mary, I think I know which brewery it is, the one he was talking to you about! It's the biggest one in Cardiff and they sponsor rugby in a big way. I might be wrong but it's my best guess. No worries. We'll put this place on the map now. Mind you, I had my doubts in the beginning but I am starting to think that taking over as manager of this pub will be a good thing for us in the long run, even though we have never done this sort of thing before." He smiled up at his ever-patient wife. "How many more do we have to call, Mary?"

She rechecked the list, re-marking the definite ones. "Just three, Twm, and I'll do those because you look a little bit stressed out at the moment."

Twm Mawr nodded agreement, closed his eyes and drifted off into to light slumber as he dreamt of the crowds that would be there on the Friday afternoon, eating and drinking at the brewery's expense.

Thursday was the busiest they had been since they took over the management of the Lamb. They worked late into the night after closing time to make sure not a crumb would be out of place when the crowd of officials and the rugby internationals arrived on the following day. Twm Mawr smiled to himself in the certain knowledge that the people in the Bont wouldn't see another bash like this one for a very long time.

Friday dawned and grew into a warm summer's day as the local dignitaries began to arrive, some of the men in top hats and tails and their ladies in flowing dresses and large picture hats. As one of the locals said, it looked like a day out at the Ascot races as they strutted up and down the paved courtyard in front of the pub awaiting the arrival of the brewery party.

The pub itself was decked out in flags and bunting and tables set out with all manner of food and sandwiches on snow-white table cloths. The only thing missing was a red carpet to welcome their guests. The Hunt came down the road towards the pub in red coats, looking smart on their fine horses. The Master, giving a quick toot on his hunting horn to bring the pack of hounds to heel, stood up in his stirrups and touched the brim of his hat to acknowledge the ladies waving a welcome as stirrup cups were brought out for the huntsmen, while the hounds milled around, sniffing here and there among the guests in their finery. It was indeed a grand spectacle as the local photographers clicked away like grandfather clocks to get the best possible record of the event on film.

1.30 p.m. came and went. Suddenly it was 2.45 p.m., and Twm was beginning to get a bit anxious, nervously looking at his wrist watch every few seconds. Mary, his wife, was fussing back and forth, and was slowly getting more irritable that things were not going to plan.

"Well, Twm! Where are they, then?"

"I don't know!" Twm Mawr replied, raising his hands. "I don't know, do I? Did you get the time right? You took the call, not me," he said accusingly.

"Well of course I did. I wouldn't forget something as important as this," she replied sharply. "Don't you think you should phone somebody to ask?"

"Okay, then. What was his name anyway?"

"I don't know." Mary was desperately trying to recall the exact conversation. "Come to think of it, I don't think he told me exactly who he was, only that he was from the publicity department of the brewery."

"What! You never asked him who he is? How did that happen?"

"It's okay, Twm. Don't worry about it. Everything will be okay. Just calm down a bit."

Twm Mawr was silent for a minute or so then told Mary he was going to look for the butcher and his step-brother. He found them in the bar, both holding a large double scotch. He looked at his watch and said, "These people are pretty late, don't you think?"

Will David, the butcher's step-brother said, "Twm, I know the type of people these are. After leaving the office this morning, they're probably having a slap-up lunch in a hotel somewhere and are now running a bit late."

"Ah, yes. You're right enough. That's what it is." Twm Mawr sounded grateful for any explanation, relief in his voice. He turned away, slapping the palms of his hands together in agreement and went into his private quarters muttering to himself, "That's exactly what has happened, but I'll phone anyway just to make sure. No sense in upsetting the local big shots," he said, laughing to himself. He opened his diary and dialled the number for the brewery.

"Yes," he said into the phone. "I would like to speak to your manager please."

"And who shall I say is speaking, please?" she asked politely.

"Er, this is Twm. Sorry. This is Thomas Thomas, Manager of the Lamb in Pont-nedd-fechan near Glynneath."

"One moment, please."

There was an eerie silence as he held the phone to his ear while he tried to gather his thoughts. What shall I say? I don't want to upset anyone by being pushy when I've only just moved in here. Damn, I should have waited. His mind racing on the possible consequences. He was just about to put the phone back on the cradle when there was a click as he was being transferred. Too late now! He cleared his throat. "Tom Evans speaking. I'm the assistant manager. What can I do for you today, Mr Thomas?"

"Ah. Well, um, Mr Evans, it's like this. On Monday morning of this week, my wife took a call from someone in your publicity department and…" He went on to explain, in detail, everything that had been requested.

Tom Evans listened intently and when Twm Mawr had finished his long explanation, not a sound was heard from the other end. Twm said "Hello? Mr Evans? Are you still there?"

"Oh yes, Mr Thomas, I am still here! I was just thinking… Just a minute, while I make a few inquiries." There was another long silence, during which Twm Mawr was dancing nervously from one foot to the other in his anxiety.

"Are you quite sure that you have the correct brewery, Mr Thomas?"

"Well, I think so. Now you have doubting myself. The man from the publicity department said that we buy a lot of your product, which we do, and that we sell more of your leading brand of beer than any of the others, which is also true. He also spoke, as I have mentioned to you, about international rugby players and I know your company has, in the past, sponsored rugby. So, I am guessing I've got the right one he was speaking on behalf of, Mr Evans."

"Well, then, I'm going to expand my inquiries at this end, so if you can bear with me for a few minutes, I'll come back to you as soon as possible. Could you please give me your direct telephone number and I'll call you in a couple of minutes, okay?"

Relieved, Twm Mawr gave him his number and sat back down in his armchair to await the result of his call and began to wonder what he had started, because that chap Evans didn't seem to know what the heck he was talking about.

Meanwhile, Tom Evans sat for a few minutes going over in his mind exactly what he had been told about the event planned for that day. Aloud he mused, "I know the president, chairman and the manager are given to making spot checks and inspections from time to time and the manager left me a message only this morning that he wouldn't be in for the rest of the day. So, one or all of them could be combining a spot check with this other event. I'd better get the boys here on the ball first. No sense in taking chances. If they don't turn up here, it won't harm to spruce the place up a bit and if they do appear, we are already cleaning up and we won't be caught on the hop." He picked up the internal phone. "Oh hi, Sue. Could you page the foremen of each section right away, please! I need to have a brief meeting with them. Okay, thanks." Five minutes later every department was busy cleaning up their section.

His next call was to Head Office. "Hello, this is Mr Evans, Assistant Manager, Cardiff division. Could you let me know the whereabouts of the company President and also the Chairman of the Board?"

"Certainly. The President is in Europe on a short holiday since yesterday and won't be back in the country until the end of the month. The Chairman is in London attending a conference and we have no idea where the Manager is at the moment. Is there anything else I can assist you with?"

He sat bolt upright in alarm as the information sank in. "Yes, there is! Do you know where the publicity boys are today?"

"Well, according to my latest information, they are not doing anything this morning, and because it is Friday, they only work in the morning up to midday, so I'm pretty sure they would have all left here for the weekend. Why do you ask?"

"Oh nothing. I was just curious, that's all. Bye!"

She stared at the silent phone in puzzlement. It appeared that Trefor Plough's scheme was working to perfection.

Tom Evans rocked slowly back and forth in his chair as he thought about the ingenuity of what was happening. "Whoever thought this one up is bluddy brilliant. I wonder what this poor sod did to deserve this prank?" he murmured, as he dialled the Glynneath number. "I would like to speak to Mr Twm Thomas please."

Twm Mawr, who had grabbed the phone on its first ring, replied, "Speaking!"

"Er, Mr Thomas. This is Tom Evans, the Assistant Manager from Cardiff, returning your earlier telephone call as promised. Yes. Well, I have some rather disturbing news for you." He went on to relate what he had found out and where everyone of importance would be that day…

"You mean they are not coming?" Twm Mawr interrupted, in panic.

"That's correct. They are not coming to your pub and never intended to either, more's the pity."

"What?" Twm Mawr yelped. The explanation, as yet, had not sunk in. "What do you mean, 'never intended to'?"

"Calm down a minute, Mr Thomas, please. Let me explain again," Tom Evans said softly. "As I previously mentioned to you, I have been in touch with our people all over the place to find out what was going on and where everyone was today. I'm afraid, for whatever reason, you have been the victim of a cruel practical joke. I am sure if you think hard about it, you will surely know who it is. I am sorry for you, Mr Thomas, but you now have the full picture." Hearing no sound from the other end of the phone, he quietly replaced the receiver. In his explanation, he had omitted to mention that he, too, had been drawn into and had fallen foul of the joker's brilliance.

Twm Mawr slumped back in his chair, the phone hanging limply in his hand, his mind in a complete whirl as to who would be capable of doing this to him. "Who, who, who could do this to me? I sound like a bluddy *gwdihw* about the place," he growled out loud. He looked up: his wife Mary was standing in the doorway, her arms folded, impatiently waiting for an answer.

"Well? Where the 'ell are they, then?"

Twm Mawr turned towards her, his face a picture of dismay. "We've been bluddy had, Mary! They're not coming and they never were coming here!"

"NOT COMING!" her voice rose almost to a scream. "Not bluddy coming after all this work and preparation. What about all the cost of putting this on? What am I going to tell all these people here? Tell me that! We're going to look proper fools after this is over."

"Mary, Mary, listen to me," Twm Mawr said wearily. "We've been had. All this was somebody's idea of a practical joke and we're caught up in the middle of it."

"Practical joke?" Mary almost screamed it at him, gritting her teeth. "You said a bluddy practical joke? What the 'ell are you talking about?"

"Well, you saw me on the phone. That was the Assistant Manager from the brewery in Cardiff and he just called his Head Office and they informed him that nothing had been arranged for this Friday, or any other Friday for that matter." Twm Mawr was in total despair as he began to realise the enormity of the scheme someone had created. "Mary, will you go and find the butcher and his stepbrother. I want to talk to them first."

She spun on her heel, her tight lips and face a picture of controlled anger. She quickly found the stepbrothers, speaking to the Master of the Hunt. She smiled tightly, and said, "Excuse me, gentlemen, but Twm would like to speak urgently to you both. He's back in the kitchen." She led the way through the passage to the back room and sat down at the table across from her husband. "Right you are, Twm. Tell them what you told me. The whole story, mind!"

"Tell us what?" asked the butcher, quickly getting a feeling of imminent disaster. "What's happened?"

Twm Mawr looked up. "Nobody's coming here today after all." he announced dejectedly. "Nobody at all! We've been set up. It's somebody's idea of a practical joke, that's what it is. Something to make us all look foolish."

The stepbrothers looked at each other, silent, their mouths hanging open.

"Well, I'll be damned." The butcher was the first to break the silence. "Now who the 'ell –" he started to say, when both of them in unison blurted out "Trefor Plough!"

The butcher, in temper said, "I'll get the police on it right away!"

His stepbrother reached out and held his arm as he reached for the phone. "Now, Rhys, don't be so silly. You cannot prove it was him or anybody else for that matter!"

"I just know it's him, that's good enough for me. That's all I need to know," he shouted. "This is his style. I can see his stamp all over it."

"You might very well be right, but as I said, you'll never in this world be able to prove it, and I think we should keep our voices down for the sake of future business for Twm and Mary. We must keep all this to ourselves, okay?"

"That bluddy man," fumed the butcher. "I'll 'ave him for this, making bluddy fools of all of us!" He continued to rant about Trefor Plough.

Twm Mawr and Mary stood white-faced and open-mouthed at the ferocity of the butcher's outburst. Twm asked, weakly, "what I want to know is, why me? What have I done to anyone?"

"I think it's because of me," the butcher said in a suddenly calm tone. "I've got a feeling it is because of the way I told him that he couldn't run a pub and shouldn't be in charge of one." He stopped pacing and pointed a finger at Twm. "You were there. You heard what I said to him." He began pacing again punching one meaty fist into his other hand as if to emphasise each statement he made, then muttering: "I'll 'ave him. I'll bluddy kick 'im in the pants if I 'ave 'alf a chance." He stopped pacing. "Boys, this isn't doing us any good. We might as well tell everyone to tuck in before the food spoils. We'll just have to keep all this nonsense under our hats. Okay?"

"What about the cost of all this?" Mary looked anxiously from one to the other. "We'll have to charge them something, don't you think?"

"We can't do that, Mary, because we have already told everyone already it is a free bash. We'll just have to tell them that the brewery just called to say they would not be able to make it today, and they have apologised for the inconvenience. As I see it, that's all we can do now." Twm Mawr was rapidly getting his colour and composure back. He straightened up and squared his shoulders. "Come on. We can sort out the blame later." He led the way through the hallway to greet their guests.

The butcher, his face beet-red from anger and humiliation, followed him out, still muttering, "I'm sure it was him. He's got to be responsible for this!"

Outside the four of them circulated amongst the invited guests and asked everyone to be good enough and make a start on the buffet, as they'd had this phone call from the brewery. It was a bit disappointing that they were not able to be there, but these things happen with some large companies.

Only a few of the guests made any complaints, while everybody else tucked in with gusto and a large appetite to clear most of the buffet in short order.

The butcher sat on his own at the end of the long bar, a large malt whisky clenched tightly in his meaty fist as if he had Trefor Plough by the throat. All sorts of schemes of retribution ran through his mind as he discarded them one after another in frustration until he knew full well that he had been outsmarted, and brilliantly too. He made a vow: "I'll bluddy 'ave him, I will! I will!" He rose to his feet and called out to Twm Mawr, further down the bar. "Hey, boys! Let's have a few drinks, is it? To 'ell with him up in Rhyd-y-groes!"

"That's more like it," said Twm Mawr. "C'mon boys, let's have a bit of a singsong." Turning words into action he broke into song, and the others in the bar picked up the rendition instantly, with Twm's fine tenor voice leading, they pushed all thoughts of recent catastrophic event to the back of their minds.

Saturday afternoon in the bar of the Plough Inn, little bits and pieces of the events in the valley below began to filter through. Although some of the stories were total distortions of the actual truth, others were spot on the mark. It appeared that the butcher, who had had more than a few drinks, was telling some people in the bar that Trefor Plough was responsible for the fiasco at the Lamb in the Bont on Friday afternoon, and that he personally would get his revenge on Trefor. He thought he was speaking quietly, but in his cups, he was loud enough to be heard in the next county.

Trefor, from his position behind the bar, was delighted to hear how his scheme had progressed and began asking seemingly innocent questions about the events of the day before. It was difficult to pretend ignorance in front of Old John and of course Fred, but after such a brilliant practical joke he was just bubbling over inside.

Fred came back in from the betting shop next door.

"How's the donkeys going, Fred?" Trefor called out as he pulled a pint for Old John.

"If you must know… bluddy awful. I've had three losers already."

"Never mind, Fred! Here' a free pint to cheer you up a bit," Trefor said as he placed the foaming glass in front of him.

Fred became alert in a split second. 'Hello,' he thought. 'What's brought this on, then? Hey, wait a minute. I'll bet what they are saying all over is the truth. Trefor Plough got the better of the bluddy butcher in the Bont yesterday.'

"Here's good health to you, Trefor."

"And to you too," Trefor replied, all smiles.

'Damn, he's in a good mood,' thought Fred, looking closely at the landlord over the edge of his pint glass, as he swallowed some of the amber liquid. 'I wonder… Nah, I'd only have to pay him back.'

CHAPTER 32

Fred and his move to the Mount

FRED WAS IN the bar one Saturday night when he started on again about his upcoming rent increase for the Council house he and his son Colin lived in and his need to move from there, looking pointedly at the landlord as he spoke. Trefor the landlord, who was all ears and never missed a thing in the bar that directly or indirectly involved himself, chose to ignore Fred, whilst watching him covertly from under bushy brows.

"Yes," Fred repeated, a little louder this time. "A little cottage near here would suit me and our Colin down to the ground!" He cast another sideways look towards the landlord but received no indication that Trefor had even heard any of his remarks.

Willi Bray, standing with his back to the open stove door, looked across the bar in the landlord's direction, and said in his piping voice, "I'm not the one to say, but Trefor has an empty cottage on the Mount. Didn't you know that, Fred?" As usual he was poking his nose in where it was not wanted.

"Oh, aye. I had forgotten all about that one," Fred replied, looking again in the landlord's direction.

Trefor, without looking up from what he was doing, smiled

slowly and thought, 'Here we go then, negotiations for my cottage have begun.'

"Hey Trefor!" Fred called out. "Is that little cottage of yours still empty, then?"

"I suppose it is, Fred. Why do you ask?" Trefor replied, looking directly at him. "I might want to live there myself when I retire from here."

"What's wrong with this place, then? You've got everything you need right here. Why would you want to go somewhere else?" Fred's tone of voice went up a few notches in alarm at the thought of losing an opportunity to move into cheaper accommodation.

'Aha,' Trefor thought, 'now I've got him on a hook.' "Well, Fred, when I was over there last week and the sun was shining, I looked across to the Plough and thought what a wonderful view it was across the waun. From the Mount you can see for miles and the fresh air was lovely and…"

"And the lorries from the opencast back and forth keeping you awake!" he interrupted.

"So, what do you want it for, Fred?" Trefor asked him softly. "I'm told you've got a nice house and the view of the mountain behind your house is lovely."

"Ah. Well, that council house is too big for me and our Colin now and they've already said the rent is going up again – that's twice this year! And I'm not getting any younger and the bus stops right outside the door on the Mount, which will be handy for me in my old age."

Trefor laughed out loud at this lame excuse.

"Aaah! Then keep the bluddy place to yourself, then!" Fred said in frustration, as he sensed his reasons for renting the cottage slipping away like water off a duck's back.

"So how much are you prepared to pay in rent for the Mount, then, Fred?"

Fred's features brightened while his mind clicked into gear, like a well-oiled machine. "Well, you have to remember that I am almost an old-age pensioner now…"

"Come on, Fred! How much?"

"How about if I give you ten shillings a week?"

"And you pay all the rates on the property?" Trefor replied in a flash.

Fred stared at him, mouth hanging open in shock at the swift rejoinder. "How much is that, then?"

"I'll let you know, Fred."

"Well, then. When I know, I'll think about it," he replied, grinning at the landlord and winking at the others standing near him as he moved across the room to sit near Old John on the wooden settle. Head lowered, he whispered, "I think I've got him, John bach."

"Never, *byth*, Fred! He's too sharp for you, mate!"

Fairly early on the following Sunday morning, Fred was sitting near the fire reading for the umpteenth time an old copy of the *News of the World* when there was a brief knock on the back door and George Teale, from the village in the valley below Rhyd-y-groes, walked in with his two Jack Russell terriers in tow. He sat down in the chair opposite Fred, with his dogs sitting close by his feet.

Fred looked up from the paper as George said, "What about us two taking a walk up by the small lake? We might be lucky enough to see something, is it?"

"I dunno, George," Fred said. "Look at the time. I'm thinking we are too late to go up there now. The dew is coming off the grass by this time and anyway, I didn't get to bed till late last night and the Plough will be opening in less than an hour."

"Okay, then." George was determined to go somewhere for a walk. "Let's take a stroll across the waun to the Plough."

Suddenly he sniffed the air. "Der, Fred! There's a 'ell of a funny smell in yere!"

Fred was immediately on the defensive. "Damn you! Don't you dare say there's a smell in yere and especially to my face!"

"Well look, Fred! My dogs are sniffing the air too! Look at 'em." His terriers had their heads up and were casting their noses back and forth as if trying to find out where the smell was coming from. He reached down and slipped their collars and the dogs immediately raced across the floor into the empty front room and began scratching at the worn linoleum beneath the front window.

"What the 'ell!" Fred muttered, jumping to his feet and running into the front room, where the dogs sat whining, looking over their shoulders at the men coming towards them.

"Get from there!" Fred shouted, pulling both dogs away from the spot they were marking.

"George, hold these two back for a minute while I see what's there. Damn, there is a bluddy smell yere too!" he muttered, as the dogs were being pulled away. He curled his fingers under the edge of the oilcloth and pulled it back and there, flat as a pancake, lay an uncooked kipper. Fred suddenly remembered bringing it home and hiding it away from Colin, but later, when he was sober, he couldn't remember what he had done with it.

"Well, I'm damned," he said aloud. "So that's what I did with it!" He opened the front window and threw the rotten kipper out into the front garden. "Come on George, let's get out of this bluddy smell!" Suiting words to action, they ran laughing down the hill and across the waun and arrived at the Plough just after opening time.

George lost no time in letting everyone in the bar know about Fred's latest escapade. With the crowd laughing at him, Fred just shrugged his shoulders, as if it was an everyday occurrence. It seemed at that time that not a day would go by without him being involved in some calamity or other, with or without the landlord's help.

Johnny and Alan were standing in their usual spot at the far end of the bar and joined in the laughter at Fred's expense. "Damn," said Alan, "he's in the middle of it again. How's the butcher treating you, Tref? Is he still up to his old nonsense?"

"Oh, yes. He's still at it. My phone will ring anytime between 2.00 and 4.00 a.m. He tries to disguise his voice, but the message is always the same: 'Did I wake you?', then he hangs up."

Christmas had come around once again. It was the first Christmas that Fred would spend without his wife and family around him, and it was only natural to feel a little bit down in the mouth. Having very little money to spend made it appear even worse as they struggled to make ends meet. Colin was still only working sporadically but somehow managed to find a few odd jobs to keep things going. Fred, for his part, seemed to rely on his friendship of many years with their old butcher in Waun-gron to lower the price on a small scrawny duck for their Christmas dinner. Of course, as was the custom, the landlord gave out a few free pints to all his regular customers over the festive season, but since Christmas was the time when families came together, the beer Trefor gave him only increased his feeling of loneliness. The only bright spot in the Partners' lives at that time was when one of the parish councillors brought him a turkey already stuffed and cooked to perfection with the explanation that all the family had been unwell over Christmas and rather than throw the bird to waste, it was thought that perhaps his dogs could see some benefit from all that meat. Of course, the councillor knew full well that the dogs would never see or smell any of the meat and wished Fred and Colin a very Merry Christmas.

"And a Merry Christmas to you, councillor," Fred replied, delighted to receive such a welcome gift. "What a bit of luck," he murmured as he pushed the door shut with his back against it.

"Hey Colin! Come and take a look at this huge turkey from our councillor!"

Between them they made a pile of sandwiches and stuffed themselves until they could eat no more, then made their way to the Plough, belching with satisfaction almost every step of the way there.

Fred, after managing only a pint of best bitter on top of all the food he had consumed, just had to tell someone about his latest stroke of good fortune. "Well Trefor, only you and our councillor gave any thought for old Fred and our Colin this Christmas."

"What's that then, Fred?"

"Well, I've had two free pints from you, thank you very much, and would you believe it, our councillor just brought me and our Colin a 28-pound turkey, already stuffed and cooked, for us to make a meal out of. Damn, I think that was a very nice thing to do, don't you think?"

"Well, to tell you the truth, Fred, I think that was a pretty generous thing to do."

"Aye. You're right enough, too!"

Trefor looked directly at Fred, a wide smile on his round face. "And I'm willing to bet any money you like, that you won't even buy 'im a pint when you see 'im in here next."

"Oh, yes, I will!" Fred began to bluster. "You would lose your bet on that, Trefor Plough!"

"Okay, then! Let's see you put a pint over for him now and I'll see to it that he gets it the moment he comes in."

Fred stood for a few moments while his mind raced to find a way out of the landlord's challenge. "Hey, listen, Trefor! He knows me well enough to know I will buy him at least one pint. I have known him since he was a little boy coming to our house in Waun-gron to play with our Colin as kids, remember."

"There you are, boys. See what I mean?" He turned sideways

so that Fred couldn't see him winking at the other patrons. "I've said it before, you are a great believer in 'give and take'. Everybody gives and you take. Right boys?" He raised his hands, palms up, to encourage the crowd to follow his lead. A chorus of 'Aye's and 'You're right enough, Tref', came back from around the bar.

"Wait a minute! Wait a bluddy minute! Listen to me a minute!" Fred was getting totally frustrated with the badgering. "Okay then, how much is a pint of best bitter?"

"You know very well how much it costs, Fred! You've drunk enough of it to float a battleship." He was delighted with this little bit of shaming in front of everyone.

Fred dug deep into his pocket and brought out a handful of coins which he grudgingly began to count onto the bar top.

"I hope you're all satisfied now," he growled accusingly, glaring around the room, "for making an old-age pensioner feel ashamed and broke into the bargain."

"Hey, boys!" Trefor called out, ignoring Fred's plea. "He's put enough money here for two pints for the councillor!"

A chorus of cheers rang around the bar and Fred, with a big grin on his face, bowed low to the crowd. He was once again the centre of attention and the man of the moment. He knew full well that the councillor would return his two pints and probably more over time. Fred was, in some respects, like the tight-fisted 'Cardi' who only threw a crust on the incoming tide so that he could never lose what he had thrown away.

Later that night, Fred again broached the subject of the cottage on the Mount.

"Well, to tell you the truth, Fred, I think that 25 bob a week is a fair rent and I pay all the rates and taxes. How about that?"

"What! You want 25 bob a week for that terrible place? There's no room for anything, mun. I've looked through the window. It's never worth 25 shillings."

Trefor continued serving his other customers while arguing

over the rent. "Look yere, Fred. You came to me, remember! You said, it is only you and Colin and if he chips in a few bob, it won't be so bad, will it? It's far less than you are paying the council for that house on the Bryn, isn't it? 25 bob from four pounds a week is saving of…"

"Never mind that! I'll give you half of that, Tref, and not a penny more!" Fred's voice had gone up a few notches to emphasise his stance.

Trefor looked up from wiping the bar. 'It's a pretty handy place, mind," he said, trying a different tack. "As you said before, all the buses stop right outside and then, from the gate in the back garden you can go straight down the waun to Cwm Hendre Fawr where you are always telling us you go hunting foxes. From the Mount you are halfway there already."

Fred hesitated. He was reluctant to commit himself to anything at that moment until he had time to think about it. "I'll tell you what then," he hedged. "I'll meet you over there tomorrow to have a good look around the place, okay?"

"Aye, okay. Tomorrow morning it is, at 11 o'clock."

"Right you are, then." Fred downed the remains of his pint and said, "I'm off home now. Until tomorrow then." He left the bar in a hurry, as if he had just remembered something important that needed his immediate attention, leaving a few of the locals and Trefor speculating on what he would eventually pay in rent.

Most of Fred's business was public knowledge and it often seemed that he and Colin somehow gained a sort of comfort from everyone's contribution in solving their problems, or perhaps it was all their support in any discussion to arrive at a suitable solution.

Trefor and Fred played cat and mouse with each other every time he came into the Plough, until a rent agreeable to both of them was reached, at 15 shillings a week.

Eventually the Partners moved all their belongings into the cottage on the Mount, which for an outdoorsman like Fred was an ideal location. On sunny days, he would drag a chair outside of the tiny kitchen and sit near the front porch facing the sun and the dark green forestry backdrop of the mountain and dream of greater things as he looked across the waun.

'What if I had all the money, genuine, like? All that I can see from this spot would be mine. I'd be like a gentlemen farmer: a large estate, good dogs, new guns for me and our Colin,' and then he sighed. 'Ah well. It's only a dream, Fred bach.' Getting to his feet and dragging the chair behind him, he went inside to make a cup of tea.

If Fred thought that living up there on the Mount would be peaceful, he was greatly mistaken. He had known all about the lorries running to and fro to the opencast coal site on a daily basis, but he hadn't anticipated them starting work at first light and going on until early evening, six days a week. The main objection was the empty ones going back to the site, just three miles from the Mount. Each time they hit the bad patch of the road outside his cottage the empty sound of any loose parts on the box and tailgate was like the hammer on a huge gong that echoed inside the bedrooms.

Another problem with many of the older houses like the cottage was that it had no bathroom, and certainly no inside toilet: that was outside and around the corner of the cottage, facing the predominately westerly winds blowing up the valley. There was no stove either, so to get any hot water the fire needed to be lit, and it took a long time to heat even the smallest amount of water to shave or wash. Sometimes all these seemingly small problems all arrived at the same time and Fred would get frustrated and start throwing things around in a fit of pique. It was on such a day that Fred decided he was paying far too much rent for this 'bluddy shack', as he had begun to call the cottage on the Mount.

"Colin! Tonight, I'm going to tell that Trefor about this place!" Colin looked up and nodded his agreement, then went back to reading the local newspaper.

That night Fred had been drinking in the New Inn, a pub barely half a mile from where he was living, and had managed to get a lift over to the Plough. Entering the room, he swaggered up to the bar and raised his voice. "A pint of best bitter, landlord!"

"Wait your turn!" came the prompt reply. Trefor didn't even look up from what he was doing. He knew in an instant who had made the request and continued to potter about with this and that, while Fred was getting more and more impatient.

Finally, he raised his voice and almost shouted out. "Hey! Do I have to wait all night to get a bluddy pint here?"

"If you've got the money, no," replied the landlord, looking up. "Oh, it's you, Fred!" he said, pretending to be surprised at seeing him standing there.

"Certainly it's me and you knew right away who it was, too!" Fred reached boiling point in a hurry. "I want a pint of best —"

"And I want to see the colour of your money first," Trefor interrupted.

"Bluddy 'ell!" Fred exploded. "Don't you trust me?"

"NO! Now show me the coin of the realm, Mr Howells!"

Muttering angrily to himself, Fred pulled a handful of small change and cigarette packets from the depth of his pocket and began counting out the correct amount for a pint of best bitter. "Now then, I'll have that pint before I die of thirst in yere!"

Trefor, up to his usual tricks, handed him a pint of ale that had stood under the bar for some time.

Fred, also knowing the landlord's little game, having been caught with the same stunt so many times, drained about two thirds of the pint in one go before shouting. "Hey! This beer is not what I paid for! I'm not paying for this rubbish." He reached across the bar and grabbed the pile of small change before Trefor could reach it, and banged the almost-empty glass back on the bar top.

"Ooops. Sorry, Fred, that was the wrong one," Trefor said blandly, then added, "My mistake, of course."

"Aye?" Fred replied sarcastically. "Mistake, eh? You never make any of those sort of mistakes, as long as I've known you, Trefor Plough!"

"Well, that's as maybe. Here's your pint, now tip up!"

Grumbling under his breath, Fred again counted out from the pile of coins on the bar the correct amount and swept the remaining coins back into the depths of his pocket. Turning away from the bar with the glass up to his lips, he winked conspiratorially to Old John, who was standing next to him. "Oh, yes, Trefor! I want to talk to you about my rent before I have too much to drink."

"Oooh? You want to talk? Well, so do I," came the quick reply. "I am thinking of raising the rent, now that you have opened the discussion."

Fred stood stock still in shock, his mouth wide open and the glass inches from his lips. "WHAT?" His voice shot up at a high rate of knots. "Raise my rent indeed! I want to talk to you about dropping it."

"No fear. That's not going to happen. After all the pestering you did to get me to rent it to you in the first place? You've got a really lovely little place over there and such a beautiful view of Craig y Llyn and the village across the waun. Some people would give almost anything to live where you are."

"No, by damn! It's not anything like that now! Those empty opencast lorries passing the place every five minutes of the day on their way back to refill... it's enough to drive you mad with the noise when they hit that bad patch of road right outside the

Mount. It's enough to knock you out of bed in the morning!"

"But Fred, mun! You knew all about the lorries BEFORE you moved over there, didn't you? Trefor reminded him calmly.

"Aye, I did, fair play! But I didn't know about all the rain coming in!" He turned towards the crowd at the card table.

"Do you know what, boys? When it rains over there it's drier outside than it is inside..."

"Fred, listen. I've looked into this before, when Twmos Davis was living there. The guttering is slanted the wrong way so the rain coming off next door's roof runs back into my property, but I will put it right for you and Colin when I get a chance. If you are not satisfied with that, then you had better take it up with the owner of the other cottage," said Trefor, interrupting Fred's complaining.

"C'mon, Trefor! How can I do that? I would have to go to Australia to find him!" Fred was shouting by this time. He was still facing the crowd while Trefor was making gestures behind his back to encourage the others to follow his tirade as he went on, "Boys, when it rained last week I'll swear to God we had a rainbow in the bluddy kitchen!"

The crowd, following Trefor's lead, all began laughing and cheering as they enjoyed Fred's antics and he, believing he was the one making all the fun, began laughing with them. Trefor, who was thoroughly enjoying this evening's performance, said in a serious tone, "I'll tell you what, Fred, I'll drop your rent but..." he paused for effect.

Fred's face lit up momentarily. "Aye? Go on then."

"I'll have to charge you more for the amenities."

"AMENITIES! What bluddy amenities?" Fred yelled across the bar. The crowd were in absolute hysterics at this claim by the landlord.

"Well, when it rains you can at least have a shower inside. I'll bet there was no shower available in the council house," he said, a broad smile lighting up his round features.

Fred stood there speechless, with his mouth hanging open. Then he said, "You! You! You bluddy, I don't know what!" Fred was spluttering his words.

"Okay. Now calm down, Fred. We'll talk about it, okay?" Trefor had had his bit of fun and it was almost closing time; he didn't want Fred sitting there arguing the toss all night otherwise nobody would leave, expecting more fun at Fred's expense. "I'll come over tomorrow to see you and to see what can be done to put things right."

Fred seemed happy with that reply and moved across the bar to sit down beside Old John. He began bending his ear with some of his other problems and complaints.

Old John, unspeaking, listened for a while, then getting to his feet, finished his pint and disappeared through the open bar door, nodding to the landlord as he left. It didn't seem to bother Fred that Old John had walked away in the middle of his story – he would soon find somebody else to listen to his woes.

The landlord, as good as his word, went to meet Fred at the Mount cottage the following day, and after a long discussion agreed to drop the rent to twelve and six per week. It was a pittance of a rent but it was money that he wouldn't have received from anyone else, since no one in their right mind would dream of living there under those conditions.

Fred, for his part, was full of good humour that night in the Plough, bragging to all and sundry how he had made the landlord lower his rent down to Fred's idea of a suitable payment. The landlord, in good part, agreed with him, while winking at the others when Fred turned away. "Yes, you were right enough, Fred! I think I was charging you too much for that property on the Mount." His voice had a serious ring to it.

"There you are, boys!" Fred smiled happily. "See, I was right all along."

CHAPTER 33

Fred and Alan's rabbit

IT WAS THE Saturday afternoon following Fred's bet with Alan, earlier in the week, that he could catch a rabbit with a snare.

The bar in the Plough was, as usual, crowded, and the inevitable game of four-handed crib was taking place on the large kitchen table in front of the shuttered window. The TV was at full volume, presenting various horse races from across the country, which was of particular interest to the punters on their visits to and from the licensed betting shop next door to the pub. The noise in the bar was so loud that at times like this it was a benefit to be able to lipread, but this was just the way Trefor the landlord liked it.

Fred entered the room and began pushing his way through the crowd to belly up to the bar.

Trefor and Olwen, his part-time help, were serving the crowd as fast as they could pull a pint and take the money off their thirsty customers.

"Pint of best bitter!" Fred called out above the noise.

"You'll have to wait a minute!" Trefor replied sharply. "I've got to put a fresh barrel on first," he said, as he lifted the trapdoor in the floor behind the bar, preparing to climb down the wooden ladder into the depths of the cellar.

"Well, have you got a paper then? Yesterday's will do!"

Trefor pulled a face at Fred's impatience and the delay it was causing him. "NO! No, I haven't. I've only got today's paper!" He reached under the bar and threw the folded edition of the *Western Mail* across the counter to him. Fred caught the paper in one hand, and turning away, he pushed his way through the other patrons towards an empty chair on the end of the card table.

"Where's Alan?" he demanded from anyone at the table who might answer his inquiry.

"In the betting shop," Johnny replied from his seat at the game. "Why do you want to know that, then?"

"Oh, nothing," Fred said, spreading the paper wide across the end of the table and moving the numerous beer-filled pint glasses closer together, some precariously closer to the players' elbows.

"Hey Fred! Stop bluddy potching will you? Leave things be as they are!"

"I'm only making a little bit of room, that's all."

"For what?" Twm turned towards him, red-faced in irritation.

"Never you mind," Fred replied with a broad wink. Then, like some music-hall magician, he suddenly produced a rabbit from the depths of his jacket pocket and flopped the dead animal onto the newspaper in front of him. "Well, there you are boys, I did it!" Fred's tone of voice was triumphant. "I caught it on a soft wire snare up by the old Pandy mine."

"Oh aye? P'raps you bought it just to keep your promise. It looks pretty scrawny to me," said Johnny.

"No, no. I trapped it. Honest…"

At that moment Alan came back into the bar and returned

to his seat at the game, where Bobby had been playing his hand, and silently pointed to the scoreboard to show the substantial lead gained in his absence. Alan nodded his thanks and turned sideways to look at Fred.

"What have you got there, Fred? That's not my rabbit is it? It looks a bit undernourished to me. What do you say, boys?" He laughed and looked around the others for their opinions. "If that is mine," Alan went on, "you don't expect me to clean and skin it, do you?" The look on Fred's face caused another ripple of laughter from the crowd around the table.

"Hey, c'mon, Alan. That wasn't part of the bet and you know it, too! Hey boys, you were there. You remember the bet." He looked at each one for support, but didn't succeed very well in gaining any. They just grinned at him.

"C'mon, Alan. Two pints for a rabbit! That's what we agreed, right?"

"Okay, I'll tell you what…" Alan started to say.

"Two pints, Alan!" Fred was getting annoyed. He had walked many miles to get that little rabbit for a bet and it was thirsty work, which reminded him he hadn't had a drop of beer yet. He stood up and shouted across the bar above the noise. "Hey, Trefor! How about that pint, then?"

The landlord, who had just returned to his familiar place behind the bar, shouted back with a grin on his round features. "Money first, Fred! There is no charity in here, only under very special circumstances."

"Ah! Well, I'll pay you as soon as Alan pays me for this rabbit I caught for him."

Trefor raised his voice, joining in the fun of winding Fred up, and said sternly, "Money now, or no beer for you, Fred!"

Fred, getting more and more irritated, shouted: "ALAN!" turning his head towards the card table. "Alan!" he shouted above the din.

Alan looked up from the card table at Fred's pleading look and said to Trefor. "Okay landlord. Give him a pint of what he wants and I'll square with you now, in a minute."

Elated with his success in getting a pint out of Alan, Fred said to Trefor, "There you are, landlord – Alan will pay for this pint of best." Reaching for the foaming pint, he almost downed it all in one long swallow. Smacking his lips with relish at the taste of the fresh pint, he returned to his seat at the table, where the rabbit lay on the landlord's newspaper. "Now then, Alan…"

"Now then, Fred," Alan interrupted. "I'll give you another pint if you clean and skin that thing. When did you trap it, anyway?"

"About an hour ago. I came straight yere…"

"You're supposed to clean these things right away, aren't you?"

"Well, I suppose…"

"Well nothing! Clean the damn thing now and then I'll pay you, okay?"

Fred began to get angry at this delay in paying out on his bet. "We made a bluddy bet, Alan. So pay up!"

"I will," Alan replied grinning, "but you have to clean it first. I just told you. I'll give you another pint on top of the bet we made. I can't be fairer than that."

Frustrated, Fred stood up, the empty pint glass in his hand, looking daggers from one to the other of the crowd around the table. "All right, you clever sods! You all like to have a bit of sport at my expense, don't you? Right you are, Alan, I'll bluddy clean it for you and you put the money you owe me on the table right now!" He banged the empty glass down on the end of the table, and reaching into his pocket, pulled out a well-worn, razor-sharp pocket knife. He flipped the rabbit onto its back and quickly slit open the soft underbelly, then flipped it back and shook the entrails onto the landlord's newspaper. "There!" he said to Alan. "That's how you do it, right!"

The putrid smell which emanated from the rabbit's entrails was indescribable, and the effect was all the more amongst the men crowded around the card table.

"Trefor!" shouted Twm across the bar. "Look what this bluddy monkey have done now. It's bluddy stinking over yere!"

Trefor was in the middle of pulling a pint when the agitated shout from Twm reached his ears. He craned his neck to see what was going on when a whiff of something dreadful drifted under his nose.

"Well, damn it all!" he said, slamming the partly filled glass on the bar. "Now what has he done?" He left his position behind the bar and came at a run through the hallway into the bar room, where he caught the full benefit of Fred's handiwork on the card table. "You bluddy clown, Fred!" he bellowed. "That's my today's paper too! You, you…" he spluttered. "That's it! Out you go this very minute. I've had enough of your nonsense in yere!" He grabbed Fred by his coat collar and yanking him to his feet he began to drag him toward the door shouting: "Don't you ever come back in yere again…"

"Just a minute, Tref!" Fred was resisting for all he was worth and reaching for the offending rabbit at the same time. "Just a minute, mun. The smell will clear in a couple of…"

That was about as far as he got. With one last heave, Trefor shoved his customer out through the door as if he had developed wings. Fred found himself standing on the road outside the Plough Inn.

Slightly out of breath from the effort, Trefor told Fred, "I don't want you to come back here, ever! *Chi'n deall*? Understand?"

Fred stood in the middle of the road appealing to the landlord that it wasn't his fault at all. "C'mon, Tref. It was Alan's fault! He got my rag going, that's all."

"I don't care whose fault it is or was…" Then a sudden thought struck him. "Wait there a minute, Fred!" he said, and disappeared into the gloom of the passageway back into the Plough.

Optimistically, Fred's spirits lifted slightly – only to be dashed when Trefor reappeared with the large framed photograph of Fred with the huge dead otter in his arms. Fred's mouth fell open with dismay, seeing this as the last straw from the landlord.

"Here you are, Fred! I don't want anything more to do with you or your photograph," he said, holding out the picture frame. "Don't either of you come back here again!"

Fred grasped the frame with both hands. "Well Trefor, if that's the way you want it and this is all the bluddy thanks I get, then to 'ell with you too! There was no harm at all in what I did. Just a bit of a smell, that's all."

"Goodbye, Fred!" Trefor turned his back to him and closing the inner door, he returned to his usual place behind the bar. The bar was now alive with speculation as to Trefor's resolve to ban Fred from the Plough forever. Some were of the opinion that Trefor would give in and bring him back into the fold in the end, but some sided with his opinion that enough was enough this time.

Willi Bray seemed to have the final word on the subject, though. He said, "Well, I'll tell you what, boys. There is a blank spot on the wall now where Fred's picture has hung for years and years and there will be a blank spot in yere without some of his old nonsense too!"

Fred's absence from the Plough seemed to have a quieting effect, when most nights in the past would have found him in the midst of some escapade or another. He had been, basically, the unpaid entertainer for everyone, and the void created by Trefor the landlord would take some filling.

CHAPTER 34

Fred's reinstatement

JOHNNY GOT INTO Alan's car and said he had been thinking about their earlier conversation regarding Fred's reinstatement in the Plough. He said it might be a good idea to set up a petition to present to Trefor as an ultimatum.

Alan put the car in gear and turned it in the direction of the pub before he answered. "I don't think that is a good idea and I'll tell you why. Trefor was really offended by Fred's nonsense with that damn rabbit, and to tell you the truth, I'm sorry now that I ever made that bet with him. Anyway, Trefor has a lot of pride and he won't climb down easy. So giving him an ultimatum won't work. We'll just have to try a different approach."

"Okay, I can live with that. What about the silent treatment? That will surely make him take notice."

"Yes, but not like that. We can't just switch off, can we? I mean, we stand talking to him at the end of the bar nearly every time we go in there. If we did that he would smell a rat, wouldn't he? No, when we get in there, we'll just mention to whoever is there how quiet it is and go on from there, okay?"

"Good idea, Al. Everybody knows that he likes a lot of noise in the bar, so we won't give him any, and later we can mention Fred and some of his antics while he's been away from the Plough."

"Sounds like a plan. Right, let's do that!"

Entering the bar, Johnny called for two pints and then followed Alan to a table in the corner. Trefor, who always had time for a chat with them while they stood at the end of the bar, looked at the pair with a puzzled expression, and especially so when Alan got up and spoke quietly to the usual crowd around the card table. It became even more noticeable when the noise level in the room dropped the moment he went back to the corner table and Trefor began to wonder what was going on.

Bobby, coming up to the bar for a refill, turned and spoke to the crowd in general. "Has anybody seen Fred, or heard what he's been up to lately?"

Trefor's ears pricked up and he looked quickly around the room for any response.

"Well, a couple of us were in the New Inn this morning for about half an hour and had a lot of fun, with him winding someone up," said Alan, grinning like the proverbial Cheshire Cat.

Old John Shinkins, leaning against the warmth of the stove in his seat on the wooden settle, sat up and asked Alan, "So what was the noisy rascal up to now, then?"

Alan got up from his chair and walked towards him, relating the story of that morning's escapade and the closer he got to him, the quieter he spoke, until he had Old John laughing fit to bust.

Trefor, leaning forward while filling the pint glass for Bobby, strained his ears to hear any part of Alan's story but failed to hear any more than a few words about cigarette packets, which made no sense at all.

Meanwhile, Alan had moved back to his chair at the corner table and called out, "And that's not the half of it, John!"

Trefor couldn't help but be curious about Fred's latest antics in the pub across the waun, knowing as he did the many hours of fun he had brought to the Plough. He leaned over the bar and called out to Alan. "So, what nonsense was he up to today, then?"

"Nothing much, Tref, but why in the world would you want to know what he's up to? You banned him *sine die* from here, didn't you?"

"Well, yes I did, but…"

"This place won't be the same without him now!" Bobby called out from across the room.

Trefor looked at Bobby impatiently then looked at the clock on the wall and rang the bell. "Time, boys! Time to go home."

On their way home, Alan stopped his car outside Shop John and they both got out to sit on the wooden bench to await the arrival of the crowd from the bar, who were making their way slowly down the lane. They gathered around Alan and Johnny.

"Boys, we are thinking of putting together a plan to get Fred back into the Plough! Is everyone here in agreement?" A chorus of ayes answered Alan's question.

"Tonight, as you all could see, Trefor was quite interested in what Fred had been up to this morning in the New Inn. You know what they say about curiosity? It killed the cat! I think what we have to do now is keep on dropping little bits of information to keep his interest going in Fred. It's a safe bet that's he's done something silly within the past week or so. If one of us, it doesn't matter who, tells Trefor some of the story just to keep his interest going, he might soften up enough to get Fred to come back."

"What if Fred gets stubborn and says 'To 'ell with you, Trefor Plough!'?" Bobby asked, smiling. "It could happen, you know!"

Johnny and Alan looked at each other and said in unison, "'ell's bells, we never thought of that!"

"We'll just have to take that chance," said Alan. "So for the time being, we'll stick with the curiosity plan, okay?"

It was some weeks after Fred's enforced ejection from the Plough Inn that his son Colin walked into the bar on his way home from work.

"Colin, mun!" Trefor's face lit up at seeing him. "We haven't seen you in here for ages. A pint of best bitter, is it?"

"No thanks, Tref. I've just called in to clear my IOUs. I'm working regular now, so it's time to get out of debt."

"Then I am very pleased to hear that, Colin," Trefor replied holding out a meaty hand for the money he owed him.

Colin grinned and handed over a bundle of pound notes. "I think you find all of it is present and correct, Tref."

"I'm sure it is, Colin," he said, as he stuffed the money into his pocket, uncounted.

"Oh, and another thing, Tref. My father and me are moving back to Waun-gron. I have made friends with my mother and she said I can stay there until I find another place. Fred is not very well now – sometimes he has trouble breathing and I can't look after him and go to work. So he's going to stay with my sister in Waun-gron until he gets better. Daddy – um, Fred – wants to know if we can leave all our things, you know, our beds, tables and chairs, in the Mount until we can get them moved down to Waun-gron?"

"Well, of course you can," Trefor replied immediately. "Tell your father from me that you can take as long as you like."

Colin briefly touched his cap. "Thanks Tref!" Turning on his heel, he nodded to the usual crowd listening to his discussion with the landlord and left the bar.

Trefor stood for some moments, staring off into the distance, until Willi Bray broke the spell. "Well, well, boys! I never thought I would see the day when Colin would refuse a pint of best bitter, especially after coming home from a long day's work underground!"

Sometime later, via the grapevine (Willi Bray) it appeared Fred had managed to wangle his way into a room at the OAP sheltered accommodation. It was a furnished flat with medical staff on call 24 hours a day, 7 days a week if they should be needed. It suited Fred down to the ground because, as a pensioner, it was subsidised and Meals on Wheels were provided on a daily basis. But more importantly than anything else, according to Willi, it was only 200 yards from his latest haunt, the Prince of Wales pub, and to top it all off, he had managed to persuade the landlord to hang his picture of the otter on the wall in the bar. It appeared that Willi Bray was more than delighted to pass on this snippet of gossip to Trefor and the bar in general. Johnny and Alan, standing at the end of the bar, smiled at each other and Alan said, "I suppose we can tell you now, since it looks like Fred is leaving for Waun-gron so I doubt very much if we'll see anything of him once he's down there, but we were going to try and get him reinstated in the Plough."

"Oh, were you now? Well boys, to tell you the truth I was thinking of contacting him or one of the family to find out how he was keeping, but it doesn't matter now, after what Willi Bray has been saying. Fred has got a good spot down there in Waun-gron. Good luck to him, I say!"

CHAPTER 35

Fred's passing

IT WAS EXACTLY six weeks since Fred had moved into The Shelter in Waun-gron when Johnny, sitting on the windowsill of Shop John enjoying a bar of chocolate, heard the bad news about his passing. The charter bus, bringing home miners from their early morning shift, had stopped outside the shop and about a dozen workers got off. "Shomai Johnny!" Bobby and Willi and a few others walked over to him.

"'Ave you heard the news about Fred?" Bobby asked.

"No! What's that then? What trouble has he got into again?" Johnny laughed, squinting his eyes in the sunlight as he looked up at the group.

"No, mun!" Bobby said, in a low voice. "The old rascal is dead. He died yesterday morning, early, on the way to hospital. So I heard."

"Get away! I saw him only last week in the Prince of Wales on Brecon Road. He looked okay then. He was struggling a bit for his breath, mind, but he looked all right in himself."

"Well, that's what we heard first thing this morning. One of the boys I work with told me, and he thinks the funeral is on Friday afternoon." Bobby turned to leave. "I expect everybody will want to go to this one!"

"No doubt," Johnny replied, in a subdued tone. "No doubt at all."

They stood together, Johnny and about eight or nine miners, discussing in low tones the bad news they had heard. "Boys, we'll meet tonight in the Plough, then, is it? said Johnny. "I'm sure that Trefor, whatever their differences, will have got all the details by then and we'll do what we can to help."

"Aye, right enough, Johnny," said Bobby. "They will need bearers for sure, to represent the Plough, but we'll have to wait and see what the family says about who they'll want."

Most of the regulars who gathered in the men's bar that night got the full story of Fred's passing from Trefor the landlord, who had visited Fred's family. He had been informed that at some time in the middle of the night before last, the night staff had been woken up by the emergency buzzer but by the time they had got out of bed and dressed, the buzzer had stopped and the light had gone off on the panel so they didn't know immediately who was in distress. They rushed from room to room in the twelve-unit building to find out who needed their help. Unfortunately, by the time they arrived at Fred's room, they found him collapsed on the floor beside his bed. They gave him first aid and called for an ambulance, which arrived in less than five minutes. The medics continued to provide first aid and gave him oxygen, then raced at high speed to the hospital in Merthyr. In the meantime, Colin had been sent for and he went with his father in the ambulance to the hospital, but it was too late, and he had died on the way there.

"Now, there's a crying shame for you. The poor old sod was no doubt full of dust. When I saw him last week, he could hardly breathe!" Angrily Johnny criticised the Coal Board. "They have consistently refused to recognise that 'dust' is an industrial disease. "Do you know, there's not a doctor around here that will put his signature on a death certificate to say that some poor soul died of silicosis of the lungs. And another thing," he went on, "Do you remember Mock 'Cwmhwnt', Trefor?"

"Oh yes, of course! He lived in that little bungalow down on the Pandy road, on the way to Fforch y Garon."

"That's right! He got hit by a runaway journey underground. They got him to the hospital and he died there. Do you know what they put on his death certificate? Heart failure! They said that he had had a bad heart and that's what did it! Not the fact that he was all smashed up from the accident. It ended up that his widow, Peggy was awarded a ten shillings a week pension instead of a lump sum payment from the accident. And now here we are, with Fred! He worked all his life underground for a pittance, breathing in the same air as the big money boys! It doesn't make any sense, does it?" Johnny was out of breath with anger and indignation, but every one of the miners listening to his tirade was nodding in agreement.

"Now, now, Johnny!" Trefor tapped him on his arm. "Let's calm down a bit, is it? I'm sure all the boys here know how you feel about it. Here, have a drop of beer to wet your whistle." He turned to address the crowd. "What we have to do now, boys, is to get organised. I'll put up a sheet of paper on the board to make a list of who is going to the funeral and I'll find out from Colin who the family wants to be bearers. Those who want to be bearers, put your names on the list. I'll take that with me later tonight. Olwen can look after the bar for an hour."

"Yes, you're right enough, Tref." Johnny raised his glass. "Here's to Fred, boys." He took a long swallow as everyone there raised their glasses in silent tribute.

"Okay then! Let's start making a list. My car will be available."

"And mine," said Alan. "What about flowers from all the boys here?"

"Well, I'm sending a wreath myself," Trefor replied, "but

I'm willing to start another floral tribute." He reached into his trouser pocket and put two £5 notes into a glass and handed it to Alan. "Make a collection from the boys here now, and give it back to me at the end of the night, and I'll see that the flowers get delivered to the house in Waun-gron, all right?"

"Right! Thanks, Tref." Johnny raised his voice. "Now then, boys, the glass is on the bar so throw in what you can afford for a big wreath from all of us in the Plough."

As Roy was pushing a pound note into the glass and pressing the other notes down, he remarked, "If Fred knew we were having a collection for him, he would be here like a shot!" Everyone laughed, but the sound was subdued.

"Aye, aye. You're right enough, Roy," said Johnny. "Do any of you remember that Martin whatever his name was? He left the village overnight and left behind loads of debts?"

"Oh, I remember 'im," Willi Bray said. "They call it doing a moonlight flit."

"Yes, that's right! I remember him too. He'd been gone from here about a couple of years and somebody had told him we had made a collection for his family, because we had heard that he had died. Anyway, the cheeky sod showed up here at the Plough to collect it. His first words to me were, 'Heard you boys 'ave had a whip-round for me. Where is it?' I told him pretty quick where to go! The money we did collect, all those years ago, we gave to the orphans' charity." Alan laughed.

"Aye. Right enough, too!" Twm agreed. "So what time did you say the funeral is on Friday, Tref?"

"Half past three at Bryn Gaer in Waun-gron," he confirmed.

"So, we'll all meet at the Mount Pleasant pub then, is it?"

"No, that wouldn't be right, Willi," said Trefor. "Fred is in the Chapel of Rest in Waun-gron at the moment. So if everybody is in agreement, we'll meet outside there and sing a few hymns, traditional like. I've been told that the minister from Calfaria

Chapel will be giving a service in Welsh for the family and relatives inside and he will also do another service in Welsh outside. Is everyone in agreement with the arrangements so far?" He was pleased to hear a chorus of 'ayes'. "Okay, then everything is settled for the moment. If anything changes, I'll find a way to let you all know. If anyone wants a lift by car to Waun-gron, see Alan, Johnny, Twm or Will Mawr, or whoever else has a car and is attending Fred's funeral. There will be enough cars and place for everyone.

"One other thing." Trefor looked around the room. "Just a minute, boys!" he raised his voice. "Listen a minute!" The rumble of voices gradually faded away. "I would like very much for everyone to come back here after the funeral. I've arranged for food to be put on for everyone, okay. It's the least we can do. Thanks to all of you!"

There was complete silence for a moment, then Johnny spoke. "Well Trefor – and I'm sure I say this on behalf of everyone here in the Plough and those in mourning down in Waun-gron – this is most generous of you, and we want you to know that we all appreciate it tremendously and it won't be forgotten! Right, then, boys, raise your glasses! To Trefor!"

Trefor looked more than a little embarrassed when the chorus of 'To Trefor' rang out.

Johnny turned to face the landlord. "This is very big of you, Tref."

"Well, you know, it is nothing really, After all, we've all had such a lot of fun with Fred over the years. It's been like having an unpaid entertainer in here nearly every night and now the old so-and-so has gone. We're all going to miss him you know!"

"I know that, but he won't be forgotten, you mark my words." Johnny picked up his glass and drained the remains with a flourish. "Right then. I'm off home." Raising his voice, he called out, "Boys, just in case I don't see you before then –

I'll be down by Shop John at 2.30 on Friday, then. The flowers will be delivered to the Chapel with a card from all of us, okay, Tref?"

"You just leave everything to me," Trefor raised his hand, palm out.

"Right, then!" Satisfied that everything was now in place, Johnny glanced around the room, said goodnight to his brother-in-law and slipped out through the door.

Johnny was the first to arrive outside Shop John on the Friday afternoon at exactly 2.30, parking his car to wait patiently for the other mourners to arrive. Looking in his rear-view mirror, he saw two more cars pull in quietly behind him. Getting out of his car, he stretched and yawned.

"Up early, were you?" Alan asked, as he squeezed between the cars.

"Half past five, and I've been rushing around ever since."

"How many is coming?" Twm had joined them, brushing imaginary fluff off his black suit.

"I dunno, we'll just have to wait and see."Johnny glanced at his watch."It's half past two now, and we can't leave any later than five minutes to three."

"Yes," confirmed Alan. "If there's a service at the chapel and the walk up to the cemetery by 3.30, it doesn't leave us much time."

"Ah! Don't worry about the time," Twm interrupted. "It's the last funeral of the day so they won't be too pushy to finish on time."

"I suppose you're right, Twm." Johnny leaned against the car, arms folded. He glanced up the hill. "Here's a crowd coming now, look!"

They all turned to look as he spoke. "Looks like we'll need more cars." Alan said.

"Give it time, there's a few more cars to come yet." Johnny looked at his watch again. "We've still got twenty minutes."

"You're like a bluddy race official with that watch," Twm laughed, the others joining in.

"Well," replied Johnny, a bit embarrassed. "Somebody has to keep you all on track."

The crowd streaming down from the housing site had now joined them. "Are you sure we've got enough cars?" asked Willi Bray.

"Don't you worry, Willi," Alan said. "There'll be enough, and at a push we can always put you in the boot – you're only little."

"That's not funny, Alan." Willi Bray drew himself up to his full five feet.

"Just joking. Just joking." Alan patted him on the shoulder.

"I know that." Willi glared at Alan, then grinned.

Alan drifted over to where Johnny was in conversation with Twm. "Funny how little people get so aggressive if you talk about their height," he whispered to them. They both glanced across at Willi, who was holding himself as tall as he could, chest puffed out.

"Aye!" Johnny remarked. "He is a bit touchy about it, isn't he?"

"Now don't go starting a bluddy row, Alan," said Twm. Not today, anyway."

"Okay! Okay! Everybody's a bit on edge today."

"Well, it's not the best of days, is it? Here's a couple more cars. Looks like we've got enough now." Johnny glanced at his watch. "Good timing," he remarked. "It's ten minutes to. Okay boys!" he raised his voice. "Sort yourselves out."

The crowd milled around for a few moments, gradually sorting themselves into small groups around each car. "Right then – see you at the Chapel of Rest in Waun-gron. Does everybody know where that is? Right, let's go." Johnny opened the car door and climbed in, slamming the door as he started the engine. "Bang on," he said, adjusting the rear-view mirror. "Our timing is perfect." With his arm out through the window, he signalled to the others to follow. Letting out the clutch, he led the convoy of cars down to Waun-gron.

The eight cars arrived in an orderly manner at the chapel, with close to forty men to join the already-assembled crowd. "Damn!" said Johnny, touching Alan's arm. "This is going to be a big funeral."

"You can expect a good crowd. Fred was well known all over the place." Alan pointed through the crowd. "There are people over there from Ystradfellte, from that farm on the Sennybridge road, look! Standing by the Butchers Arms landlord."

"The Butchers, Penderyn? Where?" Johnny scanned the crowd. "Oh aye, I can see them."

"C'mon, let's move in a bit closer." Alan urged them to join the crowd proper as the minister appeared in the doorway of the Chapel. He raised his hands and the assembly went silent.

Mock Williams stepped forward and in his pure, low voice, began to sing '*Crugybar*':

> *O fryniau Caersalem ceir gweled*
> *Holl daith yr anialwch i gyd.*

> From Salem's hills yonder in glory
> Our course through the desert we'll view.

Immediately the assembled crowd picked up the refrain, voices uniting in the traditional four-part singing familiar to Welsh chapels, each part complementing the others with a blend of sound, raising the hairs on the necks of onlookers and singers alike with their emotion. There was complete silence at the finish except for some muffled coughing, which stopped as Mock commenced the second hymn, '*Llef*':

O Iesu mawr! Rho d'anian bur
I eiddil gwan mewn anial dir...

Come, gracious Lord, descend and dwell
By faith and love, in every breast...

This was the hymn for bass singers and they didn't disappoint
anyone. The strength of their feelings was heard in the depth of
the tones as the sounds echoed off the wall of the narrow lane
and the Chapel. When it was over, the minister again raised his
arms outstretched to the now silent crowd.

"Friends," his soft voice carried to everyone. "We are gathered
here today to remember a man who has been close to you all,
has befriended many but above all has left no enemies. A man
who worked all his life for so little reward but nevertheless kept
a cheerful disposition, even when he had nothing. He was a man
who laughed at misfortune and tried to make the best of every
situation.

"I speak now on behalf of the family, who are deeply shocked
at the suddenness of events over which we have no dominion,
in thanking you all for your support at this time; your floral
tributes, too many to mention, and last but not least, for the
friendship shown here today on this sad occasion. Let us pray:

"Ein Tad, yr hwn wyt yn y nefoedd...

Our Father, who art in heaven..."

As the prayer continued, the coffin was brought out by the
chosen bearers and placed carefully in the hearse. The family
followed the director to the first car and the bearers climbed
into the second car.

The assembled crowd, in sombre dark suits and overcoats,
formed up in front of the hearse, and at a signal from the director
they started walking slowly towards the cemetery almost two

miles away. Johnny and the other drivers opened the car doors and waited for those mourners who were unable, for one reason or another, to walk that far.

Reaching the cemetery, the cortège passed down the long avenue of trees to where a large group of other mourners waited in the late afternoon sunlight.

As family members got out of the car, close family friends stepped forward and in time-honoured tradition shook them by the hand in unspoken sympathy and condolence.

The minister intoned a final prayer as Fred was committed to the ground and the assembled crowd, with Mock Williams leading once more, sang 'Bryn Calfaria':

> *Cymer, Iesu, fi fel 'rydwyf*
> *Fyth ni allaf fod yn well.*

> Take me as I am, O Saviour
> Better I can never be.

Alan, Johnny and the other drivers waited for their passengers to return to the village as the crowd dispersed.

"How many do you think were here today?" Willi wanted to know.

"Oh, I should think about 400," Alan replied, "and that's just the men. I saw some women in the crowd too, which is a bit unusual, I thought. What do you think Johnny?"

"Well, he was pretty popular, mind. Yes, Al, there was easy 400, and there was a crowd here, too, that wasn't at the Chapel."

"Was there?" Willi expressed surprise.

"Oh yes! There were about a dozen cars on the road when we got here and I saw people from all over. Look, there's George Teale just leaving with a carful from Glynneath. This has got to be one of the biggest funerals up here for years."

"Well, the old rascal didn't have much or leave much

behind, but a lot of people have remembered him, fair play."
Johnny sighed. "I suppose we'll all go back to the Plough now,
is it?" He looked at the crowd standing near the cars. "Listen,
if anyone wants to go home first, say now and we'll drop you
off." Receiving no reply, he said. "Okay boys, everyone in and
let's get going."

"Looks like we've got more passengers than we started with."
Johnny was standing with the car doors open, watching everyone
climbing into the cars.

"Don't worry about it," Twm said quietly. "We'll jam them in
somehow. It's not too far from here to the Plough and it's unlikely
that the police will make a fuss, especially for a funeral."

Hardly a word was spoken on the way back to the Plough,
each man alone with his thoughts.

Less than ten minutes later, the line of cars rolled silently into
the parking area next to the Plough Inn. Car doors slammed and
the passengers made their way into the main bar.

Olwen, Trefor's part-time barmaid, was pulling pint after
pint of foaming beer and lining them up on the bar like soldiers
on parade. "Help yourselves, boys," she said, with a smile. "These
are on the house – Trefor's orders."

"That's very good of him," Johnny said, raising his glass in
salute. "Where is he, anyway?"

"Oh, he phoned from Waun-gron and said he would be here
in about half an hour. He's gone to the bakery down there to
pick up something, he didn't say what."

"Oh, I see. Thanks, Olwen." Johhny turned and leaned his
back against the bar.

By this time everyone in the room had taken a pint off the bar
and had found a seat to talk quietly about the day's events.

Johnny moved across to where Alan was standing at the far
end of the bar. As he approached, Alan said, "Do you know
what? This Trefor is a great landlord. All this is going to cost

him a lot of money. All the food, free drinks, the flowers and everything else."

"Well, I suppose he can afford it – and I know that is not the point," Johnny raised his hand as Alan was about to interrupt. "What I mean is, he *can* afford to do it, but he wouldn't unless he really wanted to. He does things like this not because of the money but because he belongs, like we all belong. If you think about it, we all belong to each other, otherwise we wouldn't reach out to help each other when it's needed or at times like this!" His arm swept the room. "P'raps I'm not saying this right but I think you know what I mean, Alan. He doesn't buy friendship, you can't really do that anyway. He's just generous. If you were ever stuck for money – I'm sure that will never happen! – but he would be there in a minute and no questions asked. You know, I'm out of breath after all that."

"Right enough," Alan nodded towards Willi Bray. "He says Trefor has just come back.'

"How the 'ell do you know that?"

Alan laughed. "Sign language, mate!"

Moments later, Trefor's head poked through the serving hatch into the bar. "Hello, boys! Sorry I'm late but I had to pick up some things from the bakery in Waun-gron. I'll be there in a minute."

Alan and Johnny grinned at each other.

"See!" said Johnny. "Belonging."

After a while, Trefor appeared behind the bar to help Olwen. He was still in his best suit, minus the jacket. "Okay, Olwen. I'll take over here now. The stuff is on the table in there. Lay it all out on the tables in the front room, I've put them ready. Just give me a call when it's all ready."

Olwen nodded and disappeared under the hatch/countertop. Within minutes there was a steady hum of voices as the beer started to release the tension of the day in each one of them.

"Good turnout, wasn't it, Johnny?" Trefor said, as he wiped the top of the bar in front of him.

"Yes. I was only saying earlier, that was the largest funeral for years."

"Aye. The last big one I remember was William John. He got swept out to sea – a big strong boy like that. You would never have thought it, would you? There must have been at least 500 there." He paused in his efforts to clean the bar top. "You know, it's a sad time but life must go on. I'm going to miss the old rascal around here…"

Olwen poked her head through the hatch at that moment, breaking into Trefor's maudlin mood. "Everything is ready, Tref!"

"Right you are, then!' He turned smartly to face the rest of the crowd. "Okay, boys! The food is on the tables in the front room, so go and help yourselves."

"I'm ready for this, boys." Twm belched as he put his empty glass on the table. 'I had breakfast about five this morning before work. It's no good drinking on an empty stomach, is it?"

The sight which beheld them when they opened the door into the other room stopped them in their tracks. All the tables had been pushed together to form one long table, covered with a white cloth and laden with pies, pasties, sandwiches, cold ham, pickles, buns and just about anything a person might want to eat was on there.

"What a bluddy feast!" Roy gaped at the spread. "Boys, this has cost Trefor a pretty penny!"

"Never mind gaping and blocking the doorway. Get in there," said Bobby, pushing Roy into the room. "C'mon, he said to get stuck in!" He whistled when he, too, saw the extent of the laden tables. "Bluddy 'ell! What a landlord, boys! Free beer and now this. He's the best."

Later, when everyone had eaten his fill and had returned to the main room, Johnny stood at the end of the bar, pint glass in hand, and said to Alan. "I think that something should be said about what Trefor has done here today."

"Go ahead, you." Alan replied, picking at his teeth with the end of a matchstick.

"What about you, then?"

"I'm not much of a speaker," Alan grinned, "but I know that you always want to say something."

"Well, I do like to get my two pennies' worth in there somewhere," Johhny said, a bit sheepishly.

"All right, then, do it!"

"Boys, could I have your attention, please?" Johnny tried to penetrate the general noise. "Boys, could I have…"

Suddenly Alan shouted, "SHUT UP, YOU LOT!" The room fell silent. "Go ahead, Johnny," he said, in his normal voice.

"Boys, it's just that I'd like to say a few things before anybody falls asleep from free beer and the grand feast provided by our landlord in honour of Fred on this sad occasion. It goes without saying that this is a sad day in the village, especially here, where Fred performed at his very best. How many times have we laughed till tears streamed – and I might add, not always with him, but at him. It seemed sometimes that was a bit unkind, but he always took it in good part and never, as far as I can remember anyway, held a grudge. Today marks the passing of a real character, and as he said so many times, 'I'm a legend in my own time, boys'." Johnny raised his glass. "To Fred and the memories. May peace be with you!"

Glasses raised, everyone chorused. "To Fred!"

"And finally, to our landlord, Trefor: for the fine beer, the fine food and great hospitality, may he continue to prosper! A big hand for Trefor! Thanks." He put his glass on the bar and began to applaud and the crowd followed suit.

Someone at the back of the room shouted "SPEECH!"

Trefor, beaming behind the bar, raised both hands. "Boys, boys, wait a minute!" he paused. "I am a man of few words, so I'll just say this. I did what I could because I wanted to, and that's that! Thank you all. Thank you." After more applause, he disappeared into the inner sanctum of his kitchen.

"See, now you've embarrassed him," Alan said accusingly.

"No, I haven't! Why do you say that, Al?"

"Why do you think he left the bar like that, then?"

"How do I know? P'raps he's gone to have a cup of tea!"

"Cup of tea, be damned!" Alan snorted. "You've got no imagination, have you?"

"What do you mean by that?"

"He's upset about Fred! Can't you see that?"

"Well, I didn't think of it like that."

"No imagination. C'mon, drink up. Two pints, please, Olwen."

Roy joined them at the bar.

"Olwen! A pint for Roy too, if you please"

"Right, Alan."

"I was just saying to Twm at the table. Remember that night when Fred came in here and said, 'She've bolted' – you'd swear he was talking about a bluddy horse, not his wife."

Johnny laughed. "Well, she used to say, 'I work like a bluddy horse around the place while Fred is getting drunk somewhere on my money'."

"I suppose she was right to leave him when she did, mind," Trefor murmured as he returned behind the bar in time to hear the comment. "He was 'ell of a boy, mind. If he could wangle free beer, even if it was only half a pint, he'd be there like a shot."

Johnny laughed. "Talking of free beer, I was with him one night when we were going over to the foxing club at the Croesbychan pub at the bottom of Merthyr mountain. We were in Waun-gron going down towards Maescynon when Fred said, 'Let's call in the Glan and get old Ted to give us a few samples for free'. In we went and Ted greeted Fred like he was a long-lost brother. Fred told him we had come to sample some of the best ale around. Before we knew it, Ted was pulling sample glasses of beer all along the bar. Fred would taste this one or that one, and say try these, boys. What do you think of this or that one? And old Ted would top up all the glasses again. Well, boys, we came out of there and Fred said we must have had about three pints each and only paid for one… yes, he was a 'ell of a boy all right."

"Hey, Johnny, do you remember when we were rabbiting over in Ystradfellte and we got into that pub in Penderyn? It was well after four o'clock closing time and you said we'll never get a pint in there now, it's too late. That didn't stop Fred. He said, 'Watch this.' The crowd of us got into the bar. It was crowded and the towels were on all the pumps. Fred began singing one of his favourites, 'Myfanwy'. Before you knew it, the cloths were off and the beer was flowing. Der, he had a great voice, mind."

"I'm sure we all remember when Fred got his golden handshake from the NCB. He came in here dressed like something out of an Al Capone film. Light-coloured suit, black shirt and a white tie, and shiny patent leather dancing shoes. Well, him and Colin went off to Neath Fair with Dai 'Chops'. It turned out that Fred and Colin were paying for rum and blackcurrant drinks for this woman all night, in the Bird in Hand, and then they went to have a chat outside to sort out who was going to take her home. Dai took her off in his car, but when he walked her down the lane by her house, her husband asked if she was okay. Dai looked across the lane and this chap, about six foot six tall, came out of the shadows. And according to Fred, Dai ran like 'ell back to his car! We'll have to remind him of that when he comes in next time."

Arwyn sauntered over to the bar, an empty pint glass in his

hand. 'Aye, he was 'ell of a boy, mind. I remember the time we were gathering all our rams for an early shearing one April a few years back, when he called in for a cup of tea. He said he had been up in the forestry, looking for signs of foxes with cubs. We were in the middle of lambing at the time, so it was handy to have him around. Well, he was sitting at our kitchen table, sipping his tea when he said: 'What do you think of these, boys?' He pulled back his coat to show us a pair of very wide, bright red braces with gold-coloured trouser clips. I asked him where the 'ell he had got them from. Oh! he had seen them amongst a pile of junk in that odds and ends shop down in Waun-gron and said he had paid a pound for them.

"Well, anyway, I asked him if he could give us a hand with shearing the rams. He was there like a shot, knowing right away there would be a meal or some cash at the end of it. Well, boys, everything was going well until he pushed those fancy red braces off his shoulders and let them dangle behind his back. That was when the trouble started. He had just turned one ram loose from in front of the shearer when another big ram passed right behind him. Well, you should have seen it, boys. Somehow or other, Fred's braces got tangled in the young ram's horns! The bluddy ram was trying to go one way and pulling Fred backwards, while he was doing his best to go in the other direction and the elastic in his braces were stretched to the limit as Fred tried to turn, with the ram pulling and shaking his head for all he was worth. We all stood there laughing as Fred managed to get one leg over the back of the ram. The trouble was, he was now facing towards the back end of the ram and shouting at the top of his voice: 'Hey, boys bach!' Only Jimmy by yere had the presence of mind to grab a small gate and pin the ram and Fred into the corner of the shed so we could untangle him, but those gold trouser clips were so strong, he would have been there till Sunday without Jimmy's quick thinking.

"Remember that day, Jimmy?"

"Like it was yesterday, Arwyn." Jimmy rubbed the side of his jaw with the back of his hand, a distant look in his eyes. "Aye. Like it was yesterday."

Glossary
of local terms

Arglwydd Mawr! (Welsh)	Good Lord!
bach (Welsh)	small, or an affectionate term
Bridgend	town in the south of Wales, where there is a large psychiatric hospital
byth (Welsh)	ever
cwtch (Welsh)	a hiding place or store – or, to hide or to cuddle (Everyone knows how to cuddle, but only the Welsh know how to *cwtch*)
der	well now...
Duw (Welsh)	God
flush	to have money
'full of dust'	suffering from silicosis (sometimes called 'black lung') – coal miners' disease
gassin'	talking
gwalch (Welsh)	rascal or rogue
gwas (Welsh)	servant
Haisht!	be quiet!
Jack Russell	a breed of terrier
Jill	female ferret

just now	a short time before
lurcher	a dog cross-bred to have the ideal characteristics for hunting
marking	as in a dog's actions when hunting
mun	man/fellow/mate
no light on top	simple-minded
now in a minute	later
on strap	on credit
pickies	in trouble, as in 'fallen in the thorn bushes or stinging nettles'
purse nets	green string nets with drawstrings, to catch the prey alive
ratter	a flat cloth cap
to row	to argue
scruffy	unkempt
Some hopes!	Not a chance!
stone (weight)	14 lbs
stop tap	the end of serving time
Sure to be!	Not likely!
tampin'	furious
to be 'off' with someone	to be angry
twp/twpsyn (Welsh)	stupid
wellies	knee-high rubber boots (short for Wellingtons)

Also from Y Lolfa:

£3.99

A Childhood
in a Welsh
Mining Valley

VIVIAN JONES

y Lolfa

£9.99

Tales From My Welsh Village is just one of a
whole range of publications from Y Lolfa.
For a full list of books currently in print, send
now for your free copy of our new full-colour
catalogue. Or simply surf into our website

www.ylolfa.com

for secure on-line ordering.

TALYBONT CEREDIGION CYMRU SY24 5HE
e-mail ylolfa@ylolfa.com
website www.ylolfa.com
phone (01970) 832 304
fax 832 782

Printed by Y Lolfa
Ask for a quote